Crime Files Series

General Editor: **Clive Bloom**

Since its invention in the nineteenth century, detective fiction has never been more popular. In novels, short stories, films, radio, television and now in computer games, private detectives and psychopaths, prim poisoners and overworked cops, tommy gun gangsters and cocaine criminals are the very stuff of modern imagination, and their creators one mainstay of popular consciousness. Crime Files is a ground-breaking series offering scholars, students and discerning readers a comprehensive set of guides to the world of crime and detective fiction. Every aspect of crime writing, detective fiction, gangster movie, true-crime exposé, police procedural and post-colonial investigation is explored through clear and informative texts offering comprehensive coverage and theoretical sophistication.

Published titles include:

Maurizio Ascari
A COUNTER-HISTORY OF CRIME FICTION
Supernatural, Gothic, Sensational

Hans Bertens and Theo D'haen
CONTEMPORARY AMERICAN CRIME FICTION

Anita Biressi
CRIME, FEAR AND THE LAW IN TRUE CRIME STORIES

Ed Christian (*editor*)
THE POST-COLONIAL DETECTIVE

Paul Cobley
THE AMERICAN THRILLER
Generic Innovation and Social Change in the 1970s

Michael Cook
NARRATIVES OF ENCLOSURE IN DETECTIVE FICTION
The Locked Room Mystery

Emelyne Godfrey
MASCULINITY, CRIME AND SELF-DEFENCE IN VICTORIAN LITERATURE

Christiana Gregoriou
DEVIANCE IN CONTEMPORARY CRIME FICTION

Lee Horsley
THE NOIR THRILLER

Merja Makinen
AGATHA CHRISTIE
Investigating Femininity

Fran Mason
AMERICAN GANGSTER CINEMA
From *Little Caesar* to *Pulp Fiction*

Linden Peach
MASQUERADE, CRIME AND FICTION
Criminal Deceptions

Alistair Rolls and Deborah Walker
FRENCH AND AMERICAN NOIR
Dark Crossings

Susan Rowland
FROM AGATHA CHRISTIE TO RUTH RENDELL
British Women Writers in Detective and Crime Fiction

Adrian Schober
POSSESSED CHILD NARRATIVES IN LITERATURE AND FILM
Contrary States

Lucy Sussex
WOMEN WRITERS AND DETECTIVES IN NINETEENTH-CENTURY CRIME FICTION
The Mothers of the Mystery Genre

Heather Worthington
THE RISE OF THE DETECTIVE IN EARLY NINETEENTH-CENTURY POPULAR FICTION

R.A. York
AGATHA CHRISTIE
Power and Illusion

Crime Files
Series Standing Order ISBN 978–0–333–71471–3 (hardback)
978–0–333–93064–9 (paperback)
(*outside North America only*)

You can receive future titles in this series as they are published by placing a standing order. Please contact your bookseller or, in case of difficulty, write to us at the address below with your name and address, the title of the series and the ISBN quoted above.

Customer Services Department, Macmillan Distribution Ltd, Houndmills, Basingstoke, Hampshire RG21 6XS, England

Narratives of Enclosure in Detective Fiction

The Locked Room Mystery

Michael Cook

First published 2011 by
PALGRAVE MACMILLAN

Palgrave Macmillan in the UK is an imprint of Macmillan Publishers Limited, registered in England, company number 785998, of Houndmills, Basingstoke, Hampshire RG21 6XS.

Palgrave Macmillan in the US is a division of St Martin's Press LLC, 175 Fifth Avenue, New York, NY 10010.

Palgrave Macmillan is the global academic imprint of the above companies and has companies and representatives throughout the world.

Palgrave® and Macmillan® are registered trademarks in the United States, the United Kingdom, Europe and other countries.

ISBN 978–0–230–27665–9 hardback

This book is printed on paper suitable for recycling and made from fully managed and sustained forest sources. Logging, pulping and manufacturing processes are expected to conform to the environmental regulations of the country of origin.

A catalogue record for this book is available from the British Library.

Library of Congress Cataloging-in-Publication Data
Cook, Michael, 1946–
     Narratives of enclosure in detective fiction : the locked room
     mystery / Michael Cook.
          p.   cm. — (Crime files series)
     Includes bibliographical references and index.
     ISBN 978–0–230–27665–9 (alk. paper)
     1. Detective and mystery stories—History and criticism.
     2. Rooms in literature.   3. Setting (Literature)
     4. Space in literature.   5. Place (Philosophy) in literature.
     6. Crime in literature.   I. Title.   II. Title: Locked room mystery.
     III. Series.
     PN3448.D4C559 2011
     809.3'872—dc22   2011011753

10   9   8   7   6   5   4   3   2   1
20   19   18   17   16   15   14   13   12   11

Printed and bound in Great Britain by
CPI Antony Rowe, Chippenham and Eastbourne

For Jenny, Hannah and Naomi

Contents

Illustrations

The cover illustration is of 'The Murders in the Rue Morgue' by Aubrey Beardsley, from part of a set produced for the 1894–5 edition of Edgar Allan Poe's short stories.

Acknowledgements

The diagram from *The Hollow Man* by John Dickson Carr in Chapter 5 is included by kind permission of the author's representatives, David Higham Associates, and the publishers, Penguin.

The extract from *Hancock's Half Hour* appears by kind permission of Ray Galton and Alan Simpson and the BBC.

Preface

Narratives of Enclosure is the first full-length critical study of the locked room mystery.[1] This work, therefore, should fill a gap in present research. As the title indicates, it is a book about the structure of narrative and the constituents which activate it. The detective story makes a good subject for such a study because, from the first, it has possessed a recognizable and stable narrative, and this has undoubtedly contributed to the genre's phenomenal success amongst the reading public. I have always believed that underpinning this has been an essential homogeneity, a unity of structure, theme and language which meets a deep desire in the reader. The locked room mystery, I argue, exemplifies this model by extending the puzzle story to the limit of its potential, to the extent that it becomes an abstraction of the wider genre itself. For these reasons I have confined the scope of my research to what is now commonly termed the classic puzzle story and its metaphysical counterpart. I have, however, unashamedly gone outside the genre in a few cases, most notably in the case of Dickens's 'The Signalman', where I consider the texts to be germane to some aspect of the locked room tradition. I do not expect my arguments to be free of criticism, or even dissent, but I hope above all else to show just how valuable a contribution this most iconic of mysteries has made to our understanding of the detective story since 'The Murders in the Rue Morgue' first appeared some 170 years ago.

What follows is a brief survey of the key critical texts that have prompted my arguments. I consider myself fortunate to be living at a time when the detective story is now an accepted subject for intellectual inquiry. There are those of us, longer in the tooth than we care to admit, who know that this has not always been the case. Much credit for this should go to Howard Haycraft for pioneering what has now become a vibrant and well-populated forum for the consideration of detective fiction in all its forms. Haycraft's groundbreaking *Murder for Pleasure* (1941) was the first to provide a comprehensive survey of all aspects of the genre, including the writers, notable stories and the progress of detective fiction in America, Britain and Europe. Most influential of all, however, is the chapter entitled 'The Rules of the Game', in which Haycraft builds on works by Knox and S. S. Van Dine outlining the key elements of plot required for the successful detective story. While much of the bur-den of Haycraft's argument is directed towards fair play in the laying of clues before the reader, the text also contains one of the earliest affir-mations of the genre's closed narrative style: 'That all determinative action must proceed directly and causatively from the central theme of crime-and-pursuit; and that no extraneous factors (such as stupid-ity or "forgetting") shall be allowed to prolong the plot in an essential manner.'

Tzvetan Todorov influenced many subsequent works on the genre with his 'The Typology of Detective Fiction' in *The Poetics of Prose* (1977), with its structuralist approaches. Todorov was one of the first critics to expand on the structure of narrative in the detective story and the part this played in shaping its character. His articulation of the detec-tive story's structure is couched in the language of enclosure; he cites, for instance, the use of a prologue and an epilogue as a framing device for the story of the investigation. In addition, Todorov begins to estab-lish a critical context for the enduring notion which Poe initiated – that theme, in the form of an enclosure, would reflect the structure of the narrative itself.

Contemporary with Todorov's essay is Robert Champigny's philo-sophical meditation on the detective story narrative in *What Will Have Happened* (1977). Champigny analyses both the physical and more ethe-real constituents of the detective story in order to assess how they cooperate in the overall narrative. Thus, tangible parts of the plot, such as clues, invoke more aesthetic ideas regarding concealment, mystery and interpretation; most of all, these narrative elements combine to cre-ate 'a hermeneutic tale', one which will 'sharpen the interest not just for what will happen but for what will have happened'.[2]

Two studies at the beginning of the 1980s have become seminal texts in their consideration of the relationship between theme and narra-tive; they have certainly helped to inform my understanding of this area of the genre. In his 1981 study *The Pursuit of Crime*, Dennis Porter takes up the idea of the 'hermeneutic code as a structuring force' which informs the fundamental shape of the narrative. Porter argues that the very first detective story, 'The Murders in the Rue Morgue', is a text that is dominated by its denouement and that only after settling on the outrageous solution to the mystery was Poe able to fill in the plot ret-rospectively. This 'backward construction', as Porter calls it, is another way of viewing the closed nature of the detective story narrative. What precedes the final revelation is thus constructed solely and exclusively for the purpose of furthering its conclusion. The effect is seen at its most complete, according to Porter, within the context of the conventional genre's narrative structure: 'the movement from concealment to disclosure which characterizes the genre also implies that individual works suddenly constitute themselves into wholes at their denouement'.[3] It was a rereading of Stephen Knight's *Form and Ideology in Crime Fiction* (1980) that prompted me to think about my whole approach to detective fiction. Knight takes a similar line to Porter by examining the broad ideological implications of detective fiction through its formal properties. But one of Knight's arguments, that detective fiction should 'establish the social ideologies of the works discussed'[4], made me realize that, while my approach is not an ideological one, any holistic analysis of narrative construction must take account of thematic ideas. The essays in *The Poetics of Murder* (1983), edited by Glenn Most and William Stowe, continue the work of Porter and Knight by associating detective fiction's conservative narratological structure with a wide range of sociological, political and psychoanalytical theory. In *Detective Fiction: A Collection of Critical Essays* (1980), edited by Robin Winks, however, there is a concentration on the history of the genre and, in particular, a picture of the Golden Age story as the paradigm of the puzzle story.

The idea of the intervention of theme does appear in one influential text written from a Freudian psychoanalytical standpoint by Peter Brooks, whose *Reading for the Plot* was first published in 1984. Brooks's proposition is to combine the theory of narrative, including that of detective fiction, with psychoanalysis; in particular this approach chronicles how repression and repetition are active constituents in the formation of thematic relationships with textual structures. The principal outcome of the critical attention of the early 1980s was to establish the closed nature of the genre's narrative structure. This was crucial for the development of detective story criticism because it focused attention on the narrative of the genre rather than just the manoeuvrings of the plot. This paved the way for later studies to consider detective fiction's relevance to literary theory; notable amongst these are Martin Priestman's *Detective Fiction and Literature* (1990) and *The Cunning Craft: Original Essays on Detective Fiction and Contemporary Literature* (1990), which are constructed from the point of view that the genre can be considered alongside other literary genres.

These pioneering texts, together with a growing body of criticism, have helped to place detective fiction as a regular subject for academic debate, and since the early 1990s a number of key texts have appeared on the genre. In *Detection and Its Designs: Narrative and Power in Nineteenth Century Detective Fiction* (1998), Peter Thoms explores the place of the detective in the genre's narrative structure, concluding that the power imbued by the author to this character gives a momentum to the form that drives the investigation towards solution. Heather Worthington, in *The Rise of the Detective in Early Nineteenth-Century Popular Fiction* (2005), suggests that the rise of the detective in early fiction is largely responsible for its creation and sustained popularity, and *The Art of Detective Fiction* (Chernaik et al. 2000) is a set of essays that examine the structure and appeal of the detective story as a popular genre today. Joseph Kestner, in *The Edwardian Age and the Edwardian Detective* (2000), meanwhile, has produced a work which examines the detective story as exhibiting some of the key thematic preoccupations of the Edwardian period. These include the *fin de siècle* fears about foreign invasion, the issue of masculinity and the role of literature in the enforcement of the law. David Lehman's *The Perfect Murder* (1989) is an elegantly written canter through the genre's history, and has some interesting things to say about its conventions and, more importantly for my research, about the contribution made by the locked room mystery.

There has been a growing interest in the metaphysical detective story. One volume of essays which has done much to encourage this interest is *Detecting Texts: The Metaphysical Detective Story from Poe to Modernism* (Merivale and Sweeney 1999). This work brings together such critics as John T. Irwin, Stephen Bernstein and Joel Black who, amongst others, concentrate on texts by Jorge Luis Borges, Umberto Eco, Paul Auster and Patrick Modiano. It contains one of the most succinct definitions of metaphysical detective fiction:

> A metaphysical detective story is a text that parodies or subverts traditional detective-story conventions – such as narrative closure and the detective's role as surrogate reader – with the intention, or at least the effect, of asking questions about mysteries of being and knowing which transcend the mere machinations of the mystery plot.[5]

Accordingly, many of these essays seek to compare the abstract ideas of enclosure, subversion of the form of the detective story and the nature of writing, with that of the genre's inventor, Poe, in an attempt to return to the original impulses of the form. The collection includes John Irwin's 'The Mystery to a Solution: Poe, Borges, and the Analytic Detective Story', which draws parallels with the detective fiction of Poe and Borges and cites many allusions by the latter to the former's work.

Stephen Knight's latest book, a study of transatlantic crime fiction, now in its second edition, *Crime Fiction since 1800: Detection, Death,*

Diversity (2010), is a masterly study of the history of the genre divided into the three main headings of the subtitle. This has already become an indispensable reference book and is especially interesting for its coverage of the latest trends in thematic influences.

These works, therefore, form the critical context for *Narratives of Enclosure*. By interpreting and developing some of these ideas and using the particular perspective of the locked room mystery, I hope to cast some new light on the detective genre as a whole. As a result of this research the locked room mystery emerges as a paradigm for the way in which the textual components such as narrative, theme and language come together in the wider genre. This, I contend, is because the underlying idea of enclosure, inherent in the narrative, is repeated throughout its texts by the imagery of its language, the emblematic architecture of its physical landscape and the way in which the theme engages with its text. Although the arrangement of the material is broadly chronological, in no sense is it a comprehensive survey or history of the locked room form; rather it tries to show how selected tests are representative of a body of work which has inspired and informed the detective story.[6]

Although, at times, the production of this volume has felt like a Holmes 'three pipe problem' for me personally, no book can be produced in isolation. I owe many people a huge debt of gratitude for their help and patience in the realization of a long-held dream. Firstly, the warmest thanks go to Nick Groom and Jason Hall at Exeter University; their intelligence, indispensable advice and backing for my project were such that it would not have seen the light of day without them. My thanks go to all at Palgrave Macmillan, especially the series editor Clive Bloom for all his expert advice, the anonymous reader, many of whose valuable comments have been incorporated into the text, and to Catherine Mitchell for her support.

So to my family – I am thinking of striking a new medal for long sufferance as an award to my wife Jenny, whose patience, willingness to read drafts, often at the expense of her own research, and original suggestions were instrumental in my seeing the whole thing through. My daughters Hannah and Naomi have been generous with their time throughout and have also given priceless encouragement and help. I can't thank them enough; as a result this book is dedicated to all three.

Michael Cook
michaelcookonline.com

1
Edgar Allan Poe and the Detective Story Narrative

> The problem that makes the purest appeal to logic for its solution. It highlights the 'closed' nature of the detective tale and is, unquestionably, its most traditional expression. I am speaking of what has come to be referred to as 'the locked room mystery'.
>
> Donald A. Yates, 'An Essay on Locked Rooms'[1]

> Pure reason, incapable of any limitation, is the deity itself.
>
> Hegel, 'The Life of Jesus'[2]

One of the more remarkable facts about detective fiction, a genre which has now assumed epic proportions, is its foundation of just three short stories, an experiment to be abandoned by its creator almost as quickly as it appeared. For Edgar Allan Poe, the publication of 'The Murders in the Rue Morgue' in 1841, followed by 'The Mystery of Marie Rogêt' (1842–3) and 'The Purloined Letter' (1844), was to represent the extent of his output in this field. Although he always seemed diffident about his foray into detective fiction, being 'conscious of the inherent gimmickry' of the tales, he nevertheless realized that he was in uncharted literary territory.[3] In a letter to a friend, he wrote, 'these tales of ratiocination owe most of their popularity to being something in a new key'.[4] This 'new key' was characterized by the representation of crime as an intellectual puzzle, invoking the practice of scientism in clue solving and heralding the detective as a major literary figure. So complete was Poe's innovation that the narrative structure he composed for these tales was to become a blueprint for all subsequent detective stories. Thus the locked room of 'The Murders in the Rue Morgue', as a prototype for detective fiction with its accent on enclosures, death and references to sequestered lives, not only became a paradigm for the way in which the genre would function structurally, but carried with it an idea central to Poe's Gothic texts.

Just as Poe drew on his own writing for the ideas of architectural and metaphysical enclosures, his representation of ratiocination was the product of an eclectic distillation from other literal sources, rather than a flash of personal inspiration. The fact that such techniques had been part of a long textual chain is undeniable: in Sophocles' *Oedipus the King*, for example, Oedipus conducts a series of interrogations in an attempt to discover the murderer of King Laius. Shakespeare has long been the source of inspiration for writers of detective fiction who have used his plots and made myriad references to his plays in their own works. *Hamlet* (1602), which at its most basic is the pursuit of a murderer, contains no less than six corpses, including murder by the pouring of poison into the ear. The death of Hamlet's father is also re-enacted as the subterfuge of a play within a play, a stratagem worthy of any self-respecting detective story. In *Othello* (1604) Iago lays a false trail, a familiar device of crime writers, to implicate Desdemona by placing her handkerchief with Cassio. In Voltaire's *Zadig* (1750) too, the eponymous hero escapes imprisonment by convincing his accusers that his detailed description of a lost horse and dog derives only from close examination of the animals' tracks and hair fibres.

The tradition is particularly apparent in detective fiction's more immediate precursor. William Godwin's propagandist novel *Caleb Williams* (1794) depicts a servant who is tracked by his villainous master after employing investigative methods worthy of a detective. Its relevance to detective fiction, in particular, is of an early crime story involving investigation and pursuit leading to arrest, and in these respects it lays out a narrative rubric which will be followed by its successors. Bulwer-Lytton's *Pelham* (1828) has the dénouement turn on deductions made with false logic, whilst *Eugene Aram* (1832), a novelization of an infamous eighteenth-century crime, foreshadows the inverted form of detective fiction by recounting the story of a crime from the standpoint of the criminal. It relates the story of a schoolmaster driven to murder by poverty and finally racked by remorse, and features a putative detective called Walter Lester. However, in all these novels, although detection plays a part it is not the dominant narrative. As Stephen Knight has suggested:

> Throughout this material there is evident a widespread awareness that some form of expert police work is needed in order to have any

security in identifying the mysterious criminals of the modern world. But the efforts of these emerging figures are far from authoritative in the early stories: the criminals are caught through red-handed action, or, very often, by being persuaded into confession.[5]

The Memoirs of Vidocq, which appeared in 1828–9, provides the most direct correlation with Poe.[6] It contains romanticized versions of real cases solved by a reformed criminal who went on to create the Sûreté and found one of the first private detective agencies. He was reincarnated inter alia both as Vautrin in Balzac's *Le Pére Goriot* (1834), and as Gaboriau's detective Lecocq in a series of novels. Although Eugène François Vidocq was a highly significant figure in the pre-history of detective fiction, and may even have prompted the creation of Dupin himself, his methods and character are very different from the fictional Dupin, according to Sita Schütt:

> The memoirs, full of accounts of his criminal days, followed by equally lurid adventures detailing his activities as a policeman, where detective methods are limited to various acts of provocation, disguise, and incitement to betrayal, were instant best-sellers in France and in England. Vidocq's 'police methods' had little if any of the famous Cartesian spirit of rational inquiry that were epitomized in Poe's Chevalier Dupin less than two decades later. Vidocq succeeded in capturing the contemporary imagination through his vigour, his adventures and importantly, his early accounts of 'brigandage'.[7]

It seems that this summation would have met with Poe's approval. Vidocq might have been an inspiring figure to budding detectives in real life, and authors too, but Poe was much more interested in the exercising of pure reason. In 'The Murders in the Rue Morgue', Dupin announces:

> Vidocq, for example, was a good guesser, and a persevering man. But, without educated thought, he erred continually by the very intensity of his investigations. He impaired his vision by holding the object too close. He might see, perhaps, one or two points with unusual clearness, but in doing so, he, necessarily, lost sight of the matter as a whole.[8]

Vidocq was essentially a man of action, whose hunches, energy and knowledge of the demi-monde brought him his results; his 'guesses' were not the intuitive inferences with which Poe endows Dupin. As will become clear, although Dupin does need to establish a starting point for his reasoning, it is based on the establishment of an observed fact.

So, notwithstanding the many examples of the detective art that existed throughout literary history, Poe's innovation was real enough, and, primarily, he gave the detective story a recognizable structure. Poe's engagement with the deductive elements of past texts and his own originality recalls Todorov's remark that 'every great book establishes the existence of two genres, the reality of two norms: that of the genre it transgresses, which dominated the preceding literature, and that of the genre it creates'.[9] As such, Poe's tale stands at the threshold of a genre as yet unborn, side by side with elements of storytelling lifted from the tradition of the Gothic and Sensation novels that Poe carried into much of his own work. Poe, accordingly, redirected his own sense of the Gothic, manifest by the *Tales of the Grotesque and Arabesque*, into 'The Murders in the Rue Morgue'.

He was too, the first writer to foreground the ratiocinative process as the dominant subject of narrative, to re-present the trope of deductive reasoning as a *force majeure* in literature. In 'The Murders in the Rue Morgue' the entire narrative construction is founded on this premise. Poe achieves this effect by the temporal displacement of the crime from the sequential narrative: the mystery is thus resolved in retrospect, and the text becomes the story of an investigation and the deductive methods used to unravel it. In all three Dupin stories the reader learns of the crime through retrospective accounts, either verbal or written. These are, effectively, the placing of clues that are interpreted by the detective and explained didactically at the dénouement, filling the hiatus left by the absence of knowledge about the crime. The result is to give the impression, if not the reality, of an inexorable progress to narrative closure by the resolution and full explanation of the mystery of the crime, with ratiocination as the device that Poe uses to make sense of both plot and narrative. This proved to be detective fiction's first grand illusion, because the narrative arrangement is, of course, constructed solely with its outcome in mind. As Poe himself put it, somewhat deprecatingly, 'In "The Murders in the Rue Morgue" for instance, where is the ingenuity of unravelling a web which you yourself (the author) have woven for the express purpose of unravelling?'[10] This is a point which Poe amplifies in his essay, 'The Philosophy of Composition' (1846):

> Nothing is more clear than that every plot, worth the name, must be elaborated to its *dénouement* before anything be attempted with the pen. It is only with the *dénouement* constantly in view that we can give a plot its indispensable air of consequence, or causation, by

making the incidents, and especially the tone at all points, tend to the development of intention.[11]

This concern with the objective narrative emanated from a remark made by Dickens about *Caleb Williams* with which Poe opens his essay. Godwin had indicated that the book had been conceived backwards, so that the assemblage of plot was constructed to fit the demands of the ending. Poe, it seems, followed this course in 'The Murders in the Rue Morgue' and, as Dennis Porter suggests, it had significant consequences for the detective story:

> All the details of the double murder could not have been set down before the author had first determined the nature and method of his murderer... Poe's practice that was destined to become the prototype of classic detective fiction. After the prologue devoted to a discussion of analytical thought, it is 'the web of difficulties' in all their circumstantiality with which Poe immediately confronts the reader. Accounting for those difficulties occupies the pages that follow down to the climactic moment of the unmasking of the murderer and the final explanations of the *dénouement*.[12]

Approaching 'The Murders in the Rue Morgue' from the point of view of backward construction, as Porter describes it, is a revealing exercise. Such a method helps to explain the linear nature of the detective story narrative; from this moment the detective story becomes a text that is always anticipating a future event, the solution of the crime, by looking back to a past event, the crime itself.

Backward construction also promotes the closed nature of the text, as its narrative is always focused on reaching a dénouement. But crucially, building the narrative in this way allowed complete authorial control over the development of the plot and the speed at which it was paced; more specifically, it emphasized the enclosed part of the text, the investigation. Combined with the creation of the character of the detective, this phase of the story could be extended to preserve the sanctity of the mystery until the last possible moment. A fundamental part of this artifice was also to create a place where clues could be read and false trails laid. Poe outlines just how important this feature is in his essay 'Charles Dickens' (1842):

> That the secret be well kept is obviously necessary. A failure to preserve it until the proper moment of denouement throws all into confusion, so far as regards the *effect* intended. If the mystery

leaks out, against the author's will, his purposes are immediately at odds and ends; for he proceeds upon the supposition that certain impressions *do* exist, which do *not* exist in the mind of his readers.[13]

This is the finishing touch to Poe's narrative – delay, with all its contrivances, heightens tension, desire and participation in the *dénouement* of the mystery. This artifice gives rise to one of the more enduring consequences of Poe's narrative construction. He still seems to have loaded the detective story with elements that are ripe for its subversion. Not the least of these is the preposterous idea of an orang-utan as murderer; but what Poe does with this idea is to perpetuate the illusion that the murderer could have been a man, through the various witnesses' reports of a 'voice' heard at the scene of the murder. This he achieves through the laying of equivocal clues in the investigative phase of the narrative, so that the delay in the revelation of the secret, which we have seen he advocated, becomes an integral instrument of illusion, a misprision invented solely for the working out of the plot. This opportunity was not lost on future authors, many of whom developed the detective story into a game of concealment and misrepresentation.

If the effect that such elements have on the narrative organization is to create a frame around the unsolved crime, then, in the case of 'The Murders in the Rue Morgue', because it is a locked room mystery it doubles thematically and structurally. This arises because enclosure in this sense becomes both narratory and architectural; the locked room mystery is a form which not only gives the fullest expression to the elements of closure and enclosure, but allows the greatest possible impact of ratiocination on a plot as perplexing, seemingly impossible, as it is absurd.

Poe's structure for the detective story became one of the earliest examples of setting a narrative rubric for a popular genre. Having clearly demarked his creation as one based on ratiocination, the progression of a series of logical deductions based on clues, what followed was an absolute concentration on the resolution of a mystery from inception to solution. As Robert Champigny has remarked, 'A narrative that attracts the reader's attention to some undetermined events but avoids determining them at the end is not a mystery story.'[14] This binds the detective story inextricably with hermeneutics. Champigny's definition relies on a closed narrative formula, one which permits the slow release of the truth so that, in the investigation of the crime, the fractured dissemination of hermeneutics is transmitted in the form of clues. Only when all the clues are aggregated can the true picture of what really happened be revealed.

This view is endorsed by Patricia Merivale, who has pointed out that the idea of closure and the process of investigation are elements leading to a '[s]olution, which equals the restoring, through the power of reasoning, a criminally disrupted but inherently viable Order, which equals Narrative Closure. "Closure" is, to simplify, the sort of conclusion by which the preceding narrative comes, in hindsight, to "make sense" and thus, reciprocally, to make the conclusion itself seem inevitable.'[15] This intense focus on a progressive narrative necessitates a structure which encourages the exclusion of all material that does not contribute to its central proposition. But the notion of narrative closure only takes the analysis of detective fiction so far. The desire in the text for narrative closure actually functions as a result of an *en*closed structure in three parts: the story of a crime often preceded by a thematic introduction, the conduct of the investigation, and, finally, the presentation of the solution to the mystery. Thus the main body of the narrative, the investigation of the crime, becomes enclosed by its antecedent, the crime itself, and its subsequent resolution, ensuring that the whole text is taken up with a single consequence.

The establishment of ratiocination in Poe's three works soon became a central proposition for all detective fiction; there was an expectation that Dupin's many successors should exhibit extraordinary powers of deduction to ensure a satisfactory conclusion to the tale. As a result, ratiocination ceased to be a discrete theme in itself; rather it became a central part of the investigative stage of the narrative structure of all detective fiction. This thematic void would soon be filled by other contexts consonant with the enclosed nature of the narrative. It is precisely because this formula was consistently repeated in detective fiction that themes were adopted which in some way would reinforce a structure based on the dynamics of certainty and the restoration of order. Heta Pyrrhönen has argued that this relationship emanated from Poe, who,

> [s]trove for narrative unity to produce the desired emotional effect that, in his detective stories, was the shock of murder muffled through the ironic and detached manner of its handling. Thus, he made plot construction and thematic content reflect one another by presenting composition as a problem and coupling it with viewing murder as an exercise in ratiocination. In this way, most traces of the human dimension of murder were artfully stripped away.[16]

This analysis touches on the key to Poe's creation; but rather than merely a relationship between plot construction and theme it is precisely the enclosing structure of the narrative which gives the genre its character. Because ratiocination forms the outer frames of the story, dictating the mode of the resolution and driving the actions of the principle character, its engagement with the narrative is seamless. Not only is the narrative arranged to achieve the objective of unravelling the problem of the crime, but the theme itself is the means by which this is achieved.

The opening scene of 'The Murders in the Rue Morgue' is rightly regarded as a tour de force. Dupin is walking in the street with his companion, the narrator of the story, and, without any previous discourse on the subject, Dupin is able to tell the narrator what his thoughts have been between encountering a fruiterer and the contemplation of a cobbler-turned-actor called Chantilly. This series also has literary and philosophic allusions: fruiterer – street stones – stereotomy – Epicurus – Dr Nichols – Orion – and thus to Chantilly. Crucially, Dupin is able to provide a link by association between all the disparate encounters that his companion has. This chain of deduction is outwardly impenetrable, but when explained as a rational series it seems the most natural explanation in the world. This thematic introduction on the process of ratiocination becomes, therefore, central to an understanding of the narrative construction of the story. As Poe himself makes clear, having spent the opening pages on the nature of rational thought, this preface holds the key to the story itself: 'The narrative which follows will appear to the reader somewhat in the light of a commentary upon the propositions just advanced.'[17]

What is crucial, therefore, what makes Poe's innovation unique, is the emphasis that he applies to the ratiocinative process. As Patrick Diskin has pointed out, because of certain similarities between the stories it seems that Poe was indebted to Irish author J. C. Managan for aspects of the ratiocinative technique employed in the story.[18] A passage from Managan's tale 'The Thirty Flasks', also published in the *Dublin University Magazine* in 1838, presages the opening sequence from the 'The Murders in the Rue Morgue'. In his story Managan describes the train of associations that pass through his hero's head having been suggested by a glimpse of a pair of sandalled feet in the street. The sequence runs: sandals – feet – dances – Bigottini – the opera – ballets – balls – Brussels – Waterloo – Childe Harold – Byron; it concludes with boot makers and his exorbitant bill. There are, however, key differences between Managan's and Poe's version; Managan, in fact, places his corresponding passage as an aside in his own tale, and not as integral to his story, but to Poe this extended scene is of critical importance to the conception of the detective narrative structure and its relationship with thematic ideas. It is the driving force of the narrative in the same logical way that Dupin reveals the thoughts of his companion; the various clues to revelation of the truth are a sequential path to the final unravelling. The innovation here lies not in the presence of ratiocination but in the structural importance given by Poe to Dupin's demonstration.

The device of prefacing a detective story with a demonstration of ratiocinative technique would provide the pattern for the opening of many such stories, where the detective not only demonstrates the power of the logic he possesses but adumbrates some element of the investigation to come. Conan Doyle, for instance, actually has Holmes repeat Dupin's feat at the beginning of 'The Cardboard Box' (1893) by reading the thoughts of Watson and, at the same time, actually referring to the passage in 'The Murders in the Rue Morgue'.[19] In *The Hound of the Baskervilles* (1901–2), too, the analysis of Dr Mortimer's stick leads to a detailed description of the country doctor and his pet spaniel, a canine trail which inevitably leads to the confrontation with the legendary hound.[20] Moreover, Poe's presentation establishes that the reasoning mind of Dupin, and by extension all detectives who follow, will be the catalyst by which the narrative will be resolved. This structure is itself a strong clue to the unity of the detective story narrative; the genre appears as an effective storytelling medium because in its beginning is its end and in its end is the beginning. Two of the key constituent parts of the narrative, therefore, the introduction and the resolution, engage in a reciprocal dialogue. Not only does this reinforce the framing device for the whole, but it allows for all the outstanding questions of the crime to be answered.

In the second scene of Poe's narrative we encounter the story of the crime proper, the purpose of which is to set out the problem and the salient facts surrounding it. Dupin examines a detailed newspaper account of the murder of Madame L'Espanaye and her daughter. In what would become an accepted practice for such fiction, the circumstances of the original crime often do not unfold as a sequential narrative, but are reported as a series of clue-laden, salient facts. This part of the narrative commences the ratiocinative process by posing a series of problems the solution to which will be the subject of the narrative. From this point onwards ratiocination will act upon the narrative structure, and make sense of it. In the case of 'The Murders in the Rue Morgue' the newspaper reveals that the actual crime appears as an impossible event, the murders having been committed in a room locked from the inside.

The idea for a murder committed in a room to which access from out-side is apparently impossible had, in fact, already been anticipated by Joseph Sheridan Le Fanu in 'Passage in the Secret History of an Irish Countess'. This short story was first published in the *Dublin University Magazine* of 1838, three years before Poe's tale of the murderous orang-utan appeared. Diskin also sees remarkable similarities between the stories of the crimes in Le Fanu's 'Passage in the Secret History of an Irish Countess' and 'The Murders in the Rue Morgue' hint at a possible source for some of the material in Poe's tale. Yet these points of coin-cidence only serve to throw into relief the radically different treatment given to the outcome in each story. The essential difference is that, in Poe's tale, the clues offered are an integral part of the process in that they support the detail of the conclusion. Despite being a perplexing locked room mystery, Le Fanu's tale offers clues that are incidental to the unravelling of the plot and not contingent upon their interpretation.

'Passage in the Secret History of an Irish Countess' concerns Hugh Tisdall, who visits Sir Arthur T—n in County Galway; both are addicted to gambling and consequently spend much time closeted together. One morning Tisdall is discovered murdered, without any clue as to how the murderer entered the room. In Poe's account of the murder of Madame L'Espanaye and her daughter, the initial investigators arrive at the room, 'the door of which, being found locked, with the key inside, was forced open.'[21] Le Fanu at the same point of discovery states: 'the inmates of the house being alarmed, the door was forced open ... The door had been double locked on the *inside*, in evidence of which the key still lay where it had been placed in the lock.'[22] Discussion of the mur-der weapons corresponds too. Poe relates that 'on a chair lay a razor besmeared with blood', and the doctor who describes the injuries inac-curately records that 'any large, heavy and obtuse weapon would have produced such results'.[23] Le Fanu reveals that 'near the bed were found a pair of razors belonging to the murdered man' and that the injuries showed 'one deep wound had been inflicted on the temple, apparently with some blunt instrument'.[24]

Both accounts describe the attempt to ascertain whether access to the room could have been gained by the chimney or a trapdoor. Le Fanu tells how the chimney allowed 'in its interior scarcely the possibility of ascent', and that 'the walls, ceiling and floor of the room were care-fully examined, in order to ascertain whether they contained a trap-door or other concealed mode of entrance – but no such thing appeared.'[25] Poe's representation of the reconnoitre is remarkably similar, recording that 'chimneys of all the rooms on the fourth storey were too narrow to admit the passage of a human being', and that 'a trap-door on the roof was nailed down very securely – did not appear to have been open for years'.[26] Even the topography of the crime scenes bears comparison. We learn that the body of Madame L'Espanaye, having been thrown from the window, was in a 'small paved yard in the rear of the building'[27] and, in Le Fanu's tale, the window of the room looked out 'upon a kind of courtyard, round which the old buildings stood'.[28] In both instances Tisdall's murderers and the orang-utan approach the room from this quarter.

Poe's engagement with the previous text, however, is with the plot only; the dénouement is a complete departure from that employed by Le Fanu. The solution to 'Passage in the Secret Life of an Irish Countess' unfolds openly through a sequence of events in the form of a suspenseful adventure, when the murderers attempt a similar second killing and are observed – confirming, incidentally, Knight's view, quoted earlier, that before Poe 'criminals are caught through red-handed action'.[29] The process of ratiocination thus plays no part in the disclosure of the mystery. In 'The Murders in the Rue Morgue', however, Dupin's explanation is in the form of an intellectual abstraction arrived at through a series of painstaking deductions, inferred from clues. This conclusion represents not merely the resolution of the mystery but the triumph of ratiocination over the chaos of improbability and uncertainty. There is a sense too, that arriving at the solution has strong connections with the action of intelligent reading, of making sense of clues in the same way that a text is deciphered. At the beginning of the final discourse, after visiting the scene of the crime Dupin calls in at the office of one of the daily papers and questions his companion on whether he had observed anything '*peculiar*' at the scene of the crime:

'No, nothing peculiar,' I said; 'nothing more, at least, than we both saw stated in the paper.'

'The *Gazette*,' he replied, 'has not entered, I fear into the unusual horror of the thing. But dismiss the idle opinions of this print. It appears to me that this mystery is considered insoluble, for the very reason which should cause it to be regarded as easy of solution – I mean for the *outré* character of its features.'[30]

Dupin's exhortation to dismiss opinions is a precursor to the application of reason to the accounts in the newspapers. It is, after all, from these accounts, supported by his own observations, that he solves the mystery. As his companion states, both have read the papers; the facts, amid the speculation, are there, but what is needed is interpretation. It is this interpretation that lies at the heart of Poe's structure for the detective story. Interestingly, in the second of his detective trilogy, 'The Mystery of Marie Rogêt', the action of ratiocination as textual interpretation is even more explicit. To achieve this Poe actually inverts the first part of the story so that it appears as the account of the crime followed by a thematic discourse on ratiocination. This allows a lengthy introduction made up of official reports and newspaper articles to relate the story of the crime. Dupin then rails against the quick assumptions made in both texts: 'The mass of people regard as profound only him who suggests *pungent contradictions* of the general idea. In ratiocination, not less than in literature, it is the *epigram* which is the most immediately and the most universally appreciated. In both, it is of the lowest order of merit.'[31] In both 'The Murders in the Rue Morgue' and 'The Mystery of Marie Rogêt', the truth of the mystery is presented in two ways: initially it appears in the form of a series of seemingly haphazard clues in the story of the crime, and finally in a reasoned exposition in the story's resolution.

But in the investigation, like the critical interpreter of a text, Dupin states: 'I proceeded to think thus – *a posteriori*.'[32] This a central proposition for the detective. Dupin, by a process of careful elimination, decides that the window is the only feasible means of access, and so takes this as the point from which his investigation will regress to the murder itself. This backward reasoning, from effect to cause, is a parallel of Poe's construction of the narrative; as such it resonates with the homogeneity of the detective story narrative. One of the principal reasons why the detective story appears so focused and self-contained is that its constituents of narrative enclosure and closure, theme and plot are invariably carefully dovetailed, so that all are contributing to the momentum of the text. This inference leads Dupin to examine the window and discover the faulty nail, and to note the extreme difficulty of access, which could only be achieved with 'almost præternatural' [*sic*] agility.[33] When this evidence is added to that of the peculiarly coarse hair clutched in Madame L'Espanaye's hand, the eccentricities of the voice heard by the witnesses and the particular savagery of the attacks on the women, Dupin arrives back at the scene of the attacks and the identity of the orang-utan. Thus, the idea of backward reasoning leads to a forward momentum of the narrative, and it is ratiocination and this alone, in the face of the violence of the 'murders', which is seen to triumph.

The character of Dupin is, therefore, the personification of reason, a prototype for all detectives who follow him. The authority that Poe ascribes to his detective through the deductive process emerged from his belief in the potency of writing. Poe effectively imbues Dupin with a version of his own authorial power, so that his deductions from the clues of the 'voice', the hair and the nail, enable him to assemble – effectively to 'write' – the solution to the mystery. As Gerald Kennedy has pointed out, Poe actually refers to the physical power that words possess in 'The Power of Words' (1845), emanating particularly from the ability of language to convey tangible effects from a mere arrangement of symbols.[34] The idea of authorial power raises a wholly different idea in our understanding of what is meant by the locked room. For Poe the action of writing was inextricably bound up with the many images of death, enclosure and entropy that pervade his work. It invokes the notion of the locked room of the psyche, the struggle contained within an author's mind in the exercise of writing as a creative force. Nowhere is this influence, and indeed legacy, demonstrated more vividly than in the writing of Paul Auster, particularly in *The New York Trilogy*, which is the subject of Chapter 7.

As far as Dupin is concerned, however, this power of writing is manifested by Poe's vicarious handling of his character. The final scene, therefore, becomes not only an imposition of logic over the story of the crime but a reprise of the first, both as a demonstration and a confirmation of the practical application of ratiocinative powers.

We may, therefore, annotate Poe's narrative structure in 'The Murders in the Rue Morgue' thus: (1) *thematic introduction*, as an exposition of ratiocinative techniques or the anticipation of an alternative theme; (2) *the story of the crime*, which may be contemporary with the narrative or precede it; (3) *investigation*, through a visit to the scene of the crime and the exercise of a posteriori reasoning; and (4) *resolution* as a didactic homily by the detective. This conversion of the directly experiential narrative into a carefully managed text of omissions forms the single most important structural shift for the new genre. What results is a text which exhibits an integrity born of the relationship between a tightly drawn narrative and the language of reason, with its precise and detailed hermeneutics. It is this arrangement that detaches Poe's story from the method of presenting mysteries in contemporaneous Gothic and Sensation fiction, offering the prospect that the detective tale is as much about the method by which the mystery is resolved as the solution itself. Such a method demands that explanation and resolution are repeated features of each narrative, because the denial of a solution to a mystery that has been created solely to demonstrate the deductive powers of a detective's mind would be unthinkable. In the very moment of its creation, therefore, the detective story immediately exhibited the potential for those rigidly formulaic qualities that would characterize its progress and provoke its critics.

But Poe's narrative structure in 'The Murders in the Rue Morgue' is significant too, in quite another sense: the locked room itself is the architectural realization of the genre's own enclosed narrative. Revealingly, Poe prepares the ground for this confining physical space at the beginning of 'The Murders in the Rue Morgue'. Dupin and his companion, we learn, live a cloistered existence in a 'grotesque mansion': 'Our seclusion was perfect. We admitted no visitors. Indeed the locality of our retirement had been carefully kept a secret from my own former associates; and it had been many years since Dupin had ceased to know or be known in Paris. We existed within ourselves alone.'[35] Likewise, the L'Espanayes:

> Witnesses had seen the daughter some five or six times during the six years. The two lived an exceedingly retired life – were reputed to have money.... Had never seen any person enter the door except the old lady and her daughter, a porter once or twice, and a physician some eight or ten times.... The shutters of the front windows were seldom opened. Those in the rear were always closed.[36]

In order to solve the crime, therefore, Dupin must move within two sequestered places, his own house and that of the L'Espanayes. This engagement with the world of the *intérieur* is fundamental to the concept of the detective story. Walter Benjamin went as far as to say that because *intérieur* is a separation from the external world, it is 'not just the universe of the private individual; it is also his *etui*'; as such, what it reveals about that individual and the incidence of his or her life means that it holds 'the origin of the detective story, which inquires into these traces and follows these tacks'.[37]

Benjamin's view is a reaffirmation of the closed nature of the detective narrative; it is removed from the external world in the same way that the L'Espanayes live their lives. The essence of a locked room story, therefore, is to create two quite different loci: the room itself and the space surrounding it. Mark Madoff has characterized the relationship between the two:

> The locked-room mystery is a problem of comparison – how to discover a passage between inside and outside, how to acknowledge and

explain the fact that both inside and outside are places within the same universe, though they afford perspectives of that universe as different as the killer's and the victim's.

The parallels between the detective's dilemma and the Gothic locked-room mystery also include similar definitions of 'inside' and 'outside,'... In the detective's realm, 'inside' is a place of unexpected, inexplicable peril, of chaos which seems to sweep aside even the usual laws of physics. In the detective's realm, 'outside' is a place of banal order and reason, of hopeful safety from the rage whose results stay locked inside a room. It is a place of solved cases.[38]

So, just as the conclusion impacts on the narrative structure, at the same time it makes sense of the anarchic void of the locked room by virtue of a logical solution from the external world. This double alliance of structure and thematic content, the cooperation between the physical and the narratological enclosures, appears as a major force in the working out of the detective story's closed narrative. The relentless pursuit of logic throughout the text, the exclusive nature of the depiction of enclosure brooks no intrusion from any thematic content which does not contribute to the unfolding of the narrative. Poe's schema for the detective story thus, from its very origins, associates the genre with a proposition that resolution to intractable problems is not only desirable but always possible. Much of the case for seeing the detective story as conservative, therefore, emanates from this perception of its narrative that resolution always seeks to impose a version of the truth on the questions its text poses, which invariably means a return to the status quo.

But beneath its artifices and its preoccupation with structure and reason, Poe's detective stories, perhaps surprisingly, contain distinct resonances with his *Tales of the Grotesque and Arabesque*. This relationship, however, operates at a more profound level of understanding than the merely 'outré' nature of a plot involving a murderous orang-utan; it is rather that the narrative structure of enclosure corresponds with the relationship between physical enclosures and death which appear in many of Poe's tales. Sidney Poger and Tony Magistrale have considered the whole question of this relationship in 'Poe's Children: the Conjunction of the Detective and the Gothic Tale'. Their overall conclusion is that in both forms Poe sought to resolve the interior struggles of the mind between self-control and perversity. In the Gothic tales this is manifested as the exploration of the human capacity for evil, and in the detective tale as the exorcism of the irrational through logic. So, in 'The Murders in the Rue Morgue',

> Dupin grasps one end of the chain of reason and follows it to its other end, never once breaking the logic. Even the irrationality of the ourang-outang, appearing at a fourth-story window in Poe's 'The Murders in the Rue Morgue' is not enough to defeat our detective. The ape will be traced back to its owner, it will be captured, and it will be safely imprisoned in a zoo, never to escape again.[39]

But in the case of uncontrollable horror, of course, the potential for its return is constant; thus, the closure which pervades detective stories can be seen as a positive response to the dread of death in Poe's Gothic imagination. The sense of enclosure, therefore, ubiquitous in tales such as 'The Fall of the House of Usher' (1839), 'The Pit and the Pendulum' (1842) and 'The Cask of Amontillado' (1846), receives a formalized, corrective structure in the Dupin trilogy. As Geoffrey Hartmann has stated in his essay 'Literature High and Low: The Case of the Mystery Story', which argues the case for detective fiction to be favourably compared with more explicitly literary genres, this structure is all embracing. This arises from:

> A central if puzzling feature of the mystery story. Its plot idea tends to be stronger than anything the author can make of it. The *surnaturel* is *expliqué*, and the djinni returned to the bottle by a trick. For the mystery story has always been a genre in which appalling facts are made to fit into a rational or realistic pattern.[40]

Crime and murder in the ratiocinative story, therefore, do not appear as 'appalling facts' but as intellectual puzzles to be solved. In this respect it is possible to see the detective story as brooking all alternative possibilities other than the resolution of the mystery to which its narrative is directed. This sense of completeness includes the moderation of the most extreme and even supernatural elements. Its mollifying effect on the more outré content helps to explain why theme in the detective story invariably supports the enclosing format of the narrative structure, aiding the progression of the investigation. This takes the narrative away from the unpredictability of the fantastic and towards a reasoned conclusion.

The apparent antithesis of Poe's supremely rational texts with the remainder of the *Tales of the Grotesque and Arabesque* does not prevent striking similarities in the thematic content. The architectural possibilities of enclosure are omnipresent throughout Poe's canon. In the same way that the narrative structure of 'The Murders in the Rue Morgue' encloses the mystery of the locked room, so the three Dupin tales are surrounded by Gothic tales, imbued with the presence and menace of enclosed spaces. The relationship between the two becomes thematically reciprocal. Joseph Riddel has pointed out they appear as a 'patchwork of metaphors that nets together much of the Poe canon, weaving discursive and imaginative texts and at the same time erasing the generic margins between the so-called tales of the grotesque and the tales of ratiocination'.[41]

One of the most enduring metaphors in Poe's work, which crosses these generic boundaries, is the association between death and enclosure. From 'A Decided Loss' (1832) to 'The Cask of Amontillado' (1846) the association between the two runs through his fiction like an obsessive nightmare. In such stories as 'The Pit and the Pendulum', 'The Tell-Tale Heart' (1843), 'The Oblong Box' (1844), 'The Premature Burial' (1844) and 'The Cask of Amontillado', Poe returns again and again to the world of 'The Fall of the House of Usher'. In these tales the main protagonists all seem to inhabit a locked room of a kind, be it a tangible architectural space or somewhere within their own psyche – or, very often, a correlation between the two. They create a world in which inside and outside become of extreme importance, where enclosure forms the boundary between the exterior world of the rational and the interior world of misrule. Roderick Usher's house, for instance, is a prison, a place he never leaves, which also contains the body of his sister whom he has entombed alive. In one sense she is dead and in another she is not; this enables her escape from the tomb as a wraith to confront her brother. But this escape only leads to the wider enclosure of the house itself and precipitates the destruction of its closed world, bringing about the death of Roderick. As his sister approaches him, his desperate cry is, 'Oh whither shall I fly?'[42] There is no escape from this locked room.

By 1845 Poe had abandoned his experiment with the tales of ratiocination, and the three Dupin stories remain his only examples of detective fiction. As early as 1840 he had anticipated the narrative limitations that a text based solely on ratiocination might provide, arguing that man 'perpetually finds himself...decrying instinct as an inferior faculty, while he is forced to admit its infinite superiority, in a thousand cases, over...reason'.[43] From this it is clear that Poe sees instinctual behaviour as an important counterbalance to the application of pure logical thought – so much so that in 'The Murders in the Rue Morgue' Dupin describes the prefect of police as 'too cunning to be proud. In his wisdom is no *stamen*. It is all head and no body, like the pictures of the Goddess Laverna, – or, at best all head and shoulders, like a codfish.'[44]

Poe's departure from the detective story, therefore, did not mean that he had ended his preoccupation with the literary possibilities of the sealed enclosure; rather, he altered the narrative perspective. In a story which would impact greatly on subsequent locked room stories, 'The Pit and the Pendulum', Poe's narrative depicts the sealed chamber from the perspective of an individual's struggle between rationality and instinctive behaviour. Although the more obvious connotations are with such 'mechanical device' stories as Wilkie Collins's 'A Terribly Strange Bed' (1852) and Conan Doyle's 'The Adventure of the Engineer's Thumb' (1892), Poe's story is also an examination of the psyche's reaction to the experience of the locked room. Apart from the brief opening scene, as the Inquisition condemns the narrator to death, the whole of the story is told from this perspective. Poe reinforces this view from the inside by internalizing the narrative still further. Alone, faced with darkness, fear and the unknown, the narrator's occupation of the cell becomes a struggle within himself, between reason and instinct. The conflict manifests itself as a restless urge to deduce more about his surroundings and a resignation to what seems to be an inevitable fate.

Poe introduces the process of ratiocination as a method by which the prisoner might escape from darkness into light, offering the prospect that discovery and knowledge are, in themselves, salvation. He uses techniques worthy of Dupin himself:

> My outstretched hands at length encountered some solid obstruction. It was a wall, seemingly of stone masonry – very smooth, slimy, and cold. I followed it up; stepping with all the careful distrust with which certain antique narratives had inspired me. This process, however, afforded me no means of ascertaining the dimensions of my dungeon... I therefore... tore a part of the hem from the robe and placed the fragment at full length, and at right angles to the wall. In groping my way around the prison, I could not fail to encounter this rag upon completing the circuit.[45]

The process of detection in this story, however, proves, quite literally, to be a dead end. It solves nothing. The prisoner laments that 'I had little object – certainly no hope – in these researches; but a vague curiosity prompted me to continue them.'[46] Poe's purpose in describing these ratiocinative techniques is to present the prisoner's struggle with reason, in the form of logical deduction, and its antithesis, instinctive behaviour. Gradually, the seeming impossibility of his situation has its effect; the discovery of the pit with its inviting chasm is followed by the appearance of the bladed pendulum. Escape from the pendulum by subterfuge only brings yet more danger. The prisoner's ironic cry 'Free! – And in the grasp of the Inquisition!'[47] invokes the plight of Roderick Usher's sister and the pyrrhic victory of her escape from the tomb, merely to be contained within the walls of the cell. Accordingly, the next torture begins in the form of metal walls, which emanate heat and close mechanically on their victim.

In one sense 'The Pit and the Pendulum' represents Poe's response to the detective story, a subversion of the dominance of reason, a vision of an arbitrary world of cruelty. This dislocation quite literally renders the locked room of 'The Murders in the Rue Morgue' inside out, a place where the normal rules of logic and order do not apply. But this conclusion alone would be too simplistic, in that the prisoner is condemned to torture by the Inquisition, which, as the dominant force in the outside world, should, if the detective story is to be believed, represent what passes for order. 'The Pit and the Pendulum', therefore, is a negation of the rigidly logical Dupin trilogy, arguing instead for the complementary nature of instinct and reason. As J. A. Leo Lemay has shown, the head, 'the citadel of reason', is revealed as useless without a corresponding and interdependent part.[48] Poe's own proposition, that it is possible to reimpose order through the application of logic, is debunked by the behaviour of the prisoner. His occupation of the cell is characterized by a reality where instinct and reason constantly tussle for supremacy.

The hopeful deductions made about his cell are followed by one setback after another until, mimicking death, he resigns himself body and soul to what appears to be his fate. The prisoner's dread of the pit and his submission to it is, as Jeanne Malloy has suggested, 'to acknowledge the power of the unconscious and the limitations of the intellect'.[49] At the point of death the prisoner, the body in the locked room, is reborn following his rescue by General Lasalle's French forces which have taken the city of Toledo and deposed the Inquisition. This equivocal ending depicts a state, familiar in Poe, which hovers between life and death. Does the prisoner live or die? Or is the abruptness of the ending an awakening from a dream rather than reality? Even the possibility of rebirth is in marked contrast to the fate of the L'Espanayes in 'The Murders in the Rue Morgue', where suffering and self-knowledge forms no part of a narrative focused on the nature and practice of reason alone. For Poe, the view from inside the locked room, with its connotations of suffering and death, is central to the understanding of his fiction. The fact that he discontinued the detective series is a sign that he already saw its possibilities as barren, played out because of the crucial absence of a balance between logic and emotive reaction.

At the heart of Poe's disenchantment lay a realization of the inevitable subjectivity of analysis. As William W. Stowe has argued, detectives such as Dupin 'Do not allow the objects of their investigations to question their methods or the ideological assumptions that inform them...They remain prisoners of method, brilliant technicians who can only go on repeating what they already do so well.'[50] The problem with method is that it tries to reduce rather than to amplify. It is this dichotomy that held within it the possibility for two types of detective story to coexist: the strictly ratiocinative text and that which looked beyond the reduction of all subject matter to fact. Kevin Hayes has pointed out, in his study of the effect of Poe's work on the avant-garde movements from the mid-nineteenth-century onwards, that '[t]he Power of Words' contains a 'metaphysical dialogue which suggests that once a word is uttered, it continues to exist and have influence across the infinity of space.'[51] Such a view predicates the work of a writer such as Borges as it posits the existence of texts beyond their original setting, enabling the detective formula to be presented in such a way that places its narrative in the context of a wider contingency. For Poe, however, the discrete thematic and structural interplay between ratiocination and strict narrative form had been exhausted. Perhaps, in the production of 'The Murders of the Rue Morgue', he realized that a life devoted to the exercise of pure reason, such as is lived by Dupin, is merely the opposite extreme of the destabilized dystopia represented by the locked room of the L'Espanayes' apartment. After all, the narrator describes his sepulchral life with Dupin, their own version of the locked room, by recognizing that their routine could be thought that of 'madmen'.[52] So Dupin's locked room is a quite different artifice; it is based on the equally improbable proposition of pure reason – he lives for the shadows of the evenings, and most revealingly, to exercise 'a peculiar analytical ability'.[53] Although Poe seems to have exorcized this particular demon from his own psyche, detective fiction had come to stay.

2
The Locked Compartment: Charles Dickens's 'The Signalman' and Enclosure in the Railway Mystery Story

Listen to my song, and I will not detain you long,
And then I will tell you of what I've heard.
Of a murder that's been done, by some wicked one,
And the place where it all occurred;
Between Stepney and Bow they struck the fatal blow,
To resist he tried all in vain,
Murdered by some prigs was poor Mr. Briggs
Whilst riding in a railway train.

Excerpt from a penny broadsheet *c*.1870 on the first
railway murder in1864

On the evening of Saturday, 9 July 1864, Thomas Briggs, the chief clerk of Robarts Bank in the City, boarded the 9.50 train from Fenchurch Street to Hackney. Briggs was returning home from a weekly excursion to visit a family member in Peckham, a routine journey he had made countless times, but on this particular occasion it was destined to become infamous in the annals of crime. When passengers at Hackney boarded the first class compartment formerly occupied by Briggs, they found it covered in blood, with a bag and stick belonging to Briggs and a singular hat, not Briggs's, lying between the seats. The alarm was raised. The battered body of Briggs, still alive, was found on the line between Hackney Wick and Bow; it has never been established whether he fell or was thrown from the train during the attack. Whatever the truth of these events, he died of his injuries later that evening.[1] The crime prompted the largest manhunt thus far in English legal history; eventually, with the help of forensic examination of the hat, a German émigré, an ex-gunsmith turned tailor by the name of Franz Müller, was arrested in America where he had fled after the murder. Müller was tried, convicted and eventually hanged outside Newgate on 14 November 1864. With public executions being banned in 1868, this was one of the last such spectacles.

The first murder on the British railway system, already racked by controversy because of its appalling record of accidents, brought with it a new and deeply worrying prospect, the spectre of crime. It is difficult, after a span of nearly 150 years, to appreciate the widespread alarm that the Briggs murder caused; the fact that some 50,000 people attended the execution is testament not merely to prurient curiosity but to the extent to which the case had gripped public attention. *The Annual Register* for 1864 went as far as to say that 'The murder of Thomas Briggs will be long remembered as one of the most notable events of the year – a crime which seemed to bring home to every citizen in the United Kingdom, no matter how quiet and orderly his life, the danger of a sudden and violent death.'[2]

The Briggs case was largely responsible for dispelling a hitherto widespread belief that passengers were immune from the danger of attack within the supposedly safe surroundings of a railway compartment. There was a particular reason for this reaction. In the 1860s, all trains were without a corridor or a reliable means of communication with the driver, and so they became not only a place of physical entrapment but a locus for all kinds of imagined danger. As Wolfgang Schivelbusch has remarked, 'The train compartment became a scene of crime – a crime that could take place unheard and unseen by the travelers in adjoining compartments.'[3] The railway compartment had become, in effect, a locked room where the passenger was a helpless victim of circumstance. According to Schivelbusch, this has much to do with the railway's displacement of a familiar and sedate travel environment:

> The notion that the railroad annihilates space and time is not related to that expansion of space that results from the incorporation of ever new spaces into the transport network. What is experienced as annihilated is the traditional space time continuum which was characterized by the old transport technology. Organically embedded in nature as it was, that technology, in its mimetic relationship with space, permitted the traveller to perceive that space as a living entity.[4]

Not only did the railways race through the spaces which passengers had grown accustomed to, but they created new and more sinister spaces such as cuttings, tunnels and compartments. To travel in a train, therefore, was to enhance the experience of enclosure and, although this was a response to the physical surroundings, it becomes quickly translated into a deeper psychological concern. Such an experience is brought about by loss: relinquishing control of one's actions to another, with its attendant alienation of power, intensifies the feeling that adverse consequences are more likely. The greater the degree of dislocation, the closer the exigencies of fate seem. The displacement passengers experienced in this new environment meant that the relationship with those in control of the train, the drivers and the engineers, was one of complete abstraction, without any sense of real communication. Like the victim in a conventional locked room, the passenger's ability to exercise control over his or her existence is forfeited. So the railway, a leviathan of the Industrial Revolution which had become central to Victorian life, faced a crisis of confidence. Amidst this atmosphere of near hysteria the railway mystery story emerged as a discrete form; born of an era in which anxiety was prevalent, it has, to the present day, retained a discourse of enclosure characterized by linguistic, architectural and behavioural elements.

Perhaps, therefore, one of the enduring consequences of the Briggs murder was on the imagination – the possibility that the railways had become a magnet for the mysterious and unexplained, a place particularly vulnerable to the vagaries of fate. Interestingly, in 1866, just two years after these events, the precarious state of the railways prompted Charles Dickens to assemble a collection of railway stories under the title 'Mugby Junction'.[5] Not only did these works represent some of the earliest dystopian visions of the railway, but their influence on future stories would be far reaching and profound. Dickens's seminal contribution to 'Mugby Junction', was 'The Signalman', a ghostly tale which chronicles the catastrophic consequences of psychological disturbance. Amelia Edwards's 'The Four-Fifteen Express' (1866), like 'The Signalman' a ghost story, was originally intended for inclusion in 'Mugby Junction' but far exceeded the prescribed length and eventually found its way into the rival *Routledge's Christmas Annual* of the same year. It concerns the spooky encounter with a murdered official in a railway compartment and offers an enticing view from within the enclosed chamber. These stories are not so much concerned with the conventional locked room mystery, but with the opportunities they provide to consider the metaphysical and its relationship with the idea of enclosure. In this context the human psyche appears as a metaphor for the locked room itself.

The chthonic environment of 'The Signalman' is heavy with the weight of past events; reinforced by the use of apocalyptic language, it is a place where such memories are invoked in the signalman's psyche. Every feature serves to reinforce the idea of entrapment: the deep cutting, the sunless aspect and particularly the 'black' tunnel through which the dead are brought after the accident, and the place before which the spectre appears. From the very moment that the narrator encounters the signalman the language is highly suggestive of an enfolding landscape; he describes the railwayman's figure being 'down in a deep trench' and this impression is reinforced by an extended description of the narrator's descent:[6]

> The cutting was extremely deep, and unusually precipitous. It was made through a clammy stone, that became oozier and wetter as I went down... His post was in as solitary and dismal place as ever I saw. On either side, a dripping-wet wall of jagged stone, excluding all view but a strip of sky; the perspective one way only a crooked prolongation of this great dungeon; the shorter perspective in the other direction terminating in a gloomy red light, and the gloomier entrance to a black tunnel, in whose architecture there was a barbarous, depressing, and forbidding air. So little sunlight ever found its way to this spot, that it had an earthy, deadly smell; and so much cold wind rushed through it, that it struck chill to me, as if I had left the natural world.[7]

This language of enclosure, however, is more than a mere dystopian view of an industrial landscape; it is a part of the doubling process of the text which connotes directly with the signalman's psyche. David Seed says of this passage, 'From the very start then the tunnel becomes a focus of mystery, heightened by the metaphor of enclosure (the whole cutting is a "great dungeon") and the association with death (the tunnel has "an earthy, deathly smell").'[8]

When Dickens wrote 'The Signalman', the devastating crash in the Brighton–Clayton Tunnel, which had occurred some five years before, was still a vivid memory.[9] Intriguingly, the actual setting of the Clayton Tunnel had remarkable similarities with that of 'The Signalman', and there has been speculation that it is this particular incident which was the source for the first accident described by Dickens's signalman.[10] As the locus for doom, therefore, the tunnel became emblematic and was revisited in many railway stories. In Mrs Henry Woods's 'Going Through the Tunnel'(1869), it is entering the tunnel in the dark without a lamp which exercises the passengers – fears which are proved well founded when the thief steals the Squire's pocketbook containing fifty pounds, in the darkness of the carriage.[11] Conan Doyle's 'The Adventure of the Bruce-Partington Plans' has the body of Cadogan West found in the mouth of a tunnel. This story, which features the London Underground, utilizes the obscurity of this system as a kind of nexus to connect Holmes with the spy Oberstein. It is through studying the rail network and retracing the likely route taken by the body on the roof of a train that Holmes tracks down the murderer.

The depth of the cutting has prompted Ewald Mengel to observe that '"the steep cutting" in which the major part of the action is set, reminds one of Poe's pits, cellars, and tombs'.[12] This is especially relevant when one considers the character and situation of the signalman and the fate of the prisoner in 'The Pit and the Pendulum.' As Chapter 1 has shown, Poe's writing draws a direct parallel between enclosure and death, a consequence of his own fear of being buried alive; it is this fear which returns as both conscious and unconscious features of the text. 'The Signalman', therefore, provides us with a perspective from the psyche struggling to contain the burden it carries, doubly enclosed within both its own traumatic memory and the physical landscape the signalman inhabits. In short, the text is double-headed; the internal and external considerations are entirely engaged one with the other. This symbiosis between the signalman and the environment he inhabits becomes apparent as soon as the narrator is ushered into the signalman's box, euphemistically a coffin, whose connotations of death will soon be realized when his own body is placed there. The signalman had been 'a student of natural philosophy, and had attended lectures; but he had run wild, missed his opportunities, gone down, and never risen again. He had no complaint to offer about that. He had made his bed, and he lay upon it. It was far too late to make another.'[13] Dickens's doubling here of the descent motif between the landscape of the railway and the decline of the signalman's fortunes is a reminder of the extent to which he has fallen; he has 'gone down, and never risen again'. Yet the implications are far deeper than a mere fall from grace; there is finality in the language which pervades the whole narrative. The resignation to his life, one which clearly does not meet his original aspirations, is a recognition that he has largely contributed to his own misfortune.

It transpires that the signalman receives intimations of his own death through the medium of a spectre that, crucially, he alone sees and whose appearances foreshadow the occurrence of a tragic event. While the bleak landscape of cuttings, boxes, sheds and tunnels creates a physical dungeon, the psychological entrapment the signalman feels has an even greater impact on his demeanour. Having previously had no complaint to offer about his situation, he admits to the narrator, 'I am troubled, sir, I am troubled.'[14] The signalman recounts the appearance of the spectre, which has now happened on two occasions. In the first instance the figure appears at the edge of the tunnel, covering its face with the left hand and waving the right, shouting the fateful words 'Halloa! Below there! Look out!'[15]

This first appearance of the spectre presaged the accident in the tunnel which happened a year before the signalman's encounter with the narrator. The signalman reveals the trauma he experienced as a result and only after 'six or seven months passed' did he recover from 'the surprise and shock'.[16] But this merely provokes the second appearance of the spectre, whose presence adumbrates the death of a 'beautiful young lady' who 'had died instantaneously in one of the compartments'.[17] In a scene that will again prefigure the aftermath of his own death, the body of the woman is brought into the box and laid on the floor in the same position where the signalman himself will lie. Following these premonitions of death the signalman tells the narrator that the spectre has begun to appear again; this time the fateful words are prefaced with a new phrase, 'For God's sake, clear the way!'[18] And the signalman realizes that this third appearance 'surely is a cruel haunting of *me*'.[19] On his third visit the narrator discovers that the signalman has been knocked down and killed by a train. The circumstances are, however, somewhat bizarre. It seems that the signalman had his back to the train and despite the warnings given by the driver he took no heed and was cut down. This adds to the impression that in some way the signalman is responsible for his own death by abandoning his former diligence and surrendering to the spectre's warnings, which are, significantly, repeated by the engine driver. Since the spectre appears exclusively to the signalman, the conclusion that it is a product of his unconscious is not hard to make. What repeatedly returns to haunt him is the warning of death, a death which ultimately turns out to be his own. So, while the signalman is able to come to terms with his physical surroundings, the locked room of his own psyche allows only the vision of death to escape. It is the metaphor of the landscape, this 'unnatural valley', as the narrator calls it, which reinforces the psychological disturbance at the heart of the story.[20]

The drama of 'The Signalman', however, becomes doubly charged because the text re-enacts the trauma of its author. Just as a year had passed between the crash in the story and the appearance of the narrator, similarly 'The Signalman' appeared in print for the Christmas edition of *All The Year Round* only 18 months after Dickens had been a passenger on a train involved in the notorious Staplehurst rail crash, which had claimed many lives.[21] The crash, which occurred on 9 June 1865, resulted from the inability of a flagman to give an adequate warning because his foreman had miscalculated the time of the train's approach to repair works on a viaduct. The train then jumped a gap in the rails, dragging the central and rear coaches clean off the bridge, with Dickens trapped in one of two overhanging carriages left on the viaduct. Dickens was travelling with Ellen Ternan and her mother, and all three were thrown into one corner of the dangerously tilting carriage. With great presence of mind Dickens rescued both women, clambered down into the ravine to tend the injured and the dying and even returned to the precarious carriage to rescue the manuscript of *Our Mutual Friend*.

Dickens's initial reaction to this trauma was somatic. For a short period following the crash he was unable even to speak, and, more permanently, susceptible to bouts of shaking brought on by a terror that any carriage in which he travelled had a pronounced and potentially catastrophic left-hand list. These symptoms were a tangible legacy of the accident but, such was the instinctive desire to rescue others and help those affected, the immediacy of the situation seems to have caused a denial of the terror of the moment. Four days after the event Dickens wrote to Thomas Mitton about its consequences, saying: 'I don't want to be examined at the inquest and I don't want to write about it. I could do no good either way, and I could only seem to speak about myself, which, of course I would rather not do...but in writing these scanty words of recollection I feel the shake and am obliged to stop.'[22] Dickens's conscious intent to avoid resurrecting fears by the act of writing is at variance with what seems to be the expression of unconscious fears about the railway, accidents and the prospect of death that appear in 'The Signalman'. While it would be unwise to claim that Dickens's experiences in the Staplehurst crash directly provoked the writing of this story, there remains a cogent argument for the text to be seen, partly at least, as the product of the trauma produced by his experiences. In this reading, Dickens returns to the scene of the crash through the medium of a text that draws out his more unconscious fears by a process of transference into the central character of the story. So the text can be seen as a conscious space, where authorial thoughts are also suffused with the unconscious products of the psyche.

In fact, alarm about safety on the railways had been an increasingly important issue for writers in the 1850s and 1860s; Dickens himself had written a polemical article entitled 'Need Railway Travellers be Smashed?' as early as 1851.[23] The major accidents at Warrington and Abergele in the 1860s were just the latest in a long line of such calamities. The *Saturday Review* gave vent to the general unease by talking of a 'vague sense of danger' on the railways,[24] and the *Railway News*, somewhat sarcastically, reported that 'come what may in the way of accidents, we must keep down working expenses and keep up dividends'.[25] Two articles in the *Lancet* in 1861 featured railway accidents[26] and injuries sustained on the railways;[27] this latter article is significant because it concerned the Brighton–Clayton Tunnel accident which occurred on 25 August 1861, caused by the incompetence of a signalman.[28] Dickens's close association with such calamities would undoubtedly have struck a chord with his contemporary readership; indeed the depiction of phantoms may well have been of secondary consequence to the anxiety about safety, as Simon Cooke says:

> Drawn, as if by a malign 'force' into the Signalman's presence, the narrator takes the reader into the company of a man whose appearance readers in 1866 would have found troubling. In this sense, 'The Signalman' is more than a macabre tale of the supernatural. Rather it ought to be read, I contend, as a psychological narrative, one that locates its terror not in the strange and the magical but rather in the everyday and the prosaic. Viewed in these terms, the experiences described remain anything but 'inexplicable,' at least to the original audience, for whom issues of safety rather than the supernatural were of far greater importance.[29]

Cooke's use of the term 'psychological' is interesting in that it allies the fears of safety to a sensory plane other than the physical. This is a central idea to any psychoanalytical reading of 'The Signalman'; it implies an interaction between the conscious and the unconscious. The conscious effect is characterized by those themes which are familiar constituents of the Dickens *oeuvre*. Such associations had been in Dickens's mind as early as 1848, when he describes Dombey's train journey:

> The very speed at which the train was whirled along mocked the swift course of the young life that had been borne away so steadily and so inexorably to fore-doomed end. The power that forced itself upon its iron way – its own – defiant of all paths and roads, piercing

through the heart of every obstacle, and dragging living creatures of all classes, ages and degrees behind it, was a type of the triumphant monster, Death.[30]

In successive paragraphs the train becomes 'the remorseless monster, Death' and 'the indomitable monster, Death' because the real enigma invariably lies within the psyche of the characters themselves, a psyche which encloses their deepest fears and releases these aberrations involuntarily.[31] The signalman is portrayed as exploited by a dehumanizing system, an individual of promise who has succumbed to the relentless demands of a repetitive routine. The railway, itself, is a leviathan, a post-industrial monster set in an alien landscape where people's lives are regularly put at risk.[32]

On the other hand, the unconscious manifestation of these ideas can be seen in the extent to which Dickens's own view of the railways had changed from the public concern to his individual fears. In 'Need Railway Travellers Be Smashed?' he deals with the 'outside', the visceral, external effects of the railway accident, but 'The Signalman', some 14 years later, concerns itself with the reproduction of private trauma internalized by the psyche. The shift in emphasis during the span of time between these two works comes as no surprise because of a growing interest in the nature of traumatic shock and its impact on the unconscious memory. These public concerns about the railway and its safety are reflected by the trauma of the signalman, and Dickens himself, in different ways. They reappear in the form of both a polemic about the effects of industrialization and, importantly, a poignant, personal yet unconscious fear, released by the act of writing.

So, the problems which the railway brought manifest themselves as both corporeal and psychological. Ralph Harrington sums up the likely impact on the British public of the train environment:

Just as the Victorian railway was a vast and highly visible expression of technology triumphant, the railway accident constituted a uniquely sensational and public demonstration of the price which that triumph demanded – violence, destruction, terror, injury and death. It expressed in a particularly dramatic and striking form the often traumatic nature of the encounter between the human mind and the body, and the industrial realities of the railway.[33]

This association, therefore, of the railway and the human psyche has been a part of railway culture since its early days. Thomas Keller has commented that in Victorian times 'it was thought by many that the shock experienced after a railway accident was unique because of its potentially devastating effect on the psyche'.[34] Not until William Benjamin Carpenter wrote *Principles of Mental Physiology* in 1874 was there a recognition that memory could return unconsciously:

> Any idea which has once passed through the Mind may be thus reproduced at however long an interval, through the instrumentality of suggestive action; the recurrence of any other state of consciousness with which that idea was originally linked by Association, being adequate to awaken it also from its dormant or 'latent' condition, and to bring it within the 'sphere of consciousness'.[35]

By 1889, F. X. Dercum had confirmed this view, stating that in railway accidents, 'The vastness of the destructive forces, the magnitude of the results, the imminent danger to the lives of numbers of human beings, and the hopelessness of escape from the danger gives rise to emotions which in themselves are quite sufficient to produce shock, or even death itself.'[36]

Both Carpenter's and Dercum's work stands on the threshold of Freud's concept of the unconscious and the process by which traumatic memory returns. Portraying the human psyche as a locked room is apposite because of the parallels in the rationale of psychoanalysis, where metaphor is used to explain the workings of the unconscious. In this context, Freud's metaphor of the unconscious in 'A Note upon the Mystic Writing Pad', which likens the psyche to a child's toy, the mystic writing pad, is especially relevant.[37] The pencil is applied to a celluloid surface under which a piece of paper is in loose contact with a wax pad and the writing appears as a result of this temporary contact. When the paper is erased, the writing pad itself retains an impression of previous writing, however faint and distorted, in the wax. Freud's argument was that the psyche acts as the writing pad by absorbing stimuli, and even when these are apparently forgotten or erased, they re-emerge from the unconscious, infused with fear and desire. They are never lost but merely dormant. Freud himself was well aware of this phenomenon: 'A condition has long been known and described which occurs after severe mechanical concussions, railway disasters and other accidents involving a risk to life; it has been given the name of traumatic neurosis.'[38]

A Freudian reading of the circumstances in which Dickens produced 'The Signalman', in the year following his involvement in the Staplehurst crash, would see the text as an unconscious indication of the memory, an indication which is a returning, but modified form, of the original repressed memory. Dickens's psyche, his 'writing machine', produces 'unconscious traces' throughout the narrative; often these traces are a part of a double-edged effect of the same subject, a textual site where the conscious and the unconscious meet to produce different hermeneutic outcomes. This is apparent when the signalman recalls the accident that occurred on the line: on the one hand the text resonates with the widespread public fear about railway safety, on the other, the subject of train crashes, inevitably inviting association with Dickens's personal traumatic experience. Certainly Freud himself believed that a strong connection existed between ghosts and repressed memory; in his seminal 1919 essay 'Das Unheimliche', or 'The Uncanny', Freud states:

> If psycho-analytic theory is correct in maintaining that every affect belonging to an emotional impulse, whatever its kind, is transformed, if it is repressed, into anxiety, then among instances of frightening things there must be one class in which the frightening element can be shown to be something repressed which *recurs*. This class of frightening things would then constitute the uncanny...many people experience the feeling in the highest degree in relation to death and dead bodies, to the return of the dead, and to spirits and ghosts.[39]

Srdjan Smajic in his semiotic reading of the ghost story acknowledges Freud's ideas and remarks that, 'Since ghosts evidently belong everywhere in literature – and consequently, one might say, nowhere in particular – the ghost story appears better adapted to the climate of formalist or psychoanalytic, rather than historicist, readings.'[40] Certainly the potential for both public and private trauma existed in the period when Dickens wrote 'The Signalman' in 1865.

With the development of the arguments in 'The Mystic Writing Pad' and a possible explanation as to the nature of repressed memory comes a model which may be cogently applied to 'The Signalman'. Jill Matus's article, 'Trauma, Memory, and Railway Disaster: The Dickensian Connection', reveals the relationship that existed between trauma and the Victorian concept of the unconscious.[41] This approach allows pre-Freudian ideas to be considered within a post-Freudian context, by assessing the wider problem of the effects of railway accidents from the 1860s onward. The essence of psychological studies before Freud, according to Matus, is that 'very little attention is paid to the effect on memory of traumatic shock'.[42] In 1862, *The Lancet* featured a major article entitled 'Report of the Commission: The Influence of Railway Travelling on Public Health', which, despite extolling the virtue of the railways as 'more free from actual danger to life and limb than any other mode of conveyance',[43] revealingly states that a condition described as 'cerebral congestions', a state of degeneration apparently, could be traced to rail passengers and staff specifically.[44] In essence, 'The Signalman' as a text is what Christopher Bollas has described, in his development of Freud's theories of the unconscious, as 'the articulation of heretofore inarticulate elements of psychic life, or what I term the unthought known'.[45] For Jill Matus this idea becomes, 'A question of the knowing and unknowing self – of how something can be experienced so that it is not available to ordinary consciousness but may be retrieved or re-experienced under the suspension of the will or in a trancelike state.'[46] Often the aberration is an audible or visible hallucination; thus the apparent appearance of the spectre leads the signalman to treat the ghost as real and try to rationalize its behaviour. The narrative becomes a text in which conscious awareness is preoccupied with the interpretation of unconscious manifestations, resulting in a simultaneous doubling of thematic content, the inside and outside of the same idea juxtaposed until the distinction between the two becomes indiscernible. Here we return to the two worlds of the locked room, the areas of order and chaos. In the model of the psychical locked room these boundaries are characterized by a dynamic interaction: 'Trauma vexes the boundaries between outside and inside; recent theorists have remarked that trauma is a situation in which the outside goes inside without mediation. In "The Signalman", Dickens expresses the internal dislocations associated with the external accident.'[47] In the signalman's case trauma has induced a feeling of morbid guilt regarding the fate of those who have died in the accident, quite literally haunted by the idea that he could have prevented the catastrophe. As a result he finds himself trapped in a closed physical world where he languishes in the manner of a victim. This is doubly ironic; although he believes himself to be in effect a murderer, he is at the same time a victim of his own overactive conscience. The 'pain of mind' which affects the signalman arises from 'the mental torture of a conscientious man, oppressed beyond endurance by an unintelligible responsibility involving life'.[48] Thus we may see the spectre that appears to the signalman as a manifestation of that 'mental torture', and his death comes as an inevitable consequence of his sense of guilt. The classic locked room mystery reinforces this idea by framing the victim, drawing attention to a perceived transgression; so, for example, Chapter 4 shows how Leonard Quinton espouses the heterodoxy of Eastern religion and Doomdorf incites the Indians to antisocial behaviour and takes an under-age wife; while in Chapter 5, Professor Grimaud becomes a latter-day Cain responsible for the death of not one but two brothers. Even in Borges's metaphysical world in 'Ibn-Hakam al-Bokhari, Murdered in his Labyrinth', Sa'id quite literally places himself in a physical locked room after adopting Ibn-Hakam Al-Bokhari's persona. All these victims exhibit the concentricity of one locked room within another, physically enclosed and psychically entrapped.

This idea has profound implications for detective fiction; one might posit that in the wider genre, too, there exists, if not a physical locked room, one which resides in the transgressive psyche of the victim. So, in this reading of 'The Signalman', what emerges is a view from the locked room; the fact that this particular space is the psyche does not lessen the sense of entrapment, the only outlet for which is death. As such it becomes a model for the reading of mystery from the alternative standpoint of the victim.

Because of its central preoccupation with a seemingly impenetrable mystery it is unsurprising that 'The Signalman' has been anthologized with detective stories. If the language of psychic and physical enclosure in 'The Signalman' is enough to remind us of the stock constituents of the locked room mystery, then assessing its narrative structure reveals an even deeper affinity with the detective genre.

Dickens's rubric for the narrative complements the nature of the language in the story by the careful use of constricting devices; so, despite its metaphysical themes the text is, in fact, a product of supreme artifice. There are three distinct tropes which are the foundations of the story's ordering: the spectre is contained exclusively within the signalman's story within a story; the only description of the figure is from the psyche of the signalman; the signalman's story and Dickens's tale itself are a series of repetitious incidents which increase in frequency and constrict the narrative. These elements contribute to a structure which mimics that of the classic detective story: the narrator meets the signalman, hears his story and inquires further, before a resolution, in the form of the signalman's death, closes the narrative.

Fundamental to this plan is the construction of a frame, which is a repetition of the phrase, 'Halloa! Below there!',[49] uttered by the narrator at the very beginning of the story and repeated at its conclusion, in a modified form, by the engine driver, 'Below there! Look out! Look out! For God's sake, clear the way!'[50] This framing device serves two purposes. Firstly, it supports the linguistic connotations of the phrase

'Halloa! Below there!' that is the impending death of the signalman, by its prominent positioning at the beginning and ending of the story. The weight that is attached to this phrase by the time the story is finished is crucial to its hermeneutics because what commences as an ostensibly innocent greeting at the outset becomes, through repetition and modification, inextricably linked with the fate of the crash victims, 'the beautiful young woman' and, ultimately, the signalman himself. When the narrator utters this phrase initially, the signalman mistakenly identifies him as the spectre. This is because, in his first appearance to the signalman, the spectre has used the phrase 'Halloa! Below there! Look out!'[51] When the spectre next appears the same phrase is repeated yet again and, in depicting his death, prompts the final version of the warning, which the engine driver will repeat before the signalman is run down.

The second purpose of the frame of repetition is to limit the scope of the narrative by enclosing the story of the signalman's experiences; as a result the whole reads like a story within a story. This is achieved by Dickens through a further subdivision of the frame involving the narrator's three visits. The signalman's account of his predicament, during the narrator's second visit, is held within the two other visits by the narrator. The first visit is an initiation, while the third serves to discover the circumstances of the signalman's fate. Dickens's use of repetition, the visits by the narrator, and the reprise are a means of intensification which operates in contrary motion: the intervals between the appearances of the spectre reduce while the frequency increases. This aspect of the text is critical to its overall structure; as Peter Brooks has said, 'repetition in the text is a return, a calling back or a turning back'.[52] The beginning of each of the story's three phases is marked by the narrator's return to the scene and in each of these visits the signalman's narrative is taken forward in some way. In turn these visits bind together and enclose the further repetitions, which take place as the signalman is forced into increasing incomprehension and panic by the repeated appearance of the spectre, whose gestures and warnings he cannot fully interpret.

The memory of the signalman in these hallucinations is a textually complex one; it is the nature of such traumatic re-enactments that affects perception of the chronology of events and even the sense of what has actually happened. This is precisely because the spectral hallucination is the unconscious product of a psyche haunted by a return of his past failures in preventing the crash and the death of the young woman. But, importantly, they are the return which does not recognize itself as such. The spectre's warnings make the signalman feel uneasy about his own culpability and as a result he is trapped between the consequences of any failure of responsibility and regret for the deaths on his stretch of line. There are a number of examples that express the signalman's ambivalence towards these tragedies:

> There is danger overhanging somewhere on the line. Some dreadful calamity will happen. It is not to be doubted this time, after what has gone before. But surely this is a cruel haunting of *me*. What can I do?' ... If I telegraph Danger, on either side of me, or on both, I can give no reason for it, he went on, wiping the palms of his hands. I should get into trouble, and do no good. They would think I was mad.[53]

The repeated hallucinations that the signalman experiences mark a coincidence between the psychological aspects of the story and its narrative structure. Dickens's structural device of repetition, when applied to the psyche of the signalman, serves to underline his anxiety. It is after all 'too late'; he has sunk into a literally hopeless mental and physical depression for which he alone feels largely responsible.

The framing devices and the repetitions of the text ensure too, that the scope of the narrative is limited to the confined environment where the signalman works. Such is this constriction that the reader learns nothing of the world outside the cutting, the tunnel and the signal box. The signalman has clearly fallen from grace; but apart from the enigmatic reference to his study of philosophy his former life remains a mystery. The information about the narrator, too, only serves to reinforce the atmosphere of enclosure; he 'had been shut within narrow limits all his life'.[54] This compression of the narrative, the exclusion of extraneous events, has the effect of focusing attention on the steps leading up to the climactic event of the story, the death of the signalman. Thus the structure of the narrative acts upon the text in the same way that the language of the physical landscape affects the psyche of both the signalman and the narrator. This symbiosis of structure and language is a metaphorical relationship; the exclusivity of the structure, with its increasing tautness, mirrors the mind of the signalman himself by containing the story of his fate. So the structure is a metaphor for the narrative itself, and vice versa, revealing the whole work as bound up by its concentration on the idea of enclosure at every level. By producing a text that merges the psychological with the physical, and the language with the structure, Dickens creates a discrete world where increasingly the only choice is a retreat into one's own self. The increasing ubiquity of the spectre leaves no doubt that a tragedy will ensue; the signalman's unconscious is tightening its grip upon him. What transpires from this psychic entrapment is, therefore, the notion of death.

But it is not just the physical landscape of the railway that invokes the idea of entrapment. As the murder of Thomas Briggs shows, the train itself was a place of menace and uncertainty. Peter Haining has observed: 'Within the closed doors of the carriages, as the miles pass by and the scenery constantly changes, there exists another even more important element: the other passengers. Who are they? What are their intentions? Are they innocent travellers or potential criminals?'[55] In Amelia Edwards's 'The Four-fifteen Express' the train compartment becomes a paradigm for the confinement created by so much of the enclosed railway landscape. The story concerns William Langford who returns to England after a spell abroad and immediately catches a train to East Anglia so that he can spend Christmas with his old friend Jonathan Jelf. Langford books a compartment to himself but nonetheless is joined by a John Dwerrihouse, someone he recognizes from previous visits. Dwerrihouse, solicitor to the railway company, tells Langford about his new project to extend the line and reveals that he is carrying £75,000 to seal a land purchase deal. When Dwerrihouse leaves the train at Blackwater station he forgets his cigar case; Langford chases after him and sees him talking to a fair-haired man, but as he approaches they vanish mysteriously. Langford learns later, to his amazement, that Dwerrihouse had disappeared some three months earlier together with the money and has not been seen since. Despite initial scepticism Langford produces the cigar case, which is verified as belonging to Dwerrihouse. Although the railway staff are adamant that Langford was alone in the compartment, his claims being made about the encounter reach the ears of the railway company, anxious to investigate any clue to the mystery. Langford is summoned before the railway's board and in the course of the interview spies Raikes, an under-secretary, and recognizes him as the man he saw talking to Dwerrihouse. Raikes subsequently confesses to luring Dwerrihouse away from Blackwater, stealing the money and killing him with a blow to the head. He maintains that he had no desire to kill him, but merely to stun his victim, as robbery was the only motive. Dwerrihouse's body has lain in a pit near the station covered in debris since the attack three months earlier. It seems that three months prior to Langford's trip Dwerrihouse had occupied the very same compartment when he met his fate, leaving his cigar case behind. What Langford saw is left to conjecture.

At its most perceptible level 'The Four-fifteen Express' is, of course, a ghost story in the classic mould, in which the appearance of an eternally restless spectre, aggrieved at some previous injustice, sparks a series of events until the wrong has been overturned. Edwards, therefore, at this level of understanding, invites us to accept a supernatural explanation for events surrounding Langford's journey. But this tale, one of Edwards's most anthologized stories, is also a detective story of a murder and the subsequent investigation; so strong are the elements of detection, in fact, that the whole of the text may be cogently analysed from this standpoint. Viewed from this perspective one might see the story as presenting a particular insight into the psyche of Langford. It is only when Langford encounters the enclosed world of the compartment that the facts of Dwerrihouse's murder at last come to light. The compartment appears as a representation of Langford's psyche, an apotheosis of the physical and the mental planes, a place where he comes face to face with the victim and a vision of his murderer.

In this reading the narrative that the story presents is the working out of Langford's role as detective through the medium of his psyche. The mysterious appearance of Dwerrihouse is a temporal displacement of the normally sequential narrative associated with the detective story. Indeed, after the fracturing brought about by this meeting the remainder of the story follows a conventional pattern, so the narrative purpose of this encounter would seem to be a means by which the mystery of Dwerrihouse's death is explained. In the conventional detective story this is a process of reasoning that the detective undertakes; in 'The Four-fifteen Express' the detective's psyche, the thought processes he undertakes, are realized in a visual manifestation. There is a hint as to the imperative behind Langford's experience in this passage at the end of the story where he ponders the events and the nature of his encounter on the train:

> What was it that I saw in the train? That question remains unanswered to this day. I have never been able to reply to it. I only know that it bore the living likeness of the murdered man, whose body had been lying some ten weeks under a rough pile of branches, and brambles, and rotting leaves, at the bottom of a deserted chalk pit about half way between Blackwater and Mallingford. I know that it spoke, and moved, and looked as that man spoke, and moved, and looked in life; that I heard, or seemed to hear, things related which I could never otherwise have learned; that I was guided, as it were, by that vision on the platform to the identification of the murderer; and

that, a passive instrument myself, I was destined, by means of these mysterious teachings, to bring about the ends of justice.[56]

The final sentence is highly significant. Like the generic detective he is 'destined' to secure 'justice' by revealing the facts of the case to the world. If we understand Langford's character as a supplantation of the detective figure, the mystery of the text seems clearer; the locked room of the compartment in its metaphorical form then becomes a catalyst for the furtherance of the narrative. David Lehman, when considering the legacy of Poe's locked room of the 'The Murders in the Rue Morgue', has outlined these possibilities:

> The detective unlocks the meaning of events; he discerns in them the logic of a homicidal intervention, shows where the plan went astray (if it did), explains what happened and how and why. He alone possesses the magic key.
>
> The locked room is also neutral territory, the battlefield on which the sleuth and the villain tangle. In Poe's paradigmatic case, the locked room is a point of intersection, the place where doubles and twins collide. That is its significance in narrative terms, but it owes that significance to its power as a metaphor. Locked rooms conjure up a primal trauma of imprisonment and claustrophobia.[57]

Significantly, Langford's presence in the 'battlefield' of the enclosed compartment enables an unravelling of the case; he uncovers two decisive pieces of evidence that make sense of the narrative: the very tangible clue of the cigar case, and witnessing Dwerrihouse's meeting with the murderer, Raikes. Thus the resolution which these two crucial facts bring about is nothing less than that of the conventional detective story; from this standpoint, therefore, the question of Dwerrihouse's ghostly appearance has a strictly structural, not literal, function.

This stance is reinforced by the momentum that the journey provides towards the furtherance of the narrative. Thus the compartment as a representation of the working of Langford's psyche becomes a place from which he is 'destined' to resolve the mystery that is before him. The shocking memory which haunts Dickens's signalman, prefiguring his own death, is mirrored at every turn by the physical landscape and the language of the text, while in Langford's case this traumatic intercession becomes the catalyst by which the reasoning process is triggered. This is reinforced by the experience of the train journey, with its beginnings and endings, as a parallel of the unravelling of mystery, as Joseph Kestner has pointed out: 'Railway journeys become locales of existential angst, where contingencies may arise with disconcerting regularity, a trope of life and its hazards...The railway journey may represent several elements – the journey of self-analysis in psychoanalysis, the birth trauma, the journey of life, the contingencies of existence (accidents).'[58] The ultimate 'contingency' of course, is death, as occurred in the case of Briggs. There are, in fact, parallels in Edwards's story with the murder of Thomas Briggs, whose hat, like Dwerrihouse's cigar case, was left in the compartment and whose body was also found displaced from the compartment. We might suppose, therefore, that if the railway journey is emblematic of the 'journey of life', within such a metaphor the compartment, with all its emphasis on enclosure, lies at its very heart. It is a place where the exchange of ideas and the process of reason take effect, simultaneously both public and private, and where random encounter sits alongside intimacy and solitude. This mirrors the action of the psyche, where absorption of ideas and rationale are a part of a continuous network.

Since the publication of these two seminal stories, the ideas they contain have become absorbed into much of the mystery genre. What 'The Signalman' and stories such as 'The Four-fifteen Express' have bequeathed to successive writers is the idea of associating the condition of the human psyche with the specific physical world in which it exists. This symbiotic relationship creates a nexus which defines the tenor of the narrative; so in the case of the railway mystery story, the presence of anxiety and the proliferation of enclosure inevitably overshadow the text. It can be characterized by what is often referred to rather obliquely as 'atmosphere', as in this extract from 'The Eighth Lamp' (1915), a rewriting of 'The Signalman' by Roy Vickers, a prolific writer of detective stories. The deep cuttings of 'The Signalman' are exchanged for a subterranean environment:

> He snatched the keys as he passed and then, as if to humanise the desolation, he broke into a piercing, tuneless whistle that carried him to the seventh lamp.
>
> A trifling mechanical difficulty with the seventh switch was enough to check the whistling. For a moment he stood motionless in the silence – the silence that seemed to come out of the tunnel like a dank mist and envelop him. He measured the distance to the switch of the eighth lamp. The switch of the eighth lamp was by the foot of the staircase. He need scarcely stop as he turned it – and then he would let himself take the staircase two, three, four steps at a time.
>
> *Click!*

The eighth lamp was extinguished. From the ticket-office on the street level a single ray of light made blacker the darkness of the station. But Raoul, within a couple of feet of the staircase, waited crouching.[59]

The story reprises the behaviour of the guilt-haunted psyche; it is a testament to the vision of the railways established by Dickens, in which the deep cutting becomes the literally chthonic landscape of the Underground. Vickers relives the linguistic relationship between its apocalyptic architecture and the human psyche.

George Raoul, a signalman, working on the London Underground, has killed a fellow railwayman, a rival for the hand of Jinny. He is now haunted by his actions. After the eighth lamp of the title is extinguished he witnesses an unscheduled train pass through the darkened station. He dreads the vision but, like Dickens's counterpart, because of guilt he is powerless to resist what emerges from the tunnel:

He only saw his sin in gaining possession of her – in the way that he had gained possession of her – in its naked hideousness.
    The odd fatalism of his class prevented him from shirking the lights on the down-platform. What has to be will be. The same fatalism drove him ultimately to dousing the eighth lamp and turning, like a doomed rat, to face the already rumbling horror of the tunnel.[60]

When the train reappears he sees Pete, his former workmate, whom he has killed, at the controls, and this appearance of the spectre presages his death:

More slowly than before, as if he knew that he must wait for it, the train came on. Then in his ears sounded the familiar grinding of the brakes.
    The train had stopped in the station. The faint luminosity in the driver's window grinned its welcome. Then it beckoned.
    'I'm comin' Pete.'
    From the corner by the staircase, where he had been crouching, he moved across the platform and boarded the train.[61]

The police, already on Raoul's trail because of Jinny's suspicions, find his body dead from heart failure, alongside Pete's, in a disused hole between the two stations.

Both Dickens's and Vickers's tales have been anthologized with collections of detective stories. This should not be a surprise; the detective story had, in fact, become closely associated with the language of enclosure and death to be found in Dickens's, Vickers's and Edwards's tales, as Marty Roth has observed: 'Haunted House stories and detective stories are roughly contemporary literary events. Between them are a remarkable structural similarity and a remarkable semantic difference. At the turn of the century, a corpse found in an old room belonged not to crime but, more often, to spectral influences; it belonged to the past of that room as supernatural ambience.'[62] Roth's point is that this symbiosis is not merely attributable to language, but that the 'ambience' has also found its way into the insecurity that people felt about the railways, a subject which is at the heart of Dickens's tale. In 1897, a story called 'A Mystery of the Underground' by John Oxenham was serialized in a popular weekly, concerning the activities of a serial killer on the London Underground system. Such was the willingness of the public to believe in the dangers of rail travel that the factual newspaper reporting style 'gave Londoners the jitters and earned the author notoriety'.[63] In McDonnell Bodkin's 'The Unseen Hand' (1908), the discovery of a murdered man in a locked compartment causes a reaction that arouses the widespread anxiety about safety which pervades 'The Signalman':

> The train was trembling into motion when at a word from the collector the station-master rushed on the platform and stopped it.
> An instant tumult broke out amongst the passengers. There had been an accident on the line a short time before, and the public nerves were still unstrung.[64]

Nor was the Golden Age immune from the shadow of Dickens's tale. John Dickson Carr is one among many authors who invoke the prospect of the supernatural in his classic, essentially rational, 1928 railway story, 'The Murder in Number Four', which begins thus:

> During the night run between Dieppe and Paris, on a haunted train called the Blue Arrow, there was murder done. Six passengers in the first-class carriage saw the ghost; one other passenger and the train guard failed to see it, which was why they decided the thing was a ghost. And the dead man lay between the seats of an empty compartment, his head propped up against the opposite door and his face shining goggle-eyed in the dull blue light. He had been strangled.[65]

The 'past' that Roth refers to is exemplified by 'The Signalman' and its seminal influence: to read a railway detective story is to experience a text inhabited by 'The Signalman'. This claustrophobic unease abounds in story after story during the Edwardian period: in Baroness D'Orczy's 'The Mysterious Death on the Underground Railway' (1909), in which a woman is found poisoned on the Underground, and Conan Doyle's 'The Adventure of the Bruce-Partington Plans' which appeared in 1912. Reading Canon Whitechurch's *Thrilling Stories of the Railway* (1912),[66] Conan Doyle's 'The Story of the Lost Special' (1908), 'The Story of the Man with the Watches' (1898),[67] and 'The Bruce-Partington Plans' (1908),[68] and McDonnell Bodkin's 'How He Cut His Stick'(1901)[69] is to experience a world which had its beginnings in Dickens's tale.

By highlighting the sinister and potentially threatening enclosures of the cutting, the tunnel and the compartment, and transposing these to the closed world of the psyche, Dickens had created the stock figure of a death-haunted victim. This phenomenon acts on successive literature in the same way that the imprint of the mystic writing pad does on the authorial unconscious. Dickens's narrative surrounds the text in a mystery that can be played out to fulfil the narrative structure, but not resolved; the death of the signalman remains unexplained. For Ewald Mengel, exposition is not part of the narrative structure: 'Dickens attempts to present the death of the signalman not as a mere railway accident, but as the inevitable result of a fatal pattern of predestined events, as the work of forces beyond the grasp of human control.'[70] In the pre-Freudian world, such as prevailed when Dickens wrote 'The Signalman', the reader is beguiled by the possibility of the spectre's reality and the existence of the supernatural. But given what we learn about the signalman's experience of life, his perception of failure, his guilt, it seems much more likely that the supernatural element of the story should not be taken as literal and that his fate is somehow bound up with these traumas. A psychoanalytical reading allows recognition of the likely forces at work, but it scarcely amounts to a teleological reduction, because what ultimately proves to be beyond absolute understanding is the locked room of the psyche.

3
The Body in the Library: Reading the Locked Room in Anna Katherine Green's *The Filigree Ball*

'Do you believe,' he said without preamble, 'that a room can kill?'

John Dickson Carr, *The Red Widow Murders*[1]

'Did you ever hear of a fool crime like this, in a library, a place filled with books, with nice young girls and cranky old maids? What under heavens is there in a library to bring a crime?'

Charles J. Dutton, *Murder in a Library*[2]

It is an iconic moment. Mary the housemaid enters the library and draws back the curtains to reveal the body of a blonde stretched out on the carpet. The Bantrys, hapless owners of Gossington Hall in Agatha Christie's *The Body in the Library* (1942), have no idea who she is or how she got there. So begins one of the quintessential texts of the Golden Age, so redolent of its genre that it has acquired a metonymical relationship with the classic detective story. In her Author's Foreword to *The Body in the Library*, Agatha Christie even describes the body in the library as a cliché of detective fiction. In Christie's version the private library would represent a conventional element of social privilege, while the body of an ordinary girl placed within it would be a highly improbable and sensational incursion. It is precisely this dislocation which W. H. Auden had in mind in his essay, 'The Guilty Vicarage': 'The corpse must shock not only because it is a corpse but also because, even for a corpse, it is shockingly out of place, as when a dog makes a mess on a drawing room carpet.'[3] As this unlikely juxtaposition presents the combination of murder and libraries as a violation of the sense of peace and reverential erudition, it is little wonder that the discovery in Gossington Hall brings with it a sense of personal outrage, not for the fact of the murder itself, but for its location. As Colonel Bantry demands, 'You mean to tell me, that there's dead body in my library – *my* library?'[4]

Although body after body cropped up in the libraries of Golden Age texts, this idea, which was to be repeated by so many authors of the period, had its roots in the beginnings of the detective story. As Kathleen Klein and Joseph Keller remind us, 'it was to the nineteenth century that Golden Age detective novelists looked for their formula and their starting point'.[5] The murderous events at Gossington Hall actually subscribe to a convention begun by one of Christie's favourite authors of the genre, the American writer Anna Katherine Green. Christie's regard for Green was due in part to the creation of Amelia Butterworth, the first female detective, widely recognized as a model for Miss Marple. But the libraries to be found in Green's first book, *The Leavenworth Case* (1878), and again in *The Filigree Ball* (1903) are not merely the shock invasion of crime into a genteel environment, but a pioneering development of the self-reflexive and subverting trend in the detective story. In *The Filigree Ball* the library's presence is a reminder of the importance to the detective story of reading the clues. So central is this idea to the novel that no matter what twists and turns take place the trail always leads back to the library, a place where the mystery occurs and the solution will be found. The library is a place of knowledge, not merely for the reader of books, but also the reader of clues.

Green was born in Brooklyn in 1846, into a middle-class family of New England origin; her father, significantly, was a criminal lawyer. Her life overlapped that of Sir Arthur Conan Doyle and at the time of her death in 1935 she had become one of detective fiction's great innovators. When Green graduated from Ripley College in Vermont in 1866 she returned home with hopes of becoming a poet, but was discouraged from doing so by Emerson, to whom she had sent some of her work. Against her father's wishes she took up the novel. Aside from its body in a library, *The Leavenworth Case* originated such staples of the genre as are now taken for granted: the wealthy man about to change his will, the use of ballistics evidence, a coroner's inquest, a sketch of the scene of the crime,[6] the partially burned letter and the first serial detective, Ebenezer Gryce.

In 1884 Green married a penniless actor, Charles Rohlfs, an alliance well below her own social station. Rohlfs was a somewhat mercurial figure and although the marriage was a happy one, there are faint social parallels with the first union undertaken by Veronica Moore as a young girl in *The Filigree Ball*. Although Rohlfs gave up acting on his marriage only to return to it some years later, he did pursue a significant parallel career as a craft designer and putative engineer. When the couple moved to Buffalo, a city which pioneered the use of electricity, their house was the subject of many architectural and engineering innovations which reflected Rohlf's practical skill and design abilities. It seems that these experiences from her own life found their way into Green's work and many of her stories contain mechanical contraptions which are a key part of the plot; as her biographer Patricia Maida has pointed out:

> Rohlfs was a mechanical engineer who delighted in new designs; for instance, he invented one of the first chafing dishes and built clocks with unusual timing devices. Anna shared her husband's interests, often testing out inventions of her own in fiction. We see this in such devices as the electrical system in *The Circular Study*, the airplane in *Initials Only*, the signalling device in 'the Bronze Hand', the poisoned coils in 'The Little Steel Coils.' But the deadly settle in *The Filigree Ball*, was perhaps her most controversial of devices.[7]

Frequently, Green's devices are the fanciful imposition on a predominantly rational text; indeed at the very heart of her narratives is a desire to pit an intensely rational process with sometimes abstruse elements of plot. In the depiction of triumph of reason over the seemingly uncontrollable and unlikely forces of chaos, she is, however, a natural successor to Poe in the working out of the detective narrative. But the unravelling of the secret of the diabolic machine in *The Filigree Ball*, as is the case with so many of her novels, is contingent upon the understanding of an even deeper family secret that lies at the heart of the narrative. In *The Filigree Ball*, therefore, enclosure arises from the interaction of two thematic devices: the physical architecture, which resides in the fabric of a house, and the cerebral, which relates to the psyche of the murderess, Veronica Moore. The relationship of these themes within the classic detective story structure creates an environment where discovery assumes the principal role of narrative. Catherine Ross Nickerson argues in her examination of *The Leavenworth Case* that 'Her [Green's] stories become narratives of secrecy and disclosure, structured in complex doubled ways that repeat that very deep sense that the heart of the story is "not possible" to tell.'[8]

When the novel begins, the infamous house is derelict and the family seemingly divided by a secret every bit as perplexing as the conundrum presented by the murderous library. The scandalous secret which Veronica conceals is only 'not possible to tell' because of its impropriety;

in a sense the whole mechanics of the story turn on the social niceties of scandal and probity. Since the whole purpose of the detective story is to recover such a hidden narrative and expose its contents, the task facing the detective is to comprehend, to read those parts of the story that have surfaced in order to reveal the remainder. There is, therefore, an expectation that a process of reconstruction shall take place. But in *The Filigree Ball* the experience of this chain of revelation is heightened because in place of the detective's sidekick, the Watson figure or the direct authorial voice, the narrative is filtered through the detective himself. We are, therefore, party to discoveries which otherwise might not surface until the solution phase of the narrative. So we are aware of two narratives simultaneously: the one conventionally presented as a problem, and the unfolding narrative of what really happened – not artificially delayed, but as it happens. The effect is crucial; because the clue solving is overt we receive the narrative sequentially, like the pages in a book. Thus the detective's reading of the problem is a precise doubling of our own experience. It is this repeated act of uncovering strands of narrative, the idea that we as readers are participants in the book itself and, therefore, effectively part of the narrative, that marks *The Filigree Ball* as an exemplar of Green's work.

The Filigree Ball, then, is the story of a house. In the same way as the Leavenworth home is synonymous with its family, 'Moore House' bears the name of the family who built it and still own it. This marks the house for the Moores, whatever its condition or reputation, as part of a pre-eminent physical act of enclosure; it is, after all, within its walls that people exist, families evolve and lives are shaped. This was a subject close to Green's heart; for all the acclaim that *The Leavenworth Case* and her subsequent books gave her, Green was a stalwart defender of the home and family and ostensibly her life was lived in the manner of a middle-class housewife. At the centre of this modus vivendi was the house as a home, the hub of all family life; of the many innovations which Green introduced into detective fiction it is perhaps her portrayal of the house and its importance in her characters' lives that has its most profound narratological significance, as her biographer Patricia Maida has pointed out:

> Though the old or haunted house has traditionally been a gothic motif, Green uses houses in a variety of *other* ways. There are no castles – just stalwart American structures. Some houses are simply functional dwellings, nothing more; others reveal wealth or social class . . . ; while others are true gothic places, with secret places, houses

where tragedies have occurred ... Because Green defines environment as significant to behaviour, it is appropriate that she focuses on the house. We see this in virtually every plot. Typically, a house like the Leavenworth residence (in Green's first novel) is designated not by its address, but rather by the family name – thus the 'Leavenworth house.'[9]

The close association of a house where murder occurs is, of course, a reflection of some disturbance in the continuum of life, more particularly a manifestation of some family disharmony. So rather than recite the received social nostrum associated with the circle in which she moved, many of the households she describes are entropic. In this sense Green's works read like a warning of the dangers of jeopardizing domestic stability and harmony by irrational behaviour.

The task facing the detective, therefore, is to read and understand the house; this applies as much to its fabric as it does to the lives of the people there. Frequently in Green's novels the house appears as a metaphor for the act of reading, the physical act of entry by the detective into a new and perplexing world corresponding to the opening of a book in order to read and understand its contents. So just as the house is a touchstone for Green's narrative, it is important too, as a subject for the process of investigation and reasoning. This is often manifested by the detailed descriptions of individual rooms that her books contain; in fact rooms, strange rooms, are an abiding feature of Green's novels – bizarre things tend to happen in bizarre places. It is the very fact that these spaces are outré which requires them to be read and interpreted. This is certainly the case with the moribund library in *The Filigree Ball* and Adams's singular room, which among other functions is also a library, in *The Circular Study* (1900):

Nothing in their experience (and they had both experienced much) had prepared them for the thrilling, the solemn nature of what they were here called upon to contemplate.

Shall I attempt its description?

A room small and of circular shape, hung with strange tapestries relieved here and there by priceless curios, and lit, although it was still daylight, by a jet of rose-colored light concentrated, not on the rows of books around the lower portion of the room, or on the one great picture which at another time might have drawn the eye and held the attention, but on the upturned face of a man lying on a bearskin rug with a dagger in his heart ...[10]

The idiosyncrasies of the room are almost as arresting as the sight of the body itself and occupy Gryce for much of the book. Immediately, the assumption is made that the study and its adjoining anteroom hold the key: 'Mr Gryce grew very thoughtful and entered upon another examination of the two rooms which to his mind held all the clews that would ever be given to this strange crime.'[11] He must read the significance of the rooms and their contents, the unusual circular shape, the strange coloured lighting, the high windows and singular tapestries, before he can solve the mystery of Adams's murder. And so it proves.

The Filigree Ball was Green's twentieth novel and the first of two full-length locked room stories which she wrote at the turn of the century. The narrative is divided into three books; these do not, however, correspond precisely with Poe's original schema for the detective story: Book I 'The Forbidden Room', deals with the story of the crime and the first part of the investigation; Book II, 'The Law and Its Victim', continues with the investigation by featuring the formal inquest into Veronica Moore's death and its effect on the investigation; and Book III, 'The House of Doom', completes the policeman's inquiries and presents the solution to the case.

The story, as already discussed, is narrated by an unnamed police officer who takes it upon himself to investigate the death of Veronica Moore in an unofficial capacity. As Book I opens we learn that Moore House is one of the oldest in Washington, erected as a monument to wealth and optimism, but has since acquired a sinister reputation. There is an overpowering sense in the text of these opening pages, with its extended description of the interior and the strange series of murders, that one has been plunged headlong into the space which is to be the central focus of the narrative, giving 'the long empty and slowly crumbling building an importance which has spread its fame from one end of the country to another'.[12] Thus no matter who the murderer is or their motivation, Green's keen awareness of the importance of environment will ensure that the house will act as a magnet to the events of the narrative.

In *The Filigree Ball* the house is a labyrinthine object; it has secrets that must be discovered by the solving of layer upon layer of clues in the rooms it contains until the key locus of the narrative is revealed. It acts as a metaphor for the way in which the detective story narrative itself works; essentially the detective must penetrate the concentric layers of mystery contained in the text just as he enters the locked room to discover its secrets. In *The Filigree Ball* this process is enhanced because the family secret at the centre of the story is quite literally entwined with the fabric of Moore House. So the investigation into the causality of the characters' actions is integrally linked with reading the physical signs that the building itself possesses, the most fundamental being the notoriety arising from the mystery surrounding the discovery of three bodies lying outstretched on the hearthstone of the library:

A lifeless man, lying outstretched on a certain hearthstone, might be found once in a house and awaken no special comment; but when this same discovery has been made twice, if not thrice, during the history of a single dwelling, one might surely be pardoned a distrust of its seemingly home-like apartments, and discern in its slowly darkening walls the presence of an evil which if left to itself might perish in the natural decay of the place, but which, if met and challenged, might strike again and make another blot on its thrice-crimsoned hearthstone.[13]

Another death, in similar circumstances, has now occurred; the present owner, Veronica Moore, fascinated by the old, abandoned house, recently held her marriage to fiancé Francis Jeffrey there, but the body of a man who entered the library alone was found minutes later. Now David Moore, uncle to Veronica, who lives nearby, has contacted the police because he has seen a light in one of the upper rooms of the empty house. The unnamed police officer investigates, together with his colleague Hibbard, and discovers the body of Veronica Moore in the library shot through the heart, a ribbon tied to her wrist and a gun nearby. The conclusion is drawn that she tied the gun to her wrist and shot herself, as a result of the tragedy at her wedding two weeks earlier. The police officer remains to search for the source of the light and discovers a recently extinguished candelabrum in the library. He also notes the monstrous settle which has only one part suitable for comfortable seating. In an upstairs bedroom nicknamed 'The Colonel's Own', the detective finds burned matches, candles, a wrap with a bridal bouquet and a handkerchief marked 'Veronica' with dust on it. On a mantel are finger marks in the dust, and a curious picture on the wall has been recently dusted. He concludes that these unexplained clues may cast doubt on the general consensus that Veronica's death came about by her own hand.

Veronica's half-sister, Cora Tuttle, is strangely affected by the scene of the tragedy. Jeffrey arrives with a note from his wife saying that she did not love him as she thought. He had previously courted the penniless Miss Tuttle before he turned to Veronica, a romance which took place while Veronica was at a boarding school in a western state until the age of 17. Jeffrey has received some social disapproval for his behaviour and Cora is clearly still in love with him. Uncle David, meanwhile, has taken the news calmly. During the investigation it transpires that the man who died at the wedding was a W. Pfeiffer of Denver, an uninvited guest.

Significantly, the opening pages of the novel focus on Moore House; the entry of the police officer into the house not only establishes the role of the detective but is the first act of penetration which will lead to the exposé of the family secrets. Always, in the locked room mystery, the moment when the detective first engages with the scene of the crime is pivotal, for detective fiction – and the locked room mystery in particular – is a form of literature that portrays the liminal; the resolution of the mystery it poses relies on the interaction of the exterior world with the interior, precisely on the threshold between the two. The police officer thus embarks on a journey of concentricity to uncover the multi-layered clues that lead to the solution of the crime. But physical entry into the locked room will never be enough; however many times the detective actually enters the space, he will not experience enlightenment until he enters the room cerebrally, fully cognizant of its meaning. Green understood this process well. The painstaking gathering of evidence, the step-by-step accretion of knowledge, is one of her principal narrative legacies. Indeed the passages of her novels which deal with the investigation of the crime are amongst the most thorough in the whole of the canon. This element has an impact at all levels in the detective story, but it is especially fundamental to the revelatory nature of the genre's narrative structure.

The entry of the police officer into Moore House, therefore, is characterized by a gradual progress towards 'the forbidden room', in which he encounters the story of the house's sudden evacuation after Veronica's wedding and the remnants that still remain. Eventually he and his companion reach the portals of 'the door of the room which no man entered without purpose or passed without dread' with a real sense of desire to delve into a deeper layer of understanding, 'thinking of that which had so frequently been carried out between those columns'.[14] Such is the sense of the room being at the heart of the affair that even the detective's first entry is deferred until other ground floor rooms have been examined. So, embedded within this concept is the idea of a fluctuating process of inside and outside, a state of unknowing and a state of comprehension. At this threshold, aside from the architectural enclosure, there is also a phenomenological event, the subject of which is a contemplation of the problem posed by the text. It is the space where the detective must use his powers of ratiocination; but being a transient place it can only be occupied for a special purpose for a limited time. Much of what gives the detective story its tension is the desire by the detective to rid himself of this intellectual vacuum and move on. This anomalistic psychical position has been described by Gaston Bachelard using the metaphor of the inhabitable space:

> Outside and inside are both intimate – they are always ready to be reversed, to exchange their hostility. If there exists a border-line surface between such an inside and outside, this surface is painful on both sides.... The center of 'being-there' wavers and trembles. Intimate space loses its clarity, while exterior space loses its void, void being the raw material of possibility of being.[15]

This borderline inhabited by the text of detective fiction, therefore, occupies the story of the crime and its investigation. It is a place full of uncertainty, where enlightenment is often a 'painful' process through the interpretation and misinterpretation of clues. What the unnamed police officer embarks upon by entering Moore House is a rite of passage from one world to another, where the threshold is marked by a lack of comprehension as to the nature of the truth. That understanding is only clarified when, metaphorically speaking, the detective and the reader of the text pass into the locked room and dispel the mystery. When the detective solves the crime and leaves the locked room for good, he restores the space to its former place in the exterior world.

There is, however, a strong argument for considering the classic detective story as a genre of the *intérieur*, where the narrative inevitably turns inward to consider the clues arising from a world limited by the confines of closed dwellings and limited numbers of characters. This sense of the *intérieur* and its origin can, of course, be traced to Poe. We are reminded of the enclosure motif in 'The Murders in the Rue Morgue' in which both detective and victims lead sequestered lives of isolation. Aside from the initial street scene, Dupin moves between the two interiors to assess the traces and solve the crime; the focus of attention is on his own very private dwelling and the apartment in which the L'Espanayes are killed. In a real sense this amounts to the text being not merely an exploration of a space but an understanding of it, which is an understanding of both the clues in the case but also the habits and character of the people who have occupied it.

In *The Filigree Ball*, when he enters the room, the scene of the previous deaths, the detective discovers the body of Veronica. Unlike its counterpart at Gossington Hall, Green introduces us to a library where the shock discovery of a body in such a place has long since dissipated. In common with their surroundings, the books which languish on its shelves are redolent of decay; the police officer records that 'These were not the books of today; they had stood so long in their places unnoted and untouched, that they had acquired the color of fungus, and smelt.'[16] Thus the environment of the library is likened to a tomb, and the corresponding language is associated with books: we speak of an author's *body* of work, organic implications of a cycle of life and death in the writer's art, the finality of a book completed, a story told, shelved and forgotten. In Bolingbroke Johnson's *The Widening Stain* (1942), which concerns a murder in a university library, the librarian reflects on the particular atmosphere that such place creates: 'I like it here. It makes a nice solitary retreat for me, when I want to get away from all the to-do in the catalogue room. I even like the smell, so cool and musty. That smell of dead books.'[17]

At first sight a book may appear as a paradox, a decaying physical entity which surrounds the living thoughts of the author. Yet even in this respect the idea of 'dead books' provokes the thought that there is reciprocity between the tangible and the corporeal, a sense that there is potential for the contents of books to be superseded, discredited or even forgotten, as other texts take their place and begin the cycle all over again. In the same way, the sepulchre of the library is in part a resting place for the author; in Marion Boyd's *Murder in the Stacks* (1934) the unnatural light of a library becomes 'a faint twilight singularly appropriate to these bound thoughts of writers many of whom were long since dead'.[18] Perhaps this association of books with the placing of a body emanates from the detective writer's fear that once read it becomes moribund. Auden thought this especially true of the genre: 'I forget the story as soon as I have finished it, and have no wish to read it again. If as sometimes happens, I start reading one and find after a few pages that I have read it before, I cannot go on.'[19] The detective story then, like the reading of it, is doubly eschatological. As well as its perennial concern with death, it is an end-dominated medium, a text of final outcomes; so its essential paradox, actually, is that in the process of depicting the transformation from chaos to order, its own demise as a text is assured. The doubled process of reading, by the detective and the reader, leads to what Barthes called the 'texte de désir'.[20] This desire once sated and the solution reached, the textual possibilities end.

Setting the library as the scene of a murder, therefore, has distinct parallels with detective fiction and the path of detection particularly. In this context the metaphorical possibilities are significant: libraries are places where the acquisition of knowledge is supposed to lead to understanding, and, crucially in the detective story, the stimulus for the practice of reason. So, in the detective story, books are emblematic of the way in which clues occur and have to be read; just like books they are available for view if the thought processes are available to interpret them. Green introduces a tantalizing prospect of this idea during the perusal of the library. After the discovery of Veronica's body the police officer, having sent his colleague Hibbard back to headquarters, notices that a kitchen chair has been placed in an odd place flush with the front of the bookshelves. Not only has someone spent time examining the volumes long enough to require a seat, but the detective also notices, immediately above this position, a book projecting out from the shelf. He examines it; promisingly, it has less dust on its upper edge than the others, but the title is of no interest and he replaces it: 'I replaced the book, but not so hastily as to push it one inch beyond the position in which I found it. For, if it had a tale to tell, then was it my business to leave that tale to be read by those who understood books better than I did.'[21] This is the moment when the first real engagement with a significant clue takes place; it is a subtle play on the meaning of knowledge. The police officer admits that his 'knowledge of books is limited' but by the time the investigation has finished he gains from them knowledge of a different kind, the kind that will help him solve the case.[22] As the text implies, the police officer will, in his role as detective, return to the very same place to read the clue that the bookshelves hold, when his knowledge of the case has grown and this discovery will be the signpost which will direct him towards the truth.

The pursuit of clues along a prescribed path to achieve a satisfactory resolution is a defining narrative trait for the conventional detective story. As one of the pioneers of the genre, Green's championing of the linear closed narrative would help to prescribe the way in which future writers would approach the detective story. As much as it defines its own form of the detective story, the resolved linear narrative posits, too, a fundamental distinction with the metaphysical tale. In the Borgesian library the books will invariably contain the infinite solutions to the problems of the universe; David Lehman has noted this in respect of Umberto Eco's *The Name of the Rose*:

At the heart of *The Name of the Rose* is a labyrinthine library that seems to be patterned after the one in Borges's 'The Library of Babel,' with its spiral staircases and sense of infinitude. The first sentence of

'The Library of Babel' announces that some people regard 'the universe' and 'the Library' as synonymous. Eco spins out this Borgesian conceit to an apocalyptic end in *The Name of the Rose*.[23]

But in the more finite world of conventional detective fiction, and in the Moore library specifically, the library becomes a symbol for the means by which sense can be made of a particular mystery. It represents a very different world from that of Borges, where the subject of libraries and books, such as Ts'ui Pen's infinite book in 'The Garden of Forking Paths', which once begun never ends, leads not to definition but a multitude of alternative outcomes.[24] It is not surprising, therefore, that throughout the text of *The Filigree Ball* every inference, every incident, if interpreted correctly leads back to the library and its books. Indeed, the thematic influence of the room itself, its presence as a source of signs, overshadows even its Gothicized architectural enclosure. Thus the position of the locked room as the centre of the textual labyrinth is a self-reinforcing entity, as ultimately all the signs it contains refer to itself and the secrets it contains.

The library milieu employed by Green in *The Leavenworth Case* and later in *The Filigree Ball* also provides the detective story with some nascent examples of self-reflexivity, something that would characterize the development of the genre throughout its subsequent existence. This derives directly from the context of the room as a library per se. Susan Sweeney hints at how this might be so: 'The locked room – with its imagery of enclosure and entrapment, and its reference only to elements within its own finite space – provides a perfect metaphor for the inherent self-reflexivity of the genre.'[25] In the wider sense, Sweeney's argument may be applied to portray the locked room as emblematic of the way in which the narrative of the detective story acts as an exclusive text. There exists within this context only the elements of the mystery which it confronts; all extraneous considerations are either absent or reduced to the margins of the text. But in the narrower 'finite space' in the locked room of *The Filigree Ball*, it is the pervading presence of books that is a constant reminder that detective fiction is just that, a book which itself belongs in the environment of the library. It is no coincidence that it appears in so many detective stories; murder in a library is wholly a fictional idea, which belongs not in the realms of the outside world but in the pages of a novel. By the time that Christie was writing *The Body in the Library* the implicit references made by Green had become flagrantly explicit. As the disbelieving Colonel Bantry says to his wife at the discovery of the murdered girl: ' "You've been dreaming, Dolly, that's what it is. It's that detective story you were reading – *The Clue of the Broken Match*. You know – Lord Edgbaston finds a beautiful blonde dead on the library hearthrug. Bodies are always being found in libraries in books. I've never known a case in real life." [26]

Here is the central paradox for detective fiction in a nutshell: on the one hand, the genre mimics the constituents of the real-life police investigation such as the use of forensic analysis and systematic reasoned inquiry, but, conversely, significant elements of the narrative in the classic detective story seem only to reflect its own fictionality. The remarkable 'Locked Room Lecture' by Gideon Fell, in John Dickson Carr's *The Hollow Man*, is perhaps the most celebrated example of the inter-war period.[27] The point made by Dr Fell, as Chapter 5 will show, is that the detective story is very obviously a work of fiction which has the limitation, self-imposed, of a finite number of modus operandi. The inevitable repetition that this invites is bound to call attention to other texts. Interestingly, Green's innovative adoption of libraries as a focus for the locked room created something of a double bind for the genre. By turns her narrative purports to describe the impossibility of the library deaths, but, in drawing attention to the world of fiction represented by the library, she creates yet another locked room for the story, one in which text itself is caught up in subverting its own form. It sets the detective story on a road which would culminate in a schismatic debate in the Golden Age between advocates of the hard-boiled novel and those writing in the conventional tradition about the depiction of reality.[28] By emphasizing its status as a fictional text, *The Filigree Ball* becomes its own metaphor for the locked room it depicts, a product of supreme artifice.

Much of Book II, 'The Law and Its Victim', is taken up with the coroner's inquest and the evidence given by the chief protagonists in the case. David Moore, it seems, has established an alibi for the time of Veronica's death but Francis Jeffrey and Cora Tuttle come under suspicion. On the day before her death Veronica had had a row with Jeffrey after which she exhibited signs of 'extreme mental suffering'.[29] The final argument between Veronica and Jeffrey seems to have triggered a crisis that would lead to her suicide in the Moore House library. The method by which she chooses to convey her feelings to her husband is intriguing; she uses the medium of a book from their own library to conceal a note, which reads:

I find that I do not love you as I thought. I can not live knowing this to be so. Pray God you may forgive me!

Veronica[30]

It transpires that Cora was present at Moore House when the fatal shot was fired and, previously on that day, she had tied the ribbon on Veronica's wrist (something she had done many times) thinking that it was her bonnet, and not a gun, concealed in the folds of her dress.

At the wedding Veronica received a message via one of the waiters before the ceremony, and both she and Jeffrey were seen talking to him afterwards. Certain that this waiter possesses vital evidence, the police officer learns that he has left with an army regiment and resolves to track him down.

In Book III, 'The House of Doom', the investigation concludes and the mystery is solved. The detective meets the waiter's friend, who had overheard him talking with Veronica when the name of the uninvited guest was mentioned. She asked for him to be seated in the library.

From a book hidden in the library behind the very book he had examined on the first night of the investigation, the detective learns that the deaths in the library have always benefited the master of the house, who is never present when the incidents occur. The book was written by an Englishwoman; it contains her recollections of the time when her father, Colonel Alpheus Moore, had carried out alterations to the house and how a close friend of her father's, a General Lloyd, had subsequently died seated on the settle in the library, after threatening to expose the Colonel for treachery. This treatise also emphasizes the importance to the Moore family of a particular gold filigree ball, worn on the watch chain, which contains a secret that only the master of the house shall know. The police officer remembers seeing the ball amongst other trinkets on the dressing table in 'The Colonel's Own'; he returns and he finds it and discovers a magnifying glass inside.

> In itself it was nothing but a minute magnifying glass; but when used in connection with – what? . . . Yet this was now the important point, the culminating fact which might lead to a full understanding of these many tragedies. . . . I must trust to the inspiration of the moment which suggested with almost irresistible conviction:
>
> *The picture! That inane and seemingly worthless drawing over the fire-place in The Colonel's Own, whose presence in so rich a room has always been a mystery!*
>
> Why this object should have suggested itself to me and with such instant conviction, I can not really say.[31]

This intuitive inspiration recalls a posteriori reasoning. He uses the glass on the picture he had examined previously and discovers that the hair on the portrait contains minute writing. The detective has thought the picture to be out of place ever since his first inspection of Moore House, but he has, quite literally, no understanding of why he should feel this way until he discovers the magnifying glass. In a house of secrets where many things have a story to tell, the detective has used his intuition to alight on that which seems out of place. The solution to the mystery stems from this assertion and, so from effect to cause he is able to follow the chain of clues. Using the glass he, quite literally, reads the picture which directs him to the cupboard where a cleverly hidden apparatus releases a leaden ball at great speed to deliver a fatal concussion to anyone sitting on the settle in the library below. The detective also discovers a small piece of lace at the scene of the machinery controls in the bedroom and this proves to be from Veronica Moore's clothing.

It seems that Veronica had married Pfeiffer in a fit of youthful passion when she was away at school and he had immediately made off to the Klondike to seek his fortune. Believing him dead after a false report which actually concerned his brother, Veronica returned to Washington, only for Pfeiffer to turn up on the day of the wedding. As her ancestors had done, she used the deadly apparatus to rid herself of the evidence of her past indiscretions and then committed suicide out of remorse. Hearing his wife talk in her sleep, Jeffrey had already discovered the truth. He admits that the brief letter he gave to the police was merely an enclosure for public consumption; he had kept secret Veronica's long document of confession.

The title of Book II, 'The Victim and the Law', seems to be an ambiguous play on the notion of the word 'victim'. The coroner's inquest convenes to consider the cause of Veronica's death and wrongly concludes that she may have been murdered. But the reality is, of course, that she herself is a murderer. Yet amidst this misprision there lies a fundamental truth about the nature of the detective story narrative – because for every murder there is always a second victim, the murderer. Pursued and effectively 'killed' by the detective, this second victim becomes, like the first, subject to entrapment. This is particularly so in the locked room mystery, where the central locus of attention provides an enclosure which continually draws in both murderer and victim alike. So Veronica is as much a victim of the library as any of those who have died there, and its power to attract and imprison takes on an indefinable fascination for the young bride-to-be:

Veronica Moore, rich, pretty and wilful, had long cherished a strange liking for this frowning old home of her ancestors, and, at the most critical time of her life, conceived the idea of proving to herself and to society at large that no real ban lay upon it save in the imagination of the superstitious. So, being about to marry the choice of her young heart, she caused this house to be opened for the wedding ceremony; with what result, you know.[32]

When the fatal hour comes, she returns to the library, to the physical enclosure, to end her life. The repository for her note to Jeffrey is, appropriately enough, a book with a title rich with symbolism, *Compensation*. Veronica gives her own life as reparation for the crime she has committed, and in doing so her use of the book provides a clue as to the place where she will be found, the library of Moore House. But this is not the first time that she has had recourse to the world of books. As heir to the Moore estate she has carried out the first critical act of reading in the novel, by adopting the formula handed down by her forbears. It remains, therefore, for the detective to reprise her actions in order to decipher the mystery. Thus what the detective engages in, and by extension the reader too, is not a mere reading, but a rereading, considering and understanding the very same signs as the murderer so that he himself can reproduce the crime. In this sense Frank Kermode's assertion that 'the principal object of the reader is to discover by an interpretation of clues the answer to a problem proposed at the outset', therefore, has a particular resonance with *The Filigree Ball*.[33] In a text bound up with idea of reading and a narrative conveyed by the detective himself, the roles of detective and reader become interchangeable; both adopt the inherent characteristics of the other. This rereading by the reader/detective exhibits a triple response to the thematic device of the library: we read and possess the novel in book form; within it we are conscious that its motif of the library leads us back to the medium we are using and thus to its fictionality, only to find that in the core of the narrative the police officer is also engaged in a process of rereading in which we are a participant. As Dennis Porter suggests: 'If reading detective novels is always a rereading, however, it is a rereading in which a limited number of structural constants are combined with an indefinite number of decorative variables in order to make the familiar new.'[34] The 'structural constants' that Porter speaks of have special significance in Green's texts. Her contribution to the emerging genre had undoubtedly helped to consolidate the structural narrative pioneered by Poe, but many of her 'decorative variables' such as the library became, as we have seen, not variables but familiar, recurring thematic devices which seem so grafted on to the skeleton of the detective story as to be indistinguishable from its structure.

Veronica's behaviour is entirely consonant with the overarching narrative presence of the locked room, re-enacting a parody of the family ritual by dying in the room where she and her forbears had committed their crimes. The menace of the library and the evil deed that she has committed manifests itself as a haunting; the locked room of Moore House and the guilt she feels combine to devastating effect. There are distinct parallels with the tortured psyche of Dickens's haunted signalman in the anguish which Veronica feels. In her previously unrevealed letter to Jeffrey, in a passage that could have been written by Dickens's unfortunate, she echoes all the traits of the victim of fate:

> I am haunted now, I am haunted always, by one vision, horrible but persistent. It will not leave me; it rises between us now; it has stood between us ever since I left the house with the seal of your affection on my lips. Last night it terrified me into unconscious speech. I dreamed that I saw again, and plainly, what I caught but a shadowy glimpse of in that murderous hour: a man's form seated at the end of the old settle, with his head leaning back, in silent contemplation.[35]

There is true pathos in Veronica's predicament. Despite the fact that she is a murderess, having read and acted upon the secret of the library, she is psychologically in thrall to it. The moment of release will come when the locked room of her psyche and the physical enclosure are united:

> But I shudder now in thinking of it till soul and body seem separating, and the horror which envelopes me gives such a foretaste of hell that I wonder I can contemplate the deed which, if it releases me from this earthly anguish, will only plunge me into a possibly worse hereafter. Yet I shall surely take my life before you see me again, and in that old house. If it is despair I feel, then despair will take me there.[36]

The fate experienced by Veronica displays two enduring and interlinked features of the locked room mystery. It reminds us that physical entrapment is always accompanied by a profound metaphysical event that is equally confining and that this phenomenon gives a unique insight into the view from the inside of the locked room, from which there is no escape. It is the state of last resort. Veronica's fate is an extension of the narrative imperative which states that the criminal should be removed from society; in this sense the detective story is responding to its own dynamic. In many stories the murderer is seen to return to the scene of the crime and die; in *Murder in the Stacks*, for instance, which turns on the possession of a valuable booklet, the murderer, Dr Tyndale, returns to the library in order to claim the document, only to die, as does Veronica. This re-engagement with the original central locus of the mystery is an essential part of the detective narrative process; the interaction with its principal thematic device is invariably played right to the end of a text. In other words, it is appropriate that the criminal's demise should occur in a place of reading. Susan Sweeney has outlined this relationship thus: 'The detective story, then, not only presents the most basic elements of narrative (sequence, suspense, and closure) in their purest form, but also explicitly dramatizes the act of narration in the relationship between its narrative levels and its embedded texts. In other words, the detective story reflects reading itself.'[37]

As these pages will continue to argue, the 'embedded texts' or thematic devices have specific relationships with the detective narrative structure. In the case of the locked room mystery, the theme often mimics the architectural enclosure itself; by turns it overarches the narrative and yet is contained by it. So in the case of the library the act of reading goes to the very heart of the text: just as the book contains the text of the story, the library contains the book. It is the same with reading's relationship with the narrative structure, as we have seen in *The Filigree Ball* – at every step reading plays a crucial part in advancing the narrative.

What, in effect, the detective as reader does by solving the case is to pursue a text. Thematically this device works to facilitate the narrative, enhancing the relationship between investigation and solution, so that reading and comprehension become both part of the process, as well as a subject of it. In this sense it is the companion to Dupin's strict ratiocinative method, a theme which is born out of the arrangement of the narrative itself. Ironically, what makes for a compatible whole in *The Filigree Ball*, the homogeneity between its theme and the act of reading its text, is the very thing which draws attention to its fictional state. But nonetheless this approach to structuring is emblematic of the genre – the creation of a reciprocal exchange between theme and narrative. So, by invoking the act of reading so prominently, *The Filigree Ball*, while reminding us of the detective story's essential artifice, paved the way for increasingly self-reflexive and abstruse creations. At the end of Christie's *The Body in the Library*, Miss Marple muses on the twists and turns of the case:

> Oh, yes looking down at the dead girl and feeling sorry, because it is always sad to see a young life cut short, and thinking that whoever

had done it was a very wicked person. Of course it was all very confusing her being found in Colonel Bantry's library, altogether too like
a book to be *true*. In fact, it made the wrong pattern. It wasn't, you
see *meant*, which confused us a lot.[38]

The origins of this statement lie deep in the recesses of the fictional
libraries created by Anna Katherine Green.

4
G. K. Chesterton's Enclosure of Orthodoxy in 'The Wrong Shape'

> Orthodoxy is my doxy; heterodoxy is another man's doxy.
>
> Bishop William Warburton, 'To Lord Sandwich'[1]

Ellery Queen, in his survey of early detective fiction, was moved to describe Chesterton's *The Innocence of Father Brown* (1911), his first collection of such stories, as the 'miracle book'.[2] There is just the faintest tinge of irony in this statement; this first set of clerical mysteries do indeed contain some of the most celebrated stories in the canon, but they are also perfect examples of how Chesterton sought to articulate, in fictional form, the desirable qualities of the Catholic faith: a faith which would ultimately become his own.

There are also ambivalent overtones in Chesterton's own essay, 'How to Write a Detective Story', which first appeared in the 17th October edition of *G. K.'s Weekly*[3] in 1925:

> The first and fundamental principle is that the aim of a mystery story, as of every other story, is not darkness but light. The story is written for the moment when the reader does understand...The misunderstanding is only meant as a dark outline of cloud to out the brightness of that instant of intelligibility.[4]

The essay goes on to say that 'The secret may appear complex, but it must be simple; and in this also it is a symbol of higher mysteries'.[5] The 'light' and 'higher mysteries' resonate with the language both of detection and of religious belief and it is a testament to their compatibility that Chesterton is able to use them in the same context. In Christian doctrine the term 'mystery' or *mysterium* is used variously to encompass the miracle of Christ's birth, death and resurrection, the notion of godliness and the prospect of eternal life – the essence being that these series of mysteries remain as secrets to be unfolded to the faithful through belief in the scriptures. In the locked room form of the detective story the central mystery of an apparent miracle is resolved in the manner of a revelation by the detective. Both the religious and the secular acts of revelation are played out within the context of a well-established convention, a rite which encompasses the unfolding of the mystery and the *mysterium*. This correlation with overtly religious language draws on a body of such references throughout the genre and owes much to Poe's view of the detective story; as one critic has put it, 'Poe strove to bewilder readers so that Dupin's solution might seem the miraculous sign of genius.'[6]

Critical consideration of detective fiction's relationship with Christianity has its beginnings in biblical texts; this premise leads discussion about clerical detective stories into two key areas which are fundamental to this chapter. These are the structural and thematic similarities that arise from the pedagogic storytelling present in the scriptures. Hans Robert Jauss observes that 'The abundance of literary forms and genres ascertainable in the Old and New Testaments is astonishing.'[7] Amongst these are etiological and historical prose, novellas and short stories, riddle, parable and allegory, all of which are relevant to detective fiction because of their association with the nature of storytelling. Many of these styles listed by Jauss foreground allegory as their staple narrative drive, much of which was to represent the Church in both its spiritual and physical manifestations. At a very basic level, the physical world of the Church on earth was a realization of the unseen spiritual world, and only through the divine process of the latter could the former be created. Texts deriving from the scriptures, such as Bunyan's *Pilgrim's Progress* (1678) with its triumph over the trials and tribulations of life and the temptations of sin, bring us even closer to the allegory of order's victory over chaos, an allegory to be found repeatedly in detective fiction.

The detective story, from its very beginnings, also possessed a structural orthodoxy; it is an orthodoxy born of the formulaic model of introduction, story of the crime, investigation and solution, which is entirely consonant with a genre whose purpose is the elucidation of mystery and the restoration of order. As early as 1944, Bernard De Voto stated that the detective story 'is so popular right now because it is the only current form of fiction that is pure story'.[8] This argument was amplified by Marty Roth in 1995:

> Detective fiction did not need to change because the form had already realized its virtue: to preserve classical narrative, pure story-telling, in a fallen world. According to some writers, detective fiction was the last stronghold of a plain style that had been perversely abandoned by the prevailing literary culture in the 1880's and after.[9]

The essence of this storytelling style is detective fiction's narrative structure, which relies on the crime and solution axis. It is the widespread repetition of this structure that has created a convention to the genre, and Roth has taken his argument forward by realizing the fundamental purpose of this convention: 'In literature, conventions are regarded as scaffolding, indifferent elements of framework, whereas in detective fiction they are the crucial relays of meaning and pleasure.'[10] This arises specifically from the fact that in the detective story its conventional structure coincides precisely with the demands of the plot. So, essentially, Roth's point relates directly to the hermeneutical nature of the structure: in the investigative phase, for instance, the incidence of clues forms a key part of the pleasure to be derived from reading a text, but it also doubles as a trope to further the elucidation of mystery. This returns us to the genre's storytelling character. One reason why the detective story is able to appear as such a cogent narrative is its homogeneity, the ultimate compatibility of form in all its constituents.

In this respect detective fiction mirrors the effect of the parable; both use the convention of plain storytelling to relay meaning by textual revelation. As Frank Kermode has pointed out, the connection between mystery and parable is strong: 'Riddle and parable may be much the same: "Put forth a riddle and speak a parable to the house of Israel," says Ezekiel, proposing the enigma or allegory of the eagle of divers colors and the spreading vine.'[11] What Kermode suggests is the way in which parables in the Bible propose a simplistic, even disingenuous riddle. At the end of the parable of the Good Samaritan, for instance, the reader is asked to choose which of the three protagonists encountered by the victim proved to be more of a neighbour to him. The answer, of course, is preordained. The Good Samaritan is chosen because of the knowledge, possessed by the reader, of the Christian faith. As Kermode explains, parables 'All require some interpretive action from the auditor; they call for completion; the parable-event isn't over until a satisfactory answer or explanation is given.'[12] So it is with detective fiction, whose riddle is, of course, the mystery surrounding the crime, the progress of which poses a question that the narrative must answer by confirming the triumph of order.

The Bible itself contains some passages that are redolent of the locked room; among them is the story of Bel and the Dragon from the Apocrypha. In this story, Cyrus, King of Persia, claims that Bel the Babylonian idol is, in fact, a living God who eats and drinks every day. Daniel denies this and declares his allegiance to the one true God; so the king proposes a test, and accordingly the priests of the temple lay out food and wine for Bel. The temple is cleared of people, locked and sealed, but unbeknown to the priests Daniel scatters the floor with ashes and reseals the chamber. During the night the food and drink disappear, the seal is intact and the king triumphantly proclaims vindication, only for Daniel to point to the footsteps left in the ashes by the priests who have entered the temple by a secret passage and removed the vittles. Overlying the similarity to the narrative structure of a detective story is the enclosing theme of belief in the true God. Daniel's solution to the mystery of Bel, the earliest example of detective work restoring order, reaffirms faith in 'the living God, who hath created the heaven and the earth' (Bel and the Dragon 5); it is an allegory for the salvation that God's law brings. So, at a quite different level, the biblical story exhibits a fundamental element of detective fiction – a propensity to enclose its narrative with both structural and thematic constituents which subsume the whole. In Bel and the Dragon, heterodoxy, in the form of worshipping idols such as Bel, is undermined by the duplicity of the priests who practise it.

Christian orthodoxy and the detective story share, too, the central concepts of *mysterium* and mystery. Just as the quest of the theologian concerns the truth about faith, the detective's search for the solution to the mystery of a crime is an allegorical pursuit of a truth involving the superimposition of good over evil. As William David Spencer argues: 'The mystery and *mysterium*, then, are two ways of looking at the same profoundly central issue, the human dilemma as touched by the divine. In the mystery a crime is committed, evil has intruded in a world of innocence.'[13] This is an important analogy because it links the religious *mysterium* of Christ's life with the mystery at the heart of all detective stories. In essence, the detective genre is a secularization of the great *mysterium*, of which mystery is a derivative, representing the concealing and revealing nature of the sacraments with God as orderer and focal point of unity. At the centre of both forms of mystery is the association with death. According to Derrida, this association is 'Intimately tied to the properly Christian event of *another secret* [*sic*], or more precisely of a mystery, the *mysterium tremendum*: the terrifying mystery, the dread, fear and trembling of the Christian in the experience of the sacrificial gift.'[14] Derrida hints here that death is the ultimate religious experience, an allegory for the surrender to faith. It is the association with death that has a particular resonance with detective fiction in general, and the locked room in particular. The formulaic ritual of the locked room, where the victim, isolated and yet enclosed, is at the mercy of the murderer, takes on the appearance of a sacrifice; in Christianity, it is a specific death, that of Christ's crucifixion, with its reflection of this biblical imagery of ritual death and subsequent miraculous resurrection from a confined space. In this context, the locked room murder can be seen as a repetition and ritual re-enactment of Christ's own murder.

But the association is not merely confined to structure; the biblical miracle and the detective story have a strong thematic resonance. The account of Christ's death and resurrection in the Gospels, for instance, is replete with the allegorical language of enclosure and its association with death. The ritual murder of Jesus on the cross is followed by the burial in the tomb hewn out of rock, after which the chief priests and Pharisees, on Pilate's instructions, 'made the sepulchre sure, sealing the stone and setting a watch' (Matt. 27:66). The miracle of Christ's subsequent escape from the sealed chamber is followed by yet another, this time involving the penetration of enclosed space: 'Then the same day at evening, being the first day of the week, when the doors were shut where the disciples were, assembled for fear of the Jews, came Jesus and stood in the midst...' (John 20:19). The importance of these passages for detective fiction lies not merely in the direct allusion to the mystery of the sealed chamber, but the allegorical associations prevalent in biblical texts. The passion of Christ, too, reads like the parable of the vineyard owner who sends his son to pacify his employees after other messengers have been rebuffed. The murder of the vineyard owner's son, as with Christ, is the catalyst for the eventual proclamation of good news. Christ's appearance by passing through the walls of the locked room is, therefore, the final, providential act in the cycle of murder and resurrection before the Ascension. The enactment of these two last miracles is one of the cornerstones of Christian faith, a key biblical text, because it reveals the *mysterium tremendum* of the reaffirmation of God's Law, triumph over death, even murder, and the resumption of theistic order. It is this doubling of enclosure, both thematic and structural, that allies the detective story with its biblical counterparts. What binds the parable together is the overarching concept of faith and the affirmation of the *mysterium,* while in detective fiction it is the enactment of the crime and its revelation that preoccupies the text.

The nexus that exists, therefore, between the detective story and Christian theology lies at the metaphysical level of understanding, by means of its association of eschatological ideas. Faced with the idea of death, both detective fiction and Christianity have developed ways in which this ultimate sanction can be mitigated. The key concept is that of redemption; it is given its example by the death and resurrection of Christ, so that at the heart of Christianity there remains the possibility of salvation even in the face of the most heinous sin. The parallels with the processes at work in detective fiction are strong, as Dean DeFino concludes:

> The classic detective story models itself on this eschatology. The detective enters the scene of the crime *after* the fact and, through a feat of analysis, constructs a chain of effects and causes back to the source of the crime – mode and motive – which, while not annulling the deed (the body is still dead), gives the reader a sense of intellectual control over it. The story redeems that sense of order and control by (fictionally) exposing its logic, its cause-and-effect chain, how one thing leads to another. Hence the form's popularity: it constructs a logical discourse from seeming chaos – disparate bits of evidence, cryptic clues – through an objective scientific method.[15]

The act of retrospective construction and the idea of the detective going back over past events reinforces the idea that the detective story can be read as a narrative which seeks to purge crime in the same way that Christianity redeems sin. Because locked room mysteries have a specific relationship with key biblical texts, they appear as a special kind of parable, many of which reflect the providence of God's law and the retribution it exacts on those who have sinned. This appears as a parody of Christ's ultimate miraculous triumph over death, by holding out the hope of salvation. In the case of Chesterton, his Father Brown tales, like the detective genre they inhabit, demonstrate the triumph of order. All are manipulated by his benign reason, which he represents as being part of a grander design for the future of the world. This critical recognition of an all-embracing order, summarized by Father Brown, embodies the complementarity of theme and structure when both reflect the restoration, or at least the maintenance, of the status quo.

Chesterton's Father Brown stories appeared at a time when the Catholic Church in England had been marginalized for a long period in the nineteenth century. In 1833, certain High Church adherents (notably Pusey, Keble and Newman), who believed in the authority of the episcopate and the priesthood together with the saving grace of the sacraments, formed the Oxford Movement with the aim of promoting the Catholic elements in the English religious tradition.[16] Their belief was that Roman Catholicism was the true legacy of the early undivided Church and that Protestantism represented a break in that tradition. Members of the Oxford Movement held out the hope that reforming the Church in this way would lead to a new reformation, which would leave the Catholic Church at the centre of religious life. Despite these radical ideas, as Jonathan Hill has pointed out, Newman originally favoured:

> '*The via media*', or 'middle way'. He believed that the Catholic Church had betrayed the Christian faith by adding to it over the centuries, but at the same time the Protestant Churches had stripped too much away. The Church of England should be a halfway house between the two extremes, avoiding both excesses, and remaining true to the historical roots of Christianity itself.[17]

But this moderation did not last. The more Newman delved into the details, the more he came to the conclusion that compromise was not possible. Consequently, Newman produced his *Tract 90* in 1841, which brought matters to a head. This work sought to reconcile Nonconformism with the early Christian Church by attempting to demonstrate that its fundamental beliefs could be interpreted in a Catholic, as distinct from a Protestant, sense.[18]

This document was destined to have long-lasting repercussions for the Church in England; the Church rejected Newman's radical views and, temporarily, left the Catholic faith as marginalized as ever. Newman himself finally converted to the Catholic faith in 1845; he confined his subsequent writings to the Catholic faith itself and never effectively returned to matters of reconciliation. Newman's conversion was followed by other noteworthy individuals such as Manning, de Lisle, Knox and Hopkins in the late nineteenth and early twentieth century. But the Oxford Movement, largely under the stewardship of Edward Pusey, continued its campaign, concentrating on the practice of the liturgy and the sacraments. Although encountering continued opposition, by the time Pusey died in 1882 the Oxford Movement had seen large changes in the Church of England: clerics began wearing vestments, blessing the bread and wine, and introducing ritual and mystery into the celebration of the sacraments.

The events of the nineteenth century were to have profound consequences for Chesterton, whose own life had distinct parallels with that of Newman. He formally converted to Roman Catholicism in 1922, but in truth he had espoused the faith tacitly for much of his adult life.[19] Although he was brought up in the tradition of liberal Protestantism, it was from 1896 onwards that he came under the influence of Frances Blogg, a strong Anglo-Catholic, whom he was to marry in 1901. Chesterton's conversion was by no means an isolated case. Many literary figures were to take advantage of the Catholic revival in the twentieth century; the list is impressive and includes such luminaries as Edith Sitwell, Siegfried Sassoon, Graham Greene, Evelyn Waugh, Muriel Spark, and the Anglo-Catholics C. S. Lewis and Dorothy L. Sayers.[20]

The concept of orthodoxy for Chesterton was divided between his deep abhorrence of heresy and his desire to promote the Catholic faith as the authentic Christian doctrine. Much of Chesterton's life and writing was to be devoted to the case for orthodoxy in religious belief and, in 1908, he wrote an extended work, with this title, on the nature and constancy of Christian belief, reserving particular opprobrium for Nonconformism, in which he argued: 'The Catholic Church believed that man and God both had a spiritual freedom. Calvinism took away the freedom from man, but left it to God.'[21] Chesterton was encouraged by the events of the nineteenth century to see Catholicism moving more to the mainstream of British religious life. His view of Catholicism was of an orthodoxy in which the fundamental tenets were indisputable, but the wider theology open for debate. As he put it, 'Catholics know the two or three transcendental truths on which they do agree; and take rather a pleasure in disagreeing on everything else', making dogmatic Catholicism the foundation of 'an active, fruitful, progressive and even adventurous life' of the intellect and spirit.[22]

This liberal view of orthodoxy, its capacity for debate within a fundamental belief in an ultimate, benign controlling force, is a recurring theme in Chesterton's faith and a key element in the construction of the Father Brown stories. As Adam Schwartz reveals: 'The orthodox Christians also rebutted what they saw as another central element of both literary and theological modernism: subjectivism. They maintained that truth is not the product of particular minds that varies from thinker to thinker, but is an objective reality that exists apart from individual inquirers and is meant to be discovered by them.'[23] By extension, this doctrine becomes a rubric for a world where all are acting within a transcendent spiritual enclosure: 'In allowing Christian teaching to set the lines of excellence rather than drafting them themselves, people are empowered to exercise their vital powers in ways that ennoble human nature rather than degrade it, because their behavior is in harmony with reality instead of in discord with it.'[24]

This context of orthodoxy is precisely the milieu in which Chesterton's detective operates. It is the point of difference between Father Brown and detectives such as Dupin and Sherlock Holmes; while the former is presented as one who acts as an instrument of a metaphysical power, the logic of the latter two is drawn predominantly from the forensic examination of clues. Chesterton confirms this from the very first story, 'The Blue Cross' (1911), when Father Brown states: 'Reason is always reasonable, even in the last limbo, in the lost borderland of things. I know that people charge the Church with lowering reason, but it is just the other way. Alone on earth, the Church makes reason really supreme. Alone on earth, the Church affirms that God himself is bound by reason.'[25] Identifying reason with divine power and, more particularly, the Catholic Church, is central to Chesterton's purpose; by creating the impression that reason only comes from theological sources, and that the solution to unfathomable mysteries lies within a gift from God, Chesterton represents his faith as integral to life.

From Chesterton's point of view, the natural medium for portraying such a proposition is the most orthodox and logical of narratives, the detective story. However, the schema which combines the application of logic and metaphysical ideas is fraught with contradictions; hitherto in detective fiction the presence of a force beyond logic and the tangible evidence that clues provide would have seemed anathema to writers in the genre. Yet Chesterton's portrayal of the conventional detective story, limited by temporal and secular considerations but enclosed by a greater and more mysterious universe, would find resonances in the metaphysical stories of Borges, Robbe-Grillet and Auster.

The idea of reason, as applied to Catholic thinking, is discussed by David Deavel in his essay, 'An Odd Couple? A First Glance at Chesterton and Newman', which focuses on the rationale behind the two converts' apostasy.[26] Interestingly, Deavel notes that rationality was a decisive element in their choice, and that its nature occupied their thoughts: 'this exploration of what true rationality meant for the two began by noting that rationality needs both faith and authority to guide it to its ends'.[27] There are resonances here with detective fiction being the literary form which most aligned itself with Chesterton's own feelings about the Catholic faith; its structure and certainty of purpose were a framework for portraying Catholicism as the faith which was most aligned with reason. As Deavel points out:

> It is not just the fact that one has any old Christian authority, but it is, in Chesterton's words, 'thinking a certain authority reliable; which is entirely reasonable.' The authority must be reliable. Or, in theological language, it must be infallible. The belief that reliable or infallible authority was given to each believer in an absolute way because of the Spirit's indwelling does not make much sense given the evident historical disagreements between Christians.[28]

The certitude which Chesterton sought in his faith manifested itself most strongly through his Father Brown stories, in which he was able to present the Catholic Church as an arbiter of reason and a restorer of order:

> While it is the constant tendency of the Old Adam to rebel against so universal and automatic a thing as civilization, to preach departure and rebellion, the romance of police activity keeps in some sense before the mind the fact that civilization is the most sensational of departures and the most romantic of rebellions. By dealing with the unsleeping sentinels who guard the outposts of society, it tends to remind us that we live in an unarmed camp, making war with a chaotic world, and that the criminals, the children of chaos, are nothing but traitors within our gates.[29]

This theme has been taken up by Ian Ker, who seeks to show that Newman's desire for the formation of a Catholic literature in the English language was realized by a number of different authors, showing the development of their greatest works played out against the backdrop of Catholic ways of thinking and feeling, in what was a substantially Protestant literary domain.[30] In particular, he links Chesterton to Newman as 'rejoicing in the way in which the sacred and the secular mingle in a Catholic culture'.[31] Ker claims that Chesterton's biographical essay, *Charles Dickens*, is the key text in understanding the nature of the Catholicism that captivated the author.[32] Chesterton's own primary religious experience of the world as a place of surprise and wonder becomes the outstanding feature that the convert finds in Dickens's novels. Chesterton thus characterizes Dickens as steeped in a pre-Reformation vision of life, in opposition to the Puritan-tinged world of England.

It seems, too, that both men, in turn, regarded orthodox Christianity, particularly Roman Catholicism, as a convincing counterstatement to such apparently regnant, if destructive, civilizational currents. What seems to attract Chesterton to Dickens is his sense of encompassing the excesses of joy and despair; as he puts it: 'He was delighted at the same moment that he was desperate. The two opposite things existed in him simultaneously, and each to its full strength.'[33] Chesterton seems to equate the presence of these opposites as evidence of Dickens's 'Catholicism' in its widest sense, that which embraces the broadest possible interpretation. The extension of this argument leads Chesterton to argue that in Dickens's world 'any man could be a saint if he chose',[34] a key to Chesterton's vision of a forgiving, liberalizing Catholicism. This is particularly germane to the Father Brown stories because of the priest's attempts to rehabilitate the thief Flambeau. The proposition that any man may be saved went right to the heart of Chesterton's beliefs; as Flambeau says of Father Brown, 'Only my friend told me that he knew exactly why I stole, and I have never stolen since.'[35] For Chesterton it is clear that the pursuit and capture of the criminal is not merely an end in itself; invariably there is a wider question to be answered. Catholicism is central to this idea.

The notion that Chesterton was operating from a position of orthodoxy, however, especially in England, despite the history of established Catholicism, is at best a matter of conjecture. It seems that the correlation between Catholic orthodoxy and detective fiction as literary orthodoxy reads more like an earnest effort to legitimize Chesterton's chosen faith. James Schall argues that Chesterton 'is the real "heretic" of our time' because 'perhaps 5 per cent of the world population of some seven billion are unequivocally "orthodox" in Chesterton's sense'.[36]

In the final analysis, Chesterton had found in the detective story a medium that represented Catholicism as a stable, natural faith that could be aligned with the most logical processes that mankind could undertake. The central position which Catholicism is made to occupy in the most orthodox of narrative forms, where resolution automatically follows mystery, is itself born of a backward glance at a century of heterodoxy.

Chesterton's first locked room mystery, 'The Wrong Shape', the seventh story of *The Innocence of Father Brown*, actually examines Christianity's relationship with heterodoxy. The plot concerns the murder of Leonard Quinton, who is a poet and 'a weak and waspish man', addicted to heroin, who lives with his wife in the northern suburbs of London.[37] Quinton has so immersed himself in oriental culture that his work, his house and his belongings all reflect this obsession, whilst an Indian hermit, who appears to have mystical powers, is a permanent guest, much to the disquiet of his wife and his friends. Father Brown and his associate Flambeau arrive one Whitsuntide to visit, and discover that Quinton is with his physician, Dr Harris, in the conservatory. Simultaneously, his nephew Atkinson calls in to try to borrow money but is unable to see Quinton, apart from an abortive attempt which is repulsed by both Quinton himself and Harris. Following this, Harris escorts Atkinson from the room, locks it and states that no one should enter because he has given Quinton a sedative. A little while later Harris notices through the conservatory that Quinton is lying in a peculiar way and goes with Father Brown to find out what is wrong. In the anteroom to the conservatory Harris picks up what appears to be a suicide note and, leaving this with the priest, rushes in to find Quinton dead with a curious oriental dagger in his chest. Brown declares that the note is the 'wrong shape' because it has a corner cut from it. Ultimately, Harris admits to murder because of his love for Quinton's wife; having previously drugged his victim, he stabbed him on re-entering the room whilst Brown read the suicide note.[38] The note is an odd shape because Harris has doctored Quinton's latest manuscript by tearing it and, in the process, removing some quotation marks.

On first reading, the murder of Leonard Quinton seems to fall into the emerging pattern of these stories by depicting the ritualistic, retributive death of a sinner. But closer analysis reveals a profound anxiety about the position of established Christian beliefs when confronted with heterogeneity. Chesterton makes it clear that only Christianity can be the true path: 'Buddhism is on the side of modern Pantheism and Immanence. And it is just here that Christianity is on the side of humanity and liberty and love,' a view strongly expressed throughout 'The Wrong Shape'.[39] From the very start of the story, it is the influence of oriental art and life on Quinton that dominates the text; Quinton has 'dealt much in eastern heavens, rather worse than most western hells; in eastern monarchs, whom we might possibly call maniacs'.[40] His drug addiction is entirely associated with the East, having 'suffered heavily from oriental experiments with opium'.[41] The artefacts which festoon the house also take on a sinister aspect. As Father Brown points out, 'I have seen wicked things in a Turkey carpet',[42] and the doctor points to Quinton's obsession with Eastern religion and his house guest as 'Hindoo humbug'.[43] The Indian hermit is viewed with intense suspicion throughout the whole story; interestingly, he is described as being dressed in white and yellow, which are the papal colours, a symbolic reflection of a desire to cloak heterodoxy in the guise of established faith. Moreover, Chesterton sets the story over the weekend of Whitsun with resonances of Pentecost, when early converts to Christianity wore white to demonstrate their new-found faith.

The allegory and biblical allusion in 'The Wrong Shape' has a twofold effect. Chesterton is able to uphold a Western tradition, presenting Catholicism as a reasonable, English belief system by comparison with Eastern faiths, while simultaneously reinforcing Father Brown's quest for rational answers to questions through his own supernatural religious tenets. This is made particularly evident in the text through frequent references to ideas and objects that are 'wrong'. Often anything which offends his taste is somehow evil, not only the phoney suicide note which, being the 'wrong shape', gives the title to the story, but also the alien murder weapon itself which, to Brown, 'does not look like a weapon. It looks like an instrument of torture'.[44] The notion that wrongness is associated with the unorthodox appears in other stories from *The Innocence of Father Brown*. In 'The Secret Garden' (1911), the policeman murderer, Valentin, is an atheist, as is Prince Saradine in 'The Sins of Prince Saradine' (1911). The latter, in a pale imitation of Cain, allows his brother to die in his stead at the hand of his enemies; as Father Brown says when he arrives at Saradine's house, 'We have taken a wrong turning and come to a wrong place.'[45]

The alienation of oriental culture is, however, expressed in an even more subtle way, by identifying the Western tradition of religion, which Father Brown represents, with the elements of reason. Stories such as 'The Wrong Shape' are not solely constructed around the perceived negatives of say, Hinduism, but more as an opportunity to underpin Western orthodoxy. Of the crime, Brown says, 'I do not say it was not spiritual or diabolic', implying that a supernatural force could influence events indirectly, but of the Hindu religion this possibility becomes a vague distrust in the alien other.[46] At this level the story becomes a semantic struggle between the mystic and the *mysterium*; as Father Brown says, 'The Hindu mind works in strange channels. It loves the mystic, the theatric.'[47] Chesterton overcomes this by allying Christian faith to the rational. At the end of 'The Blue Cross' Father Brown confronts the putative thief, Flambeau, with regard to the failed robbery by saying, 'You attacked reason', adding that 'It's bad theology.'[48] In fact the mistrust might well have been on the other side because during Chesterton's lifetime the Jesuits had made large numbers of converts in India, particularly amongst the lower-caste Hindus. This became a contentious issue, although some reactions proved interesting, some even suggesting that Christianity in India 'should assume an Indian form. Brahmabandhab Upadhyay, a Roman Catholic, wore the clothes of a Hindu holy man, and thought it possible to be both a Hindu and a Christian.'[49] This idea, however, was given short shrift by Catholics. But, of course, detective fiction has been here before. In the first English detective novel, Wilkie Collins's *The Moonstone*, three Brahmins set about restoring the notorious diamond to its rightful place in the sacred city of Somnauth. The struggle for possession of the diamond is played out against the British occupation of India and the threat this posed to the Hindu faith.

In Chesterton's detective fiction, there is a central paradox that belief in the mystical is a natural outcome of modern materialism and a lack of religious conviction, while Catholicism appears as the natural ally of reason. By allying Christian faith to the logic of the detective and the formulaic structure of the detective story itself, Chesterton gives his stories an authority outside the conventional appeal to faith. In this way the explanation of an apparently miraculous crime can be explained; the 'miracle' in 'The Wrong Shape' is solved by the reasoning of Father Brown, with his theological credibility greatly enhanced by the notion that such efforts are the product of man's synthesis with God. Logic, the original thematic device for enclosing and progressing the detective narrative structure, becomes, in 'The Wrong Shape', the instrument of a divinity which is the ultimate source of that logic. The detective, therefore, is an instrument of that divinity; as Father Brown says, 'A miracle is startling, but it is simple. It is power coming directly from God instead of indirectly through nature or human wills.'[50] At this point the 'miracle' of the mystery and the *mysterium* of God coalesce within the framework of detective fiction's structure. A story that begins with the description of 'eastern heavens' as 'rather worse than most western hells' ends with the affirmation of the Christian God's will.[51] Just as the thematic introduction and *dénouement* contain, respectively, the problem that oriental religion poses and the power of a Christian God to overcome it, so the narrative structure posits a secular counterpart, the story of the crime and its solution. It is orthodox storytelling carrying the revelations of an orthodox faith.

The presence of the locked room in 'The Wrong Shape' invokes the notion of the rite: the victim is isolated and exposed as if on a sacrificial altar awaiting the arrival of death, not only at the hands of his earthly assailant but through the medium of divine providence too. This arises because in the locked room mystery, however much the detective is able to explain, there is always that trace of the miraculous that lingers. The clerical locked room mystery, therefore, always appears as a tableau, echoing the practice of Christ's ritual murder and miraculous aftermath. Accordingly Quinton's death has elements of both the sacred and the secular: divine retribution for his sin of apostasy and the anger of a jealous lover.

So, central to Chesterton's project is the problem of how to reconcile the human and divine, which in the detective story becomes a struggle between the metaphysical and ratiocination. According to Christopher Routledge, this always involves the method and extent to which reason is applied:

> Although Chesterton's detective fiction breaks with the view embodied in Dupin, that the mysteries of the universe can be revealed through the ratiocinative method, he does so on the grounds that the detective's perspective does not allow him access to all the information; a limitation that means that not all mysteries can be solved. Nonetheless, Chesterton remains committed to rationalism as such, believing Catholic theology to be rationally grounded.[52]

This has, of course, profound implications for the structure of the detective story; the introduction of metaphysical elements inevitably changes both the implications of the narrative and its technique. Underlying this shift is the idea that, beyond the normal confines of the narrative, a greater force controls the application of logic by human beings. For the detective story this is a distinctly subversive development.

After the crime is solved, Father Brown's 'wrong shape' is proved right, retroactively confirming all of his other suspicions about oriental culture. He proclaims the triumph of the supposed true faith in the same way that Daniel does at the revelations surrounding Bel in the temple. In this sense the climax of 'The Wrong Shape' is a repeat of the first story in the series, 'The Blue Cross', where the thematic imperative, the symbol of the cross, proves to be resistant to efforts of criminality. It is also where Father Brown completes the narrative form by revealing the subterfuge by which he has preserved the cross from danger. While 'The Wrong Shape' considers the relative position of Eastern religion in relation to Christianity, other stories in *The Innocence of Father Brown* are more specific about Catholicism's place within the Western religious canon. More specifically this materializes as a debate between the orthodoxies, old and new. Repeatedly there are references to the shortcomings of Protestantism as perceived by Chesterton; the world of Father Brown, however, represents a belief which, through the medium of detection, is able to display reason and justice. 'The Honour of Israel Gow' (1911) concerns the expiation of the sins of a prominent Protestant Scottish family, the Glengyles. The exploits of this line have brought dishonour to the name and Chesterton allies this taint with their faith, 'for Scotland has a double dose of the poison called heredity; the sense of blood in the aristocrat, and the sense of doom in the Calvinist'.[53]

But, even more importantly, the Father Brown stories present Catholicism as central to religious life. Its status as the predominant denomination is exploited by Chesterton to the extent that, in his writing, Catholicism equates to orthodoxy; in doing so he attempts to resolve the problems of belief in superstition and the supernatural, such as the virgin birth and the resurrection, by aligning the Church with rational practice. Such a feat only becomes feasible in the literary sense when Catholicism becomes identified with that most conventional and ordered of narrative structures, detective fiction. As Robert Gillespie has said:

> In Chesterton, civilization represents a reconstruction of a lost paradise and the detective is the conserver of the best morality that men have devised, theological laws translated into secular concepts in a community of men. In Chesterton's world, where power comes directly from God or the Devil, the forces clearly are Good and Evil, and men are only the agents of these sources of power.[54]

By association with narratives that purport to restore order to the universe, theology seems all the surer for it; but this is only possible because it is Chesterton's world. The secularization of divine laws, otherwise, has had consequences for the non-clerical detective story, because the detective becomes the guardian of a secular code which has detached itself from metaphysical considerations. One of the essential differences between the secular detective story and its clerical counterpart has to do with the consequences of the outcome. The fault lines of this divide, between the religious and the secular, can even be traced within the texts of the clerical detective story itself. The law sees the criminal caught and punished in accordance with a prescribed civil code, but, while the theological sanction may encompass the secular methods, it reaches beyond to a metaphysical consideration of the moral dimension. This latter view is mitigated by the idea of redemption and the different forms this might take within different creeds. For a writer like Chesterton, writing within a Catholic context, pre-eminent amongst redemptive thought is the idea of confession, which for the faithful becomes an essential practice in the face of transgression.

To understand the importance of confession and the way it transforms a text like 'The Wrong Shape', it is illuminating to consider briefly a contrasting story from the Nonconformist tradition. At the same time that Chesterton was producing *The Innocence of Father Brown*, Melville Davisson Post, in America, was publishing what would become one of the most celebrated locked room stories, 'The Doomdorf Mystery' (1918), in a collection featuring his backwoodsman detective, Uncle Abner. Donald Yates, a noted scholar of the genre, states that ' "The Doomdorf Mystery" is a classic regarded by critics as one of the most extraordinary locked room mysteries ever written.'[55] There could hardly be a greater contrast between the two; Chesterton's liberal Catholicism was a world away from Post's Methodist Episcopalian upbringing in West Virginia.[56] He published his first fictional work, *The Strange Schemes of Randolph Mason*, about an unscrupulous lawyer, in 1896.

Post's Methodist upbringing was strict and, in keeping with the tradition prevalent in West Virginia at the time, the Bible was at the centre of spiritual life. Indeed, the scriptures were seen as the basis of all theology, and society was established within the moral principles they contained. Post's father was '[d]eeply religious, he read and studied the Bible so thoroughly that he gained considerable respect for his extensive Biblical knowledge. He instilled in his family by his example a sense of faith, justice, and honesty – traits which obviously affected the work of his author son.'[57] Such was Post's admiration for his father that he dedicated the Uncle Abner tales to him, thus: 'To MY FATHER whose unfailing faith in an ultimate justice behind the moving of events has been to the writer a wonder and an inspiration.'[58] Post, it seems, from a very early age had been steeped in the idea of two kinds of justice: the more earthly legal system and the divine justice of God. Though Methodists never claimed that a blameless life was actually ever achieved, the teaching promoted the idea that striving for perfection was the key; much of the Methodist faith is reliant on self-examination. Sin is something which corrupts mankind and only the power of God's redeeming love can effect salvation; Wesley had always rejected the Calvinist view that Christ died for the elect. As Francis Nevins suggests: 'Post filled these tales with a power and majesty echoing the language of the King James Bible, capturing the essence of evangelical Protestantism and integrating it into detective fiction with the same supreme skill that G. K. Chesterton at the same time was lavishing upon his Father Brown stories in the service of rationalist Catholicism.'[59]

In many respects Uncle Abner is the counterpart of Father Brown, a layman who nonetheless works in harmony with his faith. As much as Father Brown is self-effacing and reticent in his ways, in the early tale 'The Angel of the Lord', Uncle Abner appears as 'one of those austere, deeply religious men who were the product of the reformation. He always carried a Bible in his pocket and he read it where he pleased'.[60] Despite these physical and theological differences, Abner's approach to detective work has distinct echoes of Chesterton's sleuth whose contemporary he was; as Otto Penzler has pointed out: 'Perhaps of greatest interest is that Abner did not rely exclusively on physical clues or technical breakdowns of alibis to find the evil-doer; he investigated human character, found flaws in the spiritual make-up of a suspect, and was able to identify the culprits in a manner previously unknown to detective literature.'[61] The key point of convergence is that in the clerical detective story judgements made by the detective are contingent upon both legal and moral questions; where these two imperatives are present this invariably results in a disturbance to the narrative structure. What may be a sin does not necessarily result in a transgression of the secular law. But a question often posed by both Chesterton and Post centres on how the sinner is to be punished for breaking the moral code of his religion. This fundamental point is the reason these stories are often read as parables, recounting how sinners, and by extension criminals, receive not merely secular justice but judgement through the providence of God.

In 'The Doomdorf Mystery' the story concerns the death of another flawed character, called Doomdorf, who has behaved in a drastically antisocial way by producing a potent illegal liquor which he dispenses to the local population, with violent and criminal consequences: 'the drunken Negroes had shot old Duncan's cattle and burned his haystacks'.[62] It seems, too, from the admission of Doomdorf's woman that she was paid for by Doomdorf with a gold chain and taken as a little girl to live with him for the purposes of sexual gratification.

Doomdorf dies in a locked room when the sun's rays pass through a glass jar full of the offending liquor, setting off the trigger of his shotgun and killing him while he is asleep, whilst outside his house a circuit preacher of the hills berates Doomdorf for his behaviour, preaching fire and brimstone through passages from the book of Isaiah and beseeching God to visit retribution on him. The allegory of death from the heavens, visited upon a sinner, is performed as a miracle which, it seems, only the Deity can perpetrate. Here the crime of producing illicit liquor is transcended by the sin of corrupting others, and so when the detective,

Uncle Abner, states that Doomdorf has fallen foul of 'a certain awful law' and is asked whether this is a statute of Virginia, the reply comes, 'It is a statute of an authority somewhat higher.'[63]

The nature of secular justice is something which occupied the lawyer Post a great deal; in the Randolph Mason series, we encounter a lawyer whose philosophy appears to be without bounds other than that which follows the legal code. The upshot of this philosophy is that Mason is able to extract his clients from legal sanction by use of the most abstruse loopholes, which, while meeting the letter of the law, leave him open to the charge of moral turpitude. When confronted by a client about the morality of such advice, Mason's reaction is a rant against such metaphysical considerations:

> Moral wrong! A name used to frighten fools. There is no such thing. The law lays down the only standard by which the acts of a citizen are to be governed. What the law permits is right, else it would prohibit it. What the law prohibits is wrong, because it punishes it. This is the only lawful measure, the only measure bearing the stamp and sanction of the state. All others are spurious, counterfeit and void. The word moral is a pure metaphysical symbol possessing no more intrinsic virtue than the radical sign.[64]

As Francis Nevins has argued, the stories of Randolph Mason are consonant with the influence that Social Darwinism had at that time in America. As far as the law was concerned, this view was derived from Oliver Wendell Holmes's essay 'The Path of the Law', written in the 1890s, which examined the law as a pure entity free from any moral considerations. The principal yardstick for a lawyer was to keep a bad man just on the legal side of the law, and to put aside any moral objections he might have – and by and large this position still prevails today.

While Doomdorf is both guilty of both sin and crime, Quinton, importantly, is a heretic – he has placed himself outside the established faith and, therefore, no longer within its protection. For Chesterton this is crucial, 'For obviously a man ought to confess himself crazy before he confesses himself heretical.'[65] As far as we know, Quinton has not committed any crime, but his sin in the eyes of the Catholic Church is great. For Chesterton it is Quinton's lack of acknowledgement of his heresy that is the damning aspect of his behaviour; so the remarkable thing about 'The Wrong Shape' is that Chesterton invites us to understand his murderer, Harris, and to sympathize with him at the expense of Quinton. The clinching factor is Harris's confession. While Quinton suffers the fate that traditionally befalls heretics, Harris's subtle attempt at expiation is cleverly achieved. Father Brown invites Harris to confess and, critically, this will be accorded all the privacy of the more conventional form of penitence: 'I sometimes think that you know some details of this matter which you have not thought fit to mention. Mine is a confidential trade like yours, and I will treat anything you write for me in strict confidence. But write the whole.'[66] Despite being in a dislocated form through the medium of a letter, it is a confession made to a priest nonetheless and closes with the following lines:

> 'When I had done it the extraordinary thing happened. Nature deserted me. I felt ill. I felt just as if I had done something wrong. I think my brain is breaking up; I feel some sort of desperate pleasure in thinking I have told the thing to somebody; that I shall not have to be alone with it if I marry and have children. What is the matter with me?...Madness...or can one have remorse, just as if one were in Byron's poems! I cannot write any more. – JAMES ERSKINE HARRIS.'
>
> Father Brown carefully folded up the letter and put it in his breast pocket just as there came a loud peal at the gate bell, and the wet waterproofs of several policemen gleamed in the road outside.[67]

It is a quietly shattering climax; Chesterton invites us to consider the unthinkable in detective fiction – that the narrative should end with the prospect of the criminal law being perverted and a murderer going free. The character of Father Brown is such that he wrestles constantly with two forces at work: the Catholic Church and the criminal law. The question Chesterton poses, in one of detective fiction's supreme moments of crisis, is how to reconcile the secret of the confessional with the secular law.

At the heart of 'The Wrong Shape', therefore, lies a radical juxtaposition of conventional understanding; instead of our sympathy being directed towards Quinton, as the murder victim, Chesterton reserves this attention for Harris. This shocking development is centred on the fact that Harris confesses. Whether or not he is a Catholic is irrelevant; he has pursued the Catholic way and, crucially, acknowledged his sin and his crime. Like the text of 'The Wrong Shape' itself, the confession encompasses two distinct worlds; within the criminal code it can be read as a confession to a crime, but importantly, it is a parody of the Catholic practice of confession. Indeed we may even posit from the beginning of his letter to Father Brown that he has begun, albeit reluctantly, to recognize the faith that the priest represents:

> 'DEAR FATHER BROWN, – *Vicisti Galilæe!* Otherwise, damn your eyes, which are very penetrating ones. Can it be possible that there is something in all that stuff of yours after all?
>
> I am a man who has ever since boyhood believed in Nature and in all natural functions and instincts, whether men called them moral or immoral. Long before I became a doctor, when I was a schoolboy keeping mice and spiders, I believed that to be a good animal is the best thing in the world. But just now I am shaken; I have believed in Nature; but it seems as if Nature could betray a man. Can there be anything in your bosh? I am really getting morbid.[68]

The opening of the letter is revealing: *Vicisti Galilæe*, 'you have won, Galilean', are the wrongly attributed last words of the Emperor Julian who, although raised as a Christian, converted to a mystical form of Paganism. That Harris should quote this is a smart piece of historical reversal by Chesterton; Harris himself has clearly espoused a form of pantheistic paganism, but now at the critical moment of confession seems to be attracted by Catholicism. This latter point is the key to Harris's catharsis: by acknowledging his guilt and turning towards the priest's faith, his soul, and most probably his life, is saved. Thus Chesterton challenges conventional morality by portraying a different vision within the locked room – that of an exchange which leaves the victim damned as a heretic and the murderer redeemed.

The implications of this difference for the structure of a detective story are profound. Whereas, in a Nonconformist context such as 'The Doomdorf Mystery', the actions of a retributive God coincide more with the progression of the conventional narrative structure, the purpose of which is to identify and ultimately punish the guilty, for Chesterton, notwithstanding the murder of a heretic, the outcome of such a crime is more equivocal. But there are considerable metaphysical consequences, for as 'The Wrong Shape' ends, another story, concerning the moral position of Harris and the practice of the Catholic faith, begins. For Chesterton this is his enclosure of doctrine; he extends the text beyond its natural narrative to an area which cannot be contained within detective fiction's conventional structure.

Crucially, the act of confession in the Nonconformist faith is essentially a self-regulatory practice in which the living of an exemplary Christian life is an integral part. Confession, if one can call it that, is a constant process of self-examination so that sin can be kept under control. Clearly, Doomdorf's dissolute existence, the fact that he has made no attempt to improve his life, renders him liable for the ultimate punishment. But, critically, this moral act, the divine providence visited on Doomdorf, takes place within the framework of the conventional narrative: a rapist receives his punishment. Unlike 'The Wrong Shape', there are no mitigations such as confession to occupy us beyond the scope of the text.

The distinction between the conventional and metaphysical enclosures turns on the two consequences which the narrative has to consider. On the one hand is the crime of murder in the form of a locked room mystery; on the other there is the question of sin and the way in which Quinton has conducted his life. The former is, of course containable within the conventional narrative form; the latter, in the light of Harris's confession, is not. Chesterton's depiction of Quinton as a heretic seems to form part of his concern that in modern life people no longer committed themselves to the certainties that, say, established religion provided. His extended essay *Heretics* pinpoints the fact that heterodoxy and secularism had become so attractive to so many that, 'The word "heresy" not only means no longer being wrong; it practically means being clearheaded and courageous. The word "orthodoxy" not only no longer means being right; it practically means being wrong. All this can mean one thing, and one thing only. It means that people care less for whether they are philosophically right.'[69] The consequences for an established faith like Catholicism were fundamental:

> When the old liberals removed the gags from all the heresies, their idea was that religious and philosophical discoveries might thus be made. Their view was that cosmic truth was so important that every one ought to bear independent testimony. The modern idea is that cosmic truth is so unimportant that it cannot matter what any one says. The former freed inquiry as men loose a noble hound; the latter frees inquiry as men fling back into the sea a fish unfit for eating.[70]

We might suppose, therefore, that a text such as 'The Wrong Shape' is essentially conservative in nature; Chesterton, after all, was advocating a return to the certainties, as he saw it, that Catholicism would bring. He was writing too, as we have seen, at a time when a resurgence was taking place in Catholic belief amongst writers and intellectuals. To a high degree all this is true, but at the same time that Chesterton was depicting the demise of a heretic, he himself was doing something remarkable with the detective story. By creating an enclosure of orthodoxy which had life beyond the normal scope of the detective story narrative, he was anticipating the part that metaphysical texts would play in the evolution of detective fiction.

5
The Hollow Text: Illusion as Theme in John Dickson Carr's *The Hollow Man*

> Theatrical magic in the mystery story, as on the stage, is always a matter of worldly means, whether mechanical, manipulative, or psychological.... Exposure hurts magic, because the explanations are always and necessarily deflationary.
>
> Cushing Strout, 'Theatrical Magic and the Novel'[1]

Edward D. Hoch, a critic and prolific writer of locked room mysteries, claimed in 1981 that 'the locked room story has a long and noble history, going back to Poe's "The Murders in the Rue Morgue"'.[2] In the period after the First World War the genre began to see a return to the notion in Poe's detective fiction that theme was a direct consequence of the nature of the detective narrative structure. As Chapter 1 demonstrated, Poe's theme of ratiocination in 'The Murders in the Rue Morgue' complemented the closed nature of the story's construction by appearing as a frame for the narrative. In this respect the locked room mysteries written by John Dickson Carr between 1930 and the outbreak of the Second World War are of particular relevance.[3] Although Carr continued to write until his death in 1977, it is his novels of the 1930s, written in the genre's Golden Age, a period of increasing conventions for the genre, which exhibit some of the most notable examples of the locked room mystery anywhere.

Carr's detective stories are held in the highest regard by critics. Michael Dirda has called him, 'Unquestionably the greatest master of the locked-room mystery',[4] Carr's more recent biographer, S. T. Joshi, claims *The Arabian Nights Murder* (1936) as the 'greatest pure detective story ever written',[5] while Kingsley Amis, in his 1981 article on Carr, announced that, 'He is the acknowledged master of that classic rarity, the tale of detection in which detection is seen to take place, the clues really are shared with the reader, and crimes of majestic and multifarious impossibility are shown at last to have been possible after all, if not always very plausible.'[6] LeRoy Lad Panekin argues: 'Carr went on to create some of the most baffling plots, the funniest characters, the most boffo situations in detective fiction. He is also, along with Sayers, one of the most forthright and distinctive commentators on the nature of detective fiction.'[7]

It is precisely the abstruse nature of his plotting, the self-reflexive tension between these elements of narrative, which forms the basis of this chapter, the overriding argument being that, within the context of formulaic self-reflexivity, the notion of the detective story as an illusory game produces, in Carr's work, a distinctive relationship between theme and structure. This argument, which represents an entirely new approach to Carr's work, examines the background to Carr's fiction and includes a textual analysis of Carr's 1935 novel *The Hollow Man*, in which there is an introduction to Carr's early work, revealing the themes and influences which characterize his stories.[8] In 1983, Hoch commissioned a distinguished panel of critics, editors and authors, including such distinguished academic figures as Jacques Barzun, Howard Haycraft and Francis Nevins, to consider which story would gain their preference from the whole body of such works. The panel were unanimous in their view that *The Hollow Man* was pre-eminent in the field.[9]

The Hollow Man is the quintessential example of Carr's novels of the 1930s, demonstrating how a burlesque of the illusory nature of mystery is possible by installing illusion as the theme. As Carr put it in his most important essay on the genre, revealingly entitled, 'The Grandest Game in the World',[10] the detective story is 'a hoodwinking contest, a duel between author and reader'.[11] This conjunction of theme and structure creates a hollow text, one where the apparent tangibility of the narrative is undermined by the rational explanation that the solution provides, dispelling the illusion created by the narrative. In *The Hollow Man* Carr entwines the established format of the detective novel – the story of the crime with a thematic introduction, the investigation of the crime, the solution of the crime – with a plot steeped in the theme of illusion. The result is a paradox, a text which the argument of this chapter suggests is a burlesque of the detective story canon itself; on the one hand purporting to adhere to the genre's conventions while on the other exhibiting surprising subversions of them.

The textual analysis itself is split into the three corresponding structural constituents of the detective story structure: crime, investigation and solution. Before each of these parts there is a résumé of the plot, revealing the way in which the thematic imperatives contribute to the effect of the closed narrative.

Two distinct rationales characterize the critical context in which Carr's work must be seen, both of which occurred in the inter-war period: the burgeoning of a Golden Age of detective fiction and the emergence of the hard-boiled school of thrillers. This so-called Golden Age has been characterized by two critics as the period between the first Agatha Christie novel of 1920, *The Mysterious Affair at Styles*, and Dorothy Sayers's *In the Teeth of the Evidence* (1939).[12] These two novels mark the textual limits of a period when the corpus of detective fiction grew enormously.

Concomitant with this growth appeared the first wave of generic criticism, much of which came from writers within the genre itself – what one critic has called 'the Golden Age's own self-validating rhetoric'.[13] Whilst the template that Poe had created for the detective story continued to be a broad basis for all narrative structure, writers of detective fiction were analysing the genre and producing prescriptive texts that codified every aspect of both the plot and the narrative. As George Dove has said, in his account of the reader's experience of the detective story, echoing Carr's description of the genre as a game:

> If the detective story is a game, it can be defined in terms of two components or functions. First, there must be definitional rules that do not simply regulate the playing of the game but make it possible for the game to be played. Such rules would provide limits or frames within which innovation could take place, plus pre-understandings and defined tasks. Second, there must be a definition of the game in terms of foreground-background, space, and its identity in terms of its own history and its place among other games, its 'mystique'.[14]

In one sense the forging of these rules of the game became the preoccupation of the Golden Age. What Dove describes is a consequence of a formulaic narrative: if the structure is prescribed for all writers, then a logical step would be to prescribe the way in which the plot imposed upon it should operate. This idea became one of the key landmarks in confirming the homogeneity of the detective story, by relating the components of plot and narrative together. As the previous chapter demonstrated, detective fiction's storytelling style had already contributed to this compatibility even before the Great War began. The first attempt at prescription came from this period too, when Carolyn Wells published *The Technique of the Mystery Story* in 1913. There followed, in 1928, S. S. Van Dine's short essay entitled 'Twenty Rules for Writing

Detective Stories',[15] and a year later Ronald Knox, theologian, priest and crime writer, produced his 'Ten Commandments', or 'Decalogue', which listed the main prerequisites for the genre:

> I. The criminal must be someone mentioned in the early part of the story, but must not be anyone whose thoughts the reader has been allowed to follow.
> II. All supernatural or preternatural agencies are ruled out as a matter of course.
> III. Not more than one secret room or passage.
> IV. No hitherto undiscovered poisons may be used, nor any appliance which will need a long scientific explanation at the end.
> V. No Chinaman must figure in the story.
> VI. No accident must ever help the detective, nor must he ever have an unaccountable intuition which proves to be right.
> VII. The detective must not himself commit the crime.
> VIII. The detective must not light on any clues which are not instantly produced for the inspection of the reader.
> IX. The stupid friend of the detective, the Watson, must not conceal any thoughts which pass through his mind; his intelligence must be slightly, but very slightly, below that of the average reader.
> X. Twin brothers, and doubles generally, must not appear unless we have been duly prepared for them.[16]

S. S. Van Dine's work was even more comprehensive; in addition to Knox's entreaties, he declares that 'there must be no love interest, there must be but one culprit',[17] and 'a detective novel should contain no long descriptive passages, no literary dallying with side-issues, no subtly worked-out character analyses, no "atmospheric" preoccupations'.[18] Despite the tongue-in-cheek tone of these texts, beneath the surface lay a serious attempt to preserve the narrative sanctity of the detective story. In 1928 Anthony Berkeley founded The Detection Club, with G. K. Chesterton as its first chairman. The club included many of the most distinguished names in British fiction, whilst maintaining substantial premises and an extensive library which included manuscripts donated by members so that the club could benefit from the royalties. John Dickson Carr was an early secretary, quite an honour for an American-born author because entry into the club was strictly limited. Admission was initiated by the taking of a bizarre oath and providing the appropriate responses to certain questions based on the contents of Van Dine's and Knox's sets of rules.[19]

The presence of such carefully defined parameters inevitably gave the impression to both authors and readers that they were participating in a choreographed performance, a ritual in which the rules were of overarching importance. In the preamble to his work, Van Dine goes so far as to say, 'The detective story is a kind of intellectual game. It is more – it is a sporting event. And for the writing of detective stories there are very definite laws.'[20] Both Van Dine's and Knox's exhortations, while adding to the prescription surrounding the genre, are more cursory texts than Wells's and confine themselves to guidance on playing fair by the reader, the inadmissibility of the detective as murderer and the solving of problems through reasoned argument, rather than supernatural means. Both, for instance, insist that clues should be laid so that they may be interpreted by the reader. Wells's book, on the other hand, concentrates on the detailed description of the narrative structure, and its relationship with plot. These excerpts from the concluding chapter, 'Final Advices', are indicative of its prescriptive and all-embracing nature:

> Even polished literary craftsmanship cannot make up for the unpardonable sin of a disappointing solution. But this by no means disparages the value of literary excellence. This ought ye to have done, but not to leave the other undone. With all the power that in you lies make for literary craftsmanship; but strive equally hard to perfect a plot which though built on accepted even if hackneyed models, has a few points of absolute originality.[21]

So important is the plot that, if need be, it should be contrived to fit within the enclosed narrative, which effectively becomes a closed narrative: 'Construct the plot backward, if need be; but see to it that every incident and every episode, every speech of the characters and every hint of the author have their direct bearing on the statement of the problem or the quest of its solution.'[22]

The frequent emphasis on plot throughout Wells's text is a reminder that detective fiction's fundamental purpose is to tell a story, that of a crime and its solution, and so every component of the text is subjugated by this overarching imperative. Plot, therefore, emerges as the key storytelling component of the narrative, which, according to Wells, is at least the equal of 'literary craftmanship' and need only be differentiated from other texts by a 'few points' of originality. But even such an integral feature as plot must still be subject to the 'statement of the problem' and 'the quest of its solution'.

One important consequence of writing within such a prescriptive context, and the significant contribution made by writers to early criticism of the genre, was an increasing tendency for texts to become self-reflexive. Such was the exchange between writers on the subject that the structure and conventions of the genre became a subject in itself. A remarkable example of this self-examination exists in chapter 13 of *The Hollow Man*: Carr interrupts the solution to the murder with a chapter entitled 'The Locked Room Lecture' in which Dr Gideon Fell, breaking all the conventions of the detective story, addresses the reader directly to discuss the possibilities of the current particular case, and locked room mysteries in general. In an extended exegesis on the subject he reviews the various landmark stories since 'The Murders in the Rue Morgue' and their contribution to the form. The chapter purports to catalogue all the various tricks used by writers of locked room mysteries; thus any pretence of presenting the novel as realistic enterprise is stripped away as Fell announces to Chief Inspector Hadley and two other characters, Pettis and Rampole:

> 'I will now lecture,' said Dr Fell, inexorably, 'on the general mechanics and development of the situation which is known in detective fiction as the "hermetically sealed chamber." Harrumph. All those opposing can skip this chapter.'
>
> 'But if you're going to analyse impossible situations,' interrupted Pettis, 'why discuss detective fiction?'
>
> 'Because,' said the doctor, frankly, 'we're in a detective story, and we don't fool the reader by pretending we're not. Let's not invent elaborate excuses to drag in a discussion of detective stories. Let's candidly glory in the noblest pursuits possible to characters in a book.'[23]

Such a metafictional device exposes the artifice of the locked room mystery, described by Susan Sweeney as 'a *mise en abyme* which reveals the fictionality of the novel in which it appears'.[24] In fact, this chapter is open confirmation of Carr's desire to burlesque the very form in which he is writing. The passage, by acknowledging its own fictionality, reveals the locked room mystery as an illusion par excellence; but more importantly, as Sweeney points out, 'just as the locked room draws attention to its architecture (doors, windows, chimneys, and so on), so the detective story draws attention to its own narrative structure, in both form and content'.[25] But above all in this chapter Carr reminds us that even outside the confines of each story's narrative the locked room form remains within yet another enclosure, that of prescription. By adding specific details to the parameters laid down by writers such as Knox and Van Dine, Carr describes the absolute limits within which the locked room mystery can be created. So in every sense of the word, both narratively and generically, the locked room mystery is written within preordained limits the performance of which is akin to that of a carefully orchestrated ritual.

These limitations of narrative, however, rather than detract from the genre's appeal have contributed to a deeper understanding of the detective story, so much so that Dennis Porter argues that it is no longer possible to dismiss detective fiction narrative as formulaic because Structuralist and Formalist ideas have revealed formulaic components to all literature. In particular, he is interested in the way that the narrative structure separates the crime and its investigation:

> In the process of telling one tale a classic detective tale uncovers another. It purports to narrate the course of an investigation, but the 'open' story of the investigation gradually unravels the 'hidden' story of the crime. In other words, the initial crime in which the tale of detection is predicated is an end as well as a beginning.[26]

Porter expresses a displacement identified by the Russian Formalists as the difference between plotting and fable; crucially this separation in the detective genre manifests itself as the creation of an illusory world which, until it is dispelled by reason, masquerades as the true narrative. The reason why the initial crime is both an end and a beginning is the fact of a posteriori reasoning: the crime is the beginning of the investigation, but it is also the aim of the detective to trace the clues which lead back to it in order to discover the truth of what happened. Kathleen Klein and Joseph Keller, in the course of their constructional analysis of the detective genre, have argued that within the interaction of these two elements,

> [s]elf-contradiction is concealed behind the illusory *façade* of the deductive novel. This is that, although the detective is eventually applauded for thinking deductively, it is the criminal who, all along, has worked directly from a premise. Every move of the criminal subsequent to the murder itself flows from the hypothesis that what the murderer alone knows about the case can be kept from the rest of the world.[27]

The essence of these two distinct strands of the narrative is to maintain until the last possible moment the illusion that has been created. The bridge for the coalescence of the two narrative strands is that moment of intuitive reasoning which the detective must make in order to solve the case. Thus the satisfactory resolution of a detective narrative must always rest on what the murderer is unaware that he or she has given away. All conventional texts, therefore, turn on the premise of a break in the continuum of consciousness by the murderer. But, as we have already noted, the detective story possesses a particularly homogenous structure and thus the operation of the narrative, which supports the crime-solution momentum, is closely allied to plot. For Peter Brooks, in his approach to narrative, the detective fiction is dependent on the relationship between a uniquely pure narrative structure and plot, one in which the latter is the active constituent of the former; it is this interplay that produces the text. Because of this, detective fiction is, 'The narrative of narratives, its classical structure a laying-bare of the structure of all narrative in that it dramatises the role of *sjužet* and *fabula* and the nature of their relation. Plot, I would add, once more appears as the active process of *sjužet* working on *fabula*, the dynamic of its interpretive ordering.'[28] Brooks uses the terms *sjužet* and *fabula* as defined by the Russian Formalists and latterly by Todorov.[29] Broadly defined in detective fiction, *fabula* is the story of the crime and *sjužet* the story of the investigation. So the action of *sjužet* on *fabula* is the dynamic element which creates the story and moves the text forward, within the overall formulaic structure. It operates as repetition; the detective goes over the same ground as the criminal, retracing the steps taken by the criminal, analysing the clues left behind and solving the mystery. The crime and its investigation are, in effect, mirror images of each other with the detective story constantly operating at two levels of narrative.

Todorov has remarked that because of the interaction of the *sjužet* and *fabula*, its inherent repetition, the detective story 'tends toward a purely geometric architecture'.[30] In addition to being the foundation for the narrative structure in the genre, this 'architecture' is the basis for the enclosure of all thematic material. Todorov's separation of *sjužet* and *fabula* in the detective story, however, is less apparent in the hard-boiled series. This is because the detecting figure acts as an omniscient eye, able to act rationally to solve crimes, whereas in the hard-boiled novel the private eye is cast into a maelstrom of events as the crimes and their investigation become hopelessly entangled. In Chandler's *The Big Sleep*, for instance, the reader is conscious that Marlowe is far from being an omniscient detective; he is caught up in the labyrinthine plot, even attacked and abducted, before the final outcome. So the trail of crimes past and present frequently overlap the investigation; the solution, the culpability of the gangster Eddie Mars, is, in fact, apparent from early in the narrative. The logical dissection of the truth, the cornerstone of the conventional detective story, is made mockery of by the fact that Chandler never does reveal who killed Sternwood's chauffeur, the catalyst for the subsequent narrative.

At the deepest level the hard-boiled novel, in sharp contrast to the ratiocinative detective story, is seen, as Lee Horsley puts it, as 'a popular expression of modernist pessimism'.[31] Authors such as Chandler and Hammett exhibit a dystopian vision of the world, displaying its tendency towards random violence, corruption and anarchy. In marked contrast, the conventional detective story displays crime as a puzzle which is capable of logical analysis and, most importantly, a restoration of order. Chandler, in his now infamous essay 'The Simple Art of Murder' (1944), looking back at the inter-war period, argues that 'Fiction in any form has always intended to be realistic'.[32] He goes on to single out Hammett as a pioneer of the hard-boiled novel who 'gave murder back to the kind of people that commit it for reasons, not just to provide a corpse; and with the means at hand, not with hand-wrought duelling pistols, curare, and tropical fish'.[33] This realism, he contends, is the principal virtue of his form of the detective novel, depicting the world as it is: 'The realist in murder writes of a world in which gangsters can rule nations and almost rule cities, in which hotels and apartment houses and celebrated restaurants are owned by men who made their money out of brothels.'[34] The distinction between so-called realism and the abstraction of the conventional detective story is fundamental to the understanding of Carr's fiction; not only does it provide a context for his sustained opposition to the output of writers of hard-boiled fiction – Chandler most notable among them – but also it was critical in shaping his ideas for the detective genre.

From the very beginning of his writing career Carr railed against realism; in 1922, at the age of 15, he published a polemic against realistic writers claiming that they 'rob life of all that is beautiful'.[35] Carr assiduously resisted any temptation to write in the manner of the hard-boiled novel. In 1935, for instance, his publisher Hamish Hamilton wrote to him, challenging his fanciful style by stating that:

There is a large section of the public which fights shy of anything which is so grotesque as to seem unreal, or perhaps I should say, unlikely to happen in ordinary life. Why not try the experiment some time of taking a perfectly usual situation and exercising your ingenuity on that? Waxworks, museums, hermetically sealed rooms, eccentric clubs, etc., are all fine and dandy, but the ordinary chap like myself spends comparatively little time in them.[36]

Carr's response, however, was to write yet another fanciful, Poe-esque tale. *The Burning Court* (1937) is a story containing witchcraft, the image of a woman walking through a bricked-up doorway, and the disappearance of a corpse from a coffin in a sealed crypt.[37] In 1941, Carr described hard-boiled fiction as 'a clueless and featureless riot of gunplay',[38] and his acidic response to Chandler's essay, contained in a letter in 1944 to Frederic Dannay, one of the two writers using the nom de plume Ellery Queen, denounces the claim to realism: 'do they honestly believe people act like that in real life?[39] Or, which is more important, ought to act like that?'[40] But the significance underlying these often childlike taunts lay in the way it reflected Carr's own style through a negative association. The hard-boiled novel aptly illustrated the antithesis of his work; instead, for Carr, the detective story was the embodiment of illusion.

Illusion for Carr was a concept on two levels of understanding. It created the appropriate medium for the trickery of a locked room mystery, but at a deeper level it became a metaphor for the act of writing itself. This arose from Carr's notion of illusion not corresponding to the conventional literary notion of aesthetic illusion; he subverted the term by rejecting any pretension to portray his work as realistic. Carr found contemporary support for this view; in 1929, Marjorie Nicolson, writing from the locus of Columbia University, spoke for those academics who embraced the detective genre in a diatribe against High Modernism:

> Yes, the detective story does constitute escape; but it is escape not from life, but from literature. We grant willingly that we find in it release. Our 'revolt' – so mysteriously explained by the psychologists – is simple enough: we have revolted from an excessive subjectivity to welcome objectivity; from long-drawn-out dissections of emotion to straightforward appeal to intellect.[41]

For Nicholson, at the heart of this 'revolt' lay detective fiction's opposition to 'contemporary realism, and in these novels we return to an earlier manner. As every connoisseur knows, the charm of the pure detective story lies in its utter unreality.'[42] This debate has had a lasting effect on the perception of the detective story and still presides over much critical reaction. As David Grossvogel points out in his discourse on the relation of detective fiction to literary tradition:

> The detective story does not propose to be 'real': it proposes only, and as a game, that the mystery is located on *this side* of the unknown. It replaces the awesomeness of limits by a false beard – a mask that is only superficially menacing and can be removed in due time. It redefines mystery by counterstating it; by assuming that mystery can be overcome, it allows the reader to play at being a god with no resonance, a little as a child might be given a stethoscope to play doctor.[43]

The essence of this 'false beard' is the presence of two narratives: the conventional detective story portrays what is a rational story – what we might call the real narrative – through the medium of one which is fanciful. This is the very thing that makes the locked room mystery the apogee of this kind of masquerade, because it presents what is ultimately commonplace as impossibility. So, in *The Hollow Man* we are confronted with two narratives representing two distinct forms of perception, the miraculous and the tangible. The trick of the narrative is to sustain the idea of the former at the expense of the latter. David Lehman argues in his study of conventional detective fiction's relationship with storytelling: 'The hard-boiled novel, striving to give the illusion of "what happens in real life," renounces the "house party" murder in favor of an urban criminal milieu. The classic whodunit, being by nature indifferent to "what happens in real life," is drawn to the artificial limitations of the closed murder as a defining trait.'[44] This abstraction from the world creates an environment where concentration on the mystery of the crime assumes overriding importance; as Ross MacDonald has said in his work on the detective figure, 'neither wars nor the dissolution of governments and societies interrupt that long weekend in the country house which is often, with more or less unconscious symbolism, cut off by a failure in communications from the outside world'.[45] Lehman argues that 'The locked-room puzzle is only the most baroque form of this removal from the newspaper's version of reality,'[46] endorsing Roger Caillois's view, in his essay depicting the detective novel as a game, that 'the fateful chamber is a compartment doubly sealed', being twice removed from reality.[47] This double departure arises from the fact that the detective novel takes place in a world apart from the everyday, and the locked room, by virtue of its inaccessibility, merely compounds this sense of isolation.

In the Golden Age a single theme was frequently employed to complement the enclosed structure, providing a point of connection between *sjužet* and *fabula*. Plot itself was coloured by the thematic force chosen by the author. Carr himself designed the frontispiece for the first edition of his 1934 locked room mystery, *The White Priory Murders* (1934), about the murder of an actress, as a playbill, listing the characters as *dramatis personae*. Emphasizing the theatrical setting in this way draws parallels with the architectural similarities of the proscenium arch and the enclosure of the locked room. Interestingly, Christianna Brand copied this approach in *Death of Jezebel* (1948) and actually uses the proscenium arch as part of the locked room locus.[48] Given the restrictive context in which authors were writing, this monothematic approach allowed a more intimate relationship with the narrative structure; the singular theme is not diffused by the presence of an alternative or competing theme. This interaction invariably becomes enhanced by the appropriate selection of the theme itself, which often displays a distinct relationship with the genre's narrative structure.

Surprisingly, for an author whose thematic ideas form such a central part of his work, no specific criticism, no specific work has been published that discusses the relationship between theme and structure in Carr's output. Conversely, the overwhelming body of criticism has concentrated on the ingenuity of his plotting and the methods of his detectives; the remarks by Michael Dirda and Kingsley Amis are typical of the reception that Carr's output provokes. Dirda's essay, a chapter in a major work on crime writers, otherwise concentrates on Carr's sense of melodrama: 'In Carr's early works the atmosphere of the unnatural, the forbidden, and the genuinely mysterious dominates the storytelling.'[49] This identification with the recherché rightly invites comparisons with Poe's *Tales of the Grotesque and Arabesque*, a source, as we have seen, for the first locked room mystery. Dirda is not the only critic to recognize this: Edmund Miller has called Carr 'a gothic';[50] Marty Roth has said that Carr's works 'open as full-fledged works of Gothic fiction';[51] and in a chapter entitled 'The Legacy of Edgar Allan Poe', David Lehman devotes no less than half the space to such analogies as the sealed crypt in *The Burning Court* and the riddle of a revived corpse in *The Reader Is Warned*, as examples of macabre and bizarre references in Carr's work.[52]

Carr's biographer Douglas Greene states that he was 'unrestrained in his enthusiasm about Poe. John said that his stories have "a terrible power."'[53] There was in his make-up a yearning for the fantastical plots of the Gothic novels, and the work of Edgar Allan Poe, in particular. It is, in fact, apparent from Carr's very first book that he was returning to the literary imagination of Poe and the beginnings of the form. *It Walks by Night* (1930) is a locked room mystery written in the style of a horror fantasy with grotesque scenes, such as a beheading, and an atmosphere of criminal insanity unfolding within the context of the traditional narrative structure of the detective story. The text refers to what Carr calls 'imaginative' writers such as Baudelaire, De Quincey and Poe.[54] In this context Carr equates imagination with the bizarre in literature, and Poe in particular. The first murder takes place in a first-floor room in Paris, recalling the death of the L'Espanaye women, where the near beheading of the daughter is matched by a ritual decapitation with a sword. The case, too, is investigated by Dupin's counterpart: Henri Bencolin is an icily logical detective whose didactic tone recalls Poe's original *amicus curiae*. In the chapter entitled 'We Talked Of Poe', the relevance of a trowel to the case – recalling Dupin's own preoccupation with a nail in 'The Murders in the Rue Morgue' – is explained by reference to another story by Poe:

> 'To my mind, the most artistic scene in all literature comes from Poe. You know Poe, don't you, Raoul?' – And he smiled. 'It is in the story about the Amontillado, where Montressor takes Fortunato down into the catacombs to bury him in the wall forever, walled up with blocks of stone and bones. You're *very* familiar with that story, aren't you, Raoul? Fortunato, not knowing of his impending doom asks his companion if he is a member of the Masons.'[55]

This passage, a key moment in early Carr fiction, reveals a synergy with the ubiquitous enclosure motif in Poe and its relevance to the locked room mystery. A short time after this chapter a corpse is found walled up in a cellar and the trowel assumes a significant role in the case. Carr associates his work with Poe's tale of entombment because it embodies the spirit of narrative and thematic enclosure essential to the medium in which he is writing. It is the first indication that Carr sees the narrative of the locked room mystery as operating at two different levels, that of the fantastic and the illusory, by contrast with the rational world of the detective. The solution to these melodramatic events in *It Walks by Night*, however, is a simple example of deception; the truth in the text is replaced by an illusive reference, an incomplete relation of a narrative event. The murderer is able to enter a constantly observed room unnoticed because the eye is confused between what it wants to see and what it actually sees. The essence of the illusion is that it is a performance, taking place in full view of an audience, just as a staged conjuring trick would be.

The idea of illusion as an enactment, just as deceptive as a conjuring trick, obscuring the truth of an event, has been taken up by Cushing Strout in his 2003 article 'Theatrical Magic and the Novel':

> There is an affinity between classic fictional methods of detection and theatrical methods of deception. The detective aims to expose the criminal's deception, and the magician aims to conceal his, but both the author and the magician practice misdirection, 'directing your attention to the wrong place,' as a character explains in John Dickson Carr's first novel, *It Walks By Night*.[56]

Robert Briney's introduction, in the 1976 edition of Carr's 1938 novel *The Crooked Hinge*, is entitled 'The Art of the Magician' and he too compares Carr's work 'with all the illusionist's skill at deception'.[57] Clayton Rawson, a close friend of Carr's, actually featured a magician, The Great Merlini, in a series of four novels and seven short stories, beginning with two novels in the 1930s.[58] Rawson's works invariably turn on the performance of a conjuring trick which has relevance to the solution of a case.

The affinity that Strout outlines is strong because a conjuring trick is constructed in a similar way to the narrative structure in the detective story. Carr himself was convinced of the relationship, as a character quotes from Act I of the murdered Edouard Vautrelle's play *The Silver Mask* in *It Walks By Night*:

> The art of Murder, my dear Maurot, is the same as the art of the magician. And the art of the magician does not lie in any such nonsense as 'the hand is quicker than the eye,' but consists simply in directing your attention to the wrong place. He will cause you to be watching one hand while with the other hand, unseen though in full view, he produces his effect.[59]

Just as the conventional detective tale has three distinct parts – crime, investigation and solution – so the art of a successful magic trick contains, according to Magic Circle rules, the pledge, where the audience is shown something that appears ordinary, the turn, where the magician makes the ordinary extraordinary, and the prestige, where the illusion is completed by a baffling dénouement.[60] The obvious difference between the two, that which creates the textual tension in such a novel, is that for its full effect the conjuring trick needs to keep secret the method by which the illusion is effected, whereas the narrative structure of detective fiction is always moving towards revelation because of its association with the strictly logical ratiocination.

So this engagement operates at a far more profound level of narrative than a mere theme of magic implies; instead the crime becomes a performance of an illusion, a trick which, once it is revealed, uncovers a void at the centre of the text, and the puzzle itself merely a presentational effect of the writing. In *The Judas Window*, for instance, published under Carr's pseudonym Carter Dickson, the detective Sir Henry Merrivale repeatedly states that the murderer gained access to the locked room by the Judas window. This baffling remark implies that a spy hole, such as in a prison cell, is the key to the crime. This clue is, therefore, both a guide and misprision because the solution proves to involve a simple keyhole, conceivably a component of virtually every door. The trick is not merely in the performance of the crime, but in the capacity of the language to confound. This controlling element of the text, where meaning is deferred, echoes the closed nature of detective narratives, a fundamental device that unfolds plot sequentially, so that the ordered narrative will mirror the restoration of order that comes with the solution of the crime itself. In this sense the restoration of order becomes a denial of part of its own text; illusion becomes a kind of *mise en abyme*, the theme of illusion embedded in a text which itself is illusory. Nowhere is this interplay between theme and structure more apparent than in *The Hollow Man*.

The Hollow Man, because of its classically conventional form, divides readily into the essential generic structure: thematic introduction and story of the crime, investigation and solution. The narrative begins with the thematic introduction contained in the first chapter, entitled 'The Threat'.

The plot concerns the murders of Professor Charles Grimaud at his London house and Pierre Fley, Illusionist, found in the middle of Cagliostro Street, where he lives. The book opens at one of the regular, but informal, weekly meetings held in a room above a Bloomsbury pub where Grimaud, a professor of medieval history, is the dominant participant. Also at the meeting are Pettis, an authority on ghost stories, Mangan a journalist, Burnaby an artist and Stuart Mills, Grimaud's secretary. The conversations are intellectual exchanges usually on the subjects of medieval mysteries and the history of magic. Often these historical puzzles are resolved, usually by Grimaud, in what is described as 'the fashion of a detective story'.[61] This evening, Grimaud holds forth on his favourite subject of low magic and witchcraft. Presaging future events, he speaks of the cult of vampirism in Hungary and the belief that men could rise from their coffins. Just as he explains the contorted forms of bodies discovered in their graves as the vain struggle of prematurely buried plague victims, the gathering is interrupted by the mysterious Pierre Fley. Fley declares himself also to be interested in the discussion and murmurs darkly about three coffins and his brother. He hands Grimaud his card which reads '*Pierre Fley, Illusionist...2B Cagliostro Street, WC1.*'[62] He intimates rather threateningly to Grimaud that a visitor would call on him soon, but Grimaud's response is uncharacteristically gruff and defiant. Fley leaves and the chapter ends with a warning that the hollow man would walk on the following Saturday.

This chapter prefigures illusion as the dominant theme of *The Hollow Man*; thus the working out of both *fabula* and *sjužet* narratives in the novel will henceforth be subject to its presence. As we have already seen, the foregrounding of a story's thematic content in the opening pages is a familiar constituent of detective stories. Despite Carr's keen sense of illusion and its place in the detective story, he never forgot that the thematic imperative in detective fiction is invariably constrained by the genre's closed narrative. In *The Hollow Man* Carr makes this very clear from the first line of the book:

> To the murder of Professor Grimaud, and later the equally incredible crime in Cagliostro Street, many fantastic terms could be applied – with reason. Those of Dr. Fell's friends who like impossible situations will not find in his case-book any puzzle more baffling or more terrifying. Naturally, Superintendent Hadley never for a moment believed in goblins or wizardry. And he was quite right – unless you believe in a magic that will be explained naturally in this narrative at the proper time.[63]

Carr's introduction of the term 'reason' is a reminder from the outset that reason is the means by which the mystery will be solved; moreover, that the narrative structure will inevitably lead to that conclusion – a fact amplified by the declaration that illusion of the crime is 'a magic that will be explained naturally'. This opening foreshadows, too, the conventional framing structure of detective fiction (thematic introduction and story of the crime, investigation, resolution), signalling that Carr's approach to the structure of the detective novel, in general, and the locked room mystery in particular, was strictly orthodox.

Carr establishes the thematic subject, too, by assiduous attention to linguistic detail in the narrative. Grimaud's surviving brother, Pierre

Fley Horvath, who appears in London as Fley the Illusionist, carries a name which is the Middle English for frighten.[64] The implication of Grimaud's encounter with Fley at the beginning of the book is that illusion, in the form of an actual performing illusionist, will be his undoing. Fley's address, too, is significant: Cagliostro Street is a name rich in the history of magic. Alessandro, Conte di Cagliostro, charlatan, magician and adventurer, was an egregious figure in eighteenth-century Parisian high society; he claimed the power to make gold and diamonds from all manner of substances, such deceits frequently bringing him into dispute with the law.[65] Cagliostro travelled to all the major cities of Europe variously selling an elixir promoting long life, reading the future in a carafe of water and, most revealingly, summoning up the dead to reveal the future.

Grimaud too, leads a life of deceit, and, like Cagliostro, he also cultivates an interest in magic and witchcraft. Just as Cagliostro claims to call up the dead, Grimaud, and eventually his brother Fley, emerge from their coffins in a parody of resurrection, worthy of Poe himself. Grimaud's own name is suggestive too, of both the French *grimoire*, meaning a magician's book[66] for calling up spirits, and 'gramarye', from the Middle English 'gramery', referring to magic, occult learning and necromancy.[67] These contrived thematic details are an essential part of the illusion; the very improbability of such homogenous compatibility gives a strong anti-realist feel to the text. The effect, therefore, of these and other references to illusion is to create an affinity between the text and the narrative structure that ensures that the thematic imperative is maintained.

The next four chapters, 'The Door', 'The False Face', 'The Impossible' and 'The Jig-Saw Words', witness the full impact that illusion has on the thematic imperative: as a series they constitute the story of the crime. The action transfers to the following Saturday evening. As prophesied in chapter 1, Grimaud receives a mysterious visitor at his London house. It is, apparently, Pierre Fley, who is shown up to Grimaud's study by his housekeeper, Ernestine Dumont. Fley is singularly dressed in a long cape and a curious mask, and enters Grimaud's study to be greeted by his host. These events are observed by Grimaud's secretary, Stuart Mills, from his room across the spacious first-floor landing, who has been asked in advance by his employer to keep a watching brief on this expected visitor. A shot is heard. Meanwhile, Chief Inspector Hadley, Dr Fell and Rampole, a friend of Fell's, are being told by Mangan about the appearance of Fley a few nights earlier. As a journalist, Mangan has followed up the theatre address on Fley's card and spoken to a fellow artiste, the acrobat O'Rourke, who has told Mangan that Fley is known as 'loony' but is a very good illusionist.[68] Fley has also spoken often about coffins and told O'Rourke that once he was buried alive with two others and only one escaped, but he said enigmatically, 'I was one of the two who did not escape.'[69]

Earlier, Mangan had advised Grimaud of Fley's reputation and suggested that the police should be involved, but Grimaud told him that Fley was expected on Saturday evening and that he would protect himself by buying from Burnaby, the artist, a large painting of a bleak landscape depicting trees and gravestones. Hadley, Fell and the others decide to visit Grimaud, whom Fell knows, to check that all is well. They are confronted by the unfolding drama, and when the door is opened Grimaud is discovered in his study dying from a bullet wound, uttering some random, barely decipherable words. Fley, however, has mysteriously vanished.

The murder appears impossible: the room is sealed, the door is locked on the inside by Grimaud, no gun is apparent, the windows are unopened, the narrow chimney leads only to a roof covered with undisturbed snow. The only clues which present themselves are a quantity of burnt paper in the fireplace, a space cleared for the painting and some disjointed words from Grimaud. Mills confirms that although Ernestine Dumont came up to Grimaud's study, presumably to present Fley's card, he was surprised to see the strangely dressed Fley follow closely behind. Fley then pushed past her, turned down his collar, removed his cap, knocked at the door exchanged a few words with Grimaud and entered the room. Mills's only other observation is that Fley appeared to be wearing a false face.

It has already been established that for Carr illusion often manifests itself as a quasi-theatrical performance. *It Walks By Night* was, in fact, originally entitled *Grand Guignol*, after the bijou theatre in Paris, which, according to his biographer Douglas Greene, Carr had visited 'in 1927 or 1928'; the chapter headings themselves often contain theatrical references.[70] The performances at the Grand Guignol specialized in the bloody portrayal of apparently realistic scenes of torture and murder. These elaborate tableaux, in many ways utterly convincing, had awakened in Carr a notion that the essence of locked room mysteries lay in the creation of a convincing illusion. This was an era, too, when the West End and Broadway theatre scenes thrived, performing many detective stories, so that the socio-literary context within which Carr wrote was heavily weighted with the idea of performance. Carr, in fact, was a playwright himself who wrote for both the stage[71] and, latterly, for radio.[72] Although the theatrical influence is clear, another kind of public performance altogether also provided a rich seam of ideas for many texts. Harry Houdini's tricks drew enormous audiences, and his book on bogus magicians provided a particular appeal to Carr as it extolled the virtue of illusion at the expense of so-called supernatural phenomena.[73] In *The Plague Court Murders* (1934), Carr extols the virtue of the 'cynical' Houdini who campaigned against bogus spiritualists and promoted the art of deception.[74]

So what Mills experiences is a performance which combines the elements of the Grand Guignol and the magical illusion of Houdini. Importantly, to witness an elaborate illusion is to play a fundamental part in its effect. The misprision here is doubled: Mills is deceived by what he sees, as is the reader, who in turn is invited to accept Mills's genuine belief in what he saw. This interpretation supports Carr's view of illusion as unrelated to reality, in the sense that his texts are travesties of reality, a deception, and yet, paradoxically, purport to portray an actual event. As Werner Wolf observes, this approach to the novel became prevalent at the time Carr was writing:

> It abolishes the obligation of adopting the subjective and perhaps reflector-characters offering instead the seemingly objective perspective of the 'camera-eye.' This new technique in fact is able to further illusion in many respects. Although its means differ from those used by stream-of-consciousness novels, it also manages to imitate the limited perspective of everyday perception.[75]

It is this limited view that the detective story seeks to create, using the text to inform and conceal simultaneously. The detective genre, exemplified by the enclosure of the locked room mystery, is able to portray this kind of illusion because, in general, the plot tells the story of the crime without narratory explanation. Thus the narrative unfolds as told by the author unmodified and, accordingly, Mills relates what appears to be the probable explanation of events, when the experience of the conventions of the detective story, with its propensity to deceive, suggests that it is both a representation of illusion and merely one version of what may have happened. It is a response that is pivotal to the momentum of the *histoire*; to narrate the actuality, rather than the impression, would be, of course, to negate the entire text. Thus the narrative of the locked room mystery, at its heart, conceals yet a further enclosure – the fundamental truth of what really happens. This act of temporary obfuscation at once reveals both the strength and weakness of such a text: it maintains interest in an essentially progressive narrative, while adumbrating what the text becomes when that interest ceases.

The story of the investigation encompasses some 12 chapters, commencing with the discovery of Fley's body later the same evening, which is found in the middle of a snow-covered Cagliostro Street. He has been shot at close range but the body is surrounded by snow marked only by his own footprints, creating another impossible situation. The investigation produces some revealing facts about Grimaud and his past. It transpires that Fley and Grimaud are brothers, sons of an eminent Hungarian professor, whose real name is Horváth.[76] Some 37 years earlier, in 1898 in Hungary, together with a third brother, they committed a bank robbery, the proceeds of which were never found. All three were sentenced to 20 years imprisonment but devised a clever plan to escape, bribing the prison doctor to certify them dead, during an outbreak of plague. Plague victims were buried outside the prison grounds, so escape could be made without detection. Grimaud had the wire cutters in order to free himself and the others, but he escaped from his coffin without releasing his brothers. When rescued by an Englishman called Drayman in Transylvania, Grimaud lies as he emerges from his coffin, telling him that he is an escaping political prisoner fighting for a Transylvania free from Austrian protection. When he reveals his plans to flee the country and pursue an academic career, Drayman willingly agrees to help such a noble cause, and, after many years, eventually joins Grimaud's household in London. Unbeknown to Grimaud, however, the graves were discovered shortly after his escape and, although one brother was found to be dead, Fley survived and was taken back to prison to finish his sentence.

Included in this part of the book is the much-discussed chapter 'The Locked Room Lecture', to which reference has already been made. In creating this self-reflexive passage not only does Carr advertise the metafictional nature of his text, a denial of any pretence towards realistic fiction, but he reminds us of the conventions that detective fiction is bound by, and, by extension, its utter artificiality. For Joshi this passage confirms the illusory nature of the text:

> In defending Gaston Leroux's *The Mystery of the Yellow Room*, Carr wrote: 'Any critic dull enough to call this story improbable would apply the same term to folklore or Arthurian romance.' I am not sure that the revolutionary nature of this statement – or of Carr's entire position – has been fully appreciated; for what Carr in effect is claiming is that the detective story does not belong to the domain of realism but to that of fantasy.[77]

Although 'The Locked Room Lecture' is the most extended example of its kind in his work, Carr litters his works with similar references. Towards the end of *The Eight of Swords* (1934), a character states, 'After all, this is only a detective story'[78] and 'this is the last chapter, we want to get it over with';[79] and, in *To Wake the Dead* (1937) when Fell is asked how he would summarize events in the book, he says, 'I call it a detective story.'[80] In *The Lost Gallows* Carr is explicit in his defence of fantasy:

> We think it very bad, by some twisted process of logic, that fiction should fulfil its manifest purpose. By the use of the word 'improbable' we try to scare writers from any dangerous use of their imaginations...And yet, of course, truth will always be inferior to fiction. When we want to pay any tale of fact a particularly high compliment, we say 'It is as thrilling as a novel.'[81]

The consequence and the dilemma for detective fiction is to suppress the idea of fictionality to an extent that will make the story convincing. By overturning this basic premise, Carr's text reads like an exegesis on the problems facing the genre. Accordingly, Fell's first proposition in the chapter recognizes this basic conundrum which faces the form: he openly acknowledges that the locked room mystery, as a flight of fancy, has been criticized for being 'unconvincing'[82] and that the result of hearing the solution to such a puzzle is that the reader is in some way 'disappointed'.[83] Earlier, Fley's fellow performer, O'Rourke, had made this very point to Fell:

> It's a funny thing about people. They go to see an illusion; you tell 'em it's an illusion; they pay their money to see an illusion. And yet for some reason they get sore because it isn't *real* magic. They hear an explanation of how somebody got out of a locked box or a roped sack that they've examined, they get sore because it *was* a trick...But they never think of the cleverness it takes just to fool 'em under their noses. I think they'd like the secret of an escape to be some unholy business like real magic; something that nobody on God's earth could ever do.[84]

There are significant parallels here with the act of writing. When Carr produces a locked room mystery, he transposes the trickery of stage magic into language and exposes the extent to which illusion is a principal function of writing itself. This is particularly so in detective fiction because it emphasizes a chronological, sequential treatment of the elements of narrative as staging posts to the natural resolution of the crime.

As Robert Champigny has said, the detective story changes 'the opposition between narrative questions and answers into a tighter tension or complementarity between narrative progression and retrogression'.[85] So the elimination of a progressive and rational dialogue on events as they unfold allows the language of the text to present the imperative of the plot without hindrance. Just as the magic trick presents a credible illusion by its uninterrupted performance to a conclusion, thereby retaining its secret, the momentum of the detective narrative, with its genuine clues and false clues, delays the exegesis of the illusion. It is the enclosed nature of the narrative, a desire to hold all textual matter within its compass, which will dictate how this occurs.

So Carr did not merely repeat the locked room formula; he sensed that the constant repetition inherent in the form, with its closed narrative and its plots of enclosure, had brought it to the verge of self-parody. By exercising this self-reflexive tendency Carr demonstrates how fragile are the components which hold the narrative together, because the *dénouement* is not only the end of the investigation of the crime, but the demise of the text too. Carr uses this chapter to expose the shortcomings of a narrative structure which is based on the repetition of a rigid formula. Such a rubric is based on the existence of a seminal text. As Jean-Pierre Dupuy has pointed out in 'Self-Reference in Literature', self-reference needs a double to refer back to the original.[86] The original in this case is the seminal 'The Murders in the Rue Morgue', where the pattern for illusion is established. The grand illusion at the heart of Poe's story is the trick of the orang-utan's voice, which is described variously in the text as 'very strange', 'shrill' and 'harsh'.[87] In the Poe story this illusion operates on two levels of comprehension. It is a deception which invites the reader to imagine that the third party present in the L'Espanaye apartment, the murderer, is indeed human, perhaps even 'Italian', 'Spanish' or 'German',[88] as the story implies. But at a more profound level this deception is one of language and the power it possesses to misrepresent and confuse, and this subject will be revisited in the final chapter. What Carr records in 'The Locked Room Lecture' is the form's debt to the particular presentation of language in writing, that a mere description of an event is subject to all the imprecision and duplicity of language. Without these fault lines that allow such misrepresentation the locked room mystery becomes barren.

Carr's apparent break from tradition paradoxically aligns his work even closer to Poe, who, we remember, abandoned the detective story because he saw little prospect of its development beyond his three short stories. Certainly, after *The Hollow Man*, the conventional locked room mystery was to become increasingly and openly self-conscious. Burdened by its past and uncertain as to its future, discussion of its own history became a notable feature of such novels. In 1940, Anthony Boucher, in his novel *Nine Times Nine*, has his detective, Lieutenant Marshall, draw on the 'Locked Room Lecture' to solve a case and expose the fundamentally fictional nature of the form:

> Apparently this damned locked-room business is old stuff to mystery novelists, even though it's new in my police experience. And this novelist has an entire chapter in which he analyzes every possible solution ... I never thought I'd see the day when I tried to solve a case with a mystery novel; but damn it all, this is a mystery-novel case.[89]

Boucher draws attention not only to his work's fictionality, but to the fact that this particular kind of fiction is the form's greatest illusion of all.

The solution to *The Hollow Man* proves to be a tour de force. Through a series of enigmatic clues Dr Gideon Fell unravels the labyrinthine complexity of the plot by starting from the premise that the order of the crimes should be reversed. He does this after he discovers a discrepancy in the timing of Fley's death. Pierre Fley, in fact, is shot by Grimaud in the Cagliostro Street flat and, mortally wounded, staggers into the snow-bound street where he confronts Grimaud, who is now on the ground floor of the premises; from here he shoots Grimaud in the chest and collapses. The shot is just one of many illusions in the story; it is mistakenly interpreted as the close-range shot which kills Fley and now he lies miraculously in the middle of the road with no one near him. Grimaud returns to his house, now dying from his wound. With the aid of his faithful housekeeper Ernestine Dumont, the mother of his daughter Rosette, Grimaud makes it back to his study in time to perform the most audacious illusion of the book. To make it appear that Fley is still alive and visits him as promised, he dresses in the cape outfit and disguises his face with a mask. The *coup de théâtre* is achieved by the use of a long rectangular mirror which Grimaud has smuggled into the room under cover of a large painting, bought the afternoon of the murder, of a Hungarian landscape curiously reminiscent, as it transpires, of the area around the prison where he and his brothers were held. The mirror is placed strategically inside the door, so that Mills appears to see Fley being shown to the study door by Dumont. In fact he sees exactly what he is meant to see, the reflection of Grimaud dressed as

Fley. As 'Fley' appears to enter the room Grimaud removes his hat and mask so that Mills appears to see Grimaud welcoming Fley. Seen from the rear, Grimaud, dressed as Fley, is seen to enter the room and the attendant Dumont, having kept the door in the correct position all the while, now closes it behind the 'two' men. Grimaud burns the costume made for him by Dumont, a former theatrical seamstress, and places the mirror on a ledge in the enormous chimney. He then fires a shot for the household and the arriving Dr Fell and Inspector Hadley to hear. Grimaud expires from the original bullet wound sustained earlier, after the locked door has been broken in. To all outward appearances he has just been shot by the mysteriously absent Fley. The grand illusion is complete.

Carr even provides a diagram to show how the complicated series of reflections and lights actually work (see Figure 1). As Chapter 3 noted, it was Anna Katherine Green who pioneered the use of the sketch plan in the detective story, an innovation soon passing into common usage in the Golden Era. The sketch plan has two broad functions: it is often introduced early in a story as a guide to the layout of the crime scene, or, as in this case, to explain a complex set of circumstances. In the former case this device may be seen as a way of reinforcing the idea of enclosure by concentrating attention on the scene of the crime. This delineation, then, becomes a pictorial version of the text, in effect, a part of the narrative that deals with the crime itself. In the Golden Age its proliferation was seen as a part of the fair play prescription which urged that the reader be given as much information as possible, in order to try solve the mystery. The diagram in *The Hollow Man*, however, is quite different; the depiction of Grimaud's trick, which appears like an elaborate set of stage directions for a conjuring trick, is the final act of illusion in the book. In a quite shameless way it actually draws attention to the artifice of the effect and the fictionality of the whole preposterous affair.

The performance of the crime by Fell is the final act of repetition by the detective. In a genre which abounds in the repeated formula of narrative and plot, the repetition of the crime is more than a mere solution; it is the exposition of the way in which language has been used hitherto, that is, to obfuscate the story of the crime. In keeping with the novel's schema Fell's solution is theatrical; he only reveals the truth of events after he has repeated the illusion which Grimaud had devised.

The solution to the case, too, proves to be the reordering of temporal displacement. Because a clock in the window of a shop near Fley's

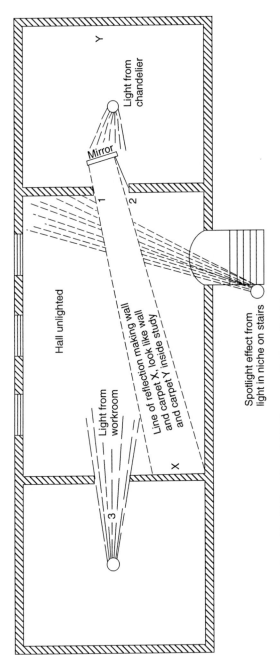

Figure 1 Diagram from *The Hollow Man* which illustrates Grimaud's trick

1. Man whose own reflection is seen by watcher, but appearing three inches taller than reflection because watcher, thirty feet away, is sitting down on a much lower level of observation.

2. Confederate who opens and shuts door.

3. Watcher. In testing this illusion, one important point must be observed. No light must fall directly *on* the mirror, else there will be a reflected dazzle to betray its presence. It will be seen that a spotlight from the niche on the stairs has been caused to fall *across* the line of the door, but not in a position to catch any reflection. No light is in the hall, and the work-room light does not penetrate far. In the study itself, the light comes from the chandelier in a very high ceiling, thus coming almost directly over the top of the mirror. It will throw, therefore, very little shadow of this mirror into the hall; and such shadow as it does throw will be obscured by the counter-shadow of the man standing before the door.

murder is some 40 minutes fast, the assumptions in the case have been based on a false chronology; the illusion created by Grimaud has succeeded because of another illusion, the false recording of time. This serendipitous event rendered Grimaud's planned illusion even more baffling. As Fell says: 'Many things in this case have turned on a matter of brief spaces of time, and how brief they are. It's a part of the same irony which described our murderer as the hollow man that the crux of the case should be a matter of mistaken time.'[90] Thus the regulation of time leads to the true understanding of events; the restoration of order which follows records the ascendancy of the narrative structure in the form of its final part, the solution, over the remainder of the text. What takes place here is the reconciliation of two levels of consciousness, what Roger Herzel has called 'the common sense, everyday world of the logically possible and the world of the seemingly miraculous which operates on different laws'.[91] By exposing the illusion created by the text, the common-sense world of the detective triumphs and, dispelling all effect that the illusion had created, the text, like the apparent figure of the murderer, is rendered hollow. This act is all the more effective because the theme of illusion corresponds to the key moment of the structure; it is the embodiment of the story of the crime. Carr, as this chapter has made clear, was writing within the precise code of a highly formulaic genre and, as such, its narrative structure will always prevail. Carr has already signified this in the very first scene of the book, in which the eminent Professor Grimaud had pronounced on his favourite subject, magic in all its forms:

> As a rule they were content to listen to his store-house of knowledge about witchcraft and sham witchcraft, wherein trickery hoaxed the credulous; his childlike love of mystification and drama, wherein he would tell a story of medieval sorcery and, at the end, abruptly explain all the puzzles in the fashion of a detective story.[92]

What Carr's text does reveal, however, is the importance of the relationship between this structure and the theme itself. If theme proves to be nothing more than a device to enhance the workings of structure, the detective story becomes eviscerated; all that remains after the story has ended are 'sterile exercises in ingenuity'.[93]

Thematic devices are, therefore, a key element in sustaining the impact of the narrative. As Peter Brooks has said, the subject of the crown lost by the Cavalier party in Conan Doyle's 'The Musgrave Ritual' (1893) leads to a deeper understanding of the narrative:

Watson says to Holmes at the start of the tale, 'These relics have a history, then?' And Holmes replies, 'So much so that they *are* history.' Between 'having a history' and 'being history,' we move to a deeper level of *fabula*, and the spatio-temporal realization of the story witnessed as Holmes plots out his points on the lawn at the last opens up a vast temporal, historical recess, another story, the history of regicide and restoration.[94]

The working of the overarching historical theme in 'The Musgrave Ritual' takes the narrative to a new and more profound level of understanding. It adds weight and substance to the narrative by infusing it with an overwhelmingly important subject such as the lost crown of England, the very symbol of authority, struggle and power. As a result the effect is felt beyond the end of the story; it has a life after the solution to the crime has emerged. In this way such themes complement the narrative they inhabit. But the very idea of theme reinforcing the narrative in 'The Musgrave Ritual' has the opposite effect in *The Hollow Man*. By installing illusion as a thematic preoccupation, Carr was able to turn the tables on the genre itself; this is because his text presented itself as the product of a prescriptive literary climate which fostered textual self-consciousness. The inevitable result was a constant awareness of the context within which writing took place and an acknowledgement that the part each narrative constituent played was of equal importance as the plot itself. Thus the depiction of writing in this form as an illusion gives rise to the conundrum that the very thing which gives the story its interest, the story of the crime, at the same time is an abstract, ephemeral game of mystery and legerdemain. *The Hollow Man* is a reminder that the texts of detective fiction contain two stories, each a version of the other; the first is always supplanted by the second as a result of the application of ratiocination. Thus illusive writing subverts the text by presenting the narrative as a deliberate misreading of events, leaving behind a void, a hollow text created by the revelation of what really happened.

6
Jorge Luis Borges and the Labyrinth of Detection

> ...And found no end, in wand'ring mazes lost.
>
> Milton, *Paradise Lost*[1]

When Jorge Luis Borges wrote the first of three detective stories in 1941, 'The Garden of Forking Paths', he did so as part of a wider initiative to mark the centenary of the publication of 'The Murders in the Rue Morgue'. This year also saw the inaugural edition of *Ellery Queen's Mystery Magazine*[2] promoting excellence in the short story, and Howard Haycraft's *Murder for Pleasure: The Life and Times of the Detective Story*, a landmark volume in the critique of the genre.[3] Borges completed his doubling of Poe's original project by adding 'Death and the Compass' in 1942 and 'Ibn-Hakam al-Bokhari, Murdered in His Labyrinth' in 1949. In the spirit of the anniversary Borges returns the detective story to its origins. In this respect, Maurice Bennett has argued that:

> The relationship between Poe and Borges, however, transcends mere similarities in metaphysical and artistic interests. Critics have noted in passing that Borges is the single most prominent perpetuator of literary forms pioneered by Poe. The detective story and the short tale that turns narrative action into philosophical speculation rank among the most notable exercises of both writers. Poe is also the author to whom Borges returns most often in praise, criticism, and explicit imitation.[4]

What Bennett speaks of here is essence: Borges's interest in Poe's detective fiction concentrated on its components, not outcomes. He perceived that Poe had based his idea on the process of reason and knowing how, from a succession of inferences, narrative could be propelled.

This approach would lead Borges into a world where the arrangement of narrative seems to matter less than its nature. His repeated deferral of the conventional detective story dénouement means that concentration is directed towards the cerebral process of investigation. In 'Death and the Compass', for instance, almost the whole narrative is taken up with the practice of Lönnrot's skills as a ratiocinative detective of the Dupin type – so much so that in all three stories there seem to be two investigations in progress: one in the body of the text and the other into the text itself. It is no surprise, therefore, that Elana Gomel has referred to Borges's stories as having the character of an 'ontological detective story'.[5] Just as the detective strives to unravel the truth of a crime, Borges seeks to discover the essence of the detective story's structure by reference to how it might appear if its formulaic structure was interrupted. This he achieves through a series of convention shifts: in all three stories fundamental features of the genre – closed narrative, restoration of order and the nature of reasoning – are examined for both their function and their alternative literary possibilities.

As if to underline this, Borges would say, many years later, in his 1978 lecture on the genre, that 'To speak of the detective story is to speak of Edgar Allan Poe.' He added, revealingly, that 'The intellectual origins of the detective story have been forgotten.'[6] Although Borges was referring specifically to the excessive violence and accent on action prevalent in the contemporary American crime novel, in truth the origins of this trend have their roots in the pre-war period, when he first contemplated writing a detective story of his own. The earthy, hard-boiled thrillers of Hammett and Chandler written in the 1930s and 1940s were already forging a new direction for the crime story, while writers such as John Dickson Carr, as we have seen, felt that these so-called realistic thrillers were a betrayal of the ratiocinative essence of the detective genre as envisaged by Poe. So Borges's detective stories were an attempt, as John Irwin has put it, to 'recover what he took to be the genre's original impulses'.[7]

Borges's actual approach to the detective story, however, seems ambivalent. There is little doubt that he held the form in high esteem:

> In this chaotic era of ours, one thing has humbly maintained the classic virtues: the detective story. For a detective story cannot be understood without a beginning, middle, and end... I would say in defense of the detective novel that it needs no defense; though now read with a certain disdain, it is safeguarding order in an era of disorder. That is a feat for which we should be grateful.[8]

Nonetheless, Borges's regard for the original vision of the detective story was based, ironically, on certainties which his work in the genre seems to question. In all three of his detective stories the established generic model, with its hermeneutic strategies and closed narratives, is consistently challenged. This results in texts that ask fundamental questions about the certitude of the genre's narrative; Borges's detective stories all seem to start as if to pursue the conventional linear pattern and then, as if viewed through a prism, the narrative distorts and ends in equivocation. As one critic has said, the metaphysical story 'flaunts its lack of closure, the failure of the detecting process', and in doing so draws attention to the frailties of a structure consistently reliant on the restoration of order.[9]

The term 'metaphysical detective story' was first coined by Howard Haycraft in 1941, who was attempting to describe the apparent contradiction of the presence of theology and logic in Chesterton's Father Brown tales.[10] This reflected the idea that in Chesterton (who was much admired by Borges), while earthly puzzles are capable of resolution, divine mysteries remain beyond human comprehension. The resuscitation of this idea by Borges dispenses with the overtly religious theme and replaces it with the unfathomable mysteries of the world. This proposition is fuelled by the myriad alternative circumstances that any one event might have, or the numerous consequences that may flow from them. These exigencies of time and space also have the effect of throwing the constancy of the detective story's structure into sharp relief. The detective story, of course, with its classic storytelling form, makes an excellent subject for an examination into the nature of narrative, so given his high esteem for detective fiction, Borges's stories seem to be born of a genuine desire to inquire rather than detract.

Borges's experimentation with the detective story tells us much about its structure. In familiar circumstances the formula which encases every investigation includes a question that requires an answer, a mystery that needs resolving. As Poe himself said, the essence of the detective story was 'unravelling a web you yourself (the author) have woven for the express purpose of unravelling'.[11] So when that solution becomes yet another question, as it does in 'Death and the Compass', Borges is testing the structure of the closed narrative either by failing to solve mysteries or, in the act of resolution, the text giving rise to other mysteries which are just as impenetrable. This conclusion is reflected in William V. Spanos's phrase, 'anti-detective story', to explain narratives like Borges's, that 'evoke the impulse to "detect" ... in order to violently frustrate it by refusing to solve the crime'.[12] This sense of endless suspension is seen by Dennis Porter from the reader's point as an interruption of the natural expectation of the linear narrative:

> The art of the popular detective novel derives from the rhythm of desire. That is, it begins by stimulating desire, proceeds to tease it through a technique of progressive revelation interrupted by systematic digression, and finally satisfies it, however unsatisfactorily, in an end that reveals all. In contrast, the tendency of much modernist fiction in the twentieth century has been to stimulate in order not to satisfy.[13]

The model of the conventional detective story which Porter describes is underpinned by the relationship between an established structure and a complementary theme. Desire is stimulated by the way that theme acts on the narrative; the resolution of the mystery, therefore, is inextricably linked to its thematic thread. In 'The Murders in the Rue Morgue', for instance, our appetite for rational explanation is awoken by Dupin's bravura demonstrations of logic in the first scene of the story and is fulfilled by his unravelling of the case at the end, while in *The Hollow Man*, the narrative not only adheres to the conventional structure of the genre but the presence of illusion as its principal theme conveys the narrative inexorably to revelation. Illusion is an essential part of the solution. In the case of Borges, however, Porter sees that gratification disappear:

> The fiction operates like a trap to catch the reader. In place of the pleasure machine of popular fiction that returns its reader to the safety of his point of departure once the thrilling circuit is completed, many modern tales are machines without exits. The end brings neither revelation and the relief of a concluded sequence nor, *a fortiori*, the return of order to community and confirmation of human mastery.[14]

But Borges's deviation from the conventions of the detective story is not entire; it runs parallel with his recognition of its essential structural relationships. This sense of writing on the threshold, from both within and without the genre, is evidence that Borges needed to step back from the formulaic straitjacket in order to appreciate and analyse its constitution. In 'Death and the Compass', for instance, if we posit what would be the logical, conventional ending to the story, Lönnrot's detective skills would lead him to capture Red Scharlach, but in Borges's version we are invited to consider the exact opposite. The effect is to create a text on the threshold, one which simultaneously carries both echoes of convention and, at the same time, subversion. It seems that Borges was not only warning that the displacement of the pure narrative of detective fiction would become a symbol for the representation of chaos and uncertainty, but also reminding us that it was a model of certitude in a literary world where structure was giving way to fragmentation and experimentation.

Tim Conley considers that this idea is no more than a mirror image of detective fiction's traditional impulse, thus retaining all of the narrative's characteristics but in juxtaposition:

> Devotee of Poe and Chesterton that he is, Borges writes detective stories in which the very fact of a crime or a pathology remains in question, and although a sense of order will finally establish itself it is often an inversion of the detective's own methodology. It is significant that the credo of Red Scharlach in 'La Muerte y la Brújula' is no different from that of a sleuth who assembles clues to determine an event... for a Lönrott [sic] it is an article of faith, but for an artful and opportunistic Scharlach it is a token of a false conversion: he is not the villain of the story in which he is written.[15]

But Borges does not merely invert detective fiction's own constituents; he actually distorts the narrative by using one of his most enduring themes, the labyrinth. Interestingly Borges's own view of his detective fiction was that, 'I have on occasion attempted the detective genre, and I'm not very proud of what I have done. I have taken it to a symbolic level, which I am not sure is appropriate.'[16] The catalyst for Conley's assertion is the labyrinth; detective fiction, with its enclosed narrative, tortuous investigation, central mystery and locked rooms has much in common with the idea of the labyrinth. In particular, as a metaphor for the locked room it is particularly significant – in the conventional locked room story the enclosed physical architecture plays an important role in underlining the closed narrative itself. Although the locked room seems, at face value, a space that is impenetrable, there is ultimately always a way in. So it is with the labyrinth. In Borges the more equivocal space of the labyrinth is more obviously open at one end, and while this corresponds with his altered state of the closed narrative, it does reflect the idea of the conventional locked room. Crucially, this allows for the contemplation of not just one solution to a mystery, but an infinite number of possibilities.

The three labyrinths that appear in Borges's detective stories are all subtle variations on the original metaphor. In 'Ibn-Hakam al-Bokhari, Murdered in his Labyrinth' the labyrinth is implicitly a locked room or at least as close to one as can be found in Borges; in 'The Garden of Forking Paths' it suggests the vision of the eternal library; and in 'Death and the Compass', a representation of the progress of inquiry leading to nothing but the infinity of time and space. Despite the presence of the labyrinth motif and its potentially open-ended form, the characters in these stories are still invariably trapped like the victim in the more recognizable locked room. This arises precisely because the physical enclosure is replaced by a metaphysical version which is unending. So, despite the fact that Borges burlesques the genre's conventions, he still recognizes the link that exists between structure and thematic content in all detective fiction. As far as the physical appearance of the labyrinth is concerned, John Irwin argues that Borges's reflection of Poe is anchored in structural and architectural similarities:

> What seems clear is that Borges's antithetical reading/rewriting of the Dupin stories registers not only the resemblance between the mystery of a locked room and the puzzle of a labyrinth, but also the resemblance between these two structures and the purloined letter. The basic similarity of the three turns upon each figure's problematic representation of the relationship between inner and outer.[17]

Both Poe and Borges use the ratiocinative detective story as the form that invites hermeneutics and the final resolution of a seemingly unfathomable mystery. To both men this heuristic approach leading to the restoration of order seems a desirable goal, but Borges differs from Poe in that his equivalent of Dupin, Lönnrot in 'Death and the Compass', is sent into the labyrinth that Red Scharlach has created to meet his destiny. This simultaneously confirms and differentiates his relationship with Poe's detective; Borges states that Lönnrot 'thought of himself as a reasoning machine, an Auguste Dupin, but there was something of the adventurer in him, even something of the gambler'.[18] By using his intellectual powers he falls into Scharlach's trap, and it is the plodding Inspector Treviranus's more mundane methods that prove to be correct. Thus Borges's story both reflects and refracts Poe's original; the price to be paid for obsession with abstract esoterica, at the expense of the facts of a case, is for the detective to fail, both physically and intellectually.

The other striking aspect of the labyrinth's structural relationship with detective fiction arises from the conjunction of inner and outer; while it is true that Borges engages with the generic narrative structure, he does so invariably from a detached perspective. So Irwin's notion of rewriting invokes the idea that in some way Borges's detective stories are forms of translation – not linguistically, but from one version of the structure to another. Moreover, the relationship between inner and outer, so critical in the locked room mystery, not only has physical parallels with the architectural references, but also what Borges saw as being integral to the detective story structure. As we have seen, if we metaphorize the journey through the labyrinth as an unending search for resolution, the detective story lapses into purposeless inquiry. So, in Borges's world, the journey through the labyrinth becomes focused on the process of epistemics, a search for the answer not to a particular problem, but how we theorize the gathering of knowledge. The labyrinth as a model, therefore, is a way in which Borges is able to emphasize the idea of inquiry. In his essay 'Unreading Borges's Labyrinth' Lawrence Schehr proposes a juxtaposition of the thematization of the labyrinth figure in Borges's detective fiction with that which Irwin outlines:

> In general critics have opted for a point of view that is normative, be it psychoanalytical, metaphysical or even structuralist. That is to say; the questions of labyrinth and text are first thematized and then through this thematization of the figure, brought back from their ex-centric position, returned to the fold, and explained as components of a normative structure.[19]

Schehr, therefore, refuses the temptation to thematize writing itself as metaphysical and proposes to view the questions of labyrinth and text as 'fundamental disruptions of and within narrative and as the trace of the irreducible paradox of representation in narrative'.[20] As this chapter argues, the idea of Borges's labyrinths, as a disturbance of narrative, is essentially thematic; they impact on Borges's work by enhancing the impression of indeterminate locus, a place where all truths are elusive. Borges challenges the idea of the pure storytelling narrative by suggesting that investigation may end in perpetual, unresolved enclosure. The labyrinth motif in Borges, therefore, is a device that militates against the search for ultimate teleological reduction.

This aspect of textual disturbance is developed by John Fraser, who sees the labyrinth in Borges as bringing about 'endlessly opening vistas of knowledge beyond knowledge, the relentless epistemological questionings, the apparent subverting of every commonsense and common-knowledge certainty'.[21] Using 'The Garden of Forking Paths' as an example, Fraser argues that Borges points out that the genre's narrative strengths, resolution and the restoration of order, are not absolutes: 'Its Chestertonian, Father Brownish aspects reminds us that every detective story or novel, even the most mystifying ones by John Dickson Carr (squaring or cubing Chesterton) ultimately ends with the assented-to solving of a mystery or mysteries, and the arrival of not at 'truth' but at specific, limited truths.'[22] It is these 'specific, limited truths' that Borges wishes to draw attention to, and they lie behind the equivocal endings to his detective stories. By hinting at the very end of 'Death and the Compass' of the possibility of a raft of alternative solutions, and the 'dizzying web of divergent, convergent and parallel times' in 'The Garden of Forking Paths', Borges lays bare the limitations of the rigidly formulaic confines of the detective story.[23]

In many respects, Fraser's reading of the labyrinth motif is similar to that of Schehr: the labyrinth as a distortion of narrative continuity. Of 'The Garden of Forking Paths' and its place in *Ficciones* he concludes that, 'Useful as the metaphor of a labyrinth is, it misrepresents *Ficciones* – and Borges – in so far as it implies a construction with a static centre and a solution. Like other major works, *Ficciones* is heuristic, an exploring.'[24] This is precisely the point effected by the Borges trilogy of detective stories: the distortion that the labyrinth provides converts the narrative into an extended, unending investigation in which any solutions are either implied, multiplied or absent.

The equivocal dénouements of Borges's detective stories, which have the effect of moving beyond the genre's conventional structural boundaries, resonate with the idea a form of translation. This ties in with the author's own attitude to linguistic translation. For Borges, therefore, each translation meant a new set of hermeneutics, one which widened the scope of the original and opened up alternative possibilities. This is precisely the relationship that Borges's detective fiction has with the wider generic canon – the certainty of the restoration of an established order is removed in favour of a world where the outcome of any particular event is not predetermined.

Borges's failure to condemn new versions of his work outright runs parallel with the theme of a perpetually evolving book, covering every possible contingency, in stories such as 'The Garden of Forking Paths'. The notion of the different potential possibilities of the text, its latent capacity to bifurcate repeatedly into a myriad of texts, is a philosophy that is underlined and reproduced by Ts'ui Pen's book, so that it becomes a text within a text. This sense of enclosure within, and yet a departure from, the conventional detective story narrative becomes Borges's

central design for the genre. Yu Tsun's ancestor Ts'ui Pen announced
that he would 'retire to construct a labyrinth'.[25] This labyrinth turns
out to be the eponymous book of the story. The book is an attempt to
construct 'a labyrinth which was truly infinite', chronicling an infinite
number of concurrent realities and times, one of which is the subject of
the story.[26]

When Yu Tsun visits Albert, the latter explains his theory of Ts'ui Pen's
book and one of the stories which it contains, that of his descendant,
Yu Tsun:

> I had wondered how a book could be infinite. The only way I could
> surmise was that it be a cyclical, or circular, volume whose last page
> would be the first, so that one might go on indefinitely ... I also pic-
> tured to myself a platonic, hereditary work, passed down from father
> to son, in which each new individual would add a chapter or with
> reverent care correct his elders' pages ... the garden of forking paths
> was the chaotic novel; the phrase 'several futures (not all)' suggested
> to me the image of a forking in *time*, rather than in space. A full
> rereading of the book confirmed my theory. In all fictions, each
> time a man meets diverse alternatives, he chooses one and elimi-
> nates the others; in the work of the impossible-to-disentangle Ts'ui
> Pen, the character chooses – simultaneously – all of them. *He creates*,
> thereby, 'several futures,' several *times*, which themselves proliferate
> and fork.[27]

Instead of eliminating all other possibilities Borges presents his detective
fiction not as a singular plot development with a closed narrative, but
as a text where alternative plots, or labyrinths converge. In both 'Death
and the Compass' and 'The Garden of Forking Paths', the plot reads
as just one of many versions of the same story. Lönnrot, at the point
of his death, invokes an alternative labyrinth where the symmetry of
Scharlach's plan is better expressed, and Scharlach himself promises to
adopt it the next time he kills him.

Borges ponders the question of the closed narrative in a literary world
where the existence of every combination of narrative and plot is a
threat to the certainty that the genre portrays. In 'The Garden of Forking Paths', the idea of a universal text enclosing all others is exemplified
by the book that Ts'ui Pen produces in order to engage with epistemics.
This is the infinite library, a never-ending repository of the entire world's
knowledge. Libraries, of course, have a very special place in the detective canon and in Borges, too. They are, for Borges, a way of giving

expression to the labyrinth, an opportunity to equate the infinite production of knowledge with the idea of never-ending space. In 'The Library of Babel' Borges actually describes how this might be configured: 'The universe (which others call the Library) is composed of an indefinite, perhaps infinite number of hexagonal galleries. In the center of each gallery is a ventilation shaft, bounded by a low railing. From any hexagon one can see the floors above and below – one after another, endlessly.[28] Ts'ui Pen's book is just such a library; like the universe it purports to be, it is so vast as to be essentially random and unfathomable. Consequently, in 'The Garden of Forking Paths' we are never quite sure which of the many versions of the story contained within the universal book we are actually witnessing. As Albert outlines in his homily on the book:

> *The Garden of Forking Paths* is an incomplete, but not false, image of the universe as conceived by Ts'ui Pen. Unlike Newton and Schopenhauer, your ancestor did not believe in a uniform and absolute time; he believed in an infinite series of times, a growing, dizzying web of divergent, convergent, and parallel times. That fabric of times that approach one another, fork, are snipped off, or are simply unknown for centuries, contains *all* possibilities. In most of those times, we do not exist; in some, you but I do not; in others, I do and you do not, in others still, we both do.[29]

Such is the dislocation we experience in the story inhabited by Albert and Yu Tsun that we are unsure whether time may be split and whether each is a version from a different rendering of the story. Albert tells Yu Tsun, the descendant of Ts'ui Pen, that despite their meeting now, 'in one of the possible pasts you are my enemy, in another my friend'.[30] As their alternative destinies coincide it appears that this Albert is Yu Tsun's friend, while the latter is his enemy. This feeling is confirmed when, just before he shoots Albert, Yu Tsun says, confusingly, 'The future is with us..., but I am your friend.'[31] Albert is sacrificed by Yu Tsun, because of the name he bears, so that he can convey a message to his spymaster in Berlin.

The Borgesian library found its most celebrated expression in Umberto Eco's *The Name of the Rose*. In Eco's novel the library, impenetrable and maze-like, deep in the centre of the monastery and presided over by the blind monk Jorge, takes on the mantle of a locked room. It is Brother William of Baskerville's task as the detective to enter the forbidden space and solve the mystery surrounding all the deaths that have taken place there. But, as David Lehman has suggested, William actually identifies Jorge as the culprit for the 'wrong reason'.[32] Having followed the clues he thinks point to a diabolical plan, he learns that no such strategy exists:

> I arrived at Jorge seeking one criminal for all the crimes and we discovered that each was committed by a different person, or by no one. I arrived at Jorge pursuing the plan of a perverse and rational mind, and there was no plan.... Where is all my wisdom, then? I behaved stubbornly, pursuing a semblance of order, when I should have known well that there is no order in the universe.[33]

William has behaved like the model that his name implies, Sherlock Holmes. In the manner of detective fiction's finest he has followed a trail of clues convinced that they are part of a grand design. But in this world such investigations are inappropriate; Borges's and Eco's libraries are very different places from the library in a conventional detective story like 'The Filigree Ball'. In Katherine Green's version, as we have seen, the library is a source of clues which the detective uncovers to arrive at a successful conclusion of a particular mystery. But to Borges, the library becomes a universal entity; far from casting light, it introduces all the random contingencies of existence into what otherwise would be a straightforward narrative. We might suppose, therefore, that the library stands as a metaphor in Borges for the difference between convention and metaphysics, a place where time and place become distorted and the familiar rules of the linear narrative do not apply.

In 'Death and the Compass' the narrative appears to embark on the form of the classic detective story: the narrative is, in fact, a chronological account of the series of murders, a particular convention of the detective story defined by Julia Kushigian as 'the linear structure of time which allows an identification of the elements step by step'.[34] Borges even provides the customary ratiocinative introduction, which prefigures the progress of the case, although he does reduce it to a mere paragraph. In Conan Doyle's only locked room mystery, 'The Speckled Band' (1892), for instance, the scene is set thus:

> Sherlock Holmes... refused to associate himself with any investigation which did not tend towards the unusual, and even the fantastic. Of all these varied cases, however, I cannot recall any which presented more singular features than that which was associated with

the well-known Surrey family of the Roylotts of Stoke Moran. . . . It is perhaps as well that the facts should now come to light, for I have reasons to know that there are widespread rumours as to the death of Dr. Roylott which tend to make the matter even more terrible than the truth.[35]

In one short preliminary paragraph the reader has learnt one of the key facts of the story, that the plot will concern itself with the death of Dr Roylott. The effect of this device is to apply a prefigured closing of the narrative, such is the convention that the plot will be enacted within these constraints and never outside them. Borges's own opening paragraph to 'Death and the Compass' has a striking similarity to that of Conan Doyle's:

Of the many problems on which Lönnrot's reckless perspicacity was exercised, none was so strange – so *rigorously* strange, one might say – as the periodic bloody deeds that culminated at the Villa Triste-le-Roy, amid the perpetual fragrance of the eucalyptus. It is true that Erik Lönnrot did not succeed in preventing the last crime, but he did, indisputably, foresee it. Nor did he divine the identity of Yarmolinsky's unlucky murderer, but he did perceive the evil series' secret shape and the part played in it by Red Scharlach.[36]

This is an example in which Borges's detective fiction uses established constituents of the detective story in a context of parody. The introduction not only purports to describe what appears to be the rubric for a conventional detective story, but for nearly the whole of its course the detective Lönnrot successfully follows clues through to a conclusion in the conventional way. However, while affirming his recognition of this structure, Borges is also telling the story of a parallel crime, the destruction of Lönnrot. Again Borges parodies the practice of detective fiction where the narrative relates two parallel stories: one which tells the story of the investigation, and the other, which eventually supplants it, the story of what really happened. In his version Borges submerges the real purpose of the narrative with a series of murders that are both interwoven into the narrative of Lönnrot's death and yet are peripheral to it. Significantly, it is the idea of the labyrinth and its potential for entrapment which Borges employs. In a subversion of detective fiction's traditional model, Scharlach pursues Lönnrot by being one step ahead of the detective, setting baited traps in the form of clues which lead to his eventual demise; it is Scharlach who supplants the role of the detective in the customary denouement:

> I swore by the god that sees with two faces, and by all the gods of fever and of mirrors, to weave a labyrinth around the man who had imprisoned my brother. I have woven it, and it has stood firm: its materials are a dead heresiologue, a compass, an eighth-century cult, a Greek word, a dagger, the rhombuses of a paint factory.[37]

Thus the labyrinth that Scharlach creates has not one but two narratives: the detective story model in which Lönnrot follows the clues set for him, and the second, unseen narrative, in which Scharlach plots his revenge for the imprisonment of his brother. The ending, therefore, makes a mockery of all the conventions which Lönnrot has observed hitherto. Unlike the conventional story the finale is the moment when the second narrative usurps the first and overturns the whole thrust of the text so far.

Lönnrot dutifully solves the riddle of the murders, but, in turn, is killed by the murderer, Red Scharlach. In an intriguing twist of Dickson Carr's illusive text the whole thrust of his investigation has been a false trail laid to entrap the detective. Borges manages the titanic volte-face of the detective's murder with just five words in the very last line of the story. Having explained the intricacies of his elaborate scheme to Lönnrot and threatened his death, even then there is still an expectation that Scharlach, gun in hand, like Roylott and countless other criminals in these stories, will be overthrown and order thus restored. But with two short sentences – 'He stepped back a few steps. Then very carefully, he fired'[38] – all generic conventions are exploded.

This absence of compliance with generic form gives Borges's texts the sense of being part of a wider presence than the confines of the detective story's narrative structure. This gives rise to the impression that each work is part of a wider text, a text so large that it incorporates all the possibilities that the individual narrative is capable of producing. In effect, the enclosing narrative of the detective story is supplanted by an infinitely wider framing structure, which impacts on the texts by subverting its conventional form. At the end of 'Death and the Compass', therefore, instead of the pre-eminent solution which puts an end to the narrative, the reader is made aware that this text is but one of many possibilities; as Scharlach says, 'The next time I kill you ... I promise you the labyrinth that consists of a single straight line that is invisible.'[39] The labyrinth is the medium through which Borges expresses this idea of the infinite text, a universal fiction which both intrudes into all fiction and in turn is modified by all subsequent writing in a never-ending cycle.

'Death and the Compass' challenges, therefore, the central artifice in the detective story that the closed nature of the narrative ends naturally in the resolution of mystery and the restoration of order. A life based on the pure exercise of reason falls foul of the arbitrariness and contrary workings of the world. Unlike the conventional detective, Lönnrot's state of being, and his fate, is defined by his failure to solve the final mystery. Lönnrot's obsession with abstract reason, his exercise of metaphysical thought at the expense of pragmatic common sense, is the path that leads to his downfall. As David Boruchoff argues, this has a profound implication for the conventional detective story:

> Just as the unrelenting practice of pure reason reveals its lack of rationality, the pursuit of the criminal by the detective becomes quite literally premeditated murder. In each of these instances Borges observes the conventions of the traditional detective tale, incorporating them, however, on the level of plot rather than that of structure. The world of 'La Muerte y la Brújula' becomes itself a critical reading of detective fiction and ... this ironic adherence to the constraints of genre bring into question the nature of genre itself.[40]

Thus, the effect of foregrounding plot in Borges is to free the text from the constraints of the detective genre's narrative structure. Although a plot involving crime, investigation and solution takes place, these elements are performed outside the conventional context of the detective story's structure; the detective is beset by his obsession with ratiocination and the solving of abstract puzzles – in other words, he is too clever for his own good. The lesson of Lönnrot's downfall seems to be that, as an epitome of the way in which crime and punishment should work, the detective story does not always correspond to our everyday experience. For David Lehman this represents an anxiety about the process of logic: 'The detective, being the paradigm of the intellectual hero, is necessarily a casualty of any such breakdown in our confidence in reason and ratiocination. The detective in a cosmos where detection is necessary but impossible to achieve is doomed from the start.'[41] That fate is to be trapped in a labyrinthine world, a world that does not conform to structural convention and is ultimately unknowable. His reasoning lands him at the centre of a labyrinth from which the only escape is death, his reward for the arrogant, assertion that, 'The mystery seemed so crystal clear to him now, he was embarrassed to have spent a hundred days on it.'[42]

The whole question of reason reflects Borges's own equivocal approach to the detective story: on the one hand it portrays the genre as a discrete and effective narrative, and yet, ironically, in its portrayal of ratiocination, it becomes a metaphor for the problematical randomness of the world. This is very similar to the world we encounter in 'The Garden of Forking Paths' and *The Name of the Rose*: the interruption to the symmetrical structure of the detective story from outside the closed world of the text leaves the narrative open to the way chance disrupts the flow of life. Just as it leads William of Baskerville to false logic, chance leads to Lönnrot's downfall, as Scharlach explains to the detective the manner of the death of Yarmolinsky, the first victim:

> The first term of the series was given me quite by chance. With some friends of mine – among them Daniel Azevedo – I had figured out a way to steal the tetrarch's sapphires. Lönnrot's, however, double-crossed us; he got drunk on the money we had advanced him and pulled the job a day early. But then he got lost in that huge hotel, and sometime around two o'clock in the he burst into Yarmolinsky's room...Azevedo told him to keep quiet; Yarmolinsky put out his hand toward the bell that would wake everyone in the hotel; Azevedo stabbed him once in the chest.[43]

The irony of this unplanned killing is that Lönnrot's original premise, which offers a 'rabbinical explanation', is proved to be wrong; from the outset the Police Commissioner, Treviranus, correctly assesses the crime as a jewel robbery gone wrong. This sets the tone for a story which is beset with the impotence of human reason; even the basis for reasoned judgement is revealed as nothing more than chance itself. Similarly, in Friedrich Dürrenmatt's 1958 novel *The Pledge*, the police commissioner directs a tirade against a writer of detective fiction:

> This fiction really infuriates me. Reality can be partially attacked by logic. Granted, we police officials are forced to proceed logically, scientifically, but the factors that muck up the works for us are so common that all too frequently only pure professional luck and chance decide the issue for us. Or against us. But in your novels chance plays no part, and if something looks like chance it's represented as some kind of destiny or divine dispensation. You writers have always sacrificed truth for the sake of your dramatic rules.[44]

Dürrenmatt's novel is in fact beset by chance. The detective Matthai, in his pursuit of a child murderer, predicts that a murder will happen and sets a trap for the culprit. Matthai waits but the murderer does not show. Unbeknown to Matthai the murderer has died in a car accident. Chance has made a mockery of his plans and Matthai continues to wait for the rest of his life.[45] His fate is similar to that of Lönnrot – the result of failing to take chance into account is essentially the end of both detectives. On the rare occasions that chance has apparently intervened in a detective story, its assimilation into the grand design of the structure has made it appear as part of the proper resolution of the plot. A celebrated example occurs in Conan Doyle's 'The Naval Treaty': Joseph Harrison is able to steal the treaty because he happens to be in Phelps's office alone by pure chance. But Harrison's fate falls into the enclosure of the structure neatly because of the feckless way he has behaved. As Holmes explains to Phelps, because Harrison 'has lost heavily in dabbling in stocks and that he is ready to do anything on earth to better his fortunes', he has behaved both criminally and amorally.[46] Thus, Harrison's fate coincides with the conventional moral thrust of the detective story, as if all had been premeditated. But in Borges this excursion into the vagaries of chance does not inevitably dissolve into the conventional detective story form. In the nightmare world of the labyrinth where any eventuality is possible, the old certainties are postponed.

The third of Borges's detective stories, 'Ibn-Hakam Al-Bokhari, Murdered in his Labyrinth', comes closest to producing a locked room mystery. In this story, Borges does not so much challenge structure but questions the artifices and conventions that detective fiction contains. In the introductory paragraphs, as the two young Englishmen approach the labyrinth, Dunraven raises the question of the unfathomable mystery surrounding the death, some 25 years earlier, of Ibn-Hakam Al-Bokhari, the chief of an African tribe, who was murdered in his heavily guarded, labyrinthine house on a cliff top in Cornwall. The death has never been adequately explained. As Dunraven explains this to his companion Unwin, the latter interrupts:

Vexed a bit, Unwin stopped him.
'Please – let's not multiply the mysteries,' he said. 'Mysteries ought to be simple. Remember Poe's purloined letter, remember Zangwill's locked room.'
'Or complex,' volleyed Dunraven. 'Remember the universe.'[47]

This dialogue, which effectively constitutes the thematic introduction, is the model of economy. Just as he does in 'Death and the Compass' Borges includes one of detective fiction's enduring methods of thematizing a text. Despite the brevity of this passage, these few lines are a signpost to key elements of the narrative.

The references to Poe's 'The Purloined Letter' and Zangwill's *The Big Bow Mystery* (1892) are intriguing; these two texts are amongst the most celebrated of the detective stories written in the manner of a *trompe l'œil*. Both are constructed around the premise that the eye may be deceived by what it sees or the psyche by what it perceives, because of the way it is presented. We have already encountered in *The Hollow Man* how Mills, the secretary, was hoodwinked into believing that he witnessed a particular scene when actually what he saw was something quite different. In 'The Purloined Letter', the trick played by the Minister is both visual and cerebral. He places the letter in full view, but the police are intent only on looking in the most obscure places; the finding of the letter is not to be achieved by ransacking the Minister's house, but by exploring the nature of his psyche.

Chapter 4 noted that the solution to the murder in 'The Wrong Shape' has similarities with the method used in Israel Zangwill's locked room novel. The detective Grodman, having given the victim a sleeping draught the night before, is summoned to the room by his landlady to help break open the door. In the instant of achieving this he bursts into the room and cuts the throat of his victim before the landlady can realize what is happening. So the crime itself is committed not in an enclosed space, but in full view of a witness, provoking memories of the overt hiding place in 'The Purloined Letter'.[48] This book is a significant milestone in the history of detective fiction because its depiction of the detective Grodman as the murderer transgresses the accepted practice in the Golden Age. He commits what he hopes will be the perfect crime, because he is bored with the commonplace cases he has solved.[49] This book seems to have been a favourite of Borges. Aside from the previous reference to the incidence of chance in the detective novel, he found the locked room mystery generally 'a problem of enduring interest',[50] with the solution to *The Big Bow Mystery* as 'ingenious' and better than that in 'The Murders in the Rue Morgue'.[51] Both these stories are illustrations of the genre's artifice of illusion, texts which deceive either by presenting a false or misleading picture of an event or by posing a conundrum the solution to which proves to be outwardly facile.[52]

This artifice is the subject of Borges's attention in 'Ibn-Hakam Al-Bokhari, Murdered in his Labyrinth'. In 'The Garden of Forking Paths'

Ts'ui Pen's labyrinthine book is emblematic of the eternal library, an unending chain of epistemics, and in 'Death and the Compass' the labyrinth takes on the form of an investigation as it progresses through the solving of clues; but in this third tale there is a physical labyrinth. John Irwin's description of the nature of labyrinths is relevant here:

> In contrast to the locked room, a labyrinth is always open from the outside but appears to be unopenable from within. It permits access to a physical body but denies it exit by subtly disrupting the link between relative and absolute bearing, by confusing the self's control of itself through the disorientation of the body. A labyrinth is in a sense a self locking enclosure that uses the directionality of the human body as the bolt in the lock.[53]

The idea of the labyrinth disrupts and contorts the concept of the locked room and its attendant loci of inside and outside; access only leads to more a problematical situation on the inside, where the clues which lead to its innermost secrets, its network of paths, are notoriously hard to read. This illegibility arises from the break in the continuity of logic that a detective story demands if clues are to be interpreted; by contrast, the labyrinth repeatedly offers so many diversions that the original problem becomes subsumed by others. In *The Big Bow Mystery* Grodman actually makes a virtue of one such diversion in order to gain open access to his victim.

This metaphor of an inside-out enclosure is particularly appropriate for a reading of 'The Purloined Letter'. In Poe's tale, ingress and egress to the Minister's house are not the problem for Dupin; it is the understanding that is the problem, the 'inside' of the labyrinthine psyche of the thief. We might propose that the labyrinth in 'Ibn-Hakam Al-Bokhari, Murdered in his Labyrinth' is a metaphor for the mind of the man who built it. In the same way that Dupin focuses on the psyche of the protagonist, Unwin surmises that because of its similarity to a spider's web the whole thing was a trap, a trap to catch a particular person. Just as we are invited to ignore appearances in *The Big Bow Mystery*, Unwin also dismisses the received wisdom that it was Ibn-Hakam Al-Bokhari who built the labyrinth, when in fact it was Sa'īd, his vizier, who had stolen the king's treasure and escaped to England. To build the labyrinth was the action of a cunning but fearful man, not that of a king.

In one sense, 'Ibn-Hakam Al-Bokhari, Murdered in his Labyrinth' is the most direct acknowledgement which Borges pays to Poe and his detective stories. The discourse between two protagonists of the story,

Unwin and Dunraven, is in fact a re-projection of the debate about the Prefect and the Minister between Dupin and his companion in 'The Purloined Letter'. Dunraven, we learn, was 'conscious of himself as the author of quite a respectable epic, though his contemporaries were incapable of so much as scanning it and its subject had yet to be revealed to him', while Unwin 'had published a study of the theorem that Fermat had not written in the margins of a page by Diophantus'.[54] These contradictory and baffling descriptions would appear to be Borges's playful way of conveying that Dunraven has the artistic temperament of the poet and Unwin the disposition of a mathematician. In 'The Purloined Letter' Dupin's and his companion's exchange reveals the essence of Poe's view on the nature of ratiocination in the detective genre:

> 'The Minister I believe has written learnedly on the Differential Calculus. He is a mathematician, and no poet.'
> 'You are mistaken; I know him well; he is both. As poet *and* mathematician, he would reason well; as mere mathematician, he could not have reasoned at all, and thus would have been at the mercy of the Prefect... The mathematics are the science of form and quantity; mathematical reasoning is merely logic applied to observation on form and quantity.'[55]

Unwin and Dunraven represent the two halves of Poe's ideal detective. They are a manifestation of the description of Dupin in 'The Murders in the Rue Morgue', about whom the narrator muses, 'I often dwelt meditatively upon the old philosophy of the Bi-Part soul, and amused myself with the fancy of a double Dupin – the creative and the resolvent.'[56] In 'Ibn-Hakam Al-Bokhari, Murdered in his Labyrinth' Dunraven acts precisely within this definition; Borges does not merely draw attention to the ambivalent qualities of the detective but to the elements of the tale itself. Not only are the detective's qualities of logical thought and understanding of human behaviour personal requirements, but they reflect the very structure of the detective story itself: 'Dunraven, who had read a great many detective novels, thought that the solution of a mystery was always a good deal less interesting than the mystery itself; the mystery had a touch of the supernatural and even the divine about it, while the solution was a sleight of hand.'[57] So Borges's story, while realizing the creative in Dunraven and the resolvent in Unwin, actually draws attention to the story of the crime and the mystery it creates. This concentration on the mystery rather than its solution is an idea pursued by Borges in both 'The Garden of Forking Paths' and 'Death and the Compass'. In both stories, when the denouement occurs, the conventional solution is replaced by an event which leads to further unresolved questions. By presenting a story that is devoid of one of its key constituents, Borges is in fact highlighting the structural tensions in the detective genre. These tensions arise, paradoxically, from the narrative symmetry of detective fiction; what Borges most admired about the genre he also viewed as undermining its appeal.

This view is not confined to Borges. Even John Dickson Carr, writing in the context of the Golden Age, recognized detective fiction's shortcomings. In 'The Locked Room Lecture' in *The Hollow Man* Dr Fell declares:

> 'Why are we dubious when we hear the explanation of the locked room? Not in the least because we are incredulous, but simply because in some vague way we are disappointed. And, from that feeling it is only natural to take an unfair step farther, and call the whole business incredible or impossible or flatly ridiculous.'[58]

The basis for these concerns is structural. Narrative closure and its concomitant enclosure are the imperatives that invite resolution, but ultimately condemn each individual text to ephemeral interest. It is precisely this conflict between mystery and exposition that Borges depicts in 'Ibn-Hakam Al-Bokhari, Murdered in his Labyrinth'. The creative Dunraven relates the mystery and is absorbed by the 'inexplicable' nature of the puzzle; Unwin the resolvent mathematician is, however, only interested in solutions.[59] Unwin represents the negation which the solution brings to the mystery narrative; he chooses 'to ignore those absurd "facts"... and think about something sensible'.[60] So Dunraven and Unwin are both a singular and double entity: single in the sense that together they possess the qualities cited by Poe as constituting the ideal detective, and double because the characteristics they display are the very dynamics of the genre's narrative structure.

In 'Ibn-Hakam Al-Bokhari, Murdered in his Labyrinth', Borges reproduces the representation of the labyrinth as a place where the progress through a physical and imagined network is a metaphor for the ratiocinative tale's quest for meaning, reflecting the fluctuating discourse between the two protagonists. In Dunraven's description the labyrinth is a place of mystery and obfuscation, a place out of its context: 'no Christian ever built such a house'.[61] But to Unwin it is the vital clue to the solution of the whole mystery. Dunraven begins his relation of the story as soon as he and Unwin enter the enclosure of the labyrinth. Significantly, they agree that 'if they always turned to the left, in less than an hour they would be at the centre of the maze'.[62] A successful navigation of the maze and the attainment of the central goal have a strong resonance with the nature of a criminal investigation. This occurs because if both the internal and external surfaces of the labyrinth are continuous then the former inevitably leads to the outer and ultimately to the exit, in the same way that clues inevitably lead, or should lead, to a solution.

The continuous nature of the labyrinth allows, too, a juxtaposition of the murderer and the victim. Inside and outside become interchangeable concepts depending on who you are or where you start from. Just as Unwin and Dunraven constitute the two halves of the detective, so Ibn-Hakam Al-Bokhari and Sa'īd are different aspects of the murderer/victim. This is emphasized by the fact that Sa'īd actually adopts Ibn-Hakam Al-Bokhari's persona as part of his deception. This double doubling takes place around the issue of access, both physical and logical, to the penetralia. The inner sanctum therefore, has a dual meaning. For the detective it is a mental journey negotiated through the application of reason; Sa'īd, however, starts at the physical centre of the labyrinth and by virtue of physical occupation is able to draw Ibn-Hakam Al-Bokhari to centre of the maze, in order to sacrifice him. Indeed, it is the imagery of the spider and the web that leads Unwin to the crime. Like the inner/outer surface of the labyrinth itself Borges reverses the idea of the locked room mystery by placing the murderer on the inside and the victim as the interloper.

Thus Borges presents 'Ibn-Hakam Al-Bokhari, Murdered in his Labyrinth' as a series of enclosures much in the same way as a conventional locked room mystery. The effect Borges achieves is brought about by structural means, the repeated use of the theme of enclosure and the narrative of closure. One further device used by Borges underlines the completeness of this concentric structure. At one level, the framing scenes featuring Unwin and Dunraven form part of the conventional detective story structure by fulfilling the introduction and resolution phase of the story. But these brief exchanges also operate at the temporal level as well. By placing the murder as a past event with little or no prospect of retribution for the murderer or proof for the detective, Borges emphasizes the abstract nature of the puzzle. It becomes framed by time and space, a *mise en abyme*, which both remains as an unsolved puzzle yet will invite investigation. By the removal of the judicial process and the ritual of punishment Borges gives expression to his desire to see the detective story restored to its intellectual origins. This relates directly to Poe and his corresponding trio of stories, and, in the same way that Dupin solves his cases, the murder of Ibn-Hakam Al-Bokhari becomes an exercise in ratiocination and nothing else. At the end of the story Borges recognizes the imperative of detective fiction to look for a solution. Despite his exigencies with the genre, he accepts that its requirements and structure require exegesis. In noting its limitations, Dunraven, the creative, says 'I accept...that my Ibn-Hakam might be Sa'īd. Such metamorphoses, you will tell me, are classic artifices of the genre.'[63]

For both Borges and Poe, the origin of the detective tale is characterized by the quest for hermeneutic inquiry and the deciphering of puzzles. Poe's stories convey a moral thrust which describes the re-establishment of conventional order, re-enacting the original creation of the world from chaos. In Borges, however, there is a more sinister overtone: he posits a universe where the logical outcome to a crime may be the triumph of evil. At the very least, the reward for consistent logical thought and the correct interpretation of clues is no guarantee of the restoration of stability. In other words, a divine presence may or may not exist, but the enactment, like the murder of Yarmolinsky, is open to the vagaries of chance.

Borges's detective stories are a reminder of Roland Barthes's plea, 'I want, I desire, quite simply a structure. Of course there is not a happiness structure; but every structure is habitable, indeed that may be its best definition.'[64] Borges demonstrates that it is indeed possible to inhabit the same structure as a Poe or a Chesterton and yet offer a quite different view of the world. His stories are testament to the fact that the enclosed world of detective fiction is just as capable of conveying complex ideas as any other generic structure. This is because Borges sees that the enduring symbols of detective fiction can be made to represent an altogether different philosophy from that which it had acquired through convention, without destroying its underlying form. Thus ratiocination does not always lead to a resolution; crime is not necessarily followed by retribution; and the enclosure of a formulaic structure can be seen as part of an infinite and unpredictable universal text. Even in Borges's most conventionally structured detective story, 'Ibn-Hakam Al-Bokhari, Murdered in his Labyrinth', the intervention of another dimension, time, prevents a definitive solution to the murder. All that transpires is that 'Ibn-Hakam might be Sa'īd'; the spectre of any number of possibilities remains.

7

The Question is the Writer Himself: Paul Auster's Locked Room in *City of Glass*

'So Inspector you can see the only person who could have done all these murders is the man sitting over there, so saying Johnny Oxford pointed his finger at...

Men are you skinny? Do you have sand kicked in your face? Wait a minute, that's not right, there's a page missing, THE LAST PAGE IS MISSING!'

'The Missing Page', Hancock's Half Hour (1960)

Paul Auster's *The New York Trilogy* – originally published as three separate novels, *City of Glass* (1985), *Ghosts* (1986) and *The Locked Room* (1986) – are works where the ultimate nightmares for detective fiction come true. These are stories where unexplained absences and strange disappearances are the norm and where the generic conventions dissolve into an endless pursuit of an unspecified mystery. In the post-Second World War period, since the appearance of Borges's three detective stories, two distinct forms of the ratiocinative detective story emerged. The conventional detective tale with its formulaic narrative of enclosure now found itself running parallel with a new form, the metaphysical detective story.[1] Successive novels by writers such as Nabokov, Robbe-Grillet, Dürrenmatt and Pynchon, amongst others, have all augmented this growing body of work.[2]

Ironically, in *The New York Trilogy* Auster adopts a practice begun by writers of conventional detective stories: he foregrounds the metafictional nature of the detective story by allying its characteristics to the nature of writing. The result is a constant round of observation, note taking, following and contemplation – a parody of the investigation made by the detective in order to locate clues and solve crimes. Not that these investigations are led by logic; in *The New York Trilogy* ratiocination seems to be a useless weapon against the tide of incoherent and puzzling events. As a result the trilogy reads like the disembodied text of a detective story, where the outer narrative constituents have been largely removed. What stimulates the reader's desire, therefore, is not the craving for resolution, but to discover the mystery itself.

In *The New York Trilogy* this literary engineering produces a concentration on form which leaves the detective story bereft of its effects. As William Little has pointed out:

> In Paul Auster's *The New York Trilogy* nothing happens again and again. To say 'nothing happens' in these detective stories is not to say that they are plotless, but rather to indicate that the plots are continually foiled by a fugitive otherness resisting apprehension by the standard procedures of systematic interrogation, empirical analysis, and deductive logic. In these texts, the detective, who is also a writer, casts nets, transcribes events, and traces marks, but his calculations and representations lead to no final illumination, no climactic discovery.[3]

In a sense Little's analysis posits the difference between the act of writing and the actions of the generic detective. Auster seems at pains to suggest the writer's impotence when applying the certainty of the language and narrative found in detective fiction to the wider world. The attempt to uncover a form of hermeneutics from the detective story's pure narrative, where progress to a preordained solution is guaranteed, fails because the contingencies of existence are not part of the genre's overall schema. In effect what Auster achieves is to throw into sharp relief the artifices of such a narrative by exposing it to the vagaries of the world. The result is to convert the narrative into an unending round of inquiry where questions and mysteries are raised but never answered. The focus, therefore, for Auster's interests are the structural elements, not their end product; as Larry McCaffery and Sinda Gregory put it, 'a form of storytelling that emphasizes the formal peculiarities of the genre and foregrounds epistemological quandaries at the same time'.[4]

Much of the way in which Auster reconfigures the detective narrative can be viewed as an abstraction, as the characters struggle to wrest themselves free from their present predicament into another version of their own persona. If one part of abstraction's meaning relates to the representation of the essence of things, then it is possible to see the trilogy as an ontological exercise. This arises because the narrative of investigation exhibited by these texts lies at the centre of the detective story; it is in itself an expression of the essence of the narrative, both structurally and heuristically. Quinn, the principal character, who, we learn, is a writer of detective stories, muses that 'it was the form that appealed to him',[5] and one part of the form, at that; as a result, the text becomes an examination of the genre's fundamentals. Its apotheosis, then, is investigation: that part of the narrative which converts ignorance into knowledge, where clues are read and reason acts to make sense of the mystery. As the opening of *City of Glass* makes clear:

> The detective is the one who looks, who listens, who moves through this morass of objects and events in search of the thought, the idea that will pull all these things together and make sense of them. In effect, the writer and the detective are interchangeable. The reader sees the world through the detective's eye, experiencing the proliferation of its details as if for the first time.[6]

Not only is the detective's craft the centre of attraction, but the writer's position is synonymous with it. The writer inquires, researches and interprets; his investigation runs parallel with that of the detective. We can suppose, therefore, that two narratives are taking place, each a mirror to the other and inextricably linked. What we witness is the tortuous procedure which investigation involves, and the consequences when it fails to bring results. So Auster's abstraction is to employ the metaphor of the detective's investigation to view the text through the creative mind of the Author. So as well as 'the question' being 'the story itself', one might easily add that, in these three stories, the question is the writer himself, and the perspective from which he writes is that of a particular locked room, that of the writer's psyche.[7] Auster articulates this ontological inquiry as the quest for a cogent narrative as Quinn turns to the detective story for inspiration:

> What he liked about these books was their sense of plenitude and economy. In the good mystery there is nothing wasted, no sentence, no word that is not significant.... Since everything seen or said, even the slightest, most trivial, can bear a connection to the outcome of the story, nothing must be overlooked. Everything becomes essence; the centre of the book shifts with each event that propels it forward. The centre, then, is everywhere, and no circumference can be drawn until the book has come to its end.[8]

Quinn sees the detective narrative as a kind of paradigm of the way in which stories are structured; its economy and its momentum are clearly things to be admired. But this passage is double-edged. As has been noted, the centre of the narrative in detective fiction is concerned with the investigation – the interpretation of clues and the search for a conclusion – but, interestingly, the passage records that the centre 'shifts with each event that propels it forward'. This, of course, can be read in two very different ways. In the conventional sense the linear narrative of the detective story moves forward with every clue that is solved; thus the centre of interest is progressed at the same speed. But what proves to be the case in *The New York Trilogy* is precisely the opposite: the 'centre' of the narrative, the inquiry, remains the only feature of the story. Auster's choice of the word 'end', too, is more equivocal than closure, which in detective fiction carries with it the connotation of resolution.

For Alison Russell, these metaphorical possibilities are a clear indication of the relationship between the detective story's themes of closure and enclosure in both the conventional and metaphysical detective story. In 'Deconstructing *The New York Trilogy*' (1990) Russell sees Auster's work as using the metaphysical detective story as a metaphor for the nature of writing itself. In the metaphysical story, indeterminate closures create an impression of never-ending texts. Russell reads this rewriting of the conventional text as a 'deferment of death for the author', to prevent the death of the self in the text when the story ends.[9] Auster's solution – to create many selves which renew the narrative – points up a key relationship between metaphysical and conventional texts, as Russell states:

> As a genre, the detective story is end-dominated, and its popularity attests to Western culture's obsession with closure. By denying closure, and by sprinkling his trilogy with references to other end-dominated texts, Auster continually disseminates the meaning of this detective story. The detective story also necessitates a movement back in time, from corpse to crime, so to speak.[10]

Auster's reliance on past texts, and the characters from them, reflects the metaphysical detective story's submersion in a literary history which is drawn from both inside and outside the conventions of the genre. This blurring of the structural boundaries does not imply that Auster's work fails to exhibit a quality of enclosure; indeed, as this chapter argues, its metafictional references are part of a self-conscious context of American literature, including Poe as the creator of the detective story. At the same time we are also conscious of Auster's own view of what it is to be a writer. We note, for instance, that for Quinn the narratives of detective fiction and writing have become intertwined; he muses on the significance of the word 'investigation' for both the writer and the private eye. He muses on the pun between the word 'eye' and the letter 'i' in upper and lower case. For a writer like Quinn it represents both his psyche and, at the same time, 'the eye of the man who looks out from himself into the world and demands that the world reveal itself to him'.[11] It seems that for the last five years Quinn has been in the 'grip of this pun'.[12] Quinn's hermetic lifestyle has become an entrapment, his psychical locked room has also taken on something of a physical guise, and he only lives in the world 'at one remove'.[13] This 'remove' is in the form of his fictional detective Max Work, whose ability to cope with the direst situations and bring things to a satisfactory conclusion causes Quinn to retreat even more into his own uncertain existence.

The books featuring Max Work are written under Quinn's nom de plume, William Wilson, which in turn evokes Poe's tale of double identity. Poe's tale of the doppelgänger not only immerses the text in the tradition of detective fiction through its inventor but, more specifically, introduces the subject of the labyrinth which will dominate Quinn's tailing of Stillman senior. In Poe's quasi-detective tale the 'rambling' school where 'William Wilson' first encounters his double is maze-like and confusing.[14] 'The huge old house, with its countless subdivisions, had several large chambers communicating with each other, where slept the greater number of students. There were, however (as must necessarily happen in a building so awkwardly planned), many little nooks or recesses, the odds and ends of the structure.'[15]

Auster substitutes the labyrinthine old house of William Wilson with the streets of New York, where Quinn, equally confused as to his identity, pursues Stillman senior in a mock pretence at detection. Quinn becomes involved with the Stillman case after he receives a couple of mysterious phone calls asking for Paul Auster, the detective. Assuming Auster's identity, he visits the Stillman apartment and meets Peter Stillman, a disturbed young man, and his wife Virginia. Virginia asks him to tail Peter's father, a former academic and writer, who is about to be released from a mental hospital where he has been for some 13 years for imprisoning and abusing Peter as a boy. Virginia, who used to be Peter's speech therapist, is very concerned that Stillman senior will try to harm Peter. Armed with a photograph of Stillman, Quinn plans to start tailing him when he leaves the train at Grand Central Station.

Before that he visits the Columbia library and reads Stillman's book, *The Garden and the Tower: Early Visions of the New World*, which is divided into two parts: 'The Myth of Paradise' and 'The Myth of Babel'.

Quinn's adoption of Auster's persona in order to take on the Stillman case, and then the role of Max Work in order to pursue it, is an attempt through the means of his nom de plume to transfer to a different dimension. The presence of Work, particularly the narrative structure that he inhabits, is the way in which Quinn is able to resolve the impasse which his writing seems to throw up. This is precisely why Quinn admires detective fiction, because in contrast with the frustration of the endless play of endless possibilities that writing offers, the genre holds out the possibility of closure to a text.

This 'escape' from the locked room of the psyche is something which has been considered by Stephen Fredman in connection with another Auster text, *The Invention of Solitude* (1982), in particular its second half, 'The Book of Memory', which Fredman calls 'a memoir-as-meditation, where Auster confronts all of his central obsessions, obsessions that return in various forms to animate his subsequent novels'.[16] Fredman argues that Auster's texts are primarily about the confining nature of writing, and utilize the metaphoric possibilities of the room as the mind, ' "the room of the book," a place where life and writing meet in an unstable, creative, and sometimes dangerous encounter'.[17] Later on, Fredman seeks to expand this idea:

> In *White Spaces*, as later in *Ghosts*, Auster represents the physicality of writing by an equation of the room with the book: 'remain in the room in which I am writing this,' he says, as though he were occupying the 'white spaces' of the page, the mind, and the room. Whichever way he turns in this symbolic architecture, the writer seems to find his physical body trapped: when he writes, it enters into the closed space of the book; when he gets up from the book, it paces the narrow confines of the room.[18]

In this reading, the writer, Auster, seems enclosed by a series of physical spaces, radiating outwards from the book itself to reflect the entrapment of his own psyche. Such a series of enclosures seems to posit a world where Auster writes, not within the constraints of generic structure, but where he is bound by a series of wider contexts; hence the shape and structure of his detective stories do not configure the conventions of the genre.

One important manifestation of the enclosures that surround Auster's writing, identified by Fredman, is his frequent recourse to the wider literary canon:

> To give such a general description of Auster's fiction in a single sentence, you could say that his books are allegories about the impossibly difficult task of writing, in which he investigates the similarly impossible task of achieving identity – through characters plagued by a double who represents the unknowable self – and that this impossible task takes place in an irrational world, governed by chance and coincidence, whose author cannot be known. And then it would be easy to construct a map of precursors and sources as a congenial modern terrain in which to situate Auster's work: the textual entrapments of Kafka, Beckett, Borges, Calvino, Ponge, Blanchot, Jabès, Celan, and Derrida; the psychological intensities of Poe, Hawthorne, Melville, Thoreau, Dickinson, Dostoevsky, and Freud.[19]

The more the writer strives to free himself of the text, the architectural and metaphysical confines of the room, and his mind, the more his search for individuality of voice becomes enmeshed in the writings of others. Auster, however, rather than shy away from what appears to be the unvarnished truth about writing, adumbrates his fictionality by frequent metafictional references, and immerses his stories in the texts of others. Quinn, therefore, sees William Wilson as 'the bridge that allowed Quinn to pass from himself into Work'.[20] This deliberate pun on the meaning of work is central to the beleaguered Quinn's purpose, as Jeffrey Nealon notes:

> For Quinn, this curious phrase 'pass from himself into Work' carries a dual meaning: first, writing under the pen name of 'Wilson' allows the writer, Quinn, to take on the active persona of the detective, Work; but, and perhaps more important, this relationship also allows Quinn's writing to pass from the always idling stages of composition into a meaningful and metaphysical realm. Quinn's passing from himself into Work allows his writing to pass from the literally limitless realm of composition (where confusion reigns because anything and everything is possible and meaningful) into the more limited realm of work.[21]

But, of course, Quinn's transfer from the confining world of his writing does not lead to the surer ground that Work, or work, provides; in fact, it has the opposite effect. The more Quinn follows Stillman around the physical space of New York, the more fruitless the excursions seem to become. Quinn has even taken to making notes in a red notebook about the day's events, but this seems utterly pointless since Stillman merely wanders the streets picking up random items that have been discarded by others. He notices, however, that Stillman also has a red notebook in which he makes a record every time he picks something up. Quinn starts to become disillusioned by both the case and by detective work in general:

> He had always imagined that the key to good detective work was a close observation of details. The more accurate the scrutiny, the more successful the results. The implication was that human behaviour could be understood, that beneath the infinite façade of gestures, tics, and silences, there was finally a coherence, an order, a source of motivation. But after struggling to take in all these surface effects, Quinn felt no closer to Stillman than when he first started following him.[22]

The world of 'Work' or work, therefore, proves to be no more illuminating than the world of writing for Quinn. The certainty that detective fiction provides, where Max Work holds sway, seems not to apply to the Stillman case. Whilst contemplating this dilemma Quinn turns to a new page in his red notebook and starts to draw a map of the area in which Stillman had wandered. Quinn decides that, after 'ransacking the chaos of Stillman's movements for some glimmer of cogency',[23] he will take Stillman's eccentric behaviour seriously, since in all the best detective stories nothing happens without reason. He then hits on the idea of tracing in outline the route that Stillman had followed on each of the days that he had been on the case. The first three shapes seem to form a rough representation of the letters O-W-E, and eventually when all the shapes emerge the letters read OWEROFBAB. Allowing for the first four days he had missed, and those yet to come, Quinn makes the 'obvious' connection and concludes that the maps spell out the letters of 'Tower of Babel'.

This result, of course, has a number of connotations: not only has the tracery delineated a circumscribed, physical space, but the literary references which flow from it, both actual and fictional, form the context for Auster's writing. The obvious biblical connection of Babel acts as a reminder of Stillman's own book, which is concerned both with the physical space of the very first garden and the concept of sin which arose from it. In particular Stillman is interested in the significance of language, his theory being that prelapsarian language had been tainted by the fall and, ever since, language has been loaded with contradiction and innuendo in order to accommodate the concept of good and evil. Stillman cites words such as 'cleave' and 'key', which each have different meanings, and Miltonian expressions 'sinister', 'serpentine' and 'delicious', as having a prelapsarian meaning free of moral connotations. The 'New Babel' of the title is seen as America, where the hope was that the Puritans would build a new world that would reverse the consequences of the Fall, and that language would become innocent again.

This quest for a pure language has strong parallels with Quinn's own immersion into the detective story. In this reading we may approach *The City of Glass* as a search for a direct and positivistic narrative where order emerges from chaos, as an alternative to the endless play of possibilities in language. The idea of an endless play of meaning is a reminder of Borges's story of the infinite episteme, 'The Library of Babel'. This story speaks of 'the formless and chaotic nature of virtually all books'[24] and shows that 'for every rational line or forthright statement there are leagues of senseless cacophony, verbal nonsense, and incoherency'.[25] Quinn's search is beginning to echo the world of Borges's detective fiction where resolution dissolves into a never-ending set of alternative possibilities, but it does not; in Quinn's case, this labyrinth proves to be a dead end, a psychical map from which there is no escape.

When Quinn meets Stillman for the first time, the latter tells him that he is inventing a new language 'that will at last say what we have to say. For our words no longer correspond to the world'.[26] Stillman uses the analogy of a broken umbrella, which we carry on calling an umbrella despite the fact that it can no longer perform its original function. So he gives everything he finds a new name to describe its present state, whether broken, transformed or putrid. As an author, Stillman is attempting to reassert control over a language which he believes is no longer adequate for a writer to describe or rationalize the world. Essentially, Stillman's mission is an ontological one; he is interested in trying to reveal the essence of something through language, rather than through the application of, say, science. This, of course, is precisely the kind of prelapsarian language that Stillman advocates in his book; he reasons that, unless we can talk accurately about everyday things, when it comes to more profound subjects we are truly lost. This is Quinn's dilemma, his search for the narrative of narratives that will adequately provide him with the clarity he seeks.

Part of Quinn's attempt to follow the narrative of the detective novel, too, prompts the maps of Stillman's perambulations. As we have seen, in doing so he is adopting the practice started by Anna Katherine Green, which was repeated throughout the detective genre, of creating sketch plans of the crime scene. Like everything else in *City of Glass* these drawings are a vestige of a practice formerly commonplace in the Golden Era, a way of circumscribing the events of the text, redirecting attention to the heart of the puzzle. In short, it is the supreme constituent of the closed narrative. But the effect of their presence in Auster's text is quite the reverse. Despite his desperate attempts to make them into something cogent, Quinn realizes that, like the language that Stillman decries, the maps ultimately tell him nothing; the shapes that he imagines form the title of Stillman's book are all outlines which contain voids. Where once detailed information would have resided in the detective story there lies yet another hiatus.

The essence of Quinn's position is that he has tried to 'pass' from the unsatisfying mode of writing to a narrative which offers the prospect of heuristic success, where the flux of creation, the jumble of 'gestures, tics and silences', is rendered sensible. Indeed, we might conclude that detective fiction is the closest thing to that paradigm of language that Stillman seeks – a kind of prelapsarian narrative that has clarity of form and a ruthless objectivity that makes its purpose plain. But Quinn discovers that the detective story, by exhibiting its metafictional qualities, leads him back into the realm of writing and away from his hoped-for escape into either Work, or work. The prospect of interpretive certainty that this narrative holds out is still part of the creative process he finds so difficult. Thus the view from his own psyche becomes locked into an unbroken circle of failed interpretation. What he has learnt is that the inadequacy of language makes it impossible for him to make any sense of the world, even in a narrative that is renowned for doing so. This is articulated by his analogy of the shapes he has created with those which appear at the end of Poe's *The Narrative of Arthur Gordon Pym of Nantucket*: 'Quinn's thoughts momentarily flew off to the concluding pages of *A. Gordon Pym* and to the discovery of the strange hieroglyphs on the inner wall of chasm – letters inscribed into the earth itself, as though they were trying to say something that could no longer be understood.'[27] In a trope that he repeats throughout the trilogy, Auster here underlines key parts of his own narrative with parallel references from previous texts. Just as Poe's tale of the stowaway adventurer culminates in the discovery of strange images on the cliff side, the canyons of New York produce their own mysterious clue. In the Poe novel, too, these hieroglyphs are part of an overriding theme of the nature, form and origin of writing and its communication with the reader. The travellers hope that this curious writing might hold the key to finding their way home but, like Quinn's own experience, it proves to be a false hope, as Pym explains their true provenance:

> I convinced him of his error, finally, by directing his attention to the floor of the fissure, where among the powder, we picked up, piece by piece, several large flakes of the marl, which had evidently been broken off by some convulsion from the surface where the indentures were found, and which had projecting points exactly fitting the indentures; thus proving them to have been the work of nature.[28]

In one particular sense, the supposed provenance of *The Narrative of Arthur Gordon Pym of Nantucket* has a remarkable similarity with that of *Don Quixote*: the preface purports to say that Pym had drawn up an account of his adventures which would be presented 'under the garb of fiction'.[29] So the novel becomes fiction dressed up as fiction in the hope that, paradoxically, it would bolster the illusion of factuality. Auster immerses himself in this method of presentation by making himself a character in the trilogy to blur the identity between the author and his fictional characters; thus he is also engaged in yet another literary game by presenting his story in the partial guise of detective fiction.

Following his meetings with Stillman, Quinn gradually loses interest in the case and embarks on aimless wandering, still trying to exercise what remains of his detective instincts. His behaviour becomes ever more erratic as he sees hidden meanings in the shape of clouds; colours in the sky, wind, dawns and dusks all have to be 'deciphered'.[30] Thus the great project of the literary detective, that of revealing meaning and an ultimate truth from the most abstruse of puzzles, retreats into an endless round of empty and fallacious reasoning. 'Quinn was nowhere now. He had nothing, he knew nothing, he knew that he knew nothing.'[31] The inadequacy of language to make sense of the world has called into question the ability of detective fiction to reduce mystery, because it reveals the extent of the artifice involved in maintaining its narrative form.

This subversion of the detective story narrative and the whole complex question of authorship in *City of Glass* is revealed in a conversation which Quinn has with Paul Auster. It seems that Auster has been doing some literary detective work of his own; he has come up with an ingenious and 'tongue in cheek'[32] theory on the provenance of *Don Quixote*. Auster argues that Cervantes went to considerable lengths to convince the reader that he was not the author. Instead Cervantes claims that his book is a true story of romances written in Arabic by Cid Hamete Benengeli and subsequently translated into Spanish. But Auster speculates that in fact Don Quixote was not mad but responsible for the whole thing, engineering the Benengeli tales and translating them himself into the Spanish. The irony of Cervantes hiring Don Quixote to translate his own memoirs does not escape him. Auster theorizes that *Don Quixote* is narrated by Sancho Panza, edited by the barber and the priest, translated into Arabic and then supposedly translated back into Spanish by Quixote himself.

These speculations about the convoluted origins of *Don Quixote* have clear consequences for the *City of Glass* and its own questions of authorship. Enclosing the whole of the text there is the 'real' Paul Auster, the writer of the whole narrative who decides to construct the novel through the medium of a number of alter egos – firstly Quinn, then Quinn's pen name, William Wilson and 'his' detective, Max Work. As if that was not enough dissemination, Auster also creates another version of himself, supposedly the head of a detective agency, who converses directly with Quinn. Even then, at the end of the novel, we are also aware of yet another character with authorial status, the narrator who records the end of Quinn. So it is possible to see in the 'other' Auster's reading of *Don Quixote* something of a parallel in *City of Glass*. As Madeleine Sorapure has suggested:

'Auster' perhaps to test his theory of *Don Quixote*, invented Quinn and wrote Quinn's red notebook himself, and then brought it to the narrator..., in order to have him write a novel. It seems a perfectly plausible plot, and one that, like 'Auster's' interpretation of *Don Quixote*, would solve the mystery of *City of Glass* itself, neatly tying up the loose ends throughout the novel by suggesting that they are there because they are supposed to be there, as part of an elaborate parody of the detective novel in which, despite the narrator's best intentions and efforts, there is no crime, no solution, and by the end no hero. In this interpretation, the author ('Auster') seems to be situated in a position of even greater mastery and authority than in the traditional detective story – a kind of metamastery – standing behind not only the events and characters in the novel but the writing of the novel itself. However, this interpretation..., implies that what the author knows and withholds from the reader is not the redeeming truth – the solution which puts the mystery to rest – but instead the fact that the whole thing is a sham, built on nothing, with Auster representing 'Auster' constructing an elaborate hoax.[33]

We have, of course, been here before: the text of Dickson Carr's *The Hollow Man* is essentially an intricately woven bluff. The narrative contains a number of misprisions which outwardly seem credible, and are recorded as such by apparently trustworthy witnesses. But in the face of the solution the bulk of the text is revealed as illusion; in fact, one might posit that the locked room mystery, the most elaborate of all detective puzzles, enacts a hoax on readers time and time again. This results from the very thing that Sorapure talks about – the authorial mastery of the detective story writer. The view that we have as readers of such texts is precisely that to which we are directed, or misdirected, by the author.

In the world of the anti-detective novel such as *City of Glass*, however, the situation is very different. What we are invited to witness is not an illusion, because that would imply an alternative, rational explanation, but an evisceration of the traditional detective narrative, one where the accustomed attainment of meaning and truth are absent. Furthermore, there is no sense that we are being deliberately deceived; the anti-detective novel flaunts its narrative void. In the *City of Glass* we witness the decline of Quinn's 'investigation' into nothingness; as the text notes, 'not only had he been sent back to the beginning, he was now before the beginning'.[34] Given the lengths that Auster goes to in order to obfuscate authorship, we are left with the sense therefore, that the real mystery lies with the author himself. In the *City of Glass* it is the 'real' Auster who encloses the text; through his various guises we experience views from his locked room, that of the creative mind. From his position of 'metamastery', as Sorapure puts it, he brings an extrinsic narrative, one which speaks of the world outside the confines of the self-contained detective story.

This narrative speaks of the problems of using such a contradictory language to impose meaning on a rigorous, closed narrative. When this bulwark of the detective story is missing, the result is a textual implosion of the kind never witnessed in the conventional form. When John Dickson Carr hoodwinks you with his controlling eye and misprisions, he always has an alternative solution to fall back on, as if to say, 'Don't worry, the structure demands that I explain.' When Auster hoaxes us the result is terminal.

The outcome of Auster's deferral of a single authorial voice leaves the characters in the novel, under their guise of writer-detectives, with a constant struggle to make sense of the world. Quinn, as detective, suffers a major crisis when he loses Stillman senior; as a result his whole reason for being is lost. Essentially, Quinn becomes a character without a purpose. He retreats to the empty Stillman apartment, into a small back room, and then eventually disappears from there. The apartment is visited by Auster and the narrator, whose presence becomes apparent at the end of the novel. They find the red notebook on the floor. We are left to speculate on the identity of the mysterious narrator: is it the real Auster, or yet another deferral of the authorial voice? Whatever the ultimate truth of this, it seems he has retold the story of Quinn from the contents of the red notebook: 'There were moments when the text was difficult to decipher, but I have done my best with it, and have refrained from any interpretations.'[35]

This 'ending' has strong parallels with the question of authorship in *Don Quixote* in which the Auster in the text is so interested. We might speculate that the *City of Glass* should be read as though the author, like Cervantes, is a mere conveyer of a document, the origins of which lie outside the author's control. This reading might lead us to the conclusion that a text devoid of the traditional trappings of the detective story, except for its metafictional references, might ultimately become a self-reflexive quest into its own existence.

Auster's retreat to the margins of the text affords what is the final view from the locked room in this study. From this perspective, the figure of Auster, the writer, becomes the enclosing thematic preoccupation of the *City of Glass*. The presence of this extrinsic narrative is not unlike the metaphysical enclosures encountered in Chesterton and Borges, in that it operates beyond the margins of the text. Thus, Auster's own psychical locked room, from which the ideas flow into the novel, reflects the series of related images of enclosure and opacity at the centre of the novel, frequently related to another text or the process of creating a text. Auster's own authorial voice, therefore, is especially resonant with the solitary confinements that appear in *City of Glass*, and throughout the trilogy. Many seem to be preoccupied with a voyage of self-discovery, which seems to equate with a life of solitude.

In the second part of the trilogy, *Ghosts*, the literary catalyst is Thoreau's *Walden*, where the image of the solitary observer is replicated when Blue sits in his room on the opposite side of the street to Black. Auster has described *Walden* as Thoreau 'exiling himself in order to find out where he was'.[36] In the chapter devoted to solitude he expresses himself in language which seems uncannily like Auster himself: 'I only know myself as a human entity; the scene, so to speak, of thoughts and affections; am sensible of a certain doubleness by which I can stand as remote from myself as another.'[37] Thoreau's confinement in the physical locked room of his cabin is a prerequisite to a journey into his psychic counterpart. This, it seems, is the ideal to which all Auster's characters should aspire, but, unlike Thoreau, only darkness and obscurity seem to await them in their own locked room. Blue's observation of Black leads him to a hitherto unconsidered review of his own life, as he struggles to repeat Thoreau's own thoughts on the nature of confinement: 'Until now, Blue has not had much chance for sitting still, and this new idleness has left him at something of a loss. For the first time in his life, he finds that he has been thrown back on himself, with nothing to grab hold of, nothing to distinguish one moment from the next.[38] The mystery of Blue's pursuit of Black is supplanted by the mystery of his own existence, and the bond he has with Black converts to interdependence and interchangeability. Blue, accordingly, begins to see Black as an alter ego, without whom he cannot function; he enters Black's room, makes his acquaintance and even acquires a copy of *Walden*. During one of their conversations Black raises the subject of 'Wakefield' (1835), Hawthorne's tale of the man who deserts his wife only to live in isolation for many years in a room nearby. Here Auster contrasts the hermitical existence of Thoreau with the solitary life of Wakefield, in the middle of a large city. The foray into Hawthorne is especially revealing; Melville described his work as possessing 'blackness', which, of course, correlates to Auster's own character, Black.[39] At the end of Hawthorne's tale, Wakefield climbs the steps of his wife's house but, rather than describe the reacquaintance of the couple after 20 years, Hawthorne leaves the outcome as a matter of conjecture:

> We will not follow our friend across the threshold. He has left us much food for thought, a portion of which shall lend its wisdom to a moral, and be shaped into a figure. Amid the seeming confusion of our mysterious world, individuals are so nicely adjusted to a system, and systems to one another, and to a whole, that, by stepping aside for a moment, a man exposes himself to fearful risk of losing his place forever. Like Wakefield, he may become, as it were, the Outcast of the Universe.[40]

The situation is a familiar one in the Auster trilogy. What confronts Wakefield is potentially the same fate that befalls Quinn, Blue and the Narrator in *The Locked Room*. All have tried to escape from the confinement of their own locked room only to cross the threshold of another where other versions of themselves exist. As a result they have become margins to the textual space they occupy. In *The Locked Room*, for instance, the narrator realizes that his nemesis, Fanshawe, 'had used me up', and that the only path to freedom and self-knowledge is to destroy what remains of Fanshawe, the red notebook: 'One by one, I tore the pages from the notebook, crumpled them in my hand, and dropped them into a trash bin on the platform' and ultimately 'I came to the last just as the train was pulling out'.[41] The reader is left wondering whether the destruction of Fanshawe's notebook is also the destruction of the narrator himself, so close is his identification with Fanshawe. No mystery has been dispelled, and, devoid of plot, the exoskeleton of detective fiction dissolves in endless deferral.

In *City of Glass*, the process of integrating the physical enclosure with that of the mind begins when Quinn retreats into the isolation of the Stillman's abandoned apartment: 'He went to one of the rooms at the back of the apartment, a small space that measured no more than ten feet by six feet. It had one wire-mesh window that gave on to a view of the airshaft, and of all the rooms it seemed to be the darkest.[42] This retreat into an enclosed physical space heralds a concomitant metaphysical reaction as Quinn reflects on his life. Auster uses the red notebook as the metaphor for the active, creative part of Quinn's mind. In tune with his surroundings, which grow gloomier with the change in the seasons, the notebook starts to run out: 'this period of growing darkness coincided with the dwindling of pages in the red notebook. Little by little, Quinn was coming to the end.'[43] The way in which Auster closes the first story of the trilogy is resonant with the dilemma that all metaphysical detective fiction poses – the presence of an unanswerable question. Quinn does not so much disappear but relocate to another dimension: 'as for Quinn, it is impossible for me to say where he is now'.[44]

At another level, Auster has Black and Blue discuss the mystifying end to Hawthorne's tale. It is interesting to note – ironic, even – that in a passage which so absorbed Auster, Hawthorne should warn about the dangers of deviating from a 'system'. It is as though his burlesque of detective fiction, of genre itself, was something which also drew attention to the soundness of the narrative structure it embraces. The characters in the *City of Glass* and the wider trilogy are trapped in a locked room from which ultimately there is no escape and, when narrative momentum fails, then an endless lapse into self-examination, an inherent self-reflexivity, is the inevitable result.

We might posit, therefore, that Auster's retreat to the margins of the text, into his own locked room, is a way of following the examples set by Thoreau and Hawthorne and the unseen narrator of *The Locked Room* (himself), who states that 'solitude became a passageway into the self, an instrument of discovery'.[45] Auster, from his detached viewpoint, treats the text as an epistemological space; it is a place where he might play

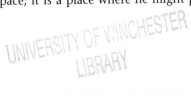

out the various conundrums which face a writer when composing a text. One reason why he uses the model of the linear narrative of detective fiction is specifically for its strong element of inquiry.

Thus Auster and his thematic imperative of the writer as locked room act on the narrative in just the same way as the themes we have encountered throughout this study. The connection between the inner and outer – more explicitly, between the self and the physical environment, the psyche and the text – is the key relationship of the whole of Auster's trilogy. The fact that the characters end up in the darkness of their own particular locked room, unable to make the narrative work, is a failure of the detective narrative itself to absorb the demands of a world outside its own closed structure. So, when it comes to the end of *The Locked Room*, Auster offers what passes for an explanation of what has gone before in the trilogy:

> The end, however, is clear to me. I have not forgotten it, and I feel lucky to have kept that much. The entire story comes down to what happened at the end, and without that end inside me now, I could not have started this book. The same holds for the two books that come before it, *City of Glass* and *Ghosts*. These three stories are finally the same story, but each one represents a different stage in my awareness of what it is about. I don't claim to have solved any problems.[46]

The end, of course, is just that – an end; it is neither resolution nor explanation. Perhaps, at the very end of his literary journey, Auster is making a fundamental point about the nature of storytelling and genre. We remember that at the very start of the *City of Glass* the detective story is admired for two divergent qualities, 'plenitude' and 'economy'. When either of these finely balanced constituents is altered, when we try to convert it into something else, by limiting its plenitude and burdening its economy, it ceases to be. From the outset it is clear that Auster has been engaged in a kind of textual game: 'What interested him about the stories he wrote was not their relation to the world, but their relation to other stories.'[47] This is precisely what Auster does: he relates detective fiction to other storytelling traditions. As Stephen Bernstein argues, 'closural, epistemological certainty that long characterised the genre is just one code dispensed with as Auster places his mystery novels within several other important textural traditions'.[48]

Thus the diffusion of authorial authenticity, the doubling of names and identity, the dislocation of the individual in an increasingly bleak and alienating landscape, and the idea of the mind as a locked room as both a physical and metaphysical place where all the mysteries of the self are enacted, are all part of Auster's inquiry into the nature of genre. He doubles the idea of investigation by placing it both within the text and outside it; his characters try to make sense of mystery by aping the detective in charge of a case, while his own, hidden voice confronts us with the failure of these characters to progress. Just like the writer he is, he asks writers' questions about the nature of writing; he interrogates detective fiction on the metaphysical questions of the self, the relationship of the individual to the world. We even have the spectacle of Quinn trying to use detective fiction's sketch plan to illuminate the puzzle that confronts him. But all along we suspect that Auster knows the answer to these questions, the impossibility of a formulaic generic structure designed to resolve a specific problem. But beyond this is the extrinsic narrative of Auster's mind as writer, who leaves us with the ultimate question: given the rudimentary tools of language, how does a writer address the mysteries that confront our psyche?

So the end of the *City of Glass* appears as a question, more puzzling than that of the most elaborate locked room mystery. But, as Stephen Bernstein has said, 'Auster is not interested in such problems or their solutions'.[49] Rather, the trilogy is constructed around the proposition that dispenses with the certainty of closure by questioning the meaning inherent in clues. Bernstein again: 'Its reader like its detectives, finally arrives at the locked room of Auster's mind .... At the close the reader, like the narrator of the final novel, is outside the writer's locked room, a room which the trilogy now completed, affords no passage whatsoever over its threshold.'[50] We are left to consider a literary world where detectives cannot detect, where investigation brings only questions, where reason brings absurdity and where end is no closure. It leaves the detective story subverted by the nature of its own locked narrative.

8
The Narrative of Enclosure

> Now, brought to this conclusion in so unequivocal a manner as
> we are, it is not our part, as reasoners, to reject it on account
> of apparent impossibilities. It is only for us to prove that these
> apparent 'impossibilities' are in reality, not such.
>
> Edgar Allan Poe, 'The Murders in the Rue Morgue'[1]

I have, during the course of this study, argued that the concept of enclosure should be recognized as having a profound effect on detective
fiction. Much of the reason for this is directly attributable to the locked
room mystery, and in particular to 'The Murders in the Rue Morgue'; its
dual status as the first modern detective story and a locked room mystery has meant that it occupies a seminal position in the canon. In this
story, as I have already demonstrated, enclosure was consonant with the
architecture of the locked room, the nature of the new narrative structure and the way in which the theme of ratiocination formed a frame
around the narrative. Crucially, the theme of logical reasoning interacts
with the narrative to fulfil the detective story's desire for closure.

Such has been the proliferation of these circumstances since the publication of Poe's work that the metaphor of enclosure can now be
seen as one of the dynamics of the genre; by this I mean that, in
addition to its more obvious imagery, it is an active constituent of
both narrative structure and thematic ideas. As ratiocination became
absorbed into the structure of the narrative, generating momentum in
the investigation phase, the detective story engaged with other thematic ideas which performed a similar function. Thus, in Chesterton,
resolution of the mystery through the application of reason by Father
Brown is seen as a gift from God, while in *The Hollow Man* the illusion of the locked room murder is matched by the illusory nature of

the narrative. In Chesterton's portrayal of the Catholic metanarrative, clearly the detective story is subsumed by an idea which purports to have universal appeal. This engagement is an early example of the way in which such enclosures have begun to infiltrate the idea of the closed narrative, even resulting in a possible challenge to the role that closure traditionally plays in 'The Wrong Shape'. So contradictions do exist even within ostensibly conventional detective fiction, particularly when the enclosing ideology actually interferes in the concept of closure and either changes or defers the application of the narrative structure. In these cases the outside world, with all its contingencies and censures, becomes the very narrative itself. This is apparent in some of Josef Škvorecký's detective stories, which I will consider later.

In this final chapter, therefore, I will revisit and amplify some of the ideas I have put forward, using some alternative textual contexts. My purpose will be to argue that the locked room mystery, with its imagery, language and narrative of enclosure, has become emblematic of the detective story itself. This will involve readdressing the three broad areas central to the idea of the locked room, which have featured throughout the study: the physical and architectural consequences of the enclosed space, the metaphor of the psyche as a locked room, especially the perspective that it provides, and the impounding narrative structure and its engagement with theme.

There are few places of greater seminal importance in the detective canon than the L'Espanaye apartment on the Rue Morgue in the Quartier St Roch. Since the appearance of this most celebrated of locked rooms, the detective story has been acutely conscious of the potential for space to confine. It does not mean, of course, that a story has to be a locked room mystery to convey the imagery of enclosure or the sense of neurotic entrapment that the form exhibits. Leaving aside 'The Speckled Band', to which I shall return later, the Holmes canon is littered with the narrative effect of confining space. In fact, many of these stories seem to have a black hole at their heart, a place of shadows, but one to which all seem inexorably drawn. In 'The Engineer's Thumb', for instance, Victor Hatherley, a hydraulic engineer, is duped by a gang of counterfeiters into repairing their press. When he discovers the fault and the real purpose behind their enterprise, he is left trapped in the press with its deadly mechanism closing on him. Hatherley's predicament rather obviously invokes the nightmare world of the prisoner in 'The Pit and the Pendulum': 'I saw that the black ceiling was coming down upon me, slowly, jerkily, but as none knew better than myself, with a force which must within a minute grind me to a shapeless pulp.

I threw myself, screaming, against the door, and dragged with my nails at the lock.'[2] We can compare this passage with Wilkie Collins's 'A Terribly Strange Bed' and its derivatives, Weatherby Chesney's 'The Horror of the Folding Bed' (1898) and Joseph Conrad's 'The Inn of the Two Witches' (1915), all of which depict the victim's sense of entrapment in the space from which there is seemingly no escape. But at least all the characters in these stories do manage to extricate themselves from their plight. Brunton's entombment, however, in 'The Musgrave Ritual', is the ultimate claustrophobic nightmare, as Holmes relates to Watson:

> I then endeavoured to raise the stone by pulling on the cravat. I could only move it slightly, and it was with the aid of one of the constables that I succeeded at last in carrying it to one side. . . .
>
> A small chamber about 7 feet deep and 4 feet square lay open to us. At one side of this was a squat, brassbound, wooden box . . . At the moment, however, we had not thought for the old chest, for our eyes were riveted upon that which crouched beside it. It was the figure of a man, clad in a suit of black, who squatted down upon his hams with his forehead sunk upon the edge of the box and his two arms thrown on each side of it.[3]

Two striking images of enclosure dominate this scene: the body of Brunton, within his impromptu grave, clutching the sealed box for which he died. The box, of course, contains the remains of the ancient crown of England; this is the final piece of the puzzle, the ultimate locked 'room' of the story, and, as I discussed in Chapter 5, at the very heart of 'The Musgrave Ritual' there is unearthed a theme of the restoration of the monarchy and its future safeguarding.

In 'The Naval Treaty', Conan Doyle employs an ingenious variation on the idea of the locked room. When Joseph Harrison steals the treaty from Percy Phelps he hides it in the room he has been occupying when visiting Phelps. On the night of the burglary, Phelps returns home having had a breakdown, and is immediately moved into Harrison's room so that Harrison's sister, to whom Phelps is engaged, may nurse him. Thus, the room which Phelps occupies for over two months is effectively inaccessible to Harrison, who is desperate to retrieve the treaty so that he can sell it to a foreign agent. It is a nice twist; on this occasion the room becomes locked to the criminal. The story then becomes a tale of two seemingly impenetrable spaces: one which Harrison does manage to enter, Phelps's office, and, ironically, his own bedroom which proves much more problematical.

But of course, the imagery of the locked room is not merely constrained by reference to a single chamber. As Chapter 3 records, it was Anna Katherine Green who introduced the rudiments of the country house murder. In *The Leavenworth Case*, a key point of the narrative, which narrows the scope of the investigation, is the fortress-like house in which Leavenworth is found. The result is that the focus is automatically turned on the Leavenworth household itself. Revealingly, after the body of Leavenworth is found in his study, the narrator, Raymond, remarks, 'The house found locked, and no one seen to leave! Evidently, then, we had not far to look for the assassin.'[4] Many of Green's subsequent stories follow the same path and are set in large houses and centre on families with a deadly secret. Conan Doyle too, began to look beyond his accustomed London setting to the large houses of wealthy owners. 'The Copper Beeches' (1892), 'The Abbey Grange' (1904), 'Wisteria Lodge' (1908) and 'The Three Gables' (1926) are among many Holmes stories that feature houses with a dark secret. This was to be an innovation that captured the imagination of the hedonistic indulgences which followed the First World War, and authors found a ready market for literature amongst readers seeking abstractions from everyday life. As Auden has suggested:

> The detective story requires:
> A closed society so that the possibility of an outside murderer (and hence of the society being totally innocent) is excluded; and closely related society so that all its members are potentially suspect ... Nature should reflect its human inhabitants, i.e., it should be the Great Good Place; for the more Eden-like it is, the greater the contradiction of murder. The country is preferable to the town, a well-to-do neighbourhood (but not too well-to-do – or there will be a suspicion of ill-gotten gains) better than a slum.[5]

The essence of Auden's point is limitation, which is a profound requirement for the classic detective story. It is one of the key points of difference with the hard-boiled thriller; as an opposition to the closed murder, a character in Anthony Berkeley's *The Poisoned Chocolates Case* (1929):

> 'I have always thought that murders may be divided into two classes, closed or open. By a closed murder I mean one committed in a certain closed circle of persons, such as a house-party, in which it is known that the murderer is limited to membership of that actual group. This

is by far the commoner form in fiction. An open murder I call one in which the criminal is not limited to any particular group but might be almost be anyone in the world. This, of course, is almost invariably what happens in real life.'[6]

The country house militates precisely against 'real life'; if it cannot define and control the milieu in which it is set, the puzzle becomes subject to unwanted contamination. The idea of the remote house is, then, symbolic of the detective novel's removal from the world outside its text, a reinforcement of the closed narrative which it characterizes. This is the theory propounded by Dickson Carr – that the conventional detective story has nothing to do with reality.[7] In Carr's case, the fact that he frequently endows this locus with a locked room mystery makes its abstraction all the more complete. The locked room mystery then becomes an ontological version of the wider genre, doubly removed, stripped of all contingency, a paradigm for the way the puzzle story concentrates on its central preoccupation.

Ironically, one of Agatha Christie's most celebrated country house stories, *4.50 from Paddington*, was not published in the inter-war period, but as late as 1957. Elspeth McGillicuddy, travelling from Scotland to visit Miss Marple, sees a woman being strangled in a passing train. The murder conjures up the prospect of one of the classic loci of the locked room, the railway compartment, but, at this point, if convention is to be followed and a tight rein kept on the scope of the narrative, Christie needs to move proceedings to the confines of Rutherford Hall. This is achieved by ensuring that no body is found on the tracks or in the train itself, so the assumption is made that the body has been thrown from the train and hidden somewhere close to the line. Miss Marple, by piecing together the facts of the murder with the train timetable, and taking into account the fact that the train in question slows down as it passes the grounds, finds that suspicion falls on Rutherford Hall as the only possible location. Interestingly, the house is shielded from the surrounding community; thus almost at once we are transported into the self-contained world of the Crackenthorpe family. The eventual discovery of the body recalls the struggles to open Brunton's underground cell; Lucy Eyelesbarrow, planted at the Hall by Miss Marple to spy on the family, and finding herself in the family mausoleum, is suspicious:

> Her eyes came to rest on the sarcophagus and stayed there.
>   That sarcophagus...

The air in the barn was faintly musty as though unaired for a long time. She went over to the sarcophagus. It had a heavy close-fitting lid. Lucy looked at it speculatively.

Then she left the barn, went to the kitchen, found a heavy crow bar, and returned. It was not an easy task, but Lucy toiled doggedly.

Slowly the lid began to rise, prised up by the crowbar.

It rose sufficiently for Lucy to see what was inside ... [8]

In the space of one story Christie foregrounds three of the recurring enclosures of detective fiction: the train compartment, the country house and the coffin. Although Christie continued writing some well-received novels up to her death in 1976, increasingly the select milieu in which her fiction resided became out of step with the developing post-war world. So in some ways *4.50 from Paddington* reads like an epitaph for the Golden Age, where death in the detective story was a discrete event, hidden away in another world and portrayed by a formulaic narrative populated with the familiar images of a certain class.

I have at various times referred to the idea of the psyche as symbolic of the locked room, and the unique perspective that it brings. This has variously encompassed the victim in 'The Pit and the Pendulum', the guilt-laden mind of the signalman, the murderer in *The Filigree Ball* and the writer in Auster's *City of Glass*. As a final reflection on this argument, I shall now turn to the particular view from the detective's psyche and look at what it has to tell us about the nature of the investigative process.

'The Speckled Band' was first published in *The Strand* magazine in February 1892, and subsequently appeared with 11 other stories we now know as *The Adventures of Sherlock Holmes*. It is Conan Doyle's only foray into the locked room mystery, discounting episodes in 'The Empty House', 'The Man with the Twisted Lip' and 'The Engineer's Thumb', which have elements of the form in them. Apart from 'The Murders in the Rue Morgue', there can be fewer detective stories which have attracted as much critical attention as Conan Doyle's story of the snake. Whole books have been devoted to its analysis with much being made, inter alia, of the Edenic serpent, the masculine sexuality of Grimesby Roylott, the theme of empire and Conan Doyle's use of the Gothic. These are, of course, perfectly valid interpretations of the story which have added much to its reputation, but I would like to suggest that the text should also be read as an exemplar of the ratiocinative technique introduced by Poe. I say this because there are strong grounds for considering the story as a partial rewriting of 'The Murders in the Rue Morgue'. Its locked room form, an animal as the agency of death, and two terrorized women are all redolent of a backward glance to Poe. Thus the two stories are also similar in their recherché plots: Dupin describes the Rue Morgue case as having an '*outré*'[9] character, and Watson says of 'The Speckled Band' case that, 'I cannot recall any which presented more singular features'.[10] We know, too, that Conan Doyle was a great admirer of Dupin; in a paean to Poe, written in 1907, he wrote:

> To him must be ascribed the monstrous progeny of writers on the detection of crime – '*quorum pars parva fui!*' [of which things I was a small part]. Each may find some little development of his own, but his main art must trace back to those admirable stories of Monsieur Dupin, so wonderful in their masterful force, their reticence, their quick dramatic point. After all, mental acuteness is the one quality which can be ascribed to the ideal detective and when that has once been admirably done, succeeding writers must necessarily be content for all time to follow in the same track.[11]

When writing the first Holmes story, *A Study in Scarlet*, he recalls, 'Poe's masterful detective, Chevalier Dupin, had from boyhood been one of my heroes. But could I bring an addition of my own?'[12] The overriding consideration seems to have been whether Holmes's own ratiocinative methods could exemplify those of Dupin. We have already seen that the essence of Dupin's craft was the practice of intuitive inference from a logical explanation of the facts:

> 'I knew, that all apparent impossibilities *must* be proved to be not such in reality.
>
> 'I proceeded to think thus – *a posteriori*. The murderers *did* escape from one of these windows. This being so, they could not have re-fastened the sashes from the inside, as they were found fastened; – the consideration which put a stop, through its obviousness, to the scrutiny of the police in this quarter. Yet the sashes *were* fastened. They *must*, then, have the power of fastening themselves. There was no escape from this conclusion.[13]

Dupin reasons from an intuitive piece of guesswork. Given all the facts to hand, this empirical method is the starting point for a regression, one which works from effect to cause. If this one proposition is correct, then the clues form a chain which confirms the original principle, as Holmes makes clear in *A Study in Scarlet*:

'I have already explained to you that what is out of the common is usually a guide rather than a hindrance. In solving a problem of this sort, the grand thing is to be able to reason backwards. That is a very useful accomplishment, and a very easy one, but people do not practise it much. In the everyday affairs of life it is more useful to reason forwards, and so the other comes to be neglected.... Most people if you describe a train of events to them, will tell you what the result would be.... There are few people, however, who, if you told them a result, would be able to evolve from their own inner consciousness what the steps were which led up to that result.'[14]

In 'The Speckled Band', Holmes gives us a demonstration. Following Helen Stoner's visit to Baker Street, he travels to Stoke Moran and examines the scene of Julia Stoner's death while Dr Roylott is in London. Holmes examines the windows and shutters in the same way that Dupin surveyed the windows of the L'Espanaye apartment, but in this case he decides that the answer lies elsewhere. His scrutiny of the adjoining bedrooms proves conclusive and, as a result, both he and Watson are able to turn the tables on Roylott. Before revealing his line of reasoning, however, Holmes admits that he has been misled into reasoning 'from insufficient data'.[15] He had wrongly surmised that the dying words of Julia Stoner, 'It was the band! The speckled band!' referred to the nearby gipsy encampment. But, after visiting the scene, like Dupin he makes the correct inference:

My attention was speedily drawn, as I have already remarked to you, to this ventilator, and to the bell-rope which hung down to the bed. The discovery that this was a dummy, and that the bed was clamped to the floor, instantly gave rise to the suspicion that the rope was there as a bridge for something passing through the hole, and coming to the bed.[16]

Thus Holmes reasons the case by virtue of retrospection from effect to cause, from his own intuitive sense to the event of the crime itself, in what would become accepted practice for the ratiocinative detective. Thus, in 'The Wrong Shape', Father Brown reasons from the premise that Quinton's so-called suicide note is the wrong shape, an inappropriate corner of paper for so momentous a confession. Gideon Fell, too, realizes that the truth of the mystery in *The Hollow Man* hangs on the question of time and the fact that witnesses were relying on a clock that was actually 40 minutes fast. This method engrained in the detective genre emanates, I contend, directly from the locked room mystery. Its presence in the first story as the pre-eminent theme partially explains this, but of more significance are Holmes's remarks that for problems 'out of the common', backward reasoning is needed to solve 'a problem of this sort'. This point has become a crucial one in understanding the approach to ratiocination in detective fiction; only an intuitive leap can be expected to activate a seamless chain of reasoning in a puzzle of extreme complexity. As Francis Nevins has put it:

> The central ritual of detective fiction is the process whereby the inexplicable, the absurd, the nightmarish are fused by the power of human intelligence into a rationally harmonious mosaic. If that view is correct, it is no wonder that the locked-room problem, in which the impossible is evoked and then dispelled with a maximum of intellectual intensity and excitement, is one of the favourite subgenres of so many distinguished writers and readers in the field.[17]

For 'the maximum of intellectual intensity', we can read the concept of backward reasoning. Having received universal adoption following its appearance in 'The Murders in the Rue Morgue', its effect has been to shape the entire central core of the genre's narrative structure. It is not only due to the process of this method, but also the fact that it creates yet another enclosure within the narrative structure. This is why this method of logic has become so widely used in the genre; it is a way in which the figure of the detective asserts his authority over the text as the agent of resolution. Peter Thoms has argued: 'Detection serves the detective's egoistic need to display his power, which derives from his storytelling skill. As a storyteller he defines his superiority, conquering the ostensible criminal by absorbing him and his deviant plot within his own controlling story, defeating his rivals by presenting a convincing narrative of explanation.'[18]

By making this intuitive leap, the detective effectively throws a frame around the investigation phase of the narrative as he is delimiting the scope of his inquiry and because the detective must control events in the investigative phase in order to fulfil the requirements of the narrative. From the moment he recognizes the significance of the bell rope and the bed, Holmes fills the frame he has created in the investigation with his hypothesis by solving a series of clues which lead back to the crime itself. One of the paradoxes of this method is that the theoretical temporal regression undergone by the detective runs counter to the progression that the clue solving actually brings to the narrative.

But this intuitive reasoning has another profound psychical dimension too: it is the moment when the detective crosses the threshold of knowledge, the limit of his consciousness. He solves the clues that operate as the fulcrum on which the detective story turns; so, in common with many other constituents of the narrative, the thrust made by the detective towards solution is built into the formulaic structure itself. This is, of course, a foundation for the idea of backward construction; the intuition that a detective uses effectively delineates a psychical boundary from which he must regress to learn the true facts of a case. In this sense the detective acts in a liminal way; what he identifies as the key to the mystery is only one step away from being below his perception. This threshold of consciousness recalls David Lehman's remark that 'If the reading of a detective novel is like the interpretation of a dream, few of the genre's conventions can have a finer symbolic resonance than the locked room.'[19] Much of this impression is gained because the locked room is removed from our conventional perception of reality; its apparent impossibility which challenges our mental capacity, the sepulchral chamber closed to view and the sense of entrapment all speak of a world that seems just beyond our level of understanding. I suggest that the position of the detective is pre-eminent in this respect. The idea of the detective as an oneiromancer is partially attributable to the fact that for much of the text he is grappling with puzzles which appear beyond the everyday level of understanding.

In 'The Speckled Band', Holmes lapses into what is a dream-like state three times during the investigation. During Helen Stoner's account of her sister's death and her own experiences he is observed 'leaning back in his chair with his eyes closed, and his head sunk in a cushion'.[20] At the end of this interview, he relapses: 'There was a long silence, during which Holmes leaned his chin upon his hands and stared into the crackling fire.'[21] After examining the bedroom used by the sisters, 'We had walked several times up and down the lawn, neither Miss Stoner nor myself liking to break in upon his thoughts before he roused himself from his reverie.'[22] Holmes's state of detachment mirrors precisely the liminal process of intuition that operates in the investigation. As he shrinks from participation in discourse with others, he is preparing his mind to engage at the furthest extent of its scope in order to make that vital breakthrough. Thus the detective has to marginalize himself, to step back from the narrative in which he is engaged, in order to regulate its worst exigencies. This becomes a recurring motif in the Holmes canon; whether it is a cocaine-induced stupor, a violin-enhanced melancholia or the intensity of the 'three pipe problem', inspiration is frequently preceded by meditation.[23]

In the conventional story the detective is often drawn to the margins of the locked room in order to examine methods of ingress and egress. In 'The Murders in the Rue Morgue', for instance, Dupin's attention is drawn to the faulty nail in the window frame and its significance in the mystery. Discovering the fact that it moved when the window was raised and resumed its position when lowered proves to be a decisive moment in Dupin's reasoning. There are numerous other examples. In 'The Judas Window' by John Dickson Carr, Sir Henry Merrivale repeatedly warns that the murderer gained access through the Judas window of the title, in other words, the keyhole; in Ellery Queen's *The Chinese Orange Mystery* (1934), the detective Richard Queen's examination of the bolted door reveals that the body of the victim shot the bolt; and Philo Vance unearths an elaborate system of string, tweezers and pins to effect a closing of the bolt from outside in Van Dine's *The Kennel Murder Case* (1933). But these discoveries on the margin of the locked room are narratively more significant when viewed as a metaphor for the progress made by the detective. The detective's realization of the point of entry becomes emblematic of the detective's breakthrough in the understanding of the case. Only by literally following in the footsteps of the murderer, by using the same method of entry, does he pass from the state of mystery to that of enlightenment.

But if the margins of understanding are at the limit of the detective's reach in the conventional tale, in the metaphysical story they appear to be out of reach altogether. Here the detective seems to function at the subliminal level; he is not in control of the events which happen around him. As we have seen, even the exercise of ratiocination is to no avail for Lönnrot in 'Death and the Compass'; in fact, following the course that ratiocination dictates only leads to his death. This is because, ultimately, unlike his conventional counterpart, he is operating in a subliminal state; he fails to see that the carefully laid clues are there as entrapment. In short, he is operating at the conventional level in a text which does not follow that structure.

In Auster's *City of Glass*, so abstracted is the narrative that Quinn finds it impossible even to engage with the task of following Stillman. The space between his work as writer and that of a real-life detective appears to be unbridgeable: 'He had lived Stillman's life, walked at his pace, seen what he had seen, and the only thing he felt now was the man's impenetrability. Instead of narrowing the distance that lay between him and Stillman, he had seen the old man slip away from him, even as he remained before his eyes.'[24] So what emerges is a profound difference between the detectives in the conventional and metaphysical tales. The reason why the detective in the latter form always seems doomed to failure is that his perception fails him. What occurs is always beyond his liminal range; there is no observable fact on which he can base his backward reasoning.

During the course of this study I have tried to show how different thematic ideas associated with the locked room have interacted with detective fiction's formulaic narrative; this conjunction has by turns been subversive and complementary but, I argue, always influential in its development. In this final reflection I want to suggest some of the ways in which the concept of the locked room and its themes have made this contribution, and its effect on the wider detective story. This will include revisiting some of the stories already included here and also looking at some which by reason of design or space have not appeared.

As theme seems to suffer from more than its fair share of misnomers, it would be as well, therefore, to iterate my definition of theme. Theme, in the sense of these chapters, is not necessarily the subject of a text, but a central idea which runs through it, engaging with the narrative and often contextualizing it. To give a simplistic example, in *The Hollow Man* the subject of the novel is the murders of Grimaud and Fley, but its theme, as I have argued, is illusion. The introduction of theme into this structural arrangement can result in an enclosure which may variously facilitate, transcend and even frustrate the detective narrative's imperative towards closure. So, while there is no doubt that the genre's formulaic narrative structure has contributed to its success, with the tantalizing journey from mystery to solution having a significant effect on the reader by increasing desire, the part played by theme in this process should not be underestimated. In fact, I would suggest that theme has played a pivotal role in the ability of the detective story to refresh itself. For instance, excellent writer though Chesterton is, it is interesting to speculate what the impact of the Father Brown series would be had the main protagonist not been a priest. It is the distinguishing mark of Catholic dogma, a force which envelopes the text and alters the way the narrative structure behaves, that both differentiates and regenerates the idea of the detective story in the reader's mind. The theme of Catholic orthodoxy is a discrete concept and, although it is not part of the formulaic narrative, it may ultimately subsume, enclose and modify it. Its association with the locked room in Chesterton's stories enables, too, a reciprocal dialogue to take place, connoting a specific relationship between with the idea of miracles and reason.

I have suggested that two broad categories of theme have emerged: those that arise from the nature of the detective story's narrative itself, which I would call intrinsic; and those which are extrinsic, reflecting a wider social, religious and ideological presence. In the former category, ratiocination in Poe's innovative trilogy, illusion in Carr's *The Hollow Man* and the concept of the labyrinth in Borges are all in some way born out of the texts they inhabit; in particular they reflect the presence of a narrative of enclosure. In 'The Murders in the Rue Morgue', for instance, Poe makes it clear from the outset that the concept of ratiocination is to be the overarching imperative which drives both narrative and plot. The celebrated scene at the beginning of the story is the preface not only for the conduct of 'The Murders in the Rue Morgue' but for the two other stories in the Dupin cycle. Poe's detective is not a man of action, he is a thinker: in 'The Purloined Letter' he outwits both Minister D— and the Prefect of police by subterfuge, and in 'The Mystery of Marie Rogêt', he solves the case from his armchair through the use of newspaper reports. Thus, in 'The Murders in the Rue Morgue', not only does ratiocination become the means by which the narrative progresses, but it forms a framing device, simultaneously enclosing and activating the investigation.

Ratiocination is one thing but another function of the puzzle story is to hoodwink the reader. This mask of illusion which covers so many detective stories actually arises from the narrative structure of the genre itself. Part of the function of this arrangement is to delay the resolution of the mystery, as Dennis Porter argues:

> The importance of 'The Murders in the Rue Morgue' from the point of view of the art of fiction is that it established the precedent for the genre in which the *dénouement* determines the order and causality of all that precedes. It is a peculiarity of detective fiction that the story of an investigation is made gradually to uncover the story of the crime which antedates it. And the business of uncovering is made to proceed via a series of steps that are carefully calculated with a view to their effect on a reader.[25]

These 'series of steps' are characterized by obfuscation and delay; as I have argued in the case of a text like *The Hollow Man*, this manifests itself as illusion. I suggest that this is the case with most detective fiction of the puzzle variety – the temporal lacuna between crime and resolution is invariably filled with an assortment of relevant material and, importantly, much that is misleading. In short, the detective story is substantially a misprision, a text which has at its heart a gigantic practical joke. This is seen in extremis in the locked room mystery because the text purports to make the impossible a likely outcome of events. So for this reason I suggest that Porter is correct to identify 'The Murders in the Rue Morgue' as the wellspring of a practice which now is widespread throughout the genre.

The classic components of this illusive kind of text are present in Christie's locked room short story, 'Problem at Sea', where she explores the possibility of the doubly sealed enclosure, the locked room surrounded by an isolated venue. This story, although published in 1974, is amongst a collection set in the inter-war period, under the title *Poirot's Early Cases*. Christie was fond of exploring different venues of enclosure in her story other than her reliable standby of the country house, so planes as well as boats – such as in *Death in the Clouds* (1935) and *Death on the Nile* (1937) – feature in her oeuvre. 'Problem at Sea' concerns the mysterious death of the wealthy and difficult Mrs Clapperton while on a cruise. She is married to a 'Colonel' Clapperton who, it appears, is a bogus officer and, actually, a former music hall artist. The dapper 'Colonel' becomes the object of a mild flirtation with two young girls and is also admired by a Miss Henderson, one of the passengers on the boat. As the boat docks at Alexandria Clapperton prepares to go ashore with the two young ladies, but suggests that his wife may want to come. He goes to her cabin door with the ladies and Poirot; he finds the door locked on the inside and his wife, whose voice sounds 'shrill and decisive' in no mood to accompany them.[26] They leave her, apparently alive and well, and go ashore. But later, when she does not appear, the door is broken down and she is found stabbed to death. The murder seems impossible, but Poirot uses the one tangible clue, the 'Colonel's' music hall background, to solve it. In a theatrical repetition of Clapperton's trick, he assembles the entire ship's company and uses a doll to indicate how the former ventriloquist threw his voice to make it sound as though his wife was still alive. Clapperton, exposed, has a heart attack and dies.

Stephen Knight has suggested that Christie's 'plain flat style' and 'anonymity of authorial voice' contribute to texts that 'continuously expose identity to be a constructed illusion'.[27] Although Knight uses these phrases in respect of detective fiction's possible connection to modernism, I suggest that they also have something fundamental to say about detective fiction's narrative structure. It has been said many times that the genre's plain storytelling style has a simplistic charm with a wide appeal. To a certain extent this is true: in order to convey a mystery and its solution to a conclusion, it must, perforce, follow this perceived path. But that is not quite the whole picture; it does not explain one of the central paradoxes of the detective story – that it relies on the obscurity of language, its sounds, its meaning and its shortcomings, in order to create its seemingly straightforward narrative. This is demonstrated in 'Problem at Sea' because Clapperton is able to imitate and, crucially, *re*produce his wife's voice – a female voice at that – in order to convince witnesses.

This imprecision in the sound of language is exactly the point which Poe poses in 'The Murders in the Rue Morgue', which I touched on Chapter 5, where utter confusion reigns amongst those present during the orang-utan's attack, when it comes to identifying the 'shrill' voice:

> The Frenchman supposes it the voice of a Spaniard, and 'might have distinguished some words *had he been acquainted with the Spanish.'* The Dutchman maintains it to have been that of a Frenchman; but we find it stated that *'not understanding French this witness was examined through an interpreter.'* The Englishman thinks it the voice of a German, and *'does not understand German.'* The Spaniard 'is sure' that it was that of an Englishman, but 'judges by the intonation' altogether, *'as he has no knowledge of the English.'* The Italian believes it the voice of a Russian, but *'has never conversed with a native of Russia.'*[28]

Poe's project is twofold. The argument over the recognition of the voice is a narrative misprision to give the illusion that the voice *is* human; the arguments are about which language is heard, nothing else. But, at another level, Poe is challenging the nature of language's ability to convey meaning accurately. The text indicates that when witnesses are confronted with an unusual sound they rationalize its meaning into something with which they are familiar, in this case a human voice. They do not read the sounds objectively, and cannot decipher the languages of their own species, let alone another. This dislocation of language is very like the situation in Auster's *City of Glass*; Stillman seeks to restore the untainted prelapsarian language, while Quinn utilizes the detective story as a model of rational narrative. But for Quinn, as well as Stillman, this proves a vain quest – despite all its supposed narrative clarity, the detective story is, at the same time, ultimately just as reliant on obfuscation for its effect as it is on resolution. Its narrative language is only designed to be clear at the chosen moment in its structure. It is the same with Clapperton's illusion: what appears plausible is not the case; what turns out to be the correct explanation, the use of ventriloquism, is, like the rampant orang-utan, abstruse in the extreme. Indeed, apart from the clue of Clapperton's music hall background given right at the start of the story, the detail that he was, in fact, a ventriloquist is not revealed, and until we reach the theatrical dénouement the text follows an entirely bogus course.

In essence, illusion can be seen as a counterpart to the narrative of what is actually revealed as the solution at the end of a detective novel. It is a second narrative, one that runs parallel with its principal, and is ultimately dispelled by it. This alternative narrative is the one which is pre-eminent in the text until it is supplanted, and is, therefore, the one with which we are most familiar.

In Colin Dexter's *The Wench Is Dead* (1989), a hospital-bound Inspector Morse takes an interest in a Victorian case about the murder of Joanna Franks, whose body was found in the Oxford Canal. Two bargemen on the boat on which she travelled were hanged for the murder. The novel has distinct similarities with 'The Mystery of Marie Rogêt' – the woman found in the water, the armchair detective – and, like Poe, Dexter based the novel on an actual event, the 1839 murder of Christina Collins as she travelled the Trent and Mersey Canal at Rugeley, Staffordshire. Joanna Franks was supposedly travelling from Coventry to London to join her second husband, Charles Franks. Her first husband, one F. T. Donavan, a stage magician, who was the 'Emperor of all the Illusionists', had died the year before. Morse goes back over the evidence and he is suspicious as to why she travelled by barge and did not take the quicker option by train. Eventually he discovers, by measuring the dress of the victim, and through speculative means checking her height, that the body found in the canal could not have been Joanna Franks. It seems that the whole incident was part of scheme to claim Joanna's life insurance. Charles Franks, who is actually Donavan, posed as her second husband to identify the body as hers. The pair had substituted the body of another woman as the victim. Thus the illusory narrative of *The Wench Is Dead* proves to be nothing more than a contrivance to conceal the underlying, authentic version, a trope to delay the outcome and to fill the hiatus between crime and solution. As Dennis Porter suggests:

> Every action sequence that occurs in a detective novel between a crime and its solution delays for a time that solution even when it appears logically required by it. Down to the level of a sentence, all telling involves the postponing of an end simply because articulate speech is linear and expresses itself in the dimension of time.[29]

I suggest that this practice is exemplified by the locked room mystery, the most extreme of all the illusions; the problem it presents is so seemingly insoluble that it obfuscates successfully the underlying narrative of what really happened. Thus, in 'Problem at Sea', *The Wench Is Dead*, *The Hollow Man* and throughout the canon there is, of necessity, an illusive void at the heart of the conventional detective story.

Stephen Knight has rightly stressed that, since the Second World War, continuity in the conventional detective story has existed cheek by jowl with a burgeoning diversity. Thematic contexts for the detective story are now encompassing a wealth of new ideas, as Knight records: in the field of gender, where novels such as P. D. James's *An Unsuitable Job for a Woman* (1972) paved the way for a less genteel representation of the woman detective, and which now include gay and lesbian texts; and in the area of race and ethnicity, which are increasingly finding a voice in the detective story. Novels by Ian Rankin, for instance, featuring the police detective Rebus, have emphasized the growing awareness of Scottish identity as the political debate about independence sharpens. These extrinsic narratives are beginning to have a distinctive effect on the performance of the detective story narrative, by permeating its closed structure and making us aware of another world outside the text.

One relatively early and remarkable example of an all-embracing ideological metanarrative is to be found in the detective fiction of Josef Škvorecký. Škvorecký was born in what is now the Czech Republic in 1924, and his experiences as a slave labourer in a German aircraft factory during the Second World War and subsequent life under the communist regime left an indelible mark and helped to shape his literature. His early works, *The End of the Nylon Age* and *The Cowards*, were banned by the government. His beliefs helped to foster a movement which culminated in the Prague Spring of 1968; and when the Soviets invaded Czechoslovakia later that year he fled to Canada, started his own publishing house, taught at Toronto University and continued his writing career.

Škvorecký's abhorrence of totalitarianism and the repression he experienced finds its way into the four volumes of detective stories produced between 1966 and 1981: *The Mournful Demeanour of Lieutenant Boruvka* (1966), *Sins for Father Knox* (1973), *The End of Lieutenant Boruvka* (1975) and *The Return of Lieutenant Boruvka* (1981). All these stories retain the element of the puzzle formula – in fact, the first set contains an ingenious locked room mystery, 'The Case of the Horizontal Trajectory' – but more importantly they reflect the mounting tensions created by an honest policeman attempting to do his job against the forces of totalitarianism. The crunch comes in *The End of Lieutenant Boruvka,* which contains just five stories and is set just before and after the Soviet invasion. According to Škvorecký, the stories are loosely based on real cases and are linked, so that the whole reads like an episodic novel.

The Author's Note to *The End of Lieutenant Boruvka* was added in 1989, just before the English version appeared in 1990. It is very clear about the context within which Škvorecký is writing. He recalls the downfall of Alexander Dubček and his reforms in a powerfully worded diatribe:

> These efforts came to an abrupt end on August 21, 1968, when half a million troops (mostly Soviet) and five thousand assault vehicles invaded the country. Dubček and members of his leadership were flown to Moscow in shackles, and only barely escaped the fate of the Hungarian leader Nagy, who was shot by the Soviets after the similar defeat of the Hungarian revolution in 1956....
>
> In the wake of this ambush, Czechoslovak citizens were subjected to a degrading Orwellization of their lives – called 'normalization' – which was aimed at forcing these once free and truly democratic people into utter obedience and demoralization.[30]

This statement does more than throw a frame around the whole text. It casts a pall on everything it contains: the conduct of investigation, the behaviour of the characters and the operation of the law; all is subject to its control. In the first story, 'Miss Peskova Regrets', a dancer is murdered after being given a lethal cocktail of LSD and alcohol. At first, a famous writer and friend of Dubček is implicated after compromising letters are found in the woman's apartment but, by carefully following a trail of clues in the manner of a conventional detective, Boruvka soon divines that someone close to the communist regime is to blame. As soon as the Lieutenant gets too close he is taken off the case and is given a reluctant lecture by his boss:

> 'Anything that harms the Party, anything that tarnishes its good name, is essentially anti-democratic, and subjective intentions are irrelevant. Even if those intentions were pure as the driven snow, objectively – ...we cannot measure them by the same standards as we do other citizens, even though of course they are completely equal otherwise.'[31]

It is made clear to Boruvka that certain indiscretions in his career would be resurrected if he did not go along with the party line. The perpetrators are untouchable and the case peters out.

'Strange Archaeology', a cold case concerning the murder of a young girl trying to escape to the West, is resolved by ingenious reference to an archaeological dig, and although Boruvka identifies the culprit he has no confidence that justice will apply the appropriate sanction. When it comes to 'Ornament in the Grass', the Soviet invasion has taken place and everywhere there is a military presence. Two teenage girls, used to teasing the boys who pursue them, are found shot dead in woodland near to where army manoeuvres are taking place. Initially, Czech troops are questioned but eventually Boruvka discovers that it is a trigger-happy Soviet soldier who committed the murders. It seems he was acting as a sentry; the girls failed to identify themselves, adopting instead their customary sexually provocative attitude, so he adhered to his strict orders and shot them. Once again, the exercising of Boruvka's detective skills proves futile. The closing lines are as ominous and bleak as any in detective fiction:

> They took him off the case with no justification whatsoever. And he – he did not demand any. He felt helpless. One night about two months after the unsolved case of the double murder in the grass – no solution was ever announced....
>
> From somewhere in the darkness he could hear a rumbling, strangely metallic sound. A dark, regular throbbing of heavy vehicles moving slowly through the streets. He raised his eyes to the stars. Large, black shadows were approaching across the sky. He had never seen such heavy air traffic after midnight.
>
> It was those distant shadows – not the detective – that finally settled the case of the ornament in the grass.[32]

In the last story, 'Pirates', Boruvka finally rebels: he obstructs the arrest of someone fleeing to the West and is himself arrested. This story is notable, too for an outburst of frustrated, impassioned self-reflexivity. We are party to a discussion between a group of intellectuals, Dubček sympathizers, as they discuss the role of writers such as Škvorecký who have fled abroad:

> 'God, how our holy émigrés carry on!' another voice was shouting. 'They leave the country, they live like pigs in clover, and instead of turning their back and saying 'good riddance!' they can't stop writing about us. The bastards probably make their living at it, so they make damn good and sure the interest doesn't dry up on them.'[33]

This is self-reflexivity in the grand tradition of the detective story, except that with a bitter ironic twist Škvorecký turns it in on himself. It is a neat *mise en abyme* which draws attention to the writer of the main text and, at the same time, expresses all the impotence and guilt of someone caught in such an equivocal position. Here self-reflexivity is not about the relationship with other texts, but about the writer's relationship with his own conscience; indeed, about the integrity of writing itself. 'Pirates' is the culmination of a group of stories where thematic dynamics not only envelope the text, but act to alter the expected outcome of the narrative. In denying narrative closure it is contextualizing the genre in a philosophy where the sanction of the law is dependent on the attitude of the state apparatus, not on solutions arrived at by a detective. Even when ratiocination triumphs, all Boruvka achieves is a pyrrhic victory. The impact of these violations of the detective narrative is all the more vivid because it is embedded in a structure which, conventionally at least, holds out the prospect of resolution and consolation. Instead, perversely, the outcome of these stories leaves the detective in the locked room, surrounded by hostile forces and with his authority disempowered. Such an act of enclosure demonstrates the effect specific contexts can bring to bear, even on texts that conform to the conventions of detective fiction. It suggests that with increasing diversity in the genre the notion of closure can no longer be guaranteed.

It is now 170 years since Poe made Dupin the archetypal reasoning detective. The appearance of 'The Murders in the Rue Morgue' gave the locked room mystery a privileged position in the detective canon, and scarcely has such a single text – a short story at that – been held in such regard as a seminal work. In the examination of every artistic genre, there is, of course, a desire to seek out the primigenial; we have a delight in the identification of starting points and the moments of great change. This has become the basis for much criticism, identifying the cultural shift, assessing influence and ascribing status; such has been the lot of Poe's original tale. With these factors in mind, I propose that because of this unique position the locked room mystery represents an archetype in the genre of detective fiction. By this I do not mean that it is a kind of miniature repetition of the whole; rather it is the original paradigm for the ratiocinative story. It represents the ultimate, perfect form of the puzzle.

However, this practice of informing the wider genre goes further. I have striven to suggest that the imagery, narrative and workings of the psyche, now widely apparent in the detective story, have their beginnings in the locked room mystery. All these constituents have a common characteristic: the idea of enclosure. The conventional detective narrative, therefore, is essentially homogenous: its imagery of entrapment and entombment corresponds with the framed narrative; and its main protagonists, the detective, the victim and the murderer, all exhibit psychical characteristics which, in turn, contribute to this idea. This homogeneity, too, has led authors to use the detective story for the purposes of displaying thematic material in a certain way. Because of its narrative stability, association of a particular theme might enhance its cause, as in the case of Chesterton and Catholicism, whereas with totalitarianism the breaking of the solvent convention seems all the more shocking.

To a high degree the locked room mystery's considerable influence on the genre, shaping its narrative and invoking its images of enclosure, is a past, if still enduring event. The locked room form continues to be a recognizable entity in the work of Edward D. Hoch, who, until his death in 2008, had written over 900 short stories in this context. Recent books by Hal White such as *The Mysteries of Reverend Dean* (2008), and *The Night of the Wolf* (2000) by the French writer Paul Halter (which was first translated into English in 2004), for instance, are a continuing testament. These contain almost exclusively 'architectural' locked room and 'impossible' crimes, and are driven narratively by the same imperatives of puzzle and illusion that guided writers of the classic Golden Age stories – but contextual circumstances are now very different. Between the wars the detective story was embarking on its first substantial round of self-examination, which would ultimately inform its future direction. The locked room mystery and its familiar constituents played a major role in that metamorphosis. So, cleverly wrought though some of these contemporary texts are, their preoccupation with the archness of plot speaks more of static generic obeisance, a form marking time rather than engaged in dynamic development. Despite this, the locked room continues to cast its shadow. As long as the detective story retains its emblematic narrative, or even vestiges of it; as long as it wrestles with puzzles and mysteries, whether the outcome brings consolation or not; as long as its imagery speaks of enclosure and self-reflexivity; and as long as it engages with themes which draw attention to its innate structure, the locked room mystery will be not merely a form *of* the detective story but its very essence.

Notes

Preface

1. If one already exists it has escaped my exhaustive researches, and so to its author I offer an unreserved apology on two grounds: firstly for any oversight on my part and secondly, because I would dearly love to have read it!
2. Robert Champigny, *What Will Have Happened* (Bloomington, University of Indiana, 1977), p. 13.
3. Dennis Porter, *The Pursuit of Crime: Art and Ideology in Detective Fiction* (New Haven: Yale University Press, 1981), p. 87.
4. Stephen Knight, *Form and Ideology in Crime Fiction* (London: Macmillan, 1980), p. 3.
5. Patricia Merivale and Susan Sweeney, 'The Game's Afoot', in *Detecting Texts: The Metaphysical Detective Story from Poe to Modernism*, ed. by Patricia Merivale and Susan Sweeney (Philadelphia: University of Pennsylvania Press, 1999), p. 2.
6. For a comprehensive bibliographical survey of locked room stories, see Robert Adey, *Locked Room Murders and Other Impossible Crimes: A Comprehensive Bibliography* (Minneapolis: Crossover Press, 1991). This is a well-researched and invaluable 'bible' to have at one's fingertips.

1 Edgar Allan Poe and the Detective Story Narrative

1. Donald A. Yates, 'An Essay on Locked Rooms', in *The Mystery Writer's Art*, ed. Francis M. Nevins, Jr. (Bowling Green: Bowling Green University Popular Press, 1970), p. 273.
2. G. W. F. Hegel, 'The Life of Jesus', *Three Essays, 1793–1795: The Tubingen Essay, Berne Fragments, The Life of Jesus*, ed. and trans. Peter Fuss and John Dobbins (Notre Dame: University of Notre Dame Press, 1984), p. 75.
3. J. Gerald Kennedy, *Poe, Death and the Life of Writing* (New Haven: Yale University Press, 1987), p. 119.
4. *The Letters of Edgar Allan Poe*, ed. John Ward Ostrom (New York: Gordian Press, 1966), p. 328.
5. Stephen Knight, *Crime Fiction since 1800: Detection, Death, Diversity* (Basingstoke: Palgrave Macmillan, 2010), pp. 24–5.
6. François Eugène Vidocq, *Memoirs of Vidocq: Master of Crime*, ed. and trans. Edwin Gile Rich (Edinburgh: AK Press/Nabat, 2003).
7. Sita A. Schütt, 'French Crime Fiction', in *The Cambridge Companion to Crime Fiction* (Cambridge: Cambridge University, 2003), pp. 60–1.
8. Edgar Allan Poe, 'The Murders in the Rue Morgue', in *Tales, Poems and Essays* (London: Collins, 1952), p. 341.
9. Tzvetan Todorov, 'The Typology of Detective Fiction', in *The Poetics of Prose*, trans. Richard Howard (Ithaca, NY: Cornell University Press, 1977), p. 43.

10. Ostrom, *The Letters of Edgar Allan Poe*, vol. 2, p. 328.
11. Poe, 'The Philosophy of Composition', in *Tales, Poems and Essays*, p. 503.
12. Porter, *The Pursuit of Crime*, pp. 26–7.
13. Poe, 'Charles Dickens', in *Tales, Poems and Essays*, p. 533.
14. Champigny, *What Will Have Happened*, p. 13.
15. Merivale, 'Gumshoe Gothics', in *Detecting Texts*, p. 102.
16. Heta Pyrrhönen, *Murder from an Academic Angle: An Introduction to the Study of the Detective Narrative* (Columbia, SC: Camden House, 1994), p. 16.
17. Poe, 'The Murders in the Rue Morgue', in *Tales, Poems and Essays*, pp. 330–1.
18. Patrick Diskin, 'Poe, Le Fanu and the Sealed Room Mystery', *Notes and Queries* 13 (September 1966), 337–9. The tale referred to by Diskin is J. C. Managan, 'The Thirty Flasks', *Dublin University Magazine* xii (October 1838), 408–24.
19. Sir Arthur Conan Doyle, 'The Cardboard Box', in *The Complete Sherlock Holmes Short Stories* (London: John Murray, 1956), pp. 923–6.
20. Sir Arthur Conan Doyle, 'The Hound of the Baskervilles', in *The Complete Sherlock Holmes Long Stories* (London: John Murray, 1954), pp. 275–82.
21. Poe, 'The Murders in the Rue Morgue', p. 335.
22. Joseph Sheridan Le Fanu, 'Passage in the Secret History of an Irish Countess', in *Death Locked In: An Anthology of Locked Room Stories*, ed. Douglas G. Greene and Robert C. S. Adey (New York: Barnes and Noble, 1994), p. 33.
23. Poe, 'The Murders in the Rue Morgue', pp. 335, 340.
24. Le Fanu, 'Passage in the Secret History of an Irish Countess', pp. 33, 34.
25. Le Fanu, 'Passage in the Secret History of an Irish Countess', p. 34.
26. Poe, 'The Murders in the Rue Morgue', p. 339.
27. Poe, 'The Murders in the Rue Morgue', p. 336.
28. Le Fanu, 'Passage in the Secret History of an Irish Countess', p. 33.
29. See note 5.
30. Poe, 'The Murders in the Rue Morgue', p. 342.
31. Poe, 'The Murders in the Rue Morgue', p. 371.
32. Poe, 'The Murders in the Rue Morgue', p. 346.
33. Poe, 'The Murders in the Rue Morgue', p. 348.
34. Kennedy, *Poe, Death and the Life of Writing*, p. 115.
35. Poe, 'The Murders in the Rue Morgue', p. 330.
36. Poe, 'The Murders in the Rue Morgue', p. 337.
37. Walter Benjamin, *The Arcades Project*, trans. Howard Eiland and Kevin McLaughlin (Cambridge, MA: Harvard University Press, 1999), p. 20.
38. Mark S. Madoff, 'Inside, Outside, and the Gothic Locked-Room Mystery', in *Gothic Fictions: Prohibition/Transgression*, ed. Kenneth W. Graham (New York: AMS, 1989), p. 50.
39. Sidney Poger and Tony Magistrale, 'Poe's Children: The Conjunction of the Detective and the Gothic Tale', *Clues* 18.1 (1997), 141–2.
40. Geoffrey Hartmann, 'Literature High and Low: The Case of the Mystery Story', in *The Poetics of Murder: Detective Fiction and Literary Theory*, ed. Glenn W. Most and William W. Stowe (San Diego: Harcourt Brace Jovanovich, 1983), p. 217.
41. Joseph N. Riddel, 'The "Crypt" of Edgar Poe', *Boundary 2* 7.3 (Spring 1979), 123.
42. Poe, 'The Fall of the House of Usher', in *Tales, Poems and Essays*, p. 140.

43. Edgar Allan Poe, 'Instinct vs. Reason – A Black Cat', in *Collected Works of Edgar Allan Poe*, ed. Thomas Ollive Mabbott, 3 vols (Cambridge, MA: Belknap Press of Harvard University Press, 1969), vol. II, p. 682.
44. Poe, 'The Murders in the Rue Morgue', p. 357.
45. Poe, 'The Pit and the Pendulum', in *Tales, Poems and Essays*, pp. 216–17.
46. Poe, 'The Pit and the Pendulum', p. 217.
47. Poe, 'The Pit and the Pendulum', p. 224.
48. J. A. Leo Lemay, 'The Psychology of "The Murders in the Rue Morgue"', *American Literature* 54 (1982), 166.
49. Jeanne M. Malloy, 'Apocalyptic Imagery and the Fragmentation of the Psyche: "The Pit and the Pendulum"', *Nineteenth-Century Literature* 46.1 (June 1991), 94.
50. William W. Stowe, 'Reason and Logic in Detective Fiction', *Semiotics* 6, 2.3 (1987), 374–5.
51. Kevin J. Hayes, 'One-Man Modernist', in *The Cambridge Companion to Edgar Allan Poe*, ed. Kevin J. Hayes (Cambridge: Cambridge University Press, 2002), p. 232.
52. Poe, 'The Murders in the Rue Morgue', p. 331.
53. Poe, 'The Murders in the Rue Morgue', p. 332.

2   The Locked Compartment: Charles Dickens's 'The Signalman' and Enclosure in the Railway Mystery Story

1. Detailed accounts of Thomas Briggs's murder appear in Arthur and Mary Sellwood's *The Victorian Railway Murders* (Newton Abbot: David & Charles, 1979), pp. 11–52; H. B. Irving's 'The First Railway Murder', in *The Railway Murders: Ten Classic True Crime Stories*, ed. Jonathan Goodman (London: Allison & Busby, 1984), pp. 13–37; John Henry Wigmore, *The Principles of Judicial Proof*, ed. H. B. Irving (London: Little, Brown and Company, 1913), p. 417; Elizabeth Anne Stanko, *The Meanings of Violence* (London: Routledge, 2003), p. 26; Ralf Roth and Marie-Noelle Polino, *The City and the Railway in Europe* (Aldershot: Ashgate Publishing, 2003), p. 249.
2. *The Annual Register 1864*.
3. Wolfgang Schivelbusch, 'The Compartment', in *The Railway Journey: The Industrialisation of Time and Space in the 19th Century* (Berkeley: University of California Press, 1986), p. 79.
4. Wolfgang Schivelbusch, 'Railroad Space and Railroad Time', *New German Critique* 14 (1978), 33.
5. 'Mugby Junction', *All The Year Round*, Christmas 1866. The entire edition is given over to the Mugby Junction stories, which are, in order of their original appearance: 'Barbox Brothers', 'Barbox and Co.', 'Main Line: The Boy at Mugby', 'No.1 Branch Line: The Signalman', by Dickens; 'No. 2 Branch Line: The Engine-Driver', by Andrew Halliday; 'No. 3 Branch Line: The Compensation House', by Charles Collins; 'No. 4 Branch Line: The Travelling Post-Office', by Hesba Stretton; 'No. 5 Branch Line: The Engineer', by Amelia B. Edwards (repr. in Charles Dickens, *Christmas Stories and Others* [London: Chapman and Hall, 1891], pp. 323–64).
6. Dickens, 'The Signalman', in *Christmas Stories and Others*, p. 312.

7. Dickens, 'The Signalman', p. 312–13.
8. David Seed, 'Mystery in Everyday Things: Charles Dickens' "The Signalman"', *Criticism* 23 (1981), 48.
9. For a description of this accident see 'Brighton–Clayton Tunnel Accident', *The Railway Times* (31 August 1861), p. 1109.
10. Norris Pope, 'Dickens's "The Signalman" and Information Problems in the Railway Age', *Technology and Culture* 42.3 (July 2001), 442.
11. Mrs Henry Woods, 'Going Through the Tunnel', in *A Treasury of Victorian Detective Stories*, ed. Everett F. Bleiler (New York: Charles Scribner's Sons, 1979), pp. 173–88.
12. Ewald Mengel, 'The Structure and Meaning of Dickens's "The Signalman"', *Studies in Short Fiction* 20.4 (1983), 272.
13. Dickens, 'The Signalman', p. 314.
14. Dickens, 'The Signalman', p. 315.
15. Dickens, 'The Signalman', p. 316.
16. Dickens, 'The Signalman', p. 317.
17. Dickens, 'The Signalman', p. 318.
18. Dickens, 'The Signalman', p. 318.
19. Dickens, 'The Signalman', p. 319.
20. Dickens, 'The Signalman', p. 317.
21. An account of the Staplehurst crash can be found in Peter Ackroyd's *Dickens* (London: Minerva, 1991). The general effects of the trauma of railway accidents in the nineteenth century are well documented in Ralph Harrington's chapter, 'The Railway Accident: Trains, Trauma and Technological Crisis in Nineteenth-Century Britain', in *Traumatic Pasts: History, Psychiatry, and Trauma in the Modern Age*, ed. Mark S. Micale and Paul Learner (Cambridge: Cambridge University Press, 2001), pp. 31–56. See also: www.york.ac.uk/inst/irs/irshome/papers/rlyacc.htm (accessed 1 March 2011).
22. Charles Dickens, *The Letters of Charles Dickens*, ed. Madeline House and others (Oxford: Oxford University Press, 1965–2000), xi, 56–7.
23. Charles Dickens, 'Need Railway Travellers be Smashed?', *Household Words* (29 November 1851), 217–21.
24. 'Editorial', *Saturday Review* (17 June 1865), p. 75.
25. 'Accidents', *Railway News* (22 October 1864), p. 411.
26. 'The Late Railway Accidents', *The Lancet* (14 September 1861), 235.
27. 'Injuries', *The Lancet* (14 September, 1861), 255–6. Notes 24 to 27 are quoted in Harrington, 'Railway Safety and Railway Slaughter: Railway Accidents, Government and Public in Victorian Britain', *Journal of Victorian Culture* 8.2 (2003), 187–207, and 'The Railway Accident'.
28. See note 9 above.
29. Simon Cooke, 'Anxious Travelers: A Contextual Reading of "The Signalman"', *Dickens Quarterly* 22.2 (2005), 107.
30. Charles Dickens, *Dombey and Son* (London: Chapman and Hall, 1890), p. 227.
31. Dickens, *Dombey and Son*, p. 227.
32. For an extended discussion on Dickens and his reaction to the legacy of the Industrial Revolution see Philip Collins, 'Dickens and Industrialisation', *Studies in English Literature, 1500–1900* 20.4 (Autumn, 1980), 651–73; Catherine Gallagher, *The Body Economic: Life, Death, and Sensation in Political Economy*

and the Victorian Novel (Princeton, NJ: Princeton University Press, 2006); Myron Magnet, *Dickens and the Social Order* (Philadelphia: University of Philadelphia Press, 1985); Mildred Newcomb, *The Imagined World of Charles Dickens* (Columbus: Ohio State University Press, 1989); Harold Bloom, ed., *Charles Dickens's Hard Times* (New York: Chelsea, 1987).

33. Harrington, 'Railway Safety and Railway Slaughter', pp. 203–4.
34. Thomas Keller, 'Railway Spine Revisited: Traumatic Neurosis or Neurotrauma?', *Journal of the History of Medicine and Allied Sciences* 50 (1995), 515.
35. William Benjamin Carpenter, *Principles of Mental Physiology* (New York: Appleton, 1890), p. 429.
36. F. X. Dercum, 'Railway Shock and Its Treatment', *Therapeutic Gazette* 13 (1889), 654.
37. Sigmund Freud, 'A Note upon the Mystic Writing Pad', *The Standard Edition of the Complete Psychological Works of Sigmund Freud*, ed. James Strachey, 24 vols (London: Hogarth Press, 1953–74), vol. 19, pp. 227–34.
38. Freud, 'Beyond the Pleasure Principle', *The Standard Edition of the Complete Psychological Works of Sigmund Freud*, vol. 18, p. 12.
39. Freud, 'The Uncanny', *The Standard Edition of the Complete Psychological Works of Sigmund Freud*, vol. 17, p. 245.
40. Srdjan Smajic, 'The Trouble with Ghost-Seeing: Vision, and Genre in the Victorian Ghost Story', *English Literary History* 70 (2004), 1107.
41. Jill L. Matus, 'Trauma, Memory, and Railway Disaster: The Dickensian Connection', *Victorian Studies* 43.3 (2001), 413–36.
42. Matus, 'Trauma, Memory, and Railway Disaster', p. 420.
43. 'Report of the Commission: The Influence of Railway Travelling on Public Health', *The Lancet* (4 January 1862), 15–19, 48–53, 78–81 (p. 16).
44. 'Report of the Commission: The Influence of Railway Travelling on Public Health', p. 80.
45. Christopher Bollas, *The Shadow of the Object: Psychoanalysis of the Unthought Known* (London: Free Association Books, 1987), p. 210.
46. Matus, 'Trauma, Memory, and Railway Disaster', p. 426.
47. Matus, 'Trauma, Memory, and Railway Disaster', p. 432.
48. Dickens, 'The Signalman', p. 319.
49. Dickens, 'The Signalman', p. 312.
50. Dickens, 'The Signalman', p. 321.
51. Dickens, 'The Signalman', p. 316.
52. Peter Brooks, *Reading for the Plot: Design and Intention in Narrative* (Cambridge, MA: Harvard University Press, 1992), p. 43.
53. Dickens, 'The Signalman', p. 319.
54. Dickens, 'The Signalman', p. 313.
55. Peter Haining, 'Introduction', in *Murder on the Railways*, ed. Peter Haining (London: Artus, 1996), p. 3.
56. Amelia B. Edwards, 'The Four-fifteen Express', in *The Phantom Coach: Collected Ghost Stories*, ed. Richard Dalby (Ashcroft, British Columbia: Ash Tree Press, 1999), p. 129.
57. David Lehman, *The Perfect Murder: A Study in Detection* (New York: The Free Press, 1989), p. 77.
58. Joseph A. Kestner, *The Edwardian Detective, 1901–1915* (Aldershot: Ashgate Publishing, 2000), p. 68.

59. Roy Vickers, 'The Eighth Lamp', in *Crime on the Lines*, ed. Bryan Morgan (London: Routledge and Kegan Paul, 1975), p. 99.

60. Vickers, 'The Eighth Lamp', p. 106.

61. Vickers, 'The Eighth Lamp', p. 106.

62. Marty Roth, *Foul and Fair Play: Reading Genre in Classic Detective Fiction* (Athens, GA: University of Georgia Press, 1995), p. 34.

63. Peter Haining, 'Foreword' to John Oxenham, 'A Mystery of the Underground', in *Murder on the Railways* (London: Artus, 1996), p. 264.

64. M. McDonnell Bodkin, 'The Unseen Hand', in *The Quests of Paul Beck* (London: T. Fisher Unwin, 1910), pp. 237–8.

65. John Dickson Carr, 'The Murder in Number Four', in *The Door to Doom*, ed. Douglas G. Greene (New York: Harper & Row, 1980), p. 94.

66. V. L. Whitechurch, *Thrilling Stories of the Railway* (London: Routledge & Kegan Paul, 1977).

67. Sir Arthur Conan Doyle, 'The Story of the Lost Special', in *The Conan Doyle Stories* (London: John Murray, 1960), pp. 551–70; 'The Story of the Man with the Watches', in ibid., pp. 590–607.

68. Conan Doyle, 'The Bruce Partington Plans', in *The Complete Sherlock Holmes Short Stories*, pp. 968–99.

69. J. McDonnell Bodkin, 'How He Cut His Stick', in *Crime on the Lines*, ed. Bryan Morgan (London: Routledge and Kegan Paul, 1975), pp. 13–21.

70. Mengel, 'The Structure and Meaning of Dickens's "The Signalman"', p. 278.

3 The Body in the Library: Reading the Locked Room in Anna Katherine Green's *The Filigree Ball*

1. John Dickson Carr, *The Red Widow Murders* (New York: Pocket Books Inc, 1940), p. 2.

2. Charles J. Dutton, *Murder in a Library* (London: Hurst and Blackett, 1931), pp. 107–8. Charles Dutton also wrote three other locked room mysteries which all feature murders in a library: *The Underwood Mystery* (1921), *The Shadow on the Glass* (1923) and *The Crooked Cross* (1926).

3. W. H. Auden, 'The Guilty Vicarage', in *The Dyer's Hand and Other Essays* (New York: Random House, 1962), p. 151.

4. Agatha Christie, *The Body in the Library* (London: Collins, 1942), p. 10.

5. Kathleen Gregory Klein and Joseph Keller, 'Deductive Detective Fiction: The Self-Destructive Genre', *Genre* 19 (Summer 1986), 164.

6. So keen was Green for us to *read* the houses in her books that she started the practice of incorporating a sketch plan of the relevant rooms at the heart of the mystery. In *The Leavenworth Case* the scene of Leavenworth's library and its relationship to other rooms is the subject of the first sketch to appear in a detective story. The line drawing is a precise, draughtsman-like way of delimiting the scope of the inquiry; given Green's capacity for detail and its interpretation, the assumption is, of course, that reading the script with the sketch is the key to solving the mystery, so the problem automatically becomes realized in another dimension. The sketch plan is also a constituent part of the way in which Green seeks to give the impression of authenticity by providing pictorial evidence. The diagram, therefore, allows the text to

operate at two levels of understanding, emphasizing that no matter where the narrative leads, no doubt should remain as to the central focus of the mystery. It is a device which Green would repeat in such important novels as *The Circular Study* and *Initials Only* (1911) and anticipates its use by Conan Doyle and the wider genre in the Golden Age, as will be demonstrated in Dickson Carr's *The Hollow Man*, which is the subject of Chapter 5. The illustrations in the first edition of *The Filigree Ball* by C. M. Relyea are of a different kind, however, depicting the discovery of Veronica's body and the drawing of the filigree ball and watch chain on the front cover of the first edition. Although no diagram of the device appears in the book, the assiduously detailed description of its mechanism actually reads like a textual realization of an unseen diagram.

7. Patricia D. Maida, *Mother of Detective Fiction: The Life and Works of Anna Katherine Green* (Bowling Green, OH: Bowling Green State University Popular Press, 1989), p. 50.
8. Catherine Ross Nickerson, 'Anna Katherine Green and the Gilded Age', in *The Web of Iniquity: Early Detective Fiction by American Women* (Durham, NC: Duke University Press, 1998), p. 71.
9. Maida, *Mother of Detective Fiction*, p. 49.
10. Anna Katherine Green, *The Circular Study* (New York: McClure, Phillips and Co., 1900), p. 10.
11. Green, *The Circular Study*, p. 26.
12. Anna Katherine Green, *The Filigree Ball* (Indianapolis: Bobbs-Merrill Company, 1903), pp. 6–7.
13. Green, *The Filigree Ball*, p. 7.
14. Green, *The Filigree Ball*, p. 18.
15. Gaston Bachelard, *The Poetics of Space*, trans. Maria Jolas (Boston: Beacon Press, 1994), pp. 217–18.
16. Green, *The Filigree Ball*, p. 22.
17. W. Bolingbroke Johnson, *The Widening Stain* (New York: Alfred A. Knopf, 1942), p. 218.
18. Marion Boyd, *Murder in the Stacks* (Boston: Lothrop, 1934), p. 10.
19. Auden, 'The Guilty Vicarage', p. 146.
20. See Roland Barthes, *The Pleasure of the Text* (New York: Hill and Wang, 1975).
21. Green, *The Filigree Ball*, pp. 32–3.
22. Green, *The Filigree Ball*, p. 32.
23. Lehman, p. 205.
24. See Chapter 6.
25. S. E. Sweeney, 'Locked Rooms: Detective Fiction, Narrative Theory, and Self-reflexivity', in *The Cunning Craft: Original Essays on Detective Fiction and Contemporary Literary Theory*, ed. Ronald G. Walker and June M. Frazer (Macomb, IL: Western Illinois University Press, 1990), p. 2.
26. Christie, *The Body in the Library*, p. 9.
27. See Chapter 5.
28. See the exchanges between John Dickson Carr and Raymond Chandler discussed in Chapter 5.
29. Green, *The Filigree Ball*, p. 159.
30. Green, *The Filigree Ball*, p. 174.
31. Green, *The Filigree Ball*, p. 320.

32. Green, *The Filigree Ball*, p. 7.
33. Sir Frank Kermode, 'Novel and Narrative', in *The Poetics of Murder*, ed. Glen W. Most and William W. Stowe (New York: Harcourt, 1983), p. 179.
34. Porter, *The Pursuit of Crime*, p. 99.
35. Green, *The Filigree Ball*, p. 395.
36. Green, *The Filigree Ball*, p. 393.
37. Sweeney, 'Locked Rooms', p. 7.
38. Christie, *The Body in the Library*, p. 154.

4   G. K. Chesterton's Enclosure of Orthodoxy in 'The Wrong Shape'

1. Bishop William Warburton, 'To Lord Sandwich', in *The Works of William Warburton*, 10 vols (London: Cadell, 1807) vol. 1, p. 372.
2. Ellery Queen, *Queen's Quorum: A History of the Detective-Crime Short Story as Revealed by the 106 Most Important Books Published in this Field since 1845* (Boston: Little, Brown, 1951). There are 12 stories in *The Innocence of Father Brown*; they are, in sequential order: 'The Blue Cross', 'The Secret Garden', 'The Queer Feet', 'The Flying Stars', 'The Invisible Man', 'The Honour of Israel Gow', 'The Wrong Shape', 'The Sins of Prince Saradine', 'The Hammer of God', 'The Eye of Apollo', 'The Sign of the Broken Sword' and 'The Three Tools of Death'.
3. *G. K.'s Weekly* was a British publication founded in 1925 (pilot edition late 1924) by G. K. Chesterton, continuing until his death in 1936. It contained much of his later journalism, and extracts from it were published as *The Outline of Sanity*.
4. G. K. Chesterton, 'How to Write a Detective Story', *The Chesterton Review* 10.2 (1984), 112.
5. Chesterton, 'How to Write a Detective Story', p. 113.
6. Kennedy, *Poe, Death and the Life of Writing*, p. 119.
7. Hans Robert Jauss, 'Theory of Genres and Medieval Literature', in *Modern Genre Theory*, ed. David Duff (Harlow: Longman, 2000), p. 137.
8. Bernard De Voto, 'Easy Chair', *Harper's Magazine* (December 1944), 37.
9. Marty Roth, *Fair and Foul Play: Reading Genre in Classic Detective Fiction* (Athens: University of Georgia Press, 1995), p. 5.
10. Roth, p. 10.
11. Frank Kermode, *The Genesis of Secrecy: On the Interpretation of Narrative* (Cambridge, MA: Harvard University Press, 1979), p. 23.
12. Kermode, *The Genesis of Secrecy*, p. 24.
13. William David Spencer, *Mysterium and Mystery: The Clerical Crime Novel* (Carbondale: Southern Illinois University Press, 1992), p. 304.
14. Jacques Derrida, *The Gift of Death*, trans. David Wills (Chicago: University of Chicago Press, 1996), p. 6.
15. Dean DeFino,'Lead Birds and Falling Birds', *Journal of Modern Literature* 27.4 (2005), 74.
16. For a concise and informative account of the Oxford Movement and Newman's involvement in particular, see: C. Brad Faught, *The Oxford Movement: A Thematic History of the Tractarians and Their Times* (Philadelphia: Pennsylvania State University Press, 2003).

17. Jonathan Hill, *The History of Christian Thought* (Oxford: Lion Publishing, 2003), p. 249.
18. For a discussion on Newman and *Tract 90* see John R. Connolly, *John Henry Newman: A View of Catholic Faith for the New Millennium* (Lanham, MD: Rowman and Littlefield, 2005), and Frank M. Turner, *Apologia Pro Vita Sua & Six Sermons* (New Haven, CT: Yale University Press, 2008).
19. For details of Chesterton's life see Maisie Ward, *Gilbert Keith Chesterton* (New York: Sheed and Ward, 1943), and Alzina Stone Dale, *The Outline of Sanity: A Life of G. K. Chesterton* (Grand Rapids, MI: Eerdmans Publishing, 1982).
20. See Adam Schwartz, 'Swords of Honor: The Revival of Orthodox Christianity in Twentieth-Century Britain', *Logos: A Journal of Catholic Thought and Culture* 4.1 (Winter 2001), 11–33 (p. 13).
21. G. K. Chesterton, 'Heretics, Orthodoxy, the Blatchford Controversies', in *The Collected Works of G. K. Chesterton*, ed. David Dooley et al., 35 vols (San Francisco: Ignatius Press, 1986), vol. I, pp. 332.
22. Chesterton, 'The Thing', *The Collected Works of G. K. Chesterton*, vol. III, pp. 265 and 299.
23. Schwartz, 'Swords of Honor', p. 15.
24. Schwartz, 'Swords of Honor', p. 17.
25. G. K. Chesterton, 'The Blue Cross', in *The Complete Father Brown* (Harmondsworth: Penguin, 1981), p. 20.
26. David Paul Deavel, 'An Odd Couple? A First Glance at Chesterton and Newman', *Logos: A Journal of Catholic Thought and Culture* 10.1 (2007), 116–35. See also Sheridan Gilley, 'Newman and Chesterton', *Chesterton Review* 32.1–2 (2006), 41–55.
27. Deavel, 'An Odd Couple?', p. 128.
28. Deavel, 'An Odd Couple?', p. 130.
29. G. K. Chesterton, 'A Defence of Detective Stories', in *The Art of the Mystery Story*, ed. Howard Haycraft (New York: Grosset and Dunlap, 1946), pp. 5–6. This essay was originally published in G. K. Chesterton, *The Defendant* (London: R. B. Johnson, 1902).
30. Ian Ker, *The Catholic Revival in English Literature, 1845–1961: Newman, Hopkins, Belloc, Chesterton, Greene, Waugh* (South Bend, IN: University of Notre Dame Press, 2003).
31. Ker, *The Catholic Revival in English Literature*, p. 101.
32. G. K. Chesterton, 'Charles Dickens', in *The Collected Works of G. K. Chesterton*, vol. XV (1989), pp. 29–210.
33. Chesterton, 'Charles Dickens', pp. 66–7.
34. Chesterton, 'Charles Dickens', p. 46.
35. Chesterton, 'The Secret of Flambeau', in *The Complete Father Brown* (Harmondsworth: Penguin, 1981), p. 588.
36. James V. Schall, 'Chesterton: The Real "Heretic": The Outstanding Eccentricity of the Peculiar Sect Called Roman Catholics', *Logos: A Journal of Catholic Thought and Culture* 9.2 (Spring 2006), 72–86 (p. 78).
37. Chesterton, 'The Wrong Shape', in *The Complete Father Brown*, p. 90.
38. This solution to the mystery of how Quinton was murdered was first used in Israel Zangwill's *The Big Bow Mystery* (1892). See also the discussion on 'Ibn-Hakam Al-Bokhari, Murdered in his Labyrinth' in Chapter 6.

39. Chesterton, 'Heretics' in 'Heretics, Orthodoxy, The Blatchford Controversies', p. 337.
40. Chesterton, 'The Wrong Shape', p. 90.
41. Chesterton, 'The Wrong Shape', p. 90.
42. Chesterton, 'The Wrong Shape', p. 92.
43. Chesterton, 'The Wrong Shape', p. 93.
44. Chesterton, 'The Wrong Shape', p. 92.
45. Chesterton, 'The Sins of Prince Saradine', in *The Complete Father Brown*, p. 107.
46. Chesterton, 'The Wrong Shape', p. 99.
47. Chesterton, 'The Wrong Shape', p. 97.
48. Chesterton, 'The Blue Cross', p. 23.
49. Kenneth and Helen Ballhatchet, 'Asia', in *The Oxford History of Christianity*, ed. John McManners (Oxford: Oxford University Press, 1990), p. 518.
50. Chesterton, 'The Wrong Shape', p. 99.
51. Chesterton, 'The Wrong Shape', p. 90.
52. Christopher Routledge, 'The Chevalier and the Priest: Deductive Method in Poe, Chesterton and Borges', *Clues* 22.1 (2001), 1–2.
53. Chesterton, 'The Honour of Israel Gow', in *The Complete Father Brown*, p. 78.
54. Robert Gillespie, 'Detections: Borges and Father Brown', *Novel: A Forum on Action* 7 (1974), 226–7.
55. Donald A. Yates, 'Melville Davisson Post', in *The Oxford Companion to Crime and Mystery Writing*, ed. Rosemary Herbert (New York: Oxford University Press, 1999), p. 349. Donald A. Yates, 'An Essay on Locked Rooms', in *The Mystery Writer's Art*, ed. Francis M. Nevins (Bowling Green, OH: Bowling Green University Popular Press, 1970), pp. 272–84 is one the earliest scholarly essays to examine the locked room mystery as a separate form.
56. Post obtained a law degree at the University of West Virginia and practised there for a dozen years. He emerged as a major figure in the state's Democratic Party politics and was instrumental in John William Davis's failed campaign for the presidency in 1924. His books were much admired by Theodore Roosevelt.
57. Charles A. Norton, *Melville Davisson Post: Man of Many Mysteries* (Bowling Green, OH: Bowling Green University Popular Press, 1973), p. 9.
58. Melville Davisson Post, 'Dedication', in *Uncle Abner: The Doomdorf Mystery* (Mattituck, NY: Amereon House, 1986).
59. Francis Nevins, 'From Darwinian to Biblical Lawyering: The Stories of Melville Davisson Post', *Legal Studies Forum* 18.2 (1994), 176–212 (p. 194).
60. Melville Davisson Post, 'The Angel of the Lord', in *Uncle Abner: The Doomdorf Mystery* (Mattituck, NY: Amereon House, 1946), p. 41.
61. Otto Penzler, 'Collecting Mystery Fiction', *Armchair Detective* 18.2 9 (1985), 168.
62. Post, 'The Doomdorf Mystery', in *Uncle Abner: The Doomdorf Mystery*, p. 14.
63. Post, 'The Doomdorf Mystery', p. 18.
64. Melville Davisson Post, 'The Grazier', in *The Man of Last Resort* (New York: G. P. Putnam's Sons, 1897), p. 252–3.
65. Chesterton, 'Heretics', p. 39.
66. Chesterton, 'The Wrong Shape', p. 99.

67. Chesterton, 'The Wrong Shape', p. 103.
68. Chesterton, 'The Wrong Shape', p. 102.
69. Chesterton, 'Heretics', p. 39.
70. Chesterton, 'Heretics', p. 39.

5   The Hollow Text: Illusion as Theme in John Dickson Carr's *The Hollow Man*

1. Cushing Strout, 'Theatrical Magic and the Novel', *Sewanee Review* 111.1 (2003), 175.
2. Edward D. Hoch, 'Introduction', in *All But Impossible: An Anthology of Locked Room & Impossible Crime Stories*, ed. Edward D. Hoch (London: Robert Hale, 1981), p. viii.
3. In all, Carr wrote 31 novels in the 1930s. As John Dickson Carr: *It Walks by Night* (1930), *The Lost Gallows* (1931), *Castle Skull* (1931), *The Corpse in the Waxworks* (1932), *Poison in Jest* (1932), *Hag's Nook* (1933), *The Mad Hatter Mystery* (1933), *The Eight of Swords* (1934), *The Blind Barber* (1934), *Death-Watch* (1935), *The Hollow Man* (1935), *The Arabian Nights Murder* (1936), *The Murder of Sir Edmund Godfrey* (1936), *The Burning Court* (1937), *The Four False Weapons* (1937), *To Wake the Dead* (1937), *The Crooked Hinge* (1938), *The Problem of the Green Capsule* (1939), *The Problem of the Wire Cage* (1939). Under the pseudonym 'Carr Dickson': *The Bowstring Murders* (1933). Under the pseudonym 'Carter Dickson': *The Plague Court Murders* (1934), *The White Priory Murders* (1934), *The Red Widow Murders* (1935), *The Unicorn Murders* (1935), *The Punch and Judy Murders* (1937), *The Peacock Feather Murders* (1937), *The Third Bullet* (1937), *The Judas Window* (1938), *Death in Five Boxes* (1938), *Fatal Descent* (1939), *The Reader is Warned* (1939).

   John Dickson Carr (1906–77), the son of a prominent lawyer and Democratic Congressman, was born into a well-to-do Pennsylvanian family, although he resisted the importunities of his father to follow him into the law. Carr first became interested in the world of letters by reading and memorizing Shakespeare while watching his father in debate at the House of Congress. His scholarship, however, was always rather inconsistent and, after a brief spell at Harvard, he entered the more liberal atmosphere of Haverford College, where he began writing both fictional prose and poetry. Carr married an Englishwoman in 1932 and spent much of the pre-war period in his adopted country. For a more comprehensive biographical account see Douglas G. Greene's *John Dickson Carr: The Man Who Explained Miracles* (New York: Otto Penzler, 1995). Carr produced a considerable body of non-fiction including essays and articles, all of which have been documented by Douglas Greene. Dennis Porter, in *The Pursuit of Crime: Art and Ideology in Detective Fiction* (New Haven: Yale University Press, 1981), has described him as 'The best known biographer of Sir Arthur Conan Doyle', a work which Carr completed in 1949.
4. Michael Dirda, 'John Dickson Carr', in *Crime and Mystery Writers*, ed. Robin Winks (New York: Scrribners, 1998), p. 113.

5. S. T. Joshi, *John Dickson Carr: A Critical Study* (Bowling Green, OH: Bowling Green State University Popular Press, 1990), p. 33.
6. Kingsley Amis, 'The Art of the Impossible: *The Door to Doom*, by John Dickson Carr', *The Times Literary Supplement* (6 June 1981), p. 8.
7. LeRoy Lad Panek, *An Introduction to the Detective Story* (Bowling Green, OH: Bowling Green State University Popular Press, 1987), pp. 130–1.
8. John Dickson Carr, *The Hollow Man* (London: Hamish Hamilton, 1935), originally published in America as John Dickson Carr, *The Three Coffins* (New York: Harper and Brothers, 1935).
9. The full list of judges comprised Robert Adey, Jack Adrian, Jacques Barzun, Jon l. Breen, Robert E. Briney, Jan Broberg, Frederick Dannay (Ellery Queen), Douglas G. Greene, Howard Haycraft, Edward D. Hoch, Marvin Lachman, Richard Levinson, William Link, Francis M. Nevins, Jr., Otto Penzler, Bill Pronzini, Julian Symons and Donald A. Yates. Hoch's description of the competition can be found in Edward D. Hoch, 'Introduction', in *All But Impossible*, ed. Edward D. Hoch (Bury St Edmunds, Suffolk: St Edmundsberry Press, 1981), pp. viii–x.
10. John Dickson Carr, 'The Grandest Game in the World', in *The Door to Doom* (New York: Harper and Row, 1980), pp. 308–25.
11. Carr, 'The Grandest Game in the World', p. 310.
12. Linda Semple and Rosalind Coward, 'Introduction', in *London Particular* (London: Pandora, 1988), p. ii. See also Julian Symons, *Bloody Murder: From the Detective Story to the Crime Novel: A History* (Harmondsworth: Penguin, 1974), p. 149.
13. David Glover, 'The Writers Who Knew Too Much: Populism and Paradox in Detective Fiction's Golden Age', in *The Art of Detective Fiction*, ed. Warren Chernaik, Martin Smales and Robert Vilain (London: MacMillan, 2000), p. 45.
14. George N. Dove, *The Reader and the Detective Story* (Bowling Green, OH: Bowling Green State University Popular Press, 1997), p. 19.
15. S. S. Van Dine, 'Twenty Rules for Writing Detective Stories', *American Magazine* 14 (September 1928), pp. 26–30; repr. in S. S. Van Dine, 'Twenty Rules for Writing Detective Stories', in *The Art of the Mystery Story*, ed. Howard Haycraft (New York: Simon and Schuster, 1946), pp. 189–93. S. S. Van Dine is the pseudonym of Willard Huntington Wright who was originally an important literary editor and art critic.
16. Ronald Knox, 'Decalogue', in *Murder For Pleasure*, ed. Howard Haycraft (D. Appleton-Century: New York, 1941), p. 256.
17. Van Dine, 'Twenty Rules', p. 26.
18. Van Dine, 'Twenty Rules', p. 30.
19. The full ritual can be found in 'The Detection Club Oath', in *The Art of the Mystery Story*, ed. Howard Haycraft (New York: Simon and Schuster, 1946) pp. 197–9.
20. Van Dine, 'Twenty Rules', p. 26.
21. Carolyn Wells, *The Technique of the Mystery Story* (Springfield, MA: The Home Correspondence School, 1913), p. 317.
22. Wells, p. 291.
23. Carr, *The Hollow Man*, pp. 186–7.
24. Sweeney, 'Locked Rooms', p. 2.

25. Sweeney, 'Locked Rooms', p. 3.
26. Porter, *The Pursuit of Crime*, p. 29.
27. Kathleen Gregory Klein and Joseph Keller, 'Deductive Detective Fiction: The Self-Destructive Genre', *Genre* 19 (1986), 156.
28. Peter Brooks, *Reading for the Plot: Design and Intention in Narrative* (Cambridge, MA: Harvard University Press, 1992) p. 25.
29. Tzvetan Todorov, 'The Typology of Detective Fiction', in *The Poetics of Prose*, trans. Richard Howard (Ithaca, NY: Cornell University Press, 1977), p. 45.
30. Todorov, 'The Typology of Detective Fiction', p. 45.
31. Lee Horsley, *The 'Noir' Thriller* (Basingstoke: Palgrave, 2001), p. 1.
32. Raymond Chandler, 'The Simple Art of Murder', *Atlantic Monthly* (December 1944), pp. 31–46; repr. in 'The Simple Art of Murder', in *The Art of the Mystery Story*, ed. Howard Haycraft (New York: Simon and Schuster, 1946), p. 222.
33. Chandler, 'The Simple Art of Murder', p. 234.
34. Chandler, 'The Simple Art of Murder', p. 236.
35. John Dickson Carr, 'As We See It', *Uniontown Daily News Standard* (4 May 1922), p. 8.
36. Douglas G. Greene, *John Dickson Carr: The Man Who Explained Miracles* (New York: Otto Penzler, 1995), p. 167.
37. John Dickson Carr, *The Burning Court* (London: Hamish Hamilton, 1937).
38. Greene, *John Dickson Carr*, p. 107.
39. Ellery Queen was the joint pseudonym of Frederic Dannay (Daniel Nathan, 1905–82) and Manfred B. Lee (Manford Lepofsky, 1905–71), a team of American detective writers, magazine editors, anthologists, bibliographers and chroniclers of detective fiction. Both were friends of Carr.
40. Greene, *John Dickson Carr*, p. 108.
41. Marjorie Nicolson, 'The Professor and the Detective', in *The Art of the Mystery Story*, ed. Howard Haycraft (New York: Simon and Schuster, 1946), pp. 113–14.
42. Nicolson, 'The Professor and the Detective', pp. 117–18.
43. David I. Grossvogel, *Mystery and Its Fictions: From Oedipus to Agatha Christie* (Baltimore, MA: The Johns Hopkins University Press, 1979), p. 40.
44. David Lehman, *The Perfect Murder* (New York: The Free Press, 1989), p. 102.
45. Ross Macdonald, 'The Writer as Detective Hero', in *The Capra Chapbook Anthology*, ed. Noel Young (Santa Barbara, CA: Capra Press, 1973), p. 80.
46. Lehman, p. 103.
47. Roger Caillois, 'The Detective Novel as Game', trans. William W. Stowe, in *The Poetics of Murder*, ed. Glen W. Most and William W. Stowe (San Diego, CA: Harcourt Brace Jovanovich, 1983), p. 3.
48. Christianna Brand, *Death of Jezebel* (New York: Cornwall Press, 1948).
49. Dirda, 'John Dickson Carr', p. 117.
50. Edmund Miller, 'Stanislav Lem and John Dickson Carr: Critics of the Scientific World-View', *Armchair Detective* 14.4 (1981), 342.
51. Marty Roth, *Foul and Fair Play* (Athens, Georgia: University of Georgia Press), p. 36.
52. Lehman, *The Perfect Murder*, pp. 71–81.
53. Greene, *John Dickson Carr*, p. 21.

54. John Dickson Carr, *It Walks By Night* (Grosset & Dunlap: New York, 1930), p. 15.

55. Carr, *It Walks By Night*, p. 137.

56. Strout, p. 169.

57. Robert E. Briney, 'The Art of the Magician', in *The Cooked Hinge* (San Diego: University Extension, University of California, 1976), p. vii.

58. Clayton Rawson, *Death from a Top Hat* (London: Collins, 1938) and Clayton Rawson, *The Footprints on the Ceiling* (London: Collins, 1939).

59. Carr, *It Walks By Night*, p. 226.

60. A comprehensive account of the performance and history of stage magic can be found in James Randi, *Conjuring: A Definitive History* (New York: St. Martin's Press, 1992).

61. Carr, *The Hollow Man*, p. 13.

62. Carr, *The Hollow Man*, p. 16.

63. Carr, *The Hollow Man*, p. 11.

64. Oxford English Dictionary online: www.oed.com/

65. For an account of Cagliostro's life see: W. R. H. Trowbridge, *Cagliostro: The Splendour and Misery of a Master of Magic* (London: George Allen and Unwin, 1926).

66. OED online: www.oed.com/

67. OED online: www.oed.com/

68. Carr, *The Hollow Man*, p. 21.

69. Carr, *The Hollow Man*, p. 22.

70. Greene, *John Dickson Carr*, p. 67.

71. Carr wrote eight stage plays between 1925 and 1949.

72. Carr wrote 92 radio plays in all between 1939 and 1957, including adaptations of 'The Pit and the Pendulum' in 1943 and 'The Black Cat' in 1944.

73. Harry Houdini, *Miracle Mongers and Their Methods* (New York: Dutton, 1922).

74. John Dickson Carr, *The Plague Court Murders* (New York: Avon Book Company, 1934), p. 7.

75. Werner Wolf, 'Illusion and Breaking Illusion in Twentieth-Century Fiction', in *Aesthetic Illusion: Theoretical and Historical Approaches*, ed. Frederick Burwick and Walter Pape (Berlin: Walter de Gruyer, 1990), p. 288.

76. The revelation of Grimaud's full name, Karoly Grimaud Horváth, before his escape from prison, lays bare the illusion that has been his life. Once again Carr uses nomenclature to reinforce the thematic content. Horváth is a name that has special resonance in 1930s literature: Ödön von Horváth, author of *Tales from the Vienna Woods*, was a well-known Hungarian playwright of his day, who, as the son of a diplomat, found himself living away from his native land in Germany. Horváth, a fervent anti-Nazi and defender of national integrity, especially in respect of his homeland, led a wandering existence in Europe in the 1930s before dying in 1938. The Carr version is a burlesque of the actual Horváth. In this context the portrayal of Horváth as a man who would leave his brother for dead in order to save his own life is a travesty of the real-life hero of Hungarian nationalism.

77. Joshi, *John Dickson Carr: A Critical Study*, p. 99.

78. John Dickson Carr, *The Eight of Swords* (New York: Harper and Brothers, 1934), p. 215.
79. Carr, *The Eight of Swords*, p. 216.
80. John Dickson Carr, *To Wake the Dead* (London: Hamish Hamilton, 1937), p. 231.
81. John Dickson Carr, *The Lost Gallows* (New York: Harper and Brothers, 1934), pp. 121–2.
82. Carr, *The Hollow Man*, p. 188.
83. Carr, *The Hollow Man*, p. 188.
84. Carr, *The Hollow Man*, p. 153.
85. Champigny, p. 59.
86. Jean-Pierre Dupuy, 'Self-Reference in Literature', *Poetics* 18 (1989), pp. 491–515.
87. Poe, 'The Murders in the Rue Morgue', pp. 337, 338.
88. Poe, 'The Murders in the Rue Morgue', pp. 337, 338.
89. Anthony Boucher, *Nine Times Nine* (New York: Duell, 1940), p. 163.
90. Carr, *The Hollow Man*, p. 227.
91. Roger Herzel, 'John Dickson Carr', in *Minor American Novelists* (Carbondale and Edwardsville: Southern Illinois University Press, 1970), p. 70.
92. Carr, *The Hollow Man*, p. 13.
93. Dirda, 'John Dickson Carr', p. 113.
94. Brooks, *Reading for the Plot*, p. 26.

6 Jorge Luis Borges and the Labyrinth of Detection

1. John Milton, *Paradise Lost*, ed. Stephen Orgel and Jonathan Goldberg (Oxford: Oxford University Press, 2004), vol. II, p. 561.
2. *Ellery Queen's Mystery Magazine*, vol. 1, Fall 1941.
3. Howard Haycraft, *Murder for Pleasure: The Life and Times of the Detective Story* (New York: D. Appleton-Century, 1941).
4. Maurice J. Bennett, 'The Detective Fiction of Poe and Borges', *Comparative Literature* 35 (1983), 262–75 (p. 263).
5. Elana Gomel, 'Mystery, Apocalypse, and Utopia: The Case of the Ontological Detective Story', *Science Fiction Studies* 22.3 (1995), 343–56.
6. Jorge Luis Borges, 'The Detective Story', *The Total Library: Non-Fiction 1922–1986*, ed. Eliot Weinberger (Harmondsworth: Penguin, 1999), p. 499.
7. John T. Irwin, 'A Clew to a Clue: Locked Rooms and Labyrinths', *Raritan* 10.4 (1991), 40.
8. Borges, 'The Detective Story', p. 499.
9. Merivale, 'Gumshoe Gothics', p. 107.
10. Haycraft, *Murder for Pleasure*, p. 76.
11. J. Gerald Kennedy, *Poe, Death and the Life of Writing* (New Haven: Yale University Press, 1987), p. 119.
12. William V. Spanos, 'The Detective and the Boundary: Some Notes on the Postmodern Literary Imagination', *Boundary* 2.1, 1 (1972), 154.
13. Porter, pp. 245–6.
14. Porter, p. 246.

15. Tim Conley, 'Borges versus Proust: Towards a Combative Literature', *Comparative Literature* 55 (2003), 42–56 (p. 53).
16. Borges, 'The Detective Story', p. 499.
17. Irwin, 'A Clew to a Clue', p. 45.
18. Jorge Luis Borges, 'Death and the Compass', in *Collected Fictions*, trans. Andrew Hurley (Harmondsworth: Penguin, 1998), p. 146.
19. Lawrence R. Schehr, 'Unreading Borges's Labyrinth', *Studies in Twentieth Century Literature* 3 (1986), 178.
20. Schehr, 'Unreading Borges's Labyrinth', p. 178.
21. John Fraser, 'Jorge Luis Borges, Alive in His Labyrinth', *Criticism* 31 (1989), 179.
22. Fraser, 'Jorge Luis Borges, Alive in His Labyrinth', p. 184.
23. Borges, 'The Garden of Forking Paths', in *Collected Fictions*, p. 145.
24. Fraser, 'Jorge Luis Borges, Alive in His Labyrinth', p. 190.
25. Borges, 'The Garden of Forking Paths', p. 124.
26. Borges, 'The Garden of Forking Paths', p. 124.
27. Borges, 'The Garden of Forking Paths', p. 125.
28. Borges, 'The Library of Babel', in *Collected Fictions*, p. 112.
29. Borges, 'The Garden of Forking Paths', p. 127.
30. Borges, 'The Garden of Forking Paths', p. 125.
31. Borges, 'The Garden of Forking Paths', p. 127.
32. David Lehman, *The Perfect Murder* (New York: The Free Press, 1989), p. 206.
33. Umberto Eco, *The Name of the Rose* (London: Picador, 1984), p. 492.
34. Julia Kushigian, 'The Detective Story Genre in Poe and Borges', *Latin American Literary Review* 11.22 (1983), 34.
35. Conan Doyle, 'The Speckled Band', in *The Complete Sherlock Holmes Short Stories*, p. 173.
36. Borges, 'Death and the Compass', p. 147.
37. Borges, 'Death and the Compass', pp. 154–5.
38. Borges, 'Death and the Compass', p. 156.
39. Borges, 'Death and the Compass', p. 156.
40. David A. Boruchoff, 'In Pursuit of the Detective Genre: "La Muerte y la Brújula" of J. L. Borges', *Inti: Revista de Literatura Hispanica* 21 (1985), 12–23 (p. 15).
41. Lehman, p. 204.
42. Borges, 'Death and the Compass', p. 153.
43. Borges, 'Death and the Compass', p. 155.
44. Friedrich Dürrenmatt, *The Pledge*, trans. Richard and Clara Winston (Harmondsworth: Penguin, 1964), p. 12.
45. See Lehman, *The Perfect Murder*, p. 204.
46. Conan Doyle, 'The Naval Treaty', *The Complete Sherlock Holmes Short Stories*, Stories, p. 534.
47. Borges, 'Ibn-H'akam Al-Bokhari, Murdered in his Labyrinth', in *Collected Fictions*, p. 256.
48. Compare this solution with that in 'The Wrong Shape' in Chapter 4.
49. *The Perfect Crime* is the sub-title of the book.
50. Jorge Luis Borges, 'Ellery Queen, *The Door Between*', in *Selected Non-Fictions* (New York: Penguin, 1999), p. 181.
51. Borges, 'Ellery Queen, *The Door Between*', p. 181.

52. Robbe-Grillet's *The Erasers* (1953) also recalls *The Big Bow Mystery* by featuring the central character, Wallas, as both detective and murderer. The novel charts the mental processes of a man who is lost in his own web of lies and the crime itself is almost incidental to the understanding of what is actually taking place. In this form of the genre, the story of the crime both encloses the story of the mental processes involved in investigation and is, in turn, enclosed by it, as the self-investigation outgrows the progress of the conventional narrative.
53. Irwin, 'A Clew to a Clue', p. 46.
54. Borges, 'Ibn-H'akam Al-Bokhari, Murdered in his Labyrinth', p. 255.
55. Poe, 'The Purloined Letter', pp. 409–10.
56. Poe, 'The Murders in the Rue Morgue', p. 332.
57. Borges, 'Ibn-H'akam Al-Bokhari, Murdered in his Labyrinth', p. 260.
58. Carr, *The Hollow Man*, p. 188.
59. Borges, 'Ibn-H'akam Al-Bokhari, Murdered in his Labyrinth', p. 259.
60. Borges, 'Ibn-H'akam Al-Bokhari, Murdered in his Labyrinth', p. 260.
61. Borges, 'Ibn-H'akam Al-Bokhari, Murdered in his Labyrinth', p. 259.
62. Borges, 'Ibn-H'akam Al-Bokhari, Murdered in his Labyrinth', p. 256.
63. Borges, 'Ibn-H'akam Al-Bokhari, Murdered in his Labyrinth', p. 262.
64. Roland Barthes, *A Lover's Discourse: Fragments*, trans. Richard Howard (New York: Farrar, 1978), p. 46.

7   The Question is the Writer Himself: Paul Auster's Locked Room in *City of Glass*

1. See Chapter 5, pp. 104–7.
2. Nabokov: *The Real Life of Sebastian Knight* (1941), *Lolita* (1955) and *Pale Fire* (1963); Robbe-Grillet: *The Erasers* (1953) and *The Voyeur* (1958); Friedrich Dürrenmatt: *The Judge and His Hangman* (1950), *Suspicion* (1951) and *The Pledge* (1959); Pynchon: *The Crying of Lot 49* (1966).
3. William G. Little, 'Nothing to Go On: Paul Auster's "City of Glass"', *Contemporary Literature* 34.2 (Summer 1993), 219.
4. Larry McCaffery and Sinda Gregory, 'An Interview with Paul Auster', *Contemporary Literature* 33.1 (Spring 1992), 2.
5. Paul Auster, *City of Glass*, in *The New York Trilogy* (London: Faber and Faber, 1987), p. 8.
6. Auster, *City of Glass*, p. 8.
7. Auster, *City of Glass*, p. 3.
8. Auster, *City of Glass*, p. 8.
9. Alison Russell, 'Deconstructing *The New York Trilogy*: Paul Auster's Anti-Detective Fiction', *Critique* 13.2 (1990), 73.
10. Russell, 'Deconstructing *The New York Trilogy*', p. 80.
11. Auster, *City of Glass*, pp. 8–9.
12. Auster, *City of Glass*, p. 9.
13. Auster, *City of Glass*, p. 9.
14. Poe, 'William Wilson', in *Tales, Poems and Essays*, p. 22.
15. Poe, 'William Wilson', p. 29.

16. Stephen Fredman, ' "How to Get Out of the Room That Is the Book?" Paul Auster and the Consequences of Confinement', *Postmodern Culture* 6.3 (May 1996), I–VI (I. 1).
17. Fredman, 'How to Get Out of the Room That Is the Book?', I. 1.
18. Fredman, 'How to Get Out of the Room That Is the Book?', II. 13.
19. Fredman, 'How to Get Out of the Room That Is the Book?', II. 10.
20. Auster, *City of Glass*, p. 6.
21. Jeffrey T. Nealon, 'Work of the Detective, Work of the Writer: Paul Auster's "City of Glass" ', in *Detecting Texts*, ed. Patricia Merivale and Susan Elizabeth Sweeney (Philadelphia: University of Pennsylvania Press, 1999), p. 119.
22. Auster, *City of Glass*, p. 67.
23. Auster, *City of Glass*, p. 69.
24. Borges, 'The Library of Babel', in *Collected Fictions*, p. 113.
25. Borges, 'The Library of Babel', p. 114.
26. Auster, *City of Glass*, p. 77.
27. Auster, *City of Glass*, p. 70.
28. Edgar Allan Poe, *The Narrative of Arthur Gordon Pym of Nantucket* (London: Penguin, 1999), p. 202.
29. Poe, *The Narrative of Arthur Gordon Pym of Nantucket*, p. 3.
30. Auster, *City of Glass*, p. 117.
31. Auster, *City of Glass*, p. 104.
32. Auster, *City of Glass*, p. 97.
33. Madeleine Sorapure, 'The Detective and the Author: City of Glass, in *Beyond the Red Notebook*, ed. Dennis Barone (Philadelphia: University of Pennsylvania Press), pp. 84–5.
34. Auster, *City of Glass*, p. 104.
35. Auster, *City of Glass*, p. 132.
36. Paul Auster, *The Invention of Solitude* (New York: Sun, 1982), p. 16.
37. Henry David Thoreau, 'Solitude', *Walden: or Life in the Woods* (New York: New American Library, 1960), p. 94.
38. Auster, *Ghosts*, p. 143.
39. Herman Melville, 'Hawthorne and His Mosses', in *The Norton Anthology of American Literature*, ed. Ronald Gottesman and others (New York: Norton, 1979), vol. I, p. 2058.
40. Nathaniel Hawthorne, 'Wakefield', in *Young Goodman Brown and Other Tales* (Oxford: Oxford University Press, 1987), pp. 132–3.
41. Auster, *The Locked Room*, in *The New York Trilogy*, p. 314.
42. Auster, *City of Glass*, p. 126.
43. Auster, *City of Glass*, p. 130.
44. Auster, *City of Glass*, p. 132.
45. Auster, *The Locked Room*, p. 278–9.
46. Auster, *The Locked Room*, p. 294.
47. Auster, *City of Glass*, pp. 3–4.
48. Stephen Bernstein, 'The Question Is the Story Itself', in *Detecting Texts*, ed. Patricia Merivale and Susan Elizabeth Sweeney (Philadelphia: University of Pennsylvania Press, 1999), p. 134.
49. Bernstein, pp. 147–8.
50. Bernstein, p. 147.

8   The Narrative of Enclosure

1. Poe, 'The Murders in the Rue Morgue', p. 345.
2. Conan Doyle, 'The Engineer's Thumb', in *The Complete Sherlock Holmes Short Stories*, p. 216–17.
3. Conan Doyle, 'The Musgrave Ritual', in *The Complete Sherlock Holmes Short Stories*, p. 412.
4. Anna Katherine Green, *The Leavenworth Case* (New York: G. P. Putnam's Sons, 1878), p. 24.
5. W. H. Auden, 'The Guilty Vicarage', in *The Dyer's Hand and Other Essays* (New York: Random House, 1962), pp. 149, 151.
6. Anthony Berkeley, *The Poisoned Chocolates Case* (New York: Doubleday Doran and Company, 1929), p. 159.
7. Lehman, p. 103.
8. Agatha Christie, *4.50 From Paddington* (London: Collins, 1957), p. 60.
9. Poe, 'The Murders in the Rue Morgue', p. 342.
10. Conan Doyle, 'The Adventure of the Speckled Band', in *The Complete Sherlock Holmes Short Stories*, p. 173.
11. Sir Arthur Conan Doyle, *Through the Magic Door* (London: Smith, Elder & Co., 1907), pp. 114–15.
12. Sir Arthur Conan Doyle, *Memories and Adventures* (Boston: Little, Brown), p. 69.
13. Poe, 'The Murders in the Rue Morgue', p. 346.
14. Conan Doyle, *A Study in Scarlet*, in *The Complete Sherlock Holmes Long Stories*, p. 134.
15. Conan Doyle, 'The Speckled Band', p. 199.
16. Conan Doyle, 'The Speckled Band', p. 199.
17. Francis M. Nevins, Jr., 'Foreword' to Donald A. Yates, 'An Essay on Locked Rooms', in *The Mystery Writer's Art*, ed. Francis M. Nevins (Bowling Green, OH: Bowling Green University Popular Press, 1970), p. 272.
18. Peter Thoms, *Detection and Its Designs: Narrative and Power in Nineteenth-Century Detective Fiction* (Athens, GA: Ohio University Press, 1998), p. 3.
19. Lehman, p. 76.
20. Conan Doyle, 'The Speckled Band', p. 178.
21. Conan Doyle, 'The Speckled Band', p. 183.
22. Conan Doyle, 'The Speckled Band', p. 192.
23. Conan Doyle, 'The Red-Headed League', in *The Complete Sherlock Holmes Short Stories* (London: John Murray, 1956), p. 43.
24. Paul Auster, *City of Glass*, in *The New York Trilogy* (London: Faber and Faber, 1987), p. 67.
25. Dennis Porter, *The Pursuit of Crime: Art and Ideology in Detective Fiction* (New Haven: Yale University Press, 1981), p. 25.
26. Agatha Christie, 'Problem at Sea' in *Poirot's Early Cases* (Glasgow: Fontana, 1987), p. 228.
27. Stephen Knight, 'The Golden Age', in *The Cambridge Companion to Crime Fiction* (Cambridge: Cambridge University Press, 2003), p. 90.
28. Poe, 'The Murders in the Rue Morgue', p. 344.
29. Porter, *The Pursuit of Crime*, p. 41.

30. Josef Škvorecký, 'Author's Note', in *The End of Lieutenant Boruvka*, trans. Paul Wilson (New York: W. W. Norton and Company, 1990).
31. Josef Škvorecký, 'Miss Peskova Regrets', in *The End of Lieutenant Boruvka*, p. 58.
32. Josef Škvorecký, 'Ornament in the Grass', in *The End of Lieutenant Boruvka*, p. 122.
33. Josef Škvorecký, 'Pirates', in *The End of Lieutenant Boruvka*, p. 166.

Select Bibliography

Auden, W. H. 'The Guilty Vicarage'. In *The Dyer's Hand and Other Essays*. New York: Random House, 1962.

Auster, Paul. *The Invention of Solitude*. New York: Sun, 1982.

Auster, Paul. *The New York Trilogy*. London: Faber and Faber, 1987.

Bachelard, Gaston. *The Poetics of Space*. Trans. Maria Jolas. Boston: Beacon Press, 1994.

Benstock, Bernard, ed. *Art in Crime Writing: Essays on Detective Fiction*. New York: St Martin's Press, 1983.

Berkeley, Anthony. *The Poisoned Chocolates Case*. New York: Doubleday Doran and Company, 1929.

Bloom, Harold *The Anxiety of Influence*. New York: Oxford University Press, 1997.

Bollas, Christopher. *The Shadow of the Object: Psychoanalysis of the Unthought Known*. London: Free Association Books, 1987.

Borges, Jorge Luis. *Collected Fictions*. Trans. Andrew Hurley. Harmondsworth: Penguin, 1998.

Borges, Jorge Luis. *Selected Non-Fictions*. Ed. Eliot Weinberger. New York: Penguin, 1999.

Boucher, Anthony. *Nine Times Nine*. New York: Duell, 1940.

Bramah, Ernest. 'The Ghost at Massingham Mansions'. In *The Eyes of Max Carrados*. George H. Doran and Company, 1924, pp. 179–208.

Brand, Christianna. *Death of Jezebel*. New York: Cornwall Press, 1948.

Brand, Christianna. *London Particular*. London: Pandora, 1988.

Breen, Jon L. 'Introduction'. In *Synod of Sleuths: Essays on Judeo-Christian Detective Fiction*. Ed. Jon L. Breen and Martin H. Greenberg. Metuchen, NJ: The Scarecrow Press, 1990, pp. v–viii.

Briggs, Julia. *Night Visitors: The Rise and Fall of the English Ghost Story*. London: Faber and Faber, 1977.

Brooks, Peter. *Reading for the Plot: Design and Intention in Narrative*. Cambridge, MA: Harvard University Press, 1992.

Bulwer-Lytton, Sir Edward. *Eugene Aram: A Tale*. Philadelphia: J. Lippincott and Co., 1865.

Bulwer-Lytton, Sir Edward. *Pelham: or Adventures of a Gentleman*. London: G. Routledge and Co., 1855.

Burwick, Frederick. 'Edgar Allan Poe: The Sublime, the Picturesque, the Grotesque, and the Arabesque'. *American Studies* 43.3 (1998), 423–36.

Caillois, Roger. 'The Detective Novel as Game'. In *The Poetics of Murder: Detective Fiction and Literary Theory*. Ed. Glenn W. Most and William W. Stowe. San Diego, CA: Harcourt Brace Jovanich, 1983.

Carr, John Dickson. 'As We See It'. *Uniontown Daily News Standard* (4 May 1922).

Carr, John Dickson. *The Burning Court*. London: Hamish Hamilton, 1937.

Carr, John Dickson. *The Eight of Swords*. New York: Harper and Brothers, 1934.

Carr, John Dickson. 'The Grandest Game in the World'. In *The Door to Doom*. New York: Harper and Row, 1980.

Carr, John Dickson. *The Hollow Man*. Harmondsworth: Penguin, 1987.

Carr, John Dickson. *It Walks By Night*. New York: Grosset & Dunlap, 1930.

Carr, John Dickson. *The Lost Gallows*. New York: Harper and Brothers, 1934.

Carr, John Dickson. *The Plague Court Murders*. New York: Avon Book Company, 1934.

Carr, John Dickson. *To Wake the Dead*. London: Hamish Hamilton, 1937.

Carr, John Dickson. *The White Priory Murders*. New York: William Morrow and Co., 1934.

Carr, John Dickson (under the pseudonym Carter Dickson). *The Judas Window*. New York: Pocket Books Inc., 1943.

Carter, Ian. *Railways and Culture in Britain: The Epitome of Modernity*. Manchester: Manchester University Press, 2001.

Cawelti, John G. *Adventure, Mystery, and Romance: Formula Stories as Art and Popular Culture*. Chicago: University of Chicago Press, 1976.

Champigny, Robert. *What Will Have Happened: A Philosophical and Technical Essay on Mystery Stories*. Bloomington: Indiana University Press, 1977.

Chandler, Raymond. *The Big Sleep*. In *Three Novels*. London: Penguin, 1993, pp. 1–165.

Chandler, Raymond. 'The Simple Art of Murder'. In *Pearls Are a Nuisance*. London: Penguin, 1964.

Chernaik, Warren, Martin Smales and Robert Vilain, eds. *The Art of Detective Fiction*. London: Palgrave Macmillan, 2000.

Chesney, Weatherby. *The Adventures of an Engineer*. London: Bowden, 1898.

Chesterton, G. K. 'Charles Dickens'. In *The Collected Works of G. K. Chesterton*. Ed. David Dooley et al. 35 vols. San Francisco: Ignatius Press, 1989, vol. XV.

Chesterton, G. K. *The Complete Father Brown*. London: Penguin, 1981.

Chesterton, G. K. 'Heretics, Orthodoxy, the Blatchford Controversies'. *The Collected Works of G. K. Chesterton*. Ed. David Dooley et al., 35 vols. San Francisco: Ignatius Press, 1986, vol. I.

Chesterton, G. K. 'How to Write a Detective Story'. *The Chesterton Review* 10.2 (1984).

Christie, Agatha. *4.50 From Paddington*. London: Collins, 1957.

Christie, Agatha. *The Body in the Library*. London: Collins, 1942.

Christie, Agatha. *The Mysterious Affair at Styles*. London: Grafton Books, 1978.

Christie, Agatha. *Poirot's Early Cases*. Glasgow: Fontana, 1987.

Collins, Philip. 'Dickens and Industrialisation'. *Studies in English Literature, 1500–1900* 20.4 (Autumn, 1980), 651–73.

Collins, Wilkie. 'The Ghost and Mrs. Zant'. In *Classic Ghost Stories*. New York: Dover, 1998, pp. 30–59.

Collins, Wilkie. *The Moonstone*. Harmondsworth: Penguin, 1966.

Collins, Wilkie. 'A Terribly Strange Bed'. In *Death Locked In*. New York: Barnes & Noble, 1987.

Cooke, Simon. 'Anxious Travelers: A Contextual Reading of "The Signalman"'. *Dickens Quarterly* 22.2 (2005), 101–9.

Coughlan, David. 'Paul Auster's "City of Glass": The Graphic Novel'. *Modern Fiction Studies* 52.4 (Winter 2006), 832–54.

Culler, Jonathan. *The Pursuit of Signs: Semiotics, Literature, Deconstruction*. Ithaca, NY: Cornell University Press, 1981.

Deavel, David Paul. 'An Odd Couple? A First Glance at Chesterton and Newman'. *Logos: A Journal of Catholic Thought and Culture* 10.1 (2007), 116–35.

DeFino, Dean. 'Lead Birds and Falling Birds'. *Journal of Modern Literature* 27.4 (2005), 73–81.

Derrida, Jacques. *Archive Fever: A Freudian Impression*. Trans. Eric Prenowitz. Chicago: University of Chicago, 1996.

Derrida, Jacques. 'French Freud: Freud and the Scene of Writing'. Trans. Jeffrey Mehlman. *Yale French Studies* 48 (1972), 74–117.

Derrida, Jacques. *The Gift of Death*. Trans. David Wills. Chicago: University of Chicago Press, 1996.

Dexter, Colin. *The Wench Is Dead*. Pan Books: London, 1989.

Dickens, Charles. *Dombey and Son*. London: Chapman and Hall, 1890.

Dickens, Charles. *The Letters of Charles Dickens*. Ed. Walter Dexter. 3 vols. London: Nonesuch Press, 1938.

Dickens, Charles. 'Mugby Junction'. In *Christmas Stories and Others*. London: Chapman and Hall, 1891, pp. 323–64.

Dickens, Charles. 'Need Railway Travellers be Smashed?' *Household Words* (29 November 1851), 217–21.

Dirda, Michael. 'John Dickson Carr'. In *Crime and Mystery Writers*. Ed. Robin Winks. New York: Scribners, 1998, pp. 113–29.

Diskin, Patrick. 'Poe, Le Fanu and the Sealed Room Mystery'. *Notes and Queries* 13 (1966), 337–9.

Dove, George N. *The Reader and the Detective Story*. Bowling Green, OH: Bowling Green State University Popular Press, 1997.

Doyle, Sir Arthur Conan. *The Complete Sherlock Holmes Long Stories*. London: John Murray, 1954.

Doyle, Sir Arthur Conan. *The Complete Sherlock Holmes Short Stories* London: John Murray, 1956.

Doyle, Sir Arthur Conan. *The Conan Doyle Stories*. London: John Murray, 1960.

Dürrenmatt, Friedrich. *The Judge and His Hangman*. In *The Inspector Barlach Mysteries*. Trans. Joel Agee. Chicago: University of Chicago Press, 2006.

Dürrenmatt, Friedrich. *The Pledge*. Trans. Richard and Clara Winston. Harmondsworth: Penguin, 1964.

Dürrenmatt, Friedrich. *Suspicion*. In *The Inspector Barlach Mysteries*. Trans. Joel Agee. Chicago: University of Chicago Press, 2006.

Eco, Umberto. *The Name of the Rose*. London: Picador, 1984.

Edwards, Amelia. 'Four-Fifteen Express'. In *The Phantom Coach; The Collected Ghost Stories*. Ashcroft, British Columbia: Ash Tree Press, 1867, pp. 110–31.

Ellery Queen's Mystery Magazine, vol. 1, Fall 1941.

Forrester, Andrew. 'Arrested on Suspicion'. In *A Treasury of Victorian Detective Stories*. Ed. Everett F. Bleiler. New York: Scribners, 1979, pp. 15–35.

Frank, Lawrence. '"The Murders in the Rue Morgue": Edgar Allan Poe's Evolutionary Reverie'. *Nineteenth-Century Literature* 50.2 (1995), 168–88.

Fraser, John. 'Jorge Luis Borges, Alive in His Labyrinth'. *Criticism* 31 (1989), 179–91.

Fredman, Stephen. '"How to Get Out of the Room That Is the Book?" Paul Auster and the Consequences of Confinement'. *Postmodern Culture* 6.3 (May 1996), 1–6.

Freeman, Michael. *Railways and the Victorian Imagination*. New Haven, CT: Yale University Press, 1999.

Freud, Sigmund. *The Standard Edition of the Complete Psychological Works of Sigmund Freud*. Ed. James Strachey. 24 vols. London: Hogarth Press, 1953–74.

Futrelle, Jacques. 'The Problem of Cell 13'. In *The Thinking Machine*. New York: Scholastic Book Services, 1964, pp. 1–52.

Gillespie, Robert. 'Detections: Borges and Father Brown'. *Novel: A Forum on Action* 7 (1974), 220–30.

Gilley, Sheridan. 'Newman and Chesterton'. *Chesterton Review* 32.1–2 (2006), 41–55.

Godwin, William. *Caleb Williams*. London: Penguin, 1988.

Gohrisch, Jana. 'Familiar Excess? Emotion and the Family in Victorian Literature'. *The Yearbook of Research in English and American Literature* 16 (2000), 163–83.

Golden, Catherine, ed. *Book Illustrated: Text, Image, and Culture, 1770–1930*. New Castle, DE: Oak Knoll Press, 2000.

Goldstein, Jan. *Console and Classify: The French Psychiatric Profession in the Nineteenth Century*. Cambridge: Cambridge University Press, 1987.

Gomel, Elana. 'Mystery, Apocalypse, and Utopia: The Case of the Ontological Detective Story'. *Science Fiction Studies* 22.3 (1995), 343–56.

Gorrara, Claire. 'Cultural Intersections: The American Hard-Boiled Detective Novel and Early French *Roman Noir*'. *Modern Language Review* 98.3 (2003), 590–601.

Goulet, Andrea. 'The Yellow Spot: Ocular Pathology and Empirical Method in Gaston Leroux's Le Mystère de la Chambre Jaune'. *Substance* 34.2 (2005), 27–46.

Green, Anna Katherine. *The Circular Study*. New York: McClure, Phillips and Co., 1900.

Green, Anna Katherine. *The Filigree Ball*. Indianapolis: Bobbs-Merrill Company, 1903.

Green, Anna Katherine. *Initials Only*. New York: A. L. Burt Company, 1911.

Green, Anna Katherine. *The Leavenworth Case*. New York: G. P. Putnam's Sons, 1878.

Greene, Douglas G. *John Dickson Carr: The Man Who Explained Miracles*. New York: Otto Penzler, 1995.

Greene, Douglas G. and Robert C. S. Adey, eds. *Death Locked In: An Anthology of Locked Room Stories*. New York: Barnes and Noble, 1994.

Greenman, David J. 'Dickens's Ultimate Achievements in the Ghost Story: "To Be Taken with a Grain of Salt" and "The Signalman"'. *Dickensian* 85.1 (1989), 40–8.

Groller, Balduin. 'Anonymous Letters'. In *Cosmopolitan Crimes: Foreign Rivals of Sherlock Holmes*. Ed. Hugh Greene. New York: Pantheon Books, 1971, pp. 232–64.

Grossvogel, David I. *Mystery and Its Fictions: From Oedipus to Agatha Christie*. Baltimore, MD: The Johns Hopkins University Press, 1979.

Gutierrz-Mouat, Ricardo. 'Borges and the Center of the Labyrinth'. *Romance Notes* 21(1981), 287–92.

Halter, Paul. *The Night of the Wolf*. trans. Robert Adey and John Pugmire. Rockville, MD: Wildside Press, 2006.

Harrington, Ralph. 'The Railway Accident: Trains, Trauma and Technological Crisis in Nineteenth-Century Britain'. In *Traumatic Pasts: History, Psychiatry, and Trauma in the Modern Age*. Ed. Mark S. Micale and Paul Learner. Cambridge: Cambridge University Press, 2001, pp. 31–56. See also: www.york.ac.uk/inst/irs/irshome/papers/rlyacc.htm (accessed 20 March 2011).

Harrington, Ralph. 'Railway Safety and Railway Slaughter: Railway Accidents, Government and Public in Victorian Britain'. *Journal of Victorian Culture* 8.2 (2003), 187–207.

Hawthorne, Nathaniel. 'Wakefield'. In *Young Goodman Brown and Other Tales*. Oxford: Oxford University Press, 1987, pp. 124–33.

Haycraft, Howard, ed. *The Art of the Mystery Story*. New York: Grosset and Dunlap, 1946.

Haycraft, Howard. *Murder for Pleasure: The Life and Times of the Detective Story*. New York: D. Appleton-Century, 1941.

Hayes, Aden W. and Khachig Tololyan. 'The Cross and The Compass: Patterns of Order in Chesterton and Borges'. *Hispanic Review*. 49.4 (1981), 395–405.

Hendershot, Cyndy. 'The Animal Without: Masculinity and Imperialism in The Island of Doctor Moreau and "The Adventure of the Speckled Band"'. *Nineteenth-Century Studies* 10 (1996), 1–32.

Herbert, Rosemary, ed. *The Oxford Companion to Crime and Mystery Writing*. New York: Oxford University Press, 1999.

Hermann, Judith. *Trauma and Recovery*. New York: Basic Books, 1992.

Herzel, Roger. 'John Dickson Carr'. In *Minor American Novelists*. Carbondale and Edwardsville: Southern Illinois University Press, 1970, pp. 67–80.

Hill, Jonathan. *The History of Christian Thought*. Oxford: Lion Publishing, 2003.

Hoch, Edward D., ed. *All But Impossible: An Anthology of Locked Room & Impossible Crime Stories*. London: Robert Hale, 1981.

Holzapfel, Tamara. 'Crime and Detection in a Defective World: The Detective Fictions of Borges and Dürrenmatt'. *Studies in Twentieth Century Literature* 3.1 (1979), 53–71.

Horsley, Lee. *The 'Noir' Thriller*. Basingstoke: Palgrave Macmillan, 2001.

Houdini, Harry. *Miracle Mongers and Their Methods*. New York: Dutton, 1922.

Hubin, Allen J. 'Melville Davisson Post'. In *The Complete Uncle Abner*. San Diego: University Extension, University of California, 1977, pp. 1–12.

Hubly, Erlene. 'The Formula Challenged: The Novels of P. D. James'. *Modern Fiction Studies* 29.3 (1983), 511–21.

'Injuries'. *The Lancet* (14 September, 1861), 255–6.

Ireland, R. W. '"An Increasing Mass of Heathens in the Bosom of a Christian Land": The Railway and Crime in the Nineteenth-Century'. *Continuity and Change* 12 (1997), 55–78.

Irving, H. B. 'The First Railway Murder'. In *The Railway Murders: Ten Classic True Crime Stories*. Ed. Jonathan Goodman. London: Allison & Busby, 1984, pp. 15–35.

Irwin, John T. 'A Clew to a Clue: Locked Rooms and Labyrinths'. *Raritan* 10.4 (1991), 40–57.

Irwin, John T. *The Mystery to a Solution: Poe, Borges, and the Analytic Detective Story*. Baltimore, MD: The Johns Hopkins University Press, 1994.

Jackson, Stanley W. 'Melancholia and Partial Insanity'. *Journal of the History of the Behavioural Sciences* 19 (1983), 179–80.

Jauss, Hans Robert. 'Theory of Genres and Medieval Literature'. In *Modern Genre Theory*. Ed. David Duff. Harlow: Longman, 2000), pp. 127–47.

Joseph, Gerhard. 'Dickens, Psychoanalysis and Film: A Roundtable'. In *Dickens on Screen*. Ed. John Glavin. Cambridge: Cambridge University Press, 2003, pp. 11–28.

Joshi, S. T. *John Dickson Carr: A Critical Study*. Bowling Green, OH: Bowling Green State University Popular Press, 1990).

Kayman, Martin A. 'The Short Story from Poe to Chesterton'. In *The Cambridge Companion to Crime Fiction*. Ed. Martin Priestman. Cambridge: Cambridge University Press, 2003.

Keller, Thomas. 'Railway Spine Revisited: Traumatic Neurosis or Neurotrauma?' *Journal of the History of Medicine and Allied Sciences* 50 (1995), 507–24.

Kennedy, J. Gerald. *Poe, Death and the Life of Writing*. New Haven, CT: Yale University Press, 1987.

Kenner, Hugh. *Paradox in Chesterton*. New York: Sheed and Ward, 1947.

Kermode, Frank. *The Genesis of Secrecy: On the Interpretation of Narrative*. Cambridge, MA: Harvard University Press, 1979.

Kestner, Joseph A. *The Edwardian Age and the Edwardian Detective*. Aldershot: Ashgate, 2000.

Klein, Kathleen Gregory and Joseph Keller. 'Deductive Detective Fiction: The Self-Destructive Genre'. *Genre* 19 (1986), 155–72.

Knight, Mark. 'Chesterton, Dostoevsky and Freedom'. *English Literature in Transition* 43.1 (2000), 37–50.

Knight, Stephen. *Crime Fiction since 1800: Detection, Death, Diversity*. Basingstoke: Palgrave Macmillan, 2010.

Knight, Stephen. *Form and Ideology in Crime Fiction*. London: Macmillan, 1980.

Kostal, Rande. W. *Law and English Railway Capitalism 1825–1875*. Oxford: Clarendon Press, 1994.

Kushigian, Julia. 'The Detective Story Genre in Poe and Borges'. *Latin American Literary Review* 11 (1983), 27–39.

Le Fanu, Joseph Sheridan. 'The Fortunes of Sir Robert Ardagh'. *Dublin University Magazine* 11 (March 1838).

Le Fanu, Joseph Sheridan. *Ghost Stories and Mysteries*. London: Dover, 1975.

Lehman, David. *The Perfect Murder*. New York: The Free Press, 1989.

Lemay, J. A. Leo. 'The Psychology of "The Murders in the Rue Morgue"'. *American Literature* 54 (1982), 165–88.

Leroux, Gaston. *The Mystery of the Yellow Room*. New York: Charles Scribner's Sons, 1928.

Little, William G. 'Nothing to Go On: Paul Auster's "City of Glass"'. *Contemporary Literature* 34.2 (Summer 1993), 219–39.

Macdonald, Ross. 'The Writer as Detective Hero'. In *The Capra Chapbook Anthology*. Ed. Noel Young. Santa Barbara, CA: Capra Press, 1973, pp. 79–97.

Madoff, Mark S. 'Inside, Outside, and the Gothic Locked-Room Mystery'. In *Gothic Fictions: Prohibition/Transgression*. Ed. Kenneth W. Graham. New York: AMS, 1989, pp. 49–62.

Maida, Patricia D. *The Mother of Detective Fiction: The Life and Works of Anna Katherine Green*. Bowling Green, OH: Bowling Green State University Popular Press, 1989.

Malloy, Jeanne M. 'Apocalyptic Imagery and the Fragmentation of the Psyche: "The Pit and the Pendulum"'. *Nineteenth-Century Literature* 46.1 (June 1991), 82–95.

Managan, J. C. 'The Thirty Flasks'. *Dublin University Magazine* 12 (October 1838), 408–24.

Matchett, Willoughby. 'Thomas Griffiths Wainewright, A Notable Dickens Model'. *Dickensian* 2 (1906), 33–6.

Matus, Jill L. 'Trauma, Memory, and Railway Disaster: The Dickensian Connection'. *Victorian Studies* 43.3 (2001), 413–26.

McCaffery, Larry, and Sinda Gregory. 'An Interview with Paul Auster'. *Contemporary Literature* 33.1 (Spring 1992), 1–23.

Mengel, Ewald. 'The Structure and Meaning of Dickens's "The Signalman"'. *Studies in Short Fiction* 20.4 (1983).

Merivale, Patricia, and Susan Elizabeth Sweeney, eds. *Detecting Texts: The Metaphysical Detective Story from Poe to Modernism*. Philadelphia: University of Pennsylvania Press, 1999.

Miller, Edmund. 'Stanislav Lem and John Dickson Carr: Critics of the Scientific World-View'. *Armchair Detective* 14.4 (1981), 341–3.

Miller, J. Hillis. 'Ariadne's Thread: Repetition and the Narrative Line'. *Critical Inquiry* 3 (1976), 57–77.

Miller, J. Hillis. 'The Figure in the Carpet'. *Poetics Today* 1.3 (Spring 1980), 107–18.

Miller, Owen. 'Preface'. In *Identity of the Literary Text*. Ed. Mario J. Valdés and Owen Miller. Toronto: University of Toronto Press, 1985, pp. vii–xxi.

Most, Glenn W., and William W. Stowe eds. *The Poetics of Murder*. San Diego, CA: Harcourt Brace Jovanovich, 1983.

Nealon, Jeffrey T. 'Work of the Detective, Work of the Writer: Paul Auster's "City of Glass"'. *Modern Fiction Studies* 42.1 (Spring 1996), 91–110.

Norton, Charles A. *Melville Davisson Post: Man of Many Mysteries*. Bowling Green, OH: Bowling Green University Popular Press, 1973.

Orczy, Baroness. 'The Mysterious Death on the Underground Railway'. In *The Old Man in the Corner*. Thirsk: House of Stratus, 2003, pp. 21–40.

Ostrom, John Ward, ed. *The Letters of Edgar Allan Poe*. 2 vols. New York: Gordian Press, 1966.

Panek, LeRoy Lad. *An Introduction to the Detective Story*. Bowling Green, OH: Bowling Green State University Popular Press, 1987.

Panek, LeRoy Lad. *Watteau's Shepherds: The Detective Novel in Britain, 1914–40*. Bowling Green: Bowling Green University Popular Press, 1979.

Penzler, Otto. 'Collecting Mystery Fiction'. *Armchair Detective* 18.2 9 (1985), 152–9.

Pettitt, Clare. '"The Spirit of Craft and Money-Making": The Indignities of Literature in the 1850s'. In *Patent Inventions: Intellectual Property and the Victorian Novel*. Oxford: Oxford University Press, 2003, pp. 149–203.

Poe, Edgar Allan. *Collected Works of Edgar Allan Poe*. Ed. Thomas Ollive Mabbott. 3 vols. Cambridge, MA: Belknap Press of Harvard University Press, 1969.

Poe, Edgar Allan. *Essays and Reviews*. Ed. G. R. Thompson. New York: Library of America, 1984.

Poe, Edgar Allan. *The Narrative of Arthur Gordon Pym of Nantucket*. London: Penguin, 1999.

Poe, Edgar Allan. *Tales, Poems and Essays*. London: Collins, 1952.

Poger, Sidney, and Tony Magistrale. 'Poe's Children: The Conjunction of the Detective and the Gothic Tale'. *Clues* 18.1 (1997), 137–50.

Pollin, Burton. 'Poe's "Mystification": Its Source in *Norman Lister*'. *Mississippi Quarterly* (Spring 1972), 112–30.

Pope, Norris. 'Dickens's "The Signalman" and Information Problems in the Railway Age'. *Technology and Culture* 42.3 (July 2001), 436–61.

Porter, Dennis. *The Pursuit of Crime: Art and Ideology in Detective Fiction*. New Have, CT: Yale University Press, 1981.

Post, Melville Davisson. *The Nameless Thing*. New York: D. Appleton and Company, 1912.

Post, Melville Davisson. *Uncle Abner: The Doomdorf Mystery*. Mattituck, NY: Amereon House, 1986.

Priestman, Martin. *The Cambridge Companion to Crime Fiction*. Cambridge: Cambridge University Press, 2000.

Priestman, Martin. *Crime Fiction*. Plymouth: Northcote House, 1998.

Priestman, Martin. *Detective Fiction and Literature*. London: Macmillan, 1990.

Pyrrhönen, Heta. *Murder from an Academic Angle: An Introduction to the Study of the Detective Narrative*. Columbia, SC: Camden House, 1994.

Queen, Ellery. *Queen's Quorum: A History of the Detective-Crime Short Story as Revealed by the 106 Most Important Books Published in this Field since 1845*. Boston, MA: Little, Brown, 1951.

Rapaport, Herman. 'Review: Archive Trauma'. *Diacritics* 28.4 (1998), 68–81.

Rawson, Clayton. *Death from a Top Hat*. London: Collins, 1938.

Rawson, Clayton. *The Footprints on the Ceiling*. London: Collins, 1939.

Read, Donald. *Edwardian England*. London: Harrap, 1972.

Reilly, John M., ed. *Crime and Mystery Writers*. New York: St. Martin's Press, 1980.

Riddel, Joseph N. 'The "Crypt" of Edgar Poe'. *Boundary* 2, 7.3 (Spring 1979), 117–44.

Robbe-Grillet, Alain. *The Erasers*. London: John Calder, 1987.

Robbe-Grillet, Alain. *The Voyeur*. Trans. Richard Howard. New York: Grove Press, 1958.

Rosmarin, Adena. *The Power of Genre*. Minneapolis: University of Minnesota Press, 1985.

Roth, Marty. *Foul and Fair Play: Reading Genre in Classic Detective Fiction*. Athens: University of Georgia Press, 1995.

Roth, Ralf, and Marie-Noelle Polino. *The City and the Railway in Europe*. Aldershot: Ashgate Publishing, 2003.

Routledge, Christopher. 'The Chevalier and the Priest: Deductive Method in Poe, Chesterton and Borges'. *Clues* 22.1 (2001), 1–11.

Russell, Alison. 'Deconstructing *The New York Trilogy*: Paul Auster's Anti-Detective Fiction'. *Critique* 13.2 (1990), 71–84.

Sayers, Dorothy L. 'Introduction'. In *Tales of Detection*. Ed. Dorothy L. Sayers. London: J. M. Dent and Sons, 1940, p. vii–xiv.

Sayers, Dorothy L. *In the Teeth of the Evidence*. London: New English Library, 1961.

Scarborough, Dorothy. *The Supernatural in Modern English Fiction*. New York: G. P. Putnam's Sons, 1917.

Schehr, Lawrence R. 'Unreading Borges's Labyrinth'. *Studies in Twentieth Century Literature* 3 (1986), 177–89.

Schivelbusch, Wolfgang. 'The Compartment'. In *The Railway Journey: The Industrialisation of Time and Space in the Nineteenth-Century*. Berkeley: University of California Press, 1986, pp. 33–44.

Schivelbusch, Wolfgang. 'Railroad Space and Railroad Time'. *New German Critique* 14 (1978), 31–40.

Seed, David. 'Mystery in Everyday Things: Charles Dickens' "The Signalman"'. *Criticism* 23 (1981), 42–57.

Sellwood, Arthur, and Mary Sellwood, *The Victorian Railway Murders*. Newton Abbot: David & Charles, 1979.

Simmons, Jack. *The Express Train and Other Railway Studies*. Nairn: Thomas and Lochar, 1995.

Škvorecký, Josef. *The End of Lieutenant Boruvka*. Trans. Paul Wilson. New York: W. W. Norton & Company, 1990.

Škvorecký, Josef. *The Mournful Demeanour of Lieutenant Boruvka*. London: Victor Gollancz, 1973.

Škvorecký, Josef. *The Return of Lieutenant Boruvka*. London: Faber and Faber, 1990.

Škvorecký, Josef. *Sins For Father Knox*. London: Faber and Faber, 1990.

Smajic, Srdjan. 'The Trouble with Ghost-Seeing: Vision, and Genre in the Victorian Ghost Story'. *English Literary History* 70 (2004), 1107–35.

Spanos, William V. 'The Detective and the Boundary: Some Notes on the Postmodern Literary Imagination'. *Boundary* 2.1, 1 (1972), 147–68.

Spencer, William David. *Mysterium and Mystery: The Clerical Crime Novel*. Carbondale and Edwardsville: Southern Illinois University Press, 1989.

Stavans, Ilan. '*Borges: A Life* by James Woodall; *Collected Stories* by Jorge Luis Borges; Andrew Hurley'. *Transition* 74 (1997), 62–76.

Stockholder, Kay. 'Is Anybody at Home in the Text?' *American Imago* 57.3 (2000), 299–334.

Stowe, William W. 'Reason and Logic in Detective Fiction'. *Semiotics* 6, 2.3 (1987), 370–85.

Strout, Cushing. 'Theatrical Magic and the Novel'. *Sewanee Review* 111.1 (2003), 169–75.

Sullivan, Jack. *Elegant Nightmares: The English Ghost Story from Le Fanu to Blackwood*. Athens: Ohio University Press, 1978.

Symons, Julian. *Bloody Murder: From the Detective Story to the Crime Novel: A History*. Harmondsworth: Penguin, 1974.

Thomas, Ronald R. *Detective Fiction and the Rise of Forensic Science*. Cambridge: Cambridge University Press, 1999.

Thoms, Peter. *Detection and Its Designs: Narrative and Power in Nineteenth-Century Detective Fiction*. Athens: Ohio University Press, 1998.

Todorov, Tzvetan. *The Fantastic*. Ithaca, NY: Cornell University Press, 1973.

Todorov, Tzvetan. 'The Typology of Detective Fiction'. In *The Poetics of Prose*. Trans. Richard Howard. Ithaca, NY: Cornell University Press, 1977, pp. 42–52.

Trowbridge, W. R. H. *Cagliostro: The Splendour and Misery of a Master of Magic*. London: George Allen and Unwin, 1926.

Tytler, Graeme. 'Charles Dickens's "The Signalman": A Case of Partial Insanity?' *History of Psychiatry* 8 (1997), 421–32.

Uchiyama, Kanae. 'The Death of the Other: A Levinasian Reading of Paul Auster's *Moon Palace*'. *Modern Fiction Studies* 54.1 (Spring 2008), 115–139.

Van Dine, S. S. *The 'Canary' Murder Case*. New York: Charles Scribner's Sons, 1927.

Van Dine, S. S. 'Twenty Rules for Writing Detective Stories'. *American Magazine* (September 1928), 26–30.

Vickers, Roy. 'The Eighth Lamp'. In *Crime on the Lines*. Ed. Bryan Morgan. London: Routledge and Kegan Paul, 1975, pp. 97–109.

Vidocq, François Eugène. *Memoirs of Vidocq: Master of Crime*. Ed. and trans. Edwin Gile Rich. Edinburgh: AK Press/Nabat, 2003.

Waisman, Sergio. *Borges and Translation: The Irreverence of the Periphery*. Lewisburg, PA: Bucknell University Press, 2005.

Walker, Joseph S. 'Criminality and (Self) Discipline: The Case of Paul Auster'. *Modern Fiction Studies* 48.2 (Summer 2002), 389–421.

Walker, Ronald G., and June M. Frazer, eds. *The Cunning Craft: Original Essays on Detective Fiction and Contemporary Literature*. Macomb: Western Illinois University Press, 1990.

Ward, Maisie. *Gilbert Keith Chesterton*. New York: Sheed and Ward, 1943.

Wells, Carolyn. *The Technique of the Mystery Story*. Springfield, MA: The Home Correspondence School, 1913.

White, Hal. *The Mysteries of Reverend Dean*. Savage, Minnesota: Lighthouse Christian Publishing, 2008.

Whitechurch, Canon V. L. *Thrilling Stories of the Railway*. London: Routledge & Kegan Paul, 1977.

Winks, Robin W., ed. *Detective Fiction: A Collection of Critical Essays*. Englewood Cliffs, NJ: Prentice Hall, 1980.

Winks, Robin W., and Maureen Corrigan, eds. *Mystery and Suspense Writers: The Literature of Crime, Detection and Espionage*. 2 vols. New York: Scribner's, 1998.

Wolf, Werner. 'Illusion and Breaking Illusion in Twentieth-Century Fiction'. In *Aesthetic Illusion: Theoretical and Historical Approaches*. Ed. Frederick Burwick and Walter Pape. Berlin: Walter de Gruyer, 1990, pp. 284–97.

Worthington, Heather. *The Rise of the Detective in Early Nineteenth-Century Popular Fiction*. London: Palgrave Macmillan, 2005.

Wright, Elizabeth. *Psychoanalytic Criticism: A Reappraisal*. Cambridge: Polity Press, 1998.

Yates, Donald A. 'An Essay on Locked Rooms' In *The Mystery Writer's Art*. Ed. Francis M. Nevins, Jr. Bowling Green, OH: Bowling Green University Popular Press, 1970, pp. 272–84.

Zangwill, Israel. *The Big Bow Mystery*. London: Greenhill Books, 1892.

Index